# *49 So Fine*

## A story of beyond passion

Pierre G. Porter

Lotus 1016 Publishing & Film, Inc.
1 Union Ave., #2683, Bala Cynwyd, PA 19004

ISBN: 978-1-7353025-0-8 (Paperback Edition)
ISBN: 978-1-7353025-2-2 (Hardback Edition)
ISBN: 978-1-73530025-1-5 (eBook Edition)

Cover art and design: Marion Design

# Acknowledgements

*What makes writing so wonderful are the people who share their time and talent to help others in this creative process. Many thanks to everyone who helped me, and to those who continue to support me on my journey to create stories that challenge us to live purposefully. Hopefully, they also help us to love, laugh, cry, and heal.*

*Thank you to my editor Wayne K. Williams, Jr. for his editorial help, keen insight, and unending support in bringing this story to fruition. Because of his efforts and commitment to the book's success, as well as the invaluable input of women who understand love and lovin', this novel found its way home and is now a reality.*

*No acknowledgement would be complete however, without expressing my gratitude and appreciation to Donna Lloyd for her honesty, literary insight, and encouragement. What a wonderful and sincere voice she provided! Likewise, a heartfelt thanks to Ann Rodrigues for her editing and feedback. Finally, thank you to Tanika "T" Smith, Philly's best mixologist. Your smiles and drinks are all that. And to everyone, including the editing team, PR consultants, family and friends, my heartfelt thanks to you for your ongoing and unwavering support and encouragement, which enabled me to travel another leg on this exciting and fulfilling journey.*

*Finally, my personal thanks to the songwriters and singers of the great music of life that have made our timeless journeys of finding, losing, and desiring love memorable, generation after generation. Keep creating great music so our tomorrows will have their stories of sweet romances as great, and as oh, so special as that very music.*

Dedicated

To the great music of life, its love, its passion,
and its maturity …
A universal truth for lovers

# Contents

# Chapter 1

## MEETING HER

*We met.*
*No. I think we were introduced.*
*We talked.*
*We danced.*
*I think we exchanged numbers.*
*The night ended.*
*I was left with only the thought maybe she'd call.*
*Our time is for living.*
*Our thoughts are for sharing.*
*Remembering moments of joy that make us smile.*
*Yesterday, today, tomorrow,*
*Does it matter when the heart wants what it wants?*
*It does when its wants flow from vulnerability.*
*It doesn't when its wants flow from lust.*
*If we don't take the journey, how can we know?*
*To find love, share the pain and share the romance, day by day.*
*Songwriters write and singers sing of it.*
*Turning their songs into our memoirs*
*and our days into a life together.*
*So, I begin, perhaps for the last time, to find love,*
*At least that is always the hope.*

I was caught in her gaze, wondering if she would be the one. My eyes slowly took in her luscious, perfectly pert tits barely contained by her tight red shirt, her not-so-tiny waist, and round, tight, plump ass that fit perfectly into her white jeans. But the most captivating parts of her were those dark brown eyes staring back at me from beneath long, thick lashes and set in a lovely symmetrical face topped off with a short cut silky and curly fro, styled to fit her beauty. Her full sultry lips, built to make all of my ideas of passion a reality, made my sex throb as thoughts of exploring every inch of her light-mellow skin, darkened brown by the summer sun, played in my head. But who was she, really, beyond that sexy body? More than I would allow myself to know, still, I wanted true love. But in this moment, I only knew to ask myself the question, "Did I really want to begin again?" If I did, I needed to move toward her to say hello or find a way to be introduced. But the club was crowded, so I watched as she and her girlfriends moved to the outside deck to find seats and soak up what remained of the early evening sun. I downed the last of my drink, and, bolstered by liquid courage, I started making my way toward the deck and my inevitable destiny.

In the midst of making my move, however, I was distracted by old friends who had gathered at the bar and who were now calling me to belly-up likewise to the bar, share a couple of drinks, and catch up on some we-haven't-seen-you-lately conversation.

"Who's buying the first round?" I asked.

Kareem threw cash on the bar and called for Tress, the young bartender, to take the order for drinks for everyone: for me, a Jack Daniel's on the rocks with a splash of Coke and lemon; for Terrance, a Tanqueray and tonic on the rocks with a lemon and a lime; for Kevin, a Johnny Walker Black, neat, and for himself, a Hennessy and Coke. With that, Kareem turned to the three of us and asked, "What have you brothers been up to? I haven't seen you guys, especially you, Harold, since you moved back to Philly."

"I'd been hanging mainly in the city, but you know that I'd run through all the fine women I knew down here a while ago," I replied. Now Kareem had known me for many years and had a way of listening *through* me, not just *to* me, something he and I both knew was true but never spoke of. We accepted it for what it was, the way men do when an unspoken bond exists between them. So, as I alluded to my conquests, he smiled, truly glad to see me and the others too, of course, looked me in the eyes, and listened intently. When I finished, he spoke.

"Harold, Harold, Harold, well, brother," he said, pausing, as if preparing to replay a conversation we'd had before and to answer a question I had not yet asked. But Kareem knew me. He continued, "Yes, there are some new ones visiting the club tonight, some young ones, some fairing to the middle ones," he said referring to the ones in their late thirties and forties, "and even some very fine older sisters, too, if you are looking." Then, placing his hand on my shoulder as if asking me a question to which he already knew the answer, he said in a staccato voice, "Are you looking, Harold?" As he finished the question, all eyes trained on me, and suddenly, as if everyone were in on the joke, we all exploded in laughter. I dodged answering the question by instead asking Kareem, "Well, now brother, oh no, what have you been doing?"

Kareem knew me too well to press me, even if in jest, and replied, "Still running my construction company and buying a new car every three or four years. I know that's a waste of money, but it's what I want, and I got the cash in the bank." Kareem turned to Kevin, who stood looking on, and said, "You still working for the hospital, Kevin?"

Kevin nodded and replied emphatically, "I'll give them fifteen more years, and then I am out."

The conversations between us continued. Kareem detailed his new ride, Kevin bemoaned the long hours at the hospital and the way in which it was dominating his life, but how he reconciled the trade-off because the money and benefits were worth it all.

As usual, Terrance was doing his thing, and I always marveled at how he enjoyed his work. Then again, it was a job he loved. Truly, I enjoyed every moment catching up with these brothers, and the feeling was mutual. It certainly was a good night. Over the commotion of the crowd, I ordered the second round for us, and when Tress brought them, I gave her my American Express card and asked her to open up a tab. As much as I was enjoying talking to these good brothers, the music, as it always did, spoke to me, so I said abruptly, "Hey, watch my drink. I'm going to ask one of these fine ladies in here to dance before I go find who took me for a mental walk into her existence."

And again, in that staccato but excited voice, Kareem quickly remarked, "What … did … you … just … say," his way of poking fun at me for things I said out loud that amused him, precisely because I had said them out loud.

"Don't mind me," I said to him nonchalantly. "The songwriters are calling me to sing their songs to someone."

Kareem quipped, "There you go again, talking that bull," chuckling still as I faded into the crowd and the music enveloped me. *The DJ is playing my song*, I thought, as I walked up to a tall, fine, caramel-brown-latte-looking woman wearing a blue dress that clung to her and caught every man's attention in the club. She was a silhouette of beauty in high heels. *Beautiful legs*, I said to myself. But to her, I said, "Hello. Would you like to dance?"

"Sure," she said. She was relaxed and confident, and though she hadn't yet moved, we both began ever so noticeably to sway to the syncopation of the notes. As she answered, she looked up and eyed me steadily as if with a sense of knowing something that I ought to have already realized, too. Then, in a matter-of-fact voice, never betraying the music as it played on, she said, "You don't remember me, do you?"

I was not put off, nor did I feel one way or the other about her question, and I didn't believe she meant it to do so in any event. I simply answered, "No, I haven't been here in the club for a couple of years." I meant what I had said to Kareem earlier—I had been focused on work and my company. I missed this place.

She continued, "That was when we last talked. You were going to call me. My name is Lynn." Again, without any insinuation or barb, she spoke her words as if they were a part of the music, and likewise, I did not miss a beat, a note, or a step.

"My bad," I said. "I'm Harold. Let's dance now, Lynn, and I'll buy you a drink later."

"You're still the same," she exhaled, smiled, and diverted her eyes upward. "You know, I liked you, Harold. We talked for maybe a half hour over there in the far corner of the bar."

I heard her words as they were lifted on the notes of the music, and I appreciated her candor and her poise. "I can't believe I didn't remember your name, Lynn; how can one forget someone as fine as you?"

Now on the dance floor with Lynn, I noticed her, the sista wearing the tight red shirt, her not-so-tiny waist, and round, tight, plump ass that fit perfectly into her jeans. She was dancing close by with some guy. I wondered if he was her friend. It didn't matter. Seeing her again brought me back to my thoughts of wanting her. She must have felt me watching her, because she looked my way. I could not look away, could not avert my eyes, so our eyes made contact. We smiled at each other, but then I began noticing the eyes of other men on her. I knew then that I would have to approach her differently figuring she probably got hit on often. No problem; I've been there before and won the lady, I assured myself.

5

After ten minutes on the dance floor with fine Lynn, I was back at the bar with her. We reintroduced ourselves and talked for a while about our lives, and Lynn told me about her son who had been highly scouted by the major universities. I saw a fine sista before me, but she was a proud mother, too. I wondered what else she was. Lynn told me she had never married and had raised her son by herself. As she talked, I started to remember more. As I recalled, Lynn's father helped raise the boy while she was finishing her undergraduate and graduate studies. Now with her master's, I observed that she seemed to be doing well, and I appreciated the determination.

"Anthony is at Michigan State and doing well," she said.

We continued to share about the ups and downs of our lives and the choices we had made, for better or worse, in order to arrive where we were now. I found myself genuinely enjoying my time with her, but I did want to rush this conversation with Lynn in order to return to the bar where my friends were gesturing to me for another drink. At that moment, I realized I had yet to buy Lynn that drink I had promised her, so I signaled to my friends to give me just a minute. I said, "Lynn, let me buy you a drink," as we continued talking before I went back to the bar where my friends would have one waiting for me.

"Will you come back later, Harold?" she said, her words still music. I could hear her.

"Yes," I said, and I meant it.

Lynn watched me walk away, and after about 15 or 20 minutes had passed, I had a feeling she would remain at the other end of the bar, perhaps drinking and waiting for me to return because she wanted me.

Once I arrived back at the bar with the brothers, Kareem said to me, "Let me introduce you to some ladies who used to live in town. You'll like them. Follow me. I think they moved out on the deck."

I quickly thought to myself, *not her and her girlfriends*, but I said to Kareem, "How do you know them?"

"I see them around. Also, I did some work for one of them. Get your drink and come on. We'll say hello, and if you don't like them, we'll smoke a couple of cigars I brought with me and just hang out."

"Cool," I said.

The club was still crowded, and Kareem and I squeezed by so many unknown and unnamed ladies. As we reached the deck and headed in the direction of the ladies Kareem knew, the sista who had become my focus on this night looked up and again, our eyes made contact. I winked at her, and she smiled back at me. Kareem's former client Krista and her friends were relaxing at a table filled with drinks near the center of the deck. As Kareem and I approached, Krista got up to hug him, and then she introduced everyone. All I heard was, "This is Yvette. We grew up together." Then Kareem said, "This is my boy, Harold," as he rested his hand on my shoulder.

In that moment, standing so close to Yvette, I realized I was excited to meet her, so I pondered what to say in order to control my overly confident personality. Then Yvette reached out her hand and our hands touched. She squeezed my hand firmly, but gently. I was surprised that her grasp was so affirming as to suggest a tomorrow together, or was that just the thought I wanted for us? Warm and soft were her hands, and she held my mine for what seemed to be an extended clasp, until Kareem said, "You two still holding hands?" Unlocking them, we smiled and joined the company around us. I knew then that I had to back off, way off, and to return later. In fact, I would go back into the bar, for I knew the ladies would ask Kareem the routine questions like, "What's up with your friend?"

Knowing Kareem, he would let them know that I was a successful businessman and fun to hang out with. He would also tell them to be careful. "Harold is a passionate brother, maybe romantic, and certainly a dreamer, and he has ways with the women." For certain he would say that to them, because he always did. Kareem knew I would reply if asked, "I'm not a romantic. I just enjoy passion and perhaps a sweet romance."

Walking back to the bar, I noticed Lynn was waiting still, and I went to rejoin her there. Lynn was in her mid-forties, built like a goddess, with long silky hair to accompany an ass sculpted into a perfect dimension holding, for sure, a wonderful pussy and fully-round and obviously large tits draping her top frame. Lynn was a fine, fine bottle of wine that I could savor in my own way, experiencing the many aromas exploding my taste buds and elevating my senses beyond the normal eye-candy walking around trying to get men to notice them. Yes, she was fine and almost my height in flat shoes. Saying hello again, I wondered why I never called her, such a lovely, educated sista.

Was it my demanding work schedule back then, my commitment to growing the company along with the responsibility of having employees that made me not pursue her years ago? I liked to think so, but this time things would be different. As I sat talking, we pulled close to each other and in more than one way. Men and women can tell when the attraction is more than curiosity. There was a powerful energy in the air because our conversation turned immediately into laughter, as if already lovers, but the two of us still wanted to know why we left everything back then to chance. This time I was going to follow up and hit this fine sista. This fine lady here flirting with me was too much to deny this go-round. I was ready to dance with her, if she would allow me to be with her on a regular basis, and if she wanted to dance the dance, I was going to romance or whatever the pussy out of her. She was that fine, and I wasn't going to pass on it again, no way!

After I ordered Lynn and myself another drink, I saw Yvette walk into the bar and toward the ladies' room. I noticed her eyes scanning the bar. She saw me with Lynn, nodded, and smiled with a look of come back and talk to me—or was that my ego getting in the way? Anyway, I would do that after I firmed up with Lynn that we would meet later and catch up on the time we missed. I saw Yvette return to the deck, not looking my way at all. I let exactly twenty-five minutes pass. There is something about making a move on a lady, not too quick, but before thirty minutes. I was going to do some research on that one day, but for now I needed to wrap things up with Lynn. We exchanged numbers and social media info. We said our goodbyes, and I headed back to meet up with my friend on the deck. As I left Lynn, I resolved that this time I would commit myself to the quest. Moreover, I recognized that I really enjoyed being with her. She was witty, conversational, and I anticipated the challenge of blending two personalities into a tomorrow.

Out on the deck I saw Kareem sitting with them. I found myself a deck chair and positioned it close to Yvette. I purposely started conversing with the other women as though Yvette were not there. I noticed she was uncomfortable with the lack of attention. She had a slight frown, as if she were used to having the attention in the room. However, it was not a frown of not wanting to talk, but rather one of why aren't we talking. She would get my attention later after she pursued me, and she would. I had something to offer a woman like her. However, I would not leave without talking to her and allowing her time to tell me about herself. I would remain vague about my interests and lifestyle for the moment. While I was running those thoughts through my head, Yvette surprised me and asked if I would like a drink.

I said, "Yes." Yvette was as beautiful close up as she was from a distance. She was no Monet. She was more of a Botticelli.

"Jack Daniel's and a splash of Coke with lemon, right?" she said.

"Yes, how did you know?"

"I pay attention."

I said, "Good answer, if that's true."

She said, "It is."

"OK, I'll have a drink with you, if you'll tell me a secret," I said.

"I don't know you well enough to tell you a secret. We just met," she quipped.

"Well, what's your favorite thing?" I retorted.

"What do you mean?" she asked as she gestured with her hands.

"What do you like or do the most?" I replied.

"Why?" she asked. I noticed she became a little uncomfortable, not ready to share some personal things. She went from leaning back to straightening up and changed her demeanor, which had me wanting to probe deeper into her why.

"I'm just asking. Is it reading, walking in the park, or being kissed all over?" I asked with a smile.

"How did you come up with those three?" she said, clearly surprised.

"Guessing. Am I cold or hot?" I asked.

"I do the first two a lot. And the third? I'm a private person."

"Is that your answer? No, don't answer. I don't want to know. I was just making small talk. However, we can talk about things to come," I said as we laughed continuously.

"You're not a religious nut, are you?" Yvette asked, as if she doesn't attend church on a regular basis.

"No, not me, I was talking about calling you or you calling me. Our meeting is not a coincidence; to quote the scientist Einstein, 'Coincidence is God's way of staying anonymous.'"

Giving me a flirtatious glance from underneath those eyelashes, she responded, "Kareem said you were that kind of brother, and you date a lot of women."

"Not true," I said, and then continued after a dramatic pause. "I know a lot, but date very few. I'm reserving my time and all of me for that special one. I'll find her one day, and

I'm sure it will be by coincidence. Will you call me soon? I'm getting ready to go. I promised some friends that I would meet them back in the city. "

"Don't go," she said. "It's only 9:30, and we're having a blast talking, but maybe I'm talking too much and keeping you away from talking to everyone else."

"No. I like us together—we're like ice cream and warm cake. You're the warm cake melting my ice cream," I said with a straight face, wanting her to believe me completely.

"That sounds sweet but corny, but I like it and you," she replied playfully with a smile.

"You do?" I said, feigning surprise.

"Yes, are you surprised? You shouldn't be. It was the way you touched my hand. It made me feel warm and to want to know you, I think," she said as if she were going to bite her lip, but she didn't.

"OK, time will tell," I said, leaving her with the impression that it would be up to her to get to know me.

Yvette and Lynn were alike in many ways, but Lynn was warmer, more earthy, and reserved as if she was afraid to show vulnerability, as if not sure time would tell all her secrets. Yvette, though, she was cool and sassy with her eyes lighting up from under extended lashes. She knew what she had and that was a body that turned men into watching her move effortlessly through the club and perhaps through men's lives. However, I got the sense that she had never been really loved for who she was, just for being herself. Faking love and maybe orgasms, she seemed what some might call a transactional sister, the kind who says, "What's in it for me?" Beauty has a way of making some women that way, especially if their growing up wasn't easy. This was just our first meeting, and I was not going to assume anything because I liked her and wanted to find out more about her when she was willing to meet. I knew the call would come, although not tomorrow. She was not that kind of woman. But she would call, so I decided to stay a little while longer. It was an easy decision to stay, but little did I know it would be the easiest decision I would have to make about us. If only I had known the peaks and valleys that lay ahead.

We have all heard it said before, the words, lyrics, really, of truth, of wisdom, that baffled our own thoughts, our own logic about love, like those sung by the beguiling and beautiful Ms. Nancy Wilson. Oh, to live in her time and space would have been a dream come true, for she was certainly an angel of song and sophistication. Since I couldn't, I had to settle for being that soft-spoken man she sang about in her song, "This is All I Ask," on her latest CD, a classic, *Turned to Blue*. But another lady of song and love and not of this Earth suddenly appeared one evening many years ago as I listened to some old jazz standard on vinyl while drinking a glass of wine. Beautiful brown eyes like the eyes of an angel she had, and I, jolted out of my sofa seat, dropped my glass of wine being frightened to death. Was I dreaming wide awake? It took more than a minute to believe what I was seeing, let alone find any comfort in what had just appeared. Who was this woman, this figure out of thin air, present yes, but an apparition, too? She was singing the lyrics to the song that was playing. Her jazz voice was angelic in every way. She looked at me and said, "**I'm a friend. Please still yourself, for I have come to be a guide and comforter to you on your life journey**."

Far beyond me to speak to a figure neither here nor gone, I stuttered, "I don't understand."

"**Time is needed for you and her**."

I asked her, "Who is the woman you're referring to?"

"**She is a woman, and as opposed to your life, her youth was void of seeing love expressed freely. And for now, that is all I can share with you**."

Why she appeared on that night and to me, I don't know, except for what she conveyed to me that evening, but that was not the last night I would ever see her; she became my muse, Ms. Angel Eyes. She would become the best of me, my dream lady, and I, the gentleman in this dream about my life's journey, and I called it that, for it was surreal. But still, I would not be the gentleman yet. During this period of my life, I would return to my bad-boy impulses, an image as perceived by some. And she was there for me when I called her forward from time to time, like when I needed the best of myself and when I needed her to save me from my over self-indulgence, like now, wanting Yvette, and Lynn, and other women. Which one would be that special one I wanted? I didn't know, and the answers I sought would not be easily found, especially since my muse, Ms. Angel Eyes, wanted men to be gentlemen. And from those gentlemen, she required a certain kind of knowledge and respect of self, and I only wanted to play in my sheltered understanding with my bad-boy's sexual habits. And so I chased the Carols, the Berthas, the Dianes, and now Lynn and Yvette—to find passion. Was not the sweet joy of passion and romance that the songwriters wrote of, love's promised land? And there was none sweeter or more loving than I had found in love's promised land long ago; there, my time was spent with Bertha, a Southern beauty with a Southern name. I loved her.

I turned my thoughts back to Yvette, "Would you have lunch or dinner with me?" I said.

Yvette smiled and with some hesitancy said, "Where and when?"

"Some nice upscale restaurant in the city, and you tell me when. We can talk about it. For now, give me a kiss," I asked, with my body expression showing a sincere look of wanting to touch her lips. "I gotta go. You got my number?" I said as if I had not even asked her for a kiss, but she got it. She was quick in understanding me and my body language, it seemed.

"You want a kiss?" she retorted as if affirming my question.

"Yes, I do. The touch of your lips touching mine," I said.

"Not here," she said softly, tenderly, with her moist tongue doing a 360-degree glide around her lips.

"Then I'll wait," I said positively. "I want us to spend some time together. Do you?" I asked somehow knowing the answer.

She nodded, "I do."

Getting up from my seat, I said goodnight to everyone. Then I hand-gestured to Yvette to call me. She mouthed, "I will."

I gave Kareem a brotherly hug and said to him, "All the best to you, my brother," and I left to get to my other engagement back in the city.

## Chapter 2

## YVETTE

My cell phone rang. I answered hello, not recognizing the number on the screen. *Could it be Yvette?* The voice sounded familiar the longer we talked. We continued talking. I never asked who I was talking to until she said, "I was driving out and about Philly and thinking about you and decided to call you." I knew then it was Yvette on the other end.

"I'm glad you did. You sound different, Yvette. Are you on speaker mode? So, what's happening?" I asked.

She said, "Well, when you didn't call after two weeks, I decided to call you and ask you to have lunch with me." *Two weeks of no contact and she still wanted to meet again.* "OK, I can do that," I responded coolly.

"We can meet at a seafood restaurant near the university between classes. I think it's called Eddie's," she said.

Eddie's happened to be a favorite of mine. I've wined and dined several ladies there. Yvette, I liked her. My father would say some women you fuck and have fun with and others you take home to your mother. Yvette was the kind of woman I would have taken home to my mother, if she were still living.

"Yvette, what day would you like to meet for lunch? My week is open given I work for myself," I said.

"How about Thursday, two days from today, at one p.m.?" she said.

15

"That time works for me. Let's plan to meet then. Now that that's settled, how have you been? I've thought of you quite a lot," I continued, trying to convince her through the phone by the tone of my voice.

"Is that so, then why did I have to call you first?" she poked.

"I don't know, ego gets in my way more often than not," I confessed.

"We'll have to work on both our egos," Yvette said. "I've been thinking about you, as well. I had a dream about us being together."

I wanted to hear that, even if she was playing me with kind words. I smiled into my cell and told her I was going to call her, and I was glad she called. I started thinking back to when we first met and talked on the deck, and as we continued talking, I realized I would have to make the most of the second meeting, for it would let me know whether these feelings were about finding love again or just rock-hard passion. I hoped for the best because I wanted it to be something deeper.

The intervening weeks, though, since I had first met Yvette, had not been uneventful. I had spent a lot of time with Lynn, and she was rock-hard passion, but one Lynn was enough. Also, although I knew Lynn had her shit together, it was not hard to recognize that she was much more than tits and ass. One needs a forever-lady in his life, which is to say that I needed a forever-lady in mine. I was searching for one this go-around, but my habits were in play. I was finding myself, again, with my bad-boy habits in motion. Lynn was in play, more than tits and ass, yet here Yvette and I were talking about her classes, her children, and her exes. I made her feel comfortable because I really wanted to know more about her. I was planning our tomorrows and I was fine with all that she was sharing. Our conversation went on for about an hour before we realized how long we were talking. For the first time in a long time, I was letting someone into my personal life and business, and I hadn't even taken her out yet. I wondered what Ms. Angel Eyes would have to say about this.

Just then my cell beeped, and it was Lynn on the other line. I hit the call-you-back-in-15-minutes button. I had to hurry up and end this call with Yvette, because I knew Lynn would be calling me back, and she would keep calling until I answered.

"Yvette, I've got to return a business call. If it's OK with you, I'll call you this evening around seven p.m." She said, "OK," and I hung up.

As I hit redial to call Lynn back, I wondered where this was going, because we were having sex multiple times every day since we reconnected at the bar. She was happy, and those dark lovely ass legs suspended in the air, shaking and hollering while having multiple orgasms, ooh, I was happy laying pipe and grabbing her perfectly shaped ass. She might be a hard one to get away from. Maybe that was the reason I didn't make that call two years ago. We were baby-making fucking now, as if the strokes were going to leave us something in nine months, but I got the call from Yvette, so some changes would have to happen.

"Hello, Lynn, what's up?" I said, calling her back within 15 minutes from my text to her.

"I was just calling to say hello. I got off from work early. Can you come over? For some reason I've been thinking about all the damn sex we've been having," Lynn explained.

"Sure, are you missing me, or you just want to open your legs again?" I teased.

"Both. I got some sexy shit you can rip off me, you know the way I like it," she said.

"I don't rip off clothing. I gently remove them in an aura created by our passion for each other," I said in a serious voice.

"Right. Just bring your sexy ass over now, please," she replied, ignoring my pompous remark.

17

"OK, let me pick up something from the liquor store," I said.

"No, I got what you like; just bring your nasty ass over," she commanded, but ever so sensually.

"You know if you talk to me like that I won't come by. I'm not being a narcissist, but in this game of love and passion or vice versa, it requires a level of decorum before we end up finding ourselves lost in exploring our sexual pleasures," I explained quite frankly, immediately after which, I said, "Forget what I just said. I'm on my way." This shit was getting deep, and my acquiescence was the first sign I was in it.

"Sorry baby, you know I just want to see you," she pulled back.

"You mean sex you up?" I pushed.

"Of course, that, too," she offered.

"Lynn, I think we want to see each other because things are beginning to happen between us." I threw myself a lifeline.

"Like what?" she asked.

"Let's leave that for time to give us the answer," I said. I had thrown myself a line, and I was at least holding on to it. Then the wave hit, and I said, upping the rhetoric, "When I come to the door and ring the bell, I want you buck naked with your big-ass tits shooting out like rockets hitting me in the face."

"You think I got big tits?" she feigned humility.

"You know you do. I want us to lay on the sofa and allow me to find your cleavage, while you grab my dick as hard as you can and thrust it into your pussy," I said.

"Oh, shit," she gasped excitedly. "You don't need to ring the doorbell; it will be unlocked, and everything will be like you like it."

"See you soon," I said assuredly.

"OK, baby," she said as she hung up the phone.

Driving over to Lynn's house, my dick was hard thinking about what we were going to do. I had to figure out how to pull back just a little from her if I was going to spend time with Yvette, which is what I wanted. Pulling into Lynn's driveway, I popped a piece of gum in my mouth to freshen up my breath and sprayed on some cologne. As promised, the door was unlocked, so I called out to her, and she said, "I'm in the sunroom."

"OK," I replied. I knew then she wanted to be fucked on the sofa again and that she wanted me to bend her over, spread her ass cheeks apart, and slowly stroke that pussy. I was up for it. Lynn was not quite my height and not quite my weight, so she was work. But I was the son of a builder, and I was ready again to nail that frame two or three times before the evening was over.

"Hey, baby, do you like what you see?" Lynn said. She was moving her nearly naked form dramatically and in an overly sexualized way as she danced to the music she had playing.

"Yes, I do. Why don't you come give me some of that tight, wet pussy?" I said.

"I thought you wanted to fuck me in my cleavage and all that shit," she said.

"Who said I didn't? Let me sit on the sofa so I can find just the right fit between your tits, and you can get carried away. I know when your eyes start rolling back in your head that your hands are gonna grab something," I said.

"Oh, shut up." She laughed, moving toward me.

"Come, pretty lady, kiss me." I called, she came. Her ruby red lips, there waiting for me to finish off the invitation to lovemaking. This was going to be some good intercourse. With drinks already made, we drank, we talked, and we caressed each other passionately. Thoughts of her and me together daily, time passing, our days together, seemed like one continuous moment of two best friends being together for a long afternoon of fun. I worked this nice and slow all the while touching her in those special places, playing with her peach, and the more I played with her peach, the wetter and sweeter it became. I slid inside her just at that right moment; she exploded. Her body slicked with sweat as her screams came forth rhythmically, and we crescendoed once again into fucking ecstasy.

That was round one with this healthy babe. I looked over at her sleeping peacefully and thought about asking her to get up and fix us something to eat, but instead I decided I would prepare us something to eat so she could save her energy for round two. I continued however to watch her for a few moments longer, for she lay there beautifully resting, finding comfort, perhaps, in all her thoughts of us. Then, I got up, fixed myself a drink, and thought about what to fix for dinner. It was about 7:30 p.m., and I needed to call Yvette as promised. With Lynn sleeping stretched out naked on the sofa, I plugged my earphones into my cell and stepped out on the patio to call Yvette. She answered on the second ring. "Hello, Yvette, this is Harold."

"Yes, I know your voice."

"You do?" I asked.

"Your voice is soft and very formal, it's hard to mistake," she said. "You even sound like a White boy," she kidded.

"I don't think so. How about I sound like an educated and aware brother?" I said, self-aware.

"I shouldn't have said that. Sorry," she offered, embarrassed by her now-obviously, pedestrian remark.

"Apology accepted," I said graciously. She didn't know me, but she was getting to know me, and so as was my way, and knowing that the *Wizard of Oz* was a White dude behind a curtain, I just said matter-of-factly, "You people give them too much credit; most are not the ones you see on the TV." Then I let it go and simply asked, "Anyway, is this a good time to call you?"

"Yep, I was just waiting to see if you would call. What are you doing? Have you been busy at work?" Yvette asked, curious.

I smiled; if she only knew, this would end before it began. "Yes. I had to do some heavy lifting, but I got it done. I'm looking forward to lunch with you on Thursday. Will I get my kiss then? Your lips are very sensual," I said.

"I'm not a good kisser. My exes weren't those kinds of men," she replied.

"You're not? Don't worry, I am," I said. She let out a nervous laugh. "I'll give you a kissing lesson on Thursday." I assured her we'd make up for those earlier years void of many things, especially love.

"We'll see. Let's just enjoy lunch and see where it goes," she parried.

"Perfect," I said, then asked, "What are you doing this evening? Want to go to the movies or something?" After a momentary silence, I asked again, hoping she would say no. "No," she replied. "I got some work I brought home to complete."

"Well, then. I'll let you go, and call me tomorrow around noon," I said letting out a little sigh of relief.

"OK. You have a good night," she said.

"You as well," I said, and then hung up.

I walked back into the house to find Lynn still sleeping. So, I started to work on dinner for us. Being somewhat of an amateur chef, I prepared a spinach salad with walnuts, cranberries, bleu cheese and a balsamic dressing. For the entrée, I made a pepper Dijon crusted salmon with broccoli and twice-baked potatoes. She would awaken to a lovely meal and for dessert, her ass bent over for some more sexual romance.

I tried waking up Lynn. She was in a deep sleep. I shook her. Called her name quietly several times before, finally, she responded.

"Hey, dinner is ready," I said gently.

"OK. Let me put on something," she said, her voice thick with sleep.

"No, just sit here at the table and have a glass of pinot noir," I offered.

"OK. You know, Harold, you're too much. Two years later, I had to wait for this?" she asked rhetorically.

"Was it worth it?" I said, smiling.

"Some women wait all their whole lives for some good sex," said Lynn.

"True, I guess," I tossed out nonchalantly, knowing full well the truth of her statement.

"Yes, it's true," she emphasized and motioned her finger in the air like a conductor at the podium. "So, you, Harold," she surrendered, "can have some of this pussy anytime you want." With each word, she tapped the nail of her right index finger on the table. She held her pinot in her left hand.

I listened to the beats she made while eyeing her each tap. After a moment of silence nurtured by our eyes meeting, I said, "Let's eat and talk about you being dessert later."

"Ooh, you're nasty, Harold, but I am down with it," she said laughing.

That night, we ate, laughed, talked, and drank our fill. It was dessert time, and I suggested we go to her bedroom for round two. Afterward she moaned, "You know I can't cum anymore."

"We'll see about that," I told her.

"I don't know what you do," she confessed. "I have never cum so much and so many times. How you turn this thing into a marathon, I'll never know," she loosely queried. Her voice seemed to trail off as she spoke.

It was getting late, but I wanted to caress her warmly and kiss her, and I wanted her to kiss me in a way that passion does on its way to finding love. We made love again, still caressing each other, we fell asleep, and I never left her bed that night.

# Chapter 3

## YOU

*For your love, I'll tell the world a falsehood.*
*For you, oh, I would change my todays*
*and tomorrows to have you here*
*No longer missing you, no more tears.*
*You're my breath of a new beginning*
*For your love I'm telling the world a truth.*
*Life will steer our course, but time spent with you*
*has given me a new wanting for all that is,*
*Suspended in complete surrender to the*
*misty cloud of a love supreme.*
*You are, we are, our moment of all that can be and will be.*
*Forget me not and I will remain yours*
*in all thoughts and feeling.*
*You're my sexual healing.*
*Play Marvin one more time, or do I need*
*to tell you what love is all about*
*Falsehoods no more, truth began the moment*
*you smiled at me and I knew we were forever, if*
*forever can be, but for sure our lifetime.*
*Follow me and I you to that place that only lovers*
*know, me and you wove into we, finding ecstasy*

*Orgasmic, no, romance at its highest, truly*
*understanding Coltrane - A Love Supreme*
*Loving you is a truth, no need for falsehoods,*
*no need – for we are our today.*

Thursday morning arrived, the day of our lunch. Being a naturally early riser, I got up, fixed myself a cup of coffee, and went out on the patio. I so enjoyed this morning ritual when the weather permitted as I enjoyed the tranquility of the morning from this perch of my oversized French provincial home. It sat in an upscale neighborhood just outside the city, and I had another home, a farmhouse, in the country on 200 acres with a 40-stall stable filled with high-performance show horses—hunters and jumpers—that I leased out to a former Olympian. I stabled my six horses there, too. I was enjoying my life and all that I had worked for.

Would Yvette be the one who would join me on this amazing journey that was my life, my adventure? I didn't know, but I was going to give her all my attention for as long as she wanted it. I wondered though, what would we talk about? Should I call on Ms. Angel Eyes for help? She was a lady and knew the social norms; she would help me project to Yvette an image of a secure and confident man. If Ms. Angel Eyes designed the afternoon, she would most likely have Duke Ellington and friends providing the backdrop for the afternoon lunch affair. Ms. Angel Eyes would say, "**Be a gentleman, sing to her, if only in your thoughts, sweet words like the classic jazz tune, 'The Very Thought Of You.'**" I would try to make Yvette my everything, the woman of the song, and I'd become her very thoughts. I'd be that chameleon and not the man I was the previous night with Lynn. Ms. Angel Eyes would save any man from his bad habits if we would only listen, and for the moment, I decided to do just that.

After two cups of coffee and a scone, I showered, shaved, and put on a suit for our meetup. I considered changing my mind and wearing black jeans and a polo shirt to show that I'd been watching my diet and lifting weights. I went back and forth and finally decided to go with the jeans and a polo shirt.

Before meeting Yvette for lunch, I briefly stopped by the office. I walked into the office while on the cell and stopped by my secretary's desk for calls and scheduled appointments for later that day. I had several calls to return and a brief 11 a.m. meeting with the CFO. Then I would be on my way. My secretary had called for the valet to bring my Porsche Targa convertible to the front of the building to save some time. I didn't want to be late for lunch. On my way to lunch, I mused about that wonderful thing called love and wanted to know why love kept passing me by. I seemed to have everything except true love. But now I was thinking too much, so I turned on some old-school hip hop to keep from chastising myself. I pulled up into the restaurant parking lot. She was already there, waiting on a bench near the front door of the restaurant. She was lovely and glowing. I rolled the window down to speak. She smiled and said, "You're late."

"I apologize. Let me park," I said. I parked and walked to where she was waiting. We kissed hello and went inside. The waiter remembered me and quickly showed us to our table by the window. We talked like we really missed one another. I asked her what she would like to drink. She wasn't sure, so I ordered her a peach martini, and I ordered my usual. Seafood was on the menu, but for me, she was the dish I would take my time with. I ordered for the both of us: two snapper soups.

"What's snapper soup?" she asked, curious.

"You'll like it, and I'll tell you what's in it after you taste it." The main dish for Yvette was blackened tuna, and for me, shad roe. After I ordered, we toasted to seeing one another again.

"I like this peach martini," she said.

"I hoped you would," I said, gloating.

25

While we ate lunch, we laughed and talked and got to know each other better. I guess she felt as though she might be saying too much because in the middle of sharing yet more things about her life, her dreams, her regrets, she said rather matter-of-factly, "I don't know why I'm so comfortable with you, Harold." She looked at me, our eyes meeting just like that first night at the club. Then just as quickly, it became an afterthought, for she said, as if throwing off some unnecessary concern, "Would you order me another peach martini, though? These are so delicious."

"Sure," I said, chuckling openly. "I'll have another drink, as well." And then we both laughed. I could get used to this sound, magic really, of our laughter together.

"The food is very good. This is my first time here. Is it yours?" she asked, tapping her mouth with the cloth napkin before she spoke.

"No," I smiled sheepishly. If she only knew the crazy times I had here with other women. "I like going to nice restaurants. In fact, it's one of my favorite things," I replied.

"You and your favorite things," her eyes rolled playfully as she spoke.

"Yvette, you want to revisit that third question since you only answered the first two?" I said. It seemed the perfect time to ask.

"What do you mean?" she said, though I could tell she knew exactly what I meant.

"'The third question—do you like being kissed all over?" I said.

"I'm in need of another peach martini before I answer a question like that with an aggressive and confident man such as you," she said as if to swear playfully.

"Thanks for the compliment. It is one, right?" I asked.

"For sure. I like your style. You should have been around before my messy divorce," she mused.

"We'll leave that for another day. We're having too much fun right now," I redirected. My words faded into the air, and I reached across the small table to grab a kiss, and she leaned forward like she was on autopilot and kissed me. I had taken my shoes off a while ago, and now I was rubbing her legs and inner thighs with my left foot. She continued smiling and talking, but her voice was changing. She said, "Don't you think you should stop teasing me? I'm beginning to be aroused."

I winked at her and said, "It's hard not to be sexual with you sitting here."

"But we're in a restaurant," she said, giving a quick look around the restaurant.

"Would you prefer that we go to the unisex bathroom, slip in, lock the door, and continue?" I jested.

"I gotta confess, all I have been doing these past years was getting my kids through college and working through a divorce. Sex has never been a high priority. To be honest, I can count the number of orgasms I've had on one hand, maybe. Now you've learned all there is to know about my boring sex life in ten seconds." She picked up her drink, leaned into it, head forward and sipped a little, but her eyes looked up at me. It seemed she had taken the last step, laid herself bare. She was something else. I didn't know what that was, but I liked it and her.

"I like you," she said.

"I can tell," I replied.

"Oh, can you really?" she shot back.

"Yes, I'm gonna sex you up one day soon, Yvette, or are you a Steve Harvey ninety-day-rule kind of woman?" I asked.

"You're funny. Did you see the movie?" she said.

"Yep, I'm all those guys in one package, more aware, more swag and more experience," I said firmly and confidently.

27

"OK, I can see that," said Yvette. "Also, I blew my class sitting here with you. I'm taking a couple of coding classes at the university."

"I'm sorry," I said.

"No, that's OK. I needed some time with someone like you."

"Would you like to see the dessert menu?" I offered.

"No, I'm watching my diet. I'm on my third peach martini, and if I'm not careful, I might be your dessert," she said. She was surprising me at how playful she was.

"That certainly would be better than anything on the menu here," I proffered.

"See what I'm talking about? Only you can make that sound good to me. Twenty years ago, I would have chased you for all it's worth," she confessed proudly. She continued, "But you seem to want me, and then again, I don't think you care if I would give you some or not."

"I'll not do anything or force myself on you in any way without your consent. An understanding first, fun second, and sex third. Any two can fuck, but making and creating love fantasies, that's very different. And we'll do that when you want," I said. I sat back in my chair and took a sip of my drink.

"How do you get away with saying stuff like that to women? I'm not a stranger to sex," she said.

"No, you may not be, but I think you're a stranger to love and all its trappings. Have you ever been in love, really in love?" I asked her, and I wasn't smiling.

"Since I'm being honest, no, and I never had sex lasting over ten minutes. Three peach martinis and I'm telling you more and more about my sex life," she said.

"But you're so beautiful. I'm sure you had your sugar daddies in life caring for you in some way. Do you have one now?" I asked, exploring deeper into her history. I knew likewise she would eventually get around to asking me about the women in my life.

"Yes, I did until recently. I found out something about him, so I cut it off just before meeting you. Anyway, what does beauty and body have to do with it?" she asked.

"If you will allow me, I'll change all of that starting with a kiss," I said.

"I'm a tall order with baggage," she said, doubting herself, if only a little.

"We all will have baggage, if we live long enough," I tried to reassure her. I saw our waiter out of the corner of my eye, so I said, "Let me get the check. We can save some of this conversation for another day."

"OK," Yvette said, but she had shared a lot of herself over lunch, and I was confident that was not typically her style.

"After I pay the bill, we can go for a short walk to put some time between the drinks and driving," I said.

"I would like to walk with you," she said.

"OK. Let's go, and we'll talk about spending some time together," I said effortlessly.

# Chapter 4

## GLORIOUS SEX

Lunch with Yvette was simply great. The weeks spent sharing and sexing Lynn did not compare to one afternoon with Yvette. The time I spent with Yvette felt special. The best I could understand about how I felt was that the time spent together with her was more than just being at lunch with someone, more than just eating, more than just talking to someone. What was it, though? I had to find out what it was, if such a thing was possible. Yvette and I decided to meet again the next day at Eddie's, hopefully to continue finding ourselves. I made a 7:30 p.m. dinner reservation. It would be our first night together.

Lynn called during the day, but I had to put her on hold after many weeks of daily fucking—two, three, four, or more times throughout the night and into the glorious morning sex and yet she still couldn't get enough. But I did it; I opened that gate, and I would have to be the one who slowly closed it, even though I enjoyed pounding that pussy as much as she liked me pounding it. For now, there would be no more Lynn, not at least for several days. I needed some time to think about these two ladies.

My workday ended, and I got on the road weaving my way through rush hour traffic to meet Yvette. When I pulled into the restaurant parking lot, she was there waiting and reading a book. I tapped the horn, and she looked up, smiling. It was her smile that went through me, or maybe it was just me wanting to be with her. Anyway, I parked, walked swiftly to meet her, and embraced her with a kiss. The kiss was soft, but awkward. I would work on that. No more blue-collar kissing, that working-guy kiss, that moving past each other from work to bed to work and kids and meals in between. No more of that. To kiss a woman correctly, making her emote romantic feelings of wanting to be loved and getting her to extend lips and tongue, touching, and moving in an adagio manner was an art.

"Hello. Were you waiting long?" I asked.

"No, was just here reading a book," she answered.

"OK, time to put it away for some me-time with Harold. Ready for dinner?" I asked.

"Yes," she replied somewhat nervously, but she was excited.

The waiter, noticing me, nodded and escorted us to the same table. "You must know him," Yvette said, surprised.

"No, but I always tip twenty percent. I'm sure that helps. Yvette, what do you have a taste for this evening?" I asked.

"I'm not sure," she said.

"Let me order for you. I called earlier to see what was the fresh catch of the day. Striped bass. It's a delicious fish, and they prepare it with special herbs and lemon. The chef here is a master of flavors for the palate," I said.

"You know a lot. Please order for me. You're batting a thousand. What you ordered for me at lunch was so good. I was telling my girlfriend Kristen about the meal and about tasting snapper soup for the first time," she shared with me.

"Did you tell her we went for a walk afterward and found a park bench to sit and talk like old friends?" I questioned her.

"All that! Plus," she said.

"What's the plus?" I asked, intrigued.

She smiled and blew me a kiss. Oh, the foreplay started again. I didn't know why, but I needed her; she was fresh, sassy, and challenging. An Aries like me, I wanted her, it seemed to me, more than all the fine and educated Lynns in my life. Yvette was built for me. She was like a finely carved ice sculpture that needed to be warmed up and have the icy years melted away, the icy years of not being warmed by love and good sex. From her curly afro to her painted toenails and everything in between, I would love her into completeness and womanhood because despite her years, she was in many ways like a woman in her twenties—left brain firing hot with intelligence, drive, and ambition, right brain, young, awkward, and exciting, still unaware of exactly how to find completeness in her grownup body. It was evident listening to her. She knew little about many things surrounding love and being loved. It was like half of her was the perfect mother and perhaps, wife, but she, herself was an empty vessel; her sex life was as complete as motherhood, she may have thought. She had her kids, raised them up, and now she was done. If you don't know, you don't know. I would try to open her up not to sex, but to more than five-minute sex and to more than years of raising children and thereafter from uneventful intercourse to new experiences no longer void of the pleasures and happiness of making love and being in love. I would give her all those missed and empty years back of wanting love. Being loved fully was the goal for both of us.

When the waiter arrived at our table, I ordered the striped bass for the two of us and told the waiter to let the chef choose the sides.

"How about a bottle of Sauvignon blanc with dinner?" I asked, and the waiter smiled, knowing it paired well with the fish.

"A fine choice, sir," the waiter replied.

Yvette was all smiles. I had to ask her why the smiles. "To be honest," she said, "I have never had a man order dinner for me."

"Well, let's see how I do with dessert—or is it time for you to be the dessert?"

"You asked that yesterday," Yvette said as she leaned forward for a kiss.

"I know. I don't eat sugar a lot, but when I do, it's pleasurable," I replied.

"There you go again, making the simple exciting," she said.

"I'm talking about sugar," I said, as if I really were talking just about sugar.

"I bet you are." Yvette was caught up in a deep breath and moving her body to suggest that eating and thinking of herself as sugar just might be pleasurable.

"How was class today?" I asked, changing the subject.

"Just a class and the course will be over soon. In fact, finals are next week," she said.

"Good, so you'll be done for the balance of the year. You like festivals?" I asked.

"Yes. Why?"

"There's this Mushroom Festival every year in Kennett Square," I told her. My farmhouse wasn't very far from the town, but I decided to keep that to myself. I needed her to see me as the hard-working brother I am. Maybe letting her know that I was financially well-off might not change her thoughts about me, but I decided to open that box later—much later.

"Yvette, it is different, and you'll learn a lot about mushrooms." At that, she laughed uncontrollably, and I joined her in her laughter.

"When is it?" she asked.

"Soon. Let me google it. It's the first weekend of next month. You want to go?"

"Yes, I would go anywhere with you," she said. Those words seemed to come out of her mouth so effortlessly, but I felt them.

"Now you're blowing me up," I said, downplaying her words.

"You'll know when I blow you up," she said, which caught me off-guard. With that statement, Yvette had me shifting in my seat, trying to breathe normally. We laughed and toasted our new beginning, and then dined for about two hours before leaving the restaurant. "Come take a ride with me," I said.

"Where?"

"Didn't you say you would go anywhere with me?" I reminded her playfully, before continuing. "I'll drive us down to the canal where we can walk or take a ferry ride."

"That sounds romantic." She closed her eyes slowly as if savoring a meal before opening them, all the while smiling.

"It will be if we make it so. Let me open the car door for you," I said. Before she could respond, I had already moved toward the door to open it.

"You do that, too?" she said.

"Since I was a kid, I've been opening doors for my mother," I shared.

"Thank you," she replied.

I got in, started the car, and reached over to kiss her. Her kiss was better. As I slowly and deeply kissed her, my left hand caressed more than a handful of just one of her breasts, and then found its way to where her legs met. I gently squeezed her inner thigh on the way to feel the warmth and silky moisture of her. Her breathing went from normal to hot and bothered, but it was still only foreplay. Finishing the kiss with a suck of her neck, I put the car in drive and drove off. She was wet and animated, so I put on some old-school hip hop that had the beats of real music with soft flowing lyrics. "Hey. You OK?" I asked.

"What do you think?" she said as she buttoned her clothes, still trying to steady herself.

She leaned forward, her elbow resting on the center console, and then she put on her sunglasses, trying to hide her thoughts of what just happened. Perhaps, now hidden behind those dark lenses, were thoughts of us finding ecstasy in each other's arms soon. Were we on our way to more than just a ferry ride up the canal? Somehow, I could tell that this ride was going to go beyond passion.

# Chapter 5

# FINDING NORMAL

Weeks passed before we would say goodbye to fall and move into the new year. I was still seeing both Yvette and Lynn.

Yvette and I enjoyed being together, going to happy hours and eating out every night. She was falling hard for me, and all I was doing was being a gentleman. She started being forward in a sexual way. I had orchestrated the whole love thing growing between us. Don Juan would be proud of me, indeed. In fact, even Billy Dee Williams, Mr. Swag himself, would be especially proud. Still to this day, he could pull the young ladies. It is not what is in your pocket, but what is in your head that makes a woman go spinning in circles. Mr. Swag should hold classes with, of course, Ms. Nancy Wilson scheduled as a guest speaker. The Gentleman and the Lady would have you so refined; no ladies east or west of the Mississippi River would be safe from the social graces and romance learned from those two. Knowledge will change anyone if they want to change after getting it and being under their tutelage. Brothers would even regain the African Moorish understanding of themselves, as Kings and Princes.

All these many weeks, spending time with Yvette was a joy. Now she wanted to share herself with me, and I was ready to love her into the late night, but first we would enjoy dinner at an upscale restaurant in the city. I knew the first time our lips touched for more than just a few seconds the work needed to open her up. This woman of maturity knew not how to embrace a kiss properly, but she was wet in all her feelings for wanting now to learn, albeit later in her life. Beyond apparently and rarely being satisfied by the men she'd had in her life, she would find sexual completeness with me.

We talked about the Steve Harvey 90-day rule, but it sort of went out the window. She wanted to catch up on years lost before time and beauty would be no more. During the past weeks in between spending a lot of time together, she called me continually to make sure we would find time to be together, to have a drink, to dine out, and to help with her personal affairs. I was up for it all, because she was ready for love and to be loved—longer, more deeply, and differently. I understood her request, and I would be there to make that explosion happen. I was ready tonight to penetrate and possess her completely, filling those empty holes of passionless dreams. With this heart of mine and these arms, I was going to enthrall her and take her to where only lovers could go, driving toward the G-spot, and finding sexual healing before achieving sexual pleasures beyond her knowing. And yes, the songs would share our evening delight of passionate desires.

Yvette would be much easier to have than Lynn, even though I took my time with Yvette because she needed care and maturing, not in matters of motherhood or responsibilities, but in matters of the heart and passion, and making love. She was caught up and now wanted to experience those stories of passion, fun, and true lovemaking–from straight fucking to dancing on the ceiling. Whatever it would be, it was going to happen for as long as she wanted it to happen. She would know a lot more about many things, but for sure, she would know me and I, her. We would be joined together and perhaps forever

36

even though she would one day make that call, and she would, because of my two-year rule.

Most women at first did not care if they liked you or wanted what you have. They did not care about whatever baggage you had, married, kids, no job, etc. for two years. But at two years, women started asking themselves where was this going. Men might think we were the greatest, blowing the sisters back out regularly, but emotional creatures as they are, and while I loved them dearly, I always remembered that they had an agenda as well. For example, most of my relationships only lasted two years, and only a very few went beyond two years, but I was hoping Yvette would be one of them. I could tell from experience: Time is the unknown, and feelings are the shackles and chains that twist us up and remake us.

Maybe Yvette would be like many women who could drain the "I like you" out of a man, the kind of sista who would do just enough for you, because she just wanted what she wanted, all the time thinking she was being fair and generous only to find that she would end up running through multiple men and relationships in her life, staying for a while or longer. But when that relationship slowed down and she had not found love on their terms, she would once again be incomplete, would blame the guy, and would be ready to move on, still not having known love. Yvette told me about a city worker she dated off and on and how he took her on a trip and to ball games, but she stopped dealing with him because of what she found out about his questionable relationships with his ex-wife girlfriends, and his always investigative and controlling nature. "He was OK, I thought," she said, "but since meeting you, well ..." she paused and then continued, "... well, you totally complete me, and I have so much fun with you. Even my girlfriends who I've shared some things with are happy for me and us," she explained.

Imagine that, more truth telling. I hoped she watched her back because some men don't know how to let go when a woman finds someone else. Well, we all had history that was packed in the suitcases with which we traveled through life. Time would tell with Yvette, and this time she would know true passion. Perhaps, too, she would know love and how to love completely. So, if she did decide to move on, she would be shackled with those feelings of having been loved truly for a lifetime. True love finds us all. The journey is not without highs and lows, and life suspended in complete surrender like the musical complexities of John Coltrane's song, "A Love Supreme."

I last spoke to Yvette yesterday around 4 p.m. to let her know that we had dinner reservations for 7:30 p.m. today at Davio's. I told her I would pick her up at her place at 6:30 p.m. She told me again the Steve Harvey ninety-day rule was out the window, and we agreed that tonight, if something happened, we would just let it. I was fine with that, so I chose a restaurant that we both had never visited. That was a challenge for me, because there were few four- or five-star restaurants I had not already visited. At exactly 6:30 p.m., I rang her doorbell.

The foreplay was over with Yvette. I needed to explode my passion into her regularly, and she was ready. Maybe she was tired of me kissing and playing around with her ass and pussy in the car, at the park, on the bridge, in the movies, and while sitting side-by-side in a restaurant with my hand up her dress.

I ordered dinner for the two of us after looking over the menu. The fever, though, that Yvette and I felt left us both with very little appetite for food. In fact, we just wanted to be together tonight. So, we rushed through dinner and headed to the marina where I had a boat docked. I still hadn't told her, though, that I actually owned the boat. Instead, I let her believe that I chartered it for a couple of hours. We enjoyed drinks and laughter and the mutual excitement of me kissing her half-naked body all over while there.

After some time on the boat, we drove to her house. On the drive there, Marvin Gaye's smooth, silky voice crooned out his sexual lyrics, and Teddy Pendergrass had his back by singing "Close the Door." The ride went quickly as we listened and talked softly to each other. I pulled into her driveway and got out to open her car door. We walked close to one another and in lockstep to the entrance of her home. Once inside I told Alexa to play old school R&B. I floated over to her like a bird of prey, cloaking all of her with my body and aura of wanting to finally love her all night long. At the bottom of the steps, she said, "Let's go upstairs."

"OK," I said, but four or five steps up I turned her around, undressed her gently, and began kissing her from her lips down to her kneecaps. The smell of her lovely perfume invaded my nostrils. I loved it, and as I kissed her lightly, I found the taste of honey nestled within all her beauty. My dick was hard, and with her two legs, she was squeezing the shit out of me. I threw her legs way back, exposing her pussy to me. As I entered her, I stroked her slowly, softly, and each stroke blossomed into a beautiful story, a treasured memory. I watched her eyes widen with each stroke. This would indeed be a long story, though. Did she know that yet? The controlled panic that grew in her with each passing moment shown in her ever widening eyes, eyes she had trained on mine, and they told me she knew something different was happening. I knew she didn't know what, though. How could she know? I knew her. I knew her story. She'd never been here. This was not business as usual, was not feeding the kids and putting them to bed, was not a man humping until he was done. Her lips were tight now.

She didn't know this tempo, slower than slow, deeper than deep. No, she would not control the rhythm and the rhyme of this night. The high-pitched sounds now escaped her tight lips; she was trying to muffle those sounds, but I could hear them, and they were getting louder and louder still. I glided in her, I glided out of her, and then the dam broke. "I never been made love to like this!" she groaned. Even more suddenly came her scream, "Oh. Jesus. Fuck this pussy, baby. It's all your pussy, daddy. It's your pussy."

My head was down now. I was mining for that beautiful place she'd hidden deep inside after years of the same old thing, the same thing that made her feel the same old way. I was stroking her pussy to a beat from a drum a continent away, and as I was, to my ears, I heard the sounds of crying, but when I looked up, there were no tears, just the inexpressible passion upon her face that fought to express itself—crying but no tears, screams but no pain, joy but no smiles. Ecstasy only. Lovemaking only. Music filled the background, and she continued talking shit to me. "Go deeper baby. Be my lover, baby." Sounds of crying again. "I need this, baby. Oh, I *need* you."

Yvette was talking real shit to me, and so I whispered to her, "I got you caught up in feelings. So, let's not stop wanting and loving completely. So, give me some more of this pussy, baby. Come on, give me some more." I was doubling down on the dick now. Her only answer was, "I love you, baby. I swear I love you." We slid down the steps and laughed, then ran up the steps to the landing where I grabbed her again. This time we were on the floor in the hallway, and I propped her legs up against the wall, and I was back to loving her, kissing her, and holding both of her ass cheeks and pulling them apart for maximum penetration. She was about to cum again for the third or fifth time, I had lost count, and her eyes rolled backward in her head as she exclaimed, "Don't stop fucking me. I have never been fucked like this. What are you doing to me?"

I said, "We got more to give each other."

She said, "*I* do, baby?"

"Yes. Let me just turn this ass over and hit this from the back."

"Oh, shit!" She was hollering again. "I've never been fucked like this, baby. This is your pussy whenever you want it, baby."

I said, "Don't lie to me."

"I'm not, big daddy," she said.

"Oh, now I'm 'big daddy.' You don't know what to say, do you?" I'm sure she said those words before, but never with so much fervor in her voice and body language. Now being loved and sexed for more than two hours and, perhaps, for the first time, now moving toward the age of forty-nine. We were lovin' in cruise mode with me still guiding the throttle. I was loving her, and she was loving me back.

"I'm tired," Yvette said finally. I had to remember she was no Lynn. I would be fucking Lynn still with her lovely ass self, and I would be good with that. All smiles and loving everything we did to each other. Lynn, I had turned into a pro. All designed in every dimension for lovemaking the way I liked it, and unhappy with all others.

When Yvette and I got done with each other, if we ever would be done with each other, would we be any good for anyone else, with our thoughts of one another always coming forth? Our thoughts would be of us and our dreams of wanting one another when we were apart, if we ever would be.

I wouldn't let my ego consume me. I needed to get grounded. Yvette was resting quietly next to me, her body close and warm to mine. Though her short rest turned into a deep sleep, I was unable to sleep, so I watched a movie. I enjoyed old movies like *An Affair to Remember* with Cary Grant and Deborah Kerr, remade with Warren Beatty and Annette Benning. It was one of my favorites, and I had watched it several times. We were beginning our *Affair*, starring Harold and Yvette.

I watched movies until about 4:30 a.m. and woke her up by touching her where her two legs met, slowing raising them into the air to enjoy a slow fuck back to a crescendo of bed-rocking up against the wall and Yvette's exaggerated voice saying, "You want some more of this pussy, baby," and me saying, "You know I do." We began in the bed as I worked her to the edge of it and rolled her over, grabbed her by the neck as she held an unsupported angle with my dick all up in that sexual cavity of pleasures.

At 7 a.m. we went another round. This time I laid her upright against the mirror to let her watch herself as we played. To make it more fun, I grabbed her pussy with my right hand, finding the warmth of her while she felt my dick up in her stomach. She was gone, pussy spraying like a car wash and me in control of the buttons.

I told Yvette to stay right where she was, angled against the mirror, and that I was going to get myself an apple from the fridge. I said to her, "I know you think I'm going to do some freaky shit, but I'm not. My grandfather told me a long time ago to always eat an apple between sex, because it makes sex sweeter and longer, and ever since then, I have always eaten an apple in the midst of sex." I summed it up this way: an apple a day keeps your dick sweet, hard, and the doctor away. "Don't knock it until you try it," I added as I left the room and headed for the kitchen.

When I returned with a Fuji apple in my hand, chewing on a mouthful, she was still there angled against the mirror, seeming to have never moved from the position in which I had left her. I kissed her and hugged her from behind and went right at it again. She said, "Let's make this a quickie." I didn't hear her, and I wasn't stopping until I ate my apple, and I ate it slowly, bite by bite. Brothers, it's OK to bite the apple, again. Yvette told me she was truly enjoying sex for the first time.

Imagine her with grown babies, and she didn't know 'nothing.' Well, she would know something when I got done with her or she with me, but I was holding out hope that this time would be her last time finding love. And if she left, she would just know a lot more for the next guy, but would he want her if he knew what was on the bill of fare of sexual experiences I had planned for us? That next guy would know that it wasn't he who turned her into something new.

I walked her to the bed where she had covered herself up with a sheet, while I sat on the end of the bed in my yoga position and talked sweet nothings to her. She was half-listening to me. I asked her several questions, and she responded to none of them. She was ready to rest again for a while. I knew, because she was just uttering "umm" and "I hear you."

While Yvette slept, I fixed breakfast. I prepared veggie omelets with red roasted potatoes, rye toast, beef sausage, and coffee with heavy cream, the way she ordered it when we went out. I sliced strawberries and blueberries to refresh the palate. While making breakfast, I replayed the events of the previous night in my mind. I remembered the sweetness and fierceness of our lovemaking, and it was good. In fact, it was fun. I decided to listen to some Arthur Prysock, his great baritone voice, and I threw in my man Johnny Hartman as well. If they had let those two guys loose back in the day, there would be no need for Sinatra or Torme. Don't get me wrong, I liked those two guys a lot, but I liked Tony Bennett better. He has a Black man's *coolness*; Sinatra had big *style,* and Torme was just *nice.* Hartman had a silky, soulful voice, and Prysock had big swag in his singing—all kings of their art and genre for me. Playing on the CD, Coltrane, featuring Johnny Hartman—it couldn't get any better—or hearing Arthur rapping throughout the CD, *This Is My Beloved.*

Listening to great voices, I took my time preparing breakfast to allow Yvette some time to sleep. The sista was knocked out. I placed everything on a tray with a small vase of the flowers from the arrangement I had sent her. I carried the tray upstairs to find her awake and sitting up in the bed with the sheet around her breasts. "I can't believe you made breakfast!" she said, with a surprised and hungry smile. "I didn't hear you at all. I would have gotten up and made us breakfast."

"Next time you can," I said, and we both laughed as I placed the tray in front of her, opened the linen napkin, and placed it on her lap. I poured the first cup of coffee. I fed her the first of several bites of food and kissed her with all the tenderness I could muster

"All right, the sista Beyonce got it right. I'm taking your ass to Red Lobster after all, as a thank you for the night we had. If I had met you in my younger days, we would have a house full of babies," she said. We smiled. She took a forkful of strawberries and said, "You're sweeter than these berries."

"That was a charming thing to say," I said.

"I mean it. You're special, and I hope we'll be together. I like you," she said with hopefulness in her voice.

"The same. Time will find a place for us, I'm sure," I said. "Finish your food. I am going to change the music and bring up my tray and join you. Is there anything you'd like to hear?"

"Yes. Phyllis Hyman," she said, surprising me.

"OK. Let me go downstairs and change the music, but are you sure you want to listen to her this early? We may be back at it, again."

"I'm ready, just let us eat first. I can get used to you and this," she said.

"Check you out. Take it slow, and we'll stay together longer, if not forever," I said.

"There you go with your sweet talk, but I like it," she exclaimed.

After getting my food and changing the music, we ate our fill, talked, and wanted each other even more. There, watching her, I asked myself if we should do it again. Why not? She wanted more and I was willing, but there is something about too much too quickly. I didn't want to do that, again. We laid around in each other's arms for the rest of the day.

# Chapter 6

## FUN AT THE BEACH

On Monday, after a great weekend with Yvette, I thought a lot about her. I decided for the next month that I would spend the rest of my time with her. I began with a call to her to ask if she would like to spend the day at the beach with me. She answered on the first ring with an expressive, "Hello!"

"Wow. I deserve all that," I said chuckling.

"And more," she said. "I'm still replaying the other night with you. You took me some place different, and I loved it." Her voice sounded so passionate about our evening together.

"Hey, leave work and come go to the beach with me for the day," I said.

"Are you sure?" she said.

"I'm asking," I said.

"OK. What time?"

"I'll pick you up around noon."

"Sounds great, I'll be home waiting for you."

"Just bring your swimsuit and a change of clothes to hang out in before driving back," I suggested.

"OK. Harold, it sounds like you do this a lot," she said, though asking, sort of. She continued, "Now, I'm a water girl; find the water, you'll find me."

"I like the beach as much as you do. If you bring your music and beach speakers, I'll bring the cooler full of food and liquor, as well as towels, lounge chairs, and an umbrella," I assured her.

At about 11:45 a.m., I was in her driveway and proceeded to pack everything into the back of her silver Lexus SUV. Within fifteen minutes, we were on our way for fun in the sun, sand, and beach bars. An hour later, I pulled up to the boardwalk and unloaded the SUV and had Yvette wait while I parked the car at an econo parking lot. "All day parking for $5," the sign read. The parking lot attendant knew me, and I think the old Kolkata brother just liked watching me from his hut screw women in the car or while walking around the parking lot aimlessly. I walked toward the boardwalk where I left Yvette and gathered our beach stuff before we went off to find a spot on the beach close to the water. The beach was never very crowded during the middle of the week, which allowed me to get down to the shore, enjoy the sun, walk the boardwalk, play blackjack for a while, eat, get in a jazz set at Kelsey, and then arrive back home by 10 or 11 p.m. We got everything set up—umbrella up, lounge chairs unfolded, beach mats laid out, and cooler opened, showing off all of its goodies, and all she needed was to remove her beach coverup.

"How do you do it?" Yvette asked. "I would have had twice the amount of everything. You have this down to a science."

She was ready to relax, lounge in the sun to deepen that already darkened skin, which I was going to lotion down. While I was rubbing her body with tanning lotion, my thoughts of her ran wild. I applied lotion starting at her ankles, moved up to the buttocks, where I lingered longer than necessary, then finished her middle section, her shoulders, and then around her neck and face where she was waiting for a kiss.

"You're not going to kiss me after all that rubbing and feeling me all over?" she said incredulously.

"You want a kiss?" I asked. "Do you?" I pressed her.

"Yes. I want a lesson. I'm not tired like the other night," she admitted.

"All right, but the kiss is a statement of thoughts, a ride to somewhere driven by the touching of our lips and tongues. We must start there before we can move inwardly and then outwardly finding ecstasy from sheer kissing. I can kiss you for an hour and make you have an orgasm," I boasted.

"'You already have. And it was less than an hour," she flattered me. "I don't know what you do to me, but you better be glad it's not twenty years earlier or we would be on this beach with a bunch of kids," she confessed.

"You always say that," I replied.

"It's just the way you make me feel, but I'm OK here just with you. To give you all my attention and me," she said with all sincerity. I loved hitting that pussy, but really, it was much more than that I was after. I wanted her to know I wanted her and that she was worth my time and my attention. "What would you like? A peach martini I pre-made or a Tito's and tonic with lime, since you're not a sweet-drink kind of person?" I offered.

"The Tito's will do."

I remarked, "I'm drinking Jack Daniel's Lynchburg Lemonade cocktails this afternoon. It's my summer-in-the-sun drink." I then pulled out from a carry-all bag, which was leaning against the cooler, my old folding beach tray cheese board and filled it with cheeses, fruit, and crackers. Chicken salad and several pâtés were in the cooler on ice.

Eyeing the spread, Yvette sat up in fascination and said, "I like how you come to the beach, Harold, but I got to get us all new things. Your chairs, cooler, tray—all your stuff is old."

"OK. Go shopping, and we'll come back on Thursday," I said, hoping she would take the bait. I wanted to spend as much time as possible with her. Today was Monday, and we both left work on our office desks to enjoy more time together, and now it looked like we were going to do it again on Thursday. I told myself it is working. She wanted to be with me. The Steve Harvey rule is good for a younger person, but after raising a family as we both had, it was not about rules. Instead, it was about our values and the respect we had for one another as we traveled together, protected our space together, and cherished our time together. Being attentive to each other in this way meant sharing our thoughts and thus great moments. Yvette just might be the one who would change those bad-boy habits of mine, seemingly knitted into my DNA.

I returned my attention to her and enjoyed listening to the music she selected. We noticed that people close to us were digging our flow and the music she was playing. Nevertheless, we left them alone and kept our conversation to ourselves. We talked about social issues and how people today, except for a few, do not have the backbone like earlier individuals fighting injustice. She took the point of view that their income made them less concerned for others and my position was that society had been fed too much individualism. We debated and agreed on some things and disagreed on others, but it was an intellectual conversation bathed in a little urban vibe.

Eating and talking for over an hour, we decided to get up and take a walk along the shoreline and let the knee-high ocean waves crash against our legs. We talked and walked, getting lost in each other, without realizing that we walked almost two miles. We decided to turn around. Watching children play reminded us of our times with our children and spouses. It felt good, and just then, she stopped me for no reason, kissed and hugged me, and then touched my lips after the kiss with her long, slender index finger. She had lovely hands.

We continued walking back to our beach chairs. When we arrived, we viewed the ocean from our beach chairs. For about an hour, we sat eating the food we brought with us. Then we got up and went to the C-Beach Bar located on the beach for a drink and more beach watching. At the C-Beach Bar, Yvette excused herself to freshen up. I wanted to follow her, and I did, into the bathroom. They were the modern portable bathrooms you see on the beach these days. They were brand new and very clean. Following right behind her into the bathroom, I locked the door and didn't care who saw us walking inside together and then said to Yvette, "I want some sex."

Yvette said, "You're crazy; get out of here!"

"Nope. I want some pussy first," I said as she was busy. "Here, grab my dick," I continued, and with a mischievous look on her face that grew in intensity, she did, making it as hard as granite stone. She now had me worked up, and I was ready for her if she was willing. I turned her around, and she bent over at a slight angle. I pressed her further forward until she was at nearly a 90-degree angle with her elbows resting on the sink, and I removed what little clothing she had that blocked me from a clear dick entry into her peach from behind.

"My sweet baby, you want some of this?" Yvette whispered.

"Yes, that's why I'm in here with you," I said.

She began working me with words and her peach. "So, what you gonna do, Big Daddy? What you gonna do?"

"There you go talking that big daddy shit again."

"But you are my big daddy," she said, while she still had her elbows propped on the sink, sticking her ass out even further. I found her two tits to hold, and the fun started. She continued talking shit to me for about twenty-five minutes of fun lovin'. Then her pussy started to tighten while oozing orgasmic liquids of delight brought on by the intersection of her tight pussy and my dick sliding in and out like a piston in a well-tuned engine. We were doing it not in the park or on the beach, but in a damn portable bathroom at a beach bar with people probably wondering when we would come out to rejoin the real world of beach goers. It took a while for us to cum a couple of times and clean ourselves up before heading for the bar.

With our sunglasses on and now at the bar, we talked about what people were wearing to the beach these days and conversed with the bartender. All the female bartender could do was smile and ask, "Are you ready for a drink, now?"

"We are," I smiled back and said, "The coldest beer you got back there will do me," and Yvette said, "make it two."

The bartender said, "You two are different, but the sign on the door did say unisex and that's all."

"True," I affirmed. The DJ played reggae as we sat at the bar. We went to play Connect Four, at a table nearby shaded by a canopy that hid us from the sun in which Yvette kicked my ass. After losing six in a row, I asked a couple behind us if they wanted to play as teams since they were laughing at me. We played them and ended up, after six or eight games, even. Two or so hours later we headed back to our lounge chairs where we fell asleep. About an hour after that I nudged her awake. We packed up and headed for the SUV, where we washed off with a couple of gallons of water, which I always brought along for such occasions, and dried ourselves with extra towels we left in the SUV. We changed into our evening wear in the parking lot. Cleaned and refreshed, we were ready for an evening of eating, listening to music at Kelsey, and gambling at one of the casinos before heading home.

# Chapter 7

## A STRAWBERRY AND SEX

Wednesday morning, I called Yvette to ask her to fix dinner that night. She said, "I would love to fix us dinner and stay home for a change."

"A change it would be," I agreed and told her, "I'm having something special delivered to you today."

"No one has delivered anything to the house," she informed me.

"I know it will be there exactly at 6 p.m. Just wait for it," I assured her.

"I will, and I'll call you when I get it," she replied.

"Call me, if you want, but I'll see it when I get to the house," I said.

"What do you have me doing?" she asked.

"Fixing us dinner, which you said you wanted to do and stay home for a change," I answered, puzzled by her question.

"I did say that, and I meant it," she said, adding, "You just have me wondering, I guess."

"See you at 7:45 p.m. for drinks and dinner," I said, about to hang up.

But, she quipped, "Just drinks and dinner?"

"That's all I'm thinking for the moment, unless you can change my mind. I'll see you soon," I said, wanting to end the call before she asked more questions. I wanted it all to be a surprise, and I wanted to finish readying myself to dine with her.

"OK," she accepted, just before I hung up.

It would be 6 p.m. soon, and even though I implied she didn't have to call once she received the special delivery, I was interested to see if she would or wait to share with me what was in the box. Six o'clock came and went with no call, but I did receive a confirmation via my cell that the box was delivered. Consequently, I didn't know what to expect when she opened the front door, specifically, if she'd be wearing what was in the box. I was confident but not certain what she would do, so I would have to wait, and I was OK with whatever she decided. After all, Yvette and I were beyond just sex, not like Lynn and me—she and I started with sex and ended with sex most every time we met.

At 7:45 p.m. exactly I was at Yvette's door and ready to ring the doorbell when I noticed a note saying, "The door is unlocked. Come on in." I smiled as I read the note and anticipated what was to come next. I had set the stage by sending her a package. Now, it was on her from here, and I was going along for the ride, wherever it took us. Yvette had the sultry Phyllis Hyman extended mix, *You Know How to Love Me*, playing throughout the house. In fact, I heard it before entering. I walked in and called out to her, "Yvette. Where are you?"

"In the kitchen preparing dinner. Come on back. I got what you want to see, and maybe dessert for you," she said. There she was sexy as shit, dancing to the music, fingers popping, and her right index finger beckoning me forward. She was singing off-key and whirling dizzily, and shaking her sugar around in the kitchen.

Just then she said, "Come here and give me a kiss for you're the one I've been waiting for. ... Your smile, your magic and oh, to hear your voice whisper, come love me." The next song by Phyllis was "No One Can Love You More." Was she right?

No one could love her more? She had the right music to share our evening together. Avant and Keke Wyatt played next, "You & I."

"I got you, dearest," said Yvette, playing the house DJ role and the playlist continued into the night.

All I could say was sweet sugar in the belly for just then, that feeling began to ferment, but I would play it very cool, because, simply put, she was right.

What had been in the box—black silk lingerie with a garter belt, black stockings, and a bra, less the panties—was now on Yvette, fitting her sexy-ass body perfectly. She stood there, a statue of beauty unbound in every way and wanting to express her newfound sexual freedom. She wore five-inch heels with a print pattern to contrast with the black silk, and beginning from her stilettos, my eyes slowly rose admiring this beautiful woman standing in front of me. First, I admired her ankles, her sculpted calves, and her knees. Then my eyes smiled enjoying her smooth, waxed vaginal area that looked like it was done yesterday. My goodness, she was lovely, and I was only halfway to her lips. I wanted to kiss her and to kiss her for a long period of time.

Her lips were painted with lipstick the color of a fiery liquid red, and I was sure she would mark my whole body with those lips before the evening, or even dinner, was over. Her navel was so inviting. Curiously, I wondered why she never pierced it. More urgently, her plump tits with dark brown nipples commanded my attention. I would have more than a mouthful of those tonight and waste no part of them. Yes, passion was in the air and what was in the box had set the tone and provided more for dinner than pussy and conversation alone. A woman experiencing love, romance, and passion, call it what you will, but it was all that with dinner served hot. She had selected the five-inch heels to prance around the kitchen and to dine at an already set table. The shoes elevated her and only elongated her heavenly sculptured body. Even Michelangelo would have had a hard time creating something finer. I loved what I saw and anticipated what was to come.

"Well! Do you like what was in the box, big daddy?" Yvette asked in a sultry voice.

"'Yes. Most definitely," I replied. "Absolutely. You got me smiling with your styling and moving like Ms. Sexy Winner. I see why you didn't call me. The art of the surprise always works." Then striking a poignant, serious tone, I said, "Yvette, you really look great. Tell me, are you dinner or dessert?"

"Neither. We need to eat. Please sit down and pour us a glass of wine," Yvette instructed quietly. I barely heard her voice. The table was perfectly set with fine china, flatware, and stemware. The aroma of the food was only subdued by her scantily fitting lingerie, which only heightened my senses. I did not know what to eat first. Yvette had made it clear that we needed to eat, but doing so did not keep me from relishing how dynamic she was in every way in that black lingerie.

I focused on her elongated body and the smell of her sensual perfume—the smell of oriental fragrances, perhaps a full floral, or simply a light and fresh smell. I was lost in the evening and aura created by our being together and the perfume she had sprayed in all the right places. Wow, it aroused me even more. The scents continued to carry me afar with new smells of jasmine, or perhaps it was lavender, that may have been combined into a rich floral scent. The lady got me going, I said to myself.

She brought the food to the table, and we finally sat down to enjoy the meal she prepared for our dining pleasure. She was cool and so matter-of-fact as she sat there virtually naked, teasing me with every bite of food.

"How do you like the food?" she asked.

"'It's very good. You told me you were a very good cook, and now I have tasted it for myself. I'm wondering now how well you cook with clothes on."

"I guess you will have to wait for that experience," Yvette spoke teasingly.

"Oh, the lady is in rare form tonight. You got anymore?" I asked.

"Any more of what?" she asked, curious.

"You got me incoherent for the moment. Let's finish dinner, and I'll help you clean up."

"OK. I have dessert for you, strawberries and cream," she said knowingly.

"I'm a dessert man," I said, as if she hadn't remembered.

"I know," she said. Her head turned to look at me with a playfully smug smile.

We finished dinner, and we both got up to clear the table, but I had had enough, and she knew it. So when I said, "Come here," she came without hesitation. I caressed and marveled at her standing next to me, and then we kissed. When our lips parted, she steadied her gaze, and, with both authority and surrender in her voice, said, "I want you to fuck me."

"Sweetheart, that's not a problem," I said. "Let me jump out of these clothes, if one can jump out of clothing," and as I spoke, I was trying. Undressed, I now caressed her soft body again and the spark ignited by that touch set me in motion. With one hand behind her back, I swept her legs from under her with the other hand. I picked her up and placed her sensual body on the kitchen island, casting her legs upward and outward to the east and west, her legs in the air still wearing her stilettos. I entered and began fucking her on the kitchen island non-stop until she came twice. Between those orgasms, we found time to enjoy the completeness inside each other, I, in her and she, in my head. Lovemaking has a way of doing that to people who can find their way to Loveland.

I then moved down her body with a handful of strawberries to play with the pussy. Rubbing the outside of her vagina with a strawberry, somehow her pussy just sucked it inside her, and she panicked. She jumped off the damn island and started hollering, pleading, screaming, and running around demanding, "Get this strawberry out of me!" Just then the music stopped, and we were no longer hearing Phyllis singing "Somewhere in My Lifetime"—or was it "Hurry Up This Way Again?" Whatever it was, it was not about not feeling the loving.

I said, "You got a red snapper here," laughing at her.

"This isn't funny. Please help me. I'm a registered nurse. I can't go to the ER for something like this. Help me!" Yvette was clearly frustrated with me, her voice now many octaves higher."

"Just stop panicking. I will," I reassured her.

"I can't. How can I explain why I got a large-ass strawberry way up in my vagina? You got me fucking and doing more shit with you than I done in forty-some years. Now to be embarrassed by having to go to the ER and have some doctor get a damn strawberry out of my pussy!" she said, restraining the urge to become hysterical.

"You did this," I said, toying with her.

"How did I do this?" she snapped.

"You got the red snapper that sucked it inside you," I chuckled.

"Funny. Very funny," she said. The expression of embarrassment riddled her face. "How will I explain this?" she repeated.

"Just tell them the truth," I said casually.

"Right! This isn't funny. I'm a nurse. This is embarrassing. I'm a professional nurse, and this is unexplainable behavior to them in the ER."

"It's explainable, but I will get it out, if you just relax for thirty seconds," I said calmly, to help her relax. "Come here," I coaxed her. I lifted her back on the kitchen island and became Dr. Harold, probing inside for the red berry. "I got it. It still looks the same as before slipping inside your chamber walls."

She had had enough of kitchen sex after the strawberry incident. So we moved to the living room where I sat in a Queen Anne chair. I had her pull her cheeks apart and told her to slide on my dick. She did, but quickly said, "This is too much. It's in my stomach." I didn't hear her while one hand grabbed the pussy and the other her tits. She had me wet from her pussy oozing cream and it wasn't the cream from the strawberries and cream we never ate. We took a break before going upstairs to enjoy our sexual playtime for the remainder of the night.

"Harold," Yvette shared.

"Yes, Yvette," I answered.

"I'm in love with you," she said quietly, deliberately.

"How do you know that?" I asked.

"How does anyone know, except what their feelings tell them?" she said, still quiet, still deliberate.

"Let's talk about it in the morning. Curl up with me and let's get some sleep. We got a long and fun day at the beach tomorrow," I said, adding matter-of-factly, "I love you too, dear."

## Chapter 8

# RETURNING TO THE BEACH

*Why do we love?*
*Is it what we just do or say we want?*
*Is it something we seek, to find the love of a birth mother?*
*Or is it what we search for to understand*
*how two can become one?*
*Our days are for giving and time is for knowing one another*
*Love is the passion that drives us to ecstasy*
*And ecstasy to togetherness.*
*Why do we love? It is required to find humility, compassion*
*and forgiveness for our tomorrows together.*

We woke up late. I fixed us coffee first and started cooking breakfast. We ate and talked about the last several months together. I know I always played by the two-year rule, but we were far from the end; in fact, we were just beginning.

Yvette was all sexed up, having never felt these types of emotions before. I was not sure if it was passion she was feeling or if she was really in love. Time would tell. Past experience told me it was passion. Most of the women I have dealt with leave once the passion fades, probably because they wanted more from me than I was willing then to give back to them. Nonetheless, I felt something was intrinsically different with Yvette. Enjoyable as those relationships were, I had learned that passion could not outlast love on its own. Passion had a way of dying all on its own. It was a high and unless continually injected with euphoria, it withered away like grass in the heat of the mid-summer sun. The two people who got caught up in such, the mid-summer sun faded away those feelings. But like the late-summer rain showers and the cool air of the late season, the grass returned greener and more pleasant to roll around on, and love would be there. If it did, the passion that we were experiencing would renew itself. For it becomes love in all the maturity of a grownup in the room, for passion was the child, learning, and with time, growing up to understand love in its fullness, a fullness that would allow the two of us to become one. Where did one think the line "You complete me" came from?

My thoughts began floating in my head. I wanted to move toward that mature and loving place with Yvette. Did she truly want the same? Some say bad habits are hard to stop. I disagreed. We all just did the things we still wanted to do until we wanted to change. That change required growing beyond our immediate wants and desires and understanding. Was I beyond them? On this day, I would begin to collect all that was bothering me along with some of my bad habits, and place them in a box. I would place that box on a shelf and turn away and keep walking, never turning around. If I did, I would say I had been there before and let myself keep on moving because I had surrendered to the love of the truth, to the love I had for that special someone, to life, and to a mature mind. Would that be enough to trump any addiction or any of my bad-boy habits? The mind was the engine that powered us to drive forward, if we allowed ourselves the joy of using that God-given gift. But then there was the heart that battled the mind. The history of each of our lives was all before us, and so was mine.

I had allowed these thoughts of mine to escape me, but upon reclaiming them, I was able and willing to concede that yes, maybe she does in fact love me. I said, "Hey, lady, we need to start getting ready to head for the shore."

"I know you were sitting there as I was talking, but your mind was not concentrating on what I was telling you about me and you. You go off in thoughts like that sometimes for some reason, leaving me here all alone and wondering if those thoughts are about me or us," Yvette confided in me.

"For the record, if that's what I'm doing, it's about us and a little of me trying to find us," I said, speaking candidly.

"OK, I can handle that for our beginning is great, and I hope the ending will not be an ending, but just us and our time together," she said, and for a few moments after speaking those words she just peered into my eyes. Her countenance was peaceful, as if she were surrendering any attempt to hide what she truly felt. And then with grace and poise, she bowed her head, averting my eyes.

"That sounds great. Your feelings making you sentimental?" I asked her.

"No, just openly sharing my feelings, which you should learn to do, and stop keeping them in your head. No one knows what you're thinking—granted your actions and expressions, caring and concern for me do show it, even if it is unspoken by you. Yes, your feelings clearly show, but you make me hunt for the words. It would be easier for you to say them out loud and often from time to time. Mr. Wonderful, nice guy. I like you. I won't be our problem. It's what's in your head that will be our problem. I got you and the interest of your heart," she said. I believed she was trying to encourage me to "open up," but I had been here before. And was she even aware of her ability to change her mind on a dime? Right now, she believed her words. I, however, wasn't sure of them.

"Let me think about that," I said, finally sharing, "I am going to pack up the SUV."

"OK, Mr. Wonderful," she said.

So, I'm Mr. Wonderful, nice guy now?" I replied.

"You know when you are, big daddy," as she smiled at me.

Carrying our beach stuff to the car, I couldn't deny her words.

It was one o'clock, and we were headed for AC to enjoy the day. We packed up the car with our usual shore trappings and headed for the beach. Traffic was light, and we got there in no time. Like we had always done, we found a spot on the beach and were all set up within minutes .

Relaxing in our lounge chairs, we fixed drinks and our cheeseboard with different goodies this time. Music filled the air under our umbrella. As had become her custom, Yvette asked me again to lotion her body, which I did, but quicker this time. She had me thinking about other things all the while—about how amazing it was when someone shared his or her feelings with another, and how in such moments one really needs to pay attention to the truth being spoken to another. It was important stuff, important moments. My day here at the beach was to be about us, and maybe I would need to express my feelings to Yvette, if I could. Perhaps doing so would usher in the beginning of a lifetime of heavenly dreams that are only granted day by day. After having lain around in the sun for a couple of hours, I asked Yvette if she wanted to walk the boardwalk for the fun of it.

"Sure. I love walking with you. Remember though, Harold, you should try saying what's on your mind sometime," she said. Had she been reading my mind?

"Perhaps," I replied pensively. Then I continued, "I'm like my father, Yvette. He showed his love by his actions of devotion and providing food and shelter for the ones he cared about."

"I get that," she said, but thankfully she let the matter go for now. "Let's go and play some games. If you're lucky you might win me a teddy bear to sleep with when you're not there."

"Let's do that, Yvette," I said, happy to move on from the discussion. "I'm always there. It's a mental thing. It's how I think. I think you're always with me, sleeping alone or walking here together on the boardwalk," I said, wanting to assure her of my closeness. "Win you a teddy bear if you want. I'm good at boardwalk games. I worked at carnivals growing up," I said.

"You worked at carnivals?" laughed Yvette.

"Yep. I worked all the games of chance," I said.

"You keep on surprising me with your history, Harold. I guess the next thing then is that you will tell me you climb mountains and run with the bulls in Spain."

"I do all those things, except swim well," I admitted.

"You can't swim?" she blurted out. Her mouth agape communicated her disbelief.

"Nope, I cannot," I said.

Laughing steadily harder, she said, "Why can't country boys swim?"

"Well, to be honest, I can. You gotta learn in the military. I was Special Forces, but I hate swimming," I said, but wanting to avoid making a big deal of it.

"Whoa! You keep surprising me," she said. She smiled as she spoke. "That's all we did growing up in the city. We spent all day at the city pool. That's what city kids did, back then," Yvette said with an air of nostalgia.

"I can swim well enough to save myself, but I really don't enjoy swimming," I said.

"I'll teach you, baby, to enjoy it too, since I'm learning so much from you. Until now, I haven't found a man who shares as much as you, but we got to do some work on you expressing your feelings. I'll leave that alone for the time being. OK, baby?" she said, her soft hand beginning to stroke my arm as if to say it will be OK.

"So, what kind of prize do you want me to win for you? They're all here in the different booths. Or I can just go buy you some gold earrings in the jewelry store," I said.

"Really!" she blurted out and the hand that had been caressing my arm only moments ago, now smacked it in a playful manner.

Walking the boardwalk until we reached one of the casinos, we slipped in and went gambling. I went to the blackjack table, bought twenty-five hundred dollars in chips, and went to work winning earring money. I played the game well, and if I caught a hot streak, I would have money to buy Yvette a pair of earrings. Yvette told me she never played. I told her "I don't introduce anyone to bad habits." About an hour later, I was up fifteen hundred dollars, and decided to cash in and take Yvette shopping. Yvette was surprised.

"You're lucky. My Mr. Lucky," she marveled.

"How many names do you have for me?" I said jokingly, looking at her out of the corner of my eye.

"Only one, really. My Mr. Lover Man. It sums up all of you." As she spoke, she turned and placed her arms around my shoulders and kissed me softly, gently, deeply. I hadn't been thinking about it, but it seemed she had taken notes. I really enjoyed her kissing me; she was a quick learner. That I wasn't expecting it made it linger on my lips and in my mind. At the same time, her kiss and comments, ironically, made me conflicted. The kiss was great, but this woman was dropping those lines. At least part of me felt they were just that, lines, yet a part of me felt her heart in them. I had to find the extent of the truth in her words. Time tells all, my father would remind me. "Give it time, Harold. Through the rights and wrongs, love always stands up," he would say, and I wanted her love to stand up; at least I wanted to believe it could, but old habits die hard.

We shopped and found her a pair of 18-carat gold earrings with pave diamonds, a rare find at that price. She wanted them and I paid $1,200 for them, but I did not care. It was casino money. I did not mind even spending my hard-earned money on her.

With our winnings, we walked backed to our chairs on the beach and spent the remainder of the day there. At about six o'clock that evening, we packed up and headed to the SUV. Yvette sure was happy being with me. I could see it palpably in everything she did, in every gesture. I wondered how long this would last, given my first impression of her.

We did our gallons of water shower. Although I could easily afford a very nice room, I liked day-tripping to the beach this way. It reminded me of my earlier years enjoying simple fun and simple pleasures when I had no dough, just my dreams. Now all cleaned up, we changed into our evening wear and headed for Kelsey's, our favorite place to eat and to listen to some jazz or karaoke before driving home from another day trip to the beach.

## Chapter 9

# ME AND LYNN—MORE THAN A PASSING GLOW OF LOVE

I kept hanging out with Yvette and Lynn through the fall and the winter, and with spring approaching, I continued sharing great moments and great sex together more often with Yvette. Meanwhile, I was spending less and less time together with Lynn because her job demanded such a great deal of her. Regardless of her demanding schedule, however, Lynn said she wanted more than the once or twice a week that I was still seeing her. As I was missing all her sexiness as well as her beautiful ass, I would have to back off of Yvette just a little so I could enjoy some crazy sex all night long with Lynn. She was my addiction in a real sense, and I was becoming more conscious of this reality. Yvette was who I wanted, but Lynn was whom I needed. I would walk away from her in time or she from me, but for now I was going to keep sliding in and out of her intoxicating pussy. And Lynn knew it was intoxicating. In fact, I knew if I told her that I was seeing Yvette, Lynn wouldn't care. She had that much confidence in her shit, and she was that fine, finer than Yvette with just as much style. Two city women with different kinds of stripes, both players who would play for what they wanted because they were women who played to win. Neither one would allow the other the prize, even if they found another man to be with. They would try and keep what made them sexually satisfied. They have men and could probably have any they wanted, but I was what Lynn wanted for now. Neither Lynn nor Yvette would settle for less. They could find someone to be happy with, but without the sex to captivate the body and without the romance to captivate the mind, such perceived happiness would be difficult to sustain for them, or me, and as well for most women.

Yes, a woman could give a guy some pussy, and a man could just get a nut, but the truth, the unspoken tormenting truth, is that men and women want both. I was no different from Yvette or Lynn, but at some point, I would have to make a choice. For now, I was going to continue this affair with both women. In the end, I hoped to be with Yvette. Time would tell, but right now I was knocking on Lynn's front door with a bottle of tequila and my Jack Daniel's. We would toast to me promising to spend more time with her. She knew what she was, and I knew why I didn't call her for two years, a reality that now seemed so long ago. A woman like Lynn was my weakness. She appealed to every bad-boy instinct in me, and despite who I wanted, here I was toasting with Lynn, anticipating the ecstasy to come.

Because I was not spending a lot of time with Lynn, I felt guilty, and so I offered to go to Manhattan to see a play and dine out with her. I called in a favor from a friend who owned a limo service and hired a limo and a driver to escort us to and from NYC the following Friday. Lynn was happy about that since I scheduled it with her sitting in the living room on the sofa next to me.

"Would you like something to eat? I fixed dinner for us," Lynn said.

"What did you fix?" I asked, because Lynn was a really good cook.

"Porterhouse steaks medium well with just a little pink the way you like it. Like my pink pussy," she said, trying to get me aroused.

"You had to say that, right?" I said.

"You once told me that you like this pink pussy," Lynn reminded me.

"No, I told you all pussy is pink inside to be exact," I corrected.

"Whatever," she dismissed my response out of hand. "Come sit at the table, your steak is ready," she added with a pleasing smile. She knew despite my remark and the insinuation I made about her decorum that I wasn't fazed beyond a certain point.

Lynn went into the kitchen but took a while to come back.

I called to her after a few moments, "I thought you said the steaks were ready."

Damn, she came out of the kitchen buck-ass naked, tits following our dinner plates.

"Take off your pants. I'm going to cut up your steak while I sit on your dick," she commanded.

"Oh, OK," I said with a chuckle and then did exactly what she told me to. Within a moment, I was seated at the table bare-assed. She cut the first piece of steak for me and straddled my dick, all the time wanting me to chew on the steak while she held the steak on the fork.

"This is some good shit, my dear," I said to Lynn. "Damn, you do my meat the way I like it." Lynn smiled just so and wrapped her legs around the dining room chair, and like that, it was on. I couldn't wait to enter inside of her.

"We'll have to eat our steaks later; now I am having dessert," Lynn laughed and smothered my face between both of her fully rounded developed breasts.

"Hey, baby," she whispered in my ear.

"What! I'm not a baby?" I managed to say, my mouth muffled deep in between her warm tits. She was working my dick now, up and down, up and down, up and down along the top part of it.

"You want some of this," she told me.

"Yep," was all I could say, answering a question she hadn't asked, and while I was, she was serving up pink pussy the way I liked it, working her way down and around my dick, gradually stretching and widening her pussy to consume it. Up and down, up and down, her hips rose up and back away ever so slightly from me only to ride down and toward me again in slow rapid successive movements. Damn, she was serving steak; yes, she was serving *me*. In that moment, I could still feel her breasts on my face and though my eyes were closed, I could feel that they were glistening. As she pushed my head back, the breath from her open mouth warmed my face, and I opened my eyes to see her eyes through mine. As in so many times in the past, she'd given me that look. There is no name for it, but every man and woman knows it. And shifting my weight in the chair and her with me, without further delay, I cupped her legs and shot right up into her pink pussy. Her head then careened back, and she forced her hips down onto mine, and hollered, "It's in, it's in, oh, way up in my stomach, Jesus! Yes," she gasped and then her legs, slowly at first, then violently, shook uncontrollably. "Oh, I'm cumming. I'm cumming. Goddam this dick is good," she shouted, her voice vibrating all the while as if trying to speak while holding onto a runaway rollercoaster.

"Keep loving me. Don't you give my dick away," she said. "You hear me?"

"No," I said, defiantly. "It's my dick, but I got you. You know I got you," I said as if it were a promise made.

As if to match that promise, in as controlled a voice as she could muster, her voice breaking up as she spoke, she said, "If I told you I love you, would you take advantage of me?"

"No, Lynn I would not," I said with equal sobriety.

But she was not done with her truth telling, and she knew this was the moment to come clean. We hadn't spent as much time together, and maybe she suspected something, maybe she didn't. Maybe she cared and maybe she didn't, but she said,

"You don't love me; you just love fucking me." Her words came seamlessly for neither of us had stopped the rhythm of our rhyme. Her hips rose and fell in a motion majestically mastered atop a piston pounding perfectly syncopated, two parts making something beautiful, though what was not yet known.

And like that, deep in the rhythm, the truth telling abounded. "That may be true," I said, "but I love you also, more than you know. I don't express my feelings openly a lot. You just got me there, and I don't want to lose you to your work or someone else. Do you understand what I'm saying?"

"I think so, but I think it was the last orgasm that has you melting love feelings on me. I like it. You're very special to me, Harold. You're the first man that has me all fucked up and wanting you all the time. I'm no small woman, and your devilish ass got me loving you too much. What are we going to do?" Lynn confessed.

"Keep fucking, of course," I said without blinking, Cheshire cat grin on my face.

"I know that, but what else?" she wanted to know.

"We'll talk about it later. Right now, lay here on the floor and prop your feet on each side of the table so I can have some more pussy," I demanded.

And, like that, "It's all yours, body and soul," she said, and propped up her feet.

"Oh, you went jazz title on me," I said excitedly.

"You're not the only person that loves jazz. My dad was a professional sax player. I listened to jazz everyday growing up," she revealed.

All this time I had known Lynn, but I hadn't known that about her. Maybe it was in front of me, but I just hadn't realized it. All the times I had come over and found jazz playing, all the times we made love to the slow curves of so many jazz notes, and I had not realized her love for music, the music I loved. I said, "I knew there was something that gave you your flare. So, you think we need each other for more than just this?" With that question, I had opened the door to trying to understand what we were, what we had, what we might become.

"Yes, I do," she said soberly. "You make me feel like a jazz singer sings."

"What in the world do you know about those voices?" I asked, still incredulous. Could she have that understanding that I cherished?

"I know if I were her, you'd be my spring," she replied.

"That's deep, personally deep. So, you listen to jazz?" I inquired. She was drawing me in.

"My dad gave me his old collection of all his albums and CDs," she confided.

"How sweet you are. You just made things harder for me," I said surprising myself by my own blatant admission. Then I repeated my earlier question to her, saying, "Where do we go from here? A song title by the way." I had asked it, knowing I didn't want an answer. Only I could truly answer it.

Lynn said, "What do you mean? I think you mean the tune on the CD, 'Where Do I Go from You,' baby."

"Yes," I said simply.

"Those songs are for us. I have that CD. Would you like me to play it?" she said.

"Sure, Lynn," I answered.

"There are songs like 'Sweet Love,' and 'A Fool In Love,' which is me right now loving you. Don't hurt me because I'll do anything to have your love," she said, stringing along an impressive list of songs to make her point.

"You know there are a lot of great tunes on that CD," I said.

"I know the songs on that CD," Lynn said.

It seemed she felt there was a moment here to make this connection with me, so she let me know her jazz history. More than she knew, she wasn't wrong. She had said earlier that I was not very expressive with my feelings, but maybe this is how I expressed them, felt them; it was through the music. That she picked up on it, consciously or not, made an impression on me. "Lynn, believe me, I know all these songs. My muse, Ms. Angel Eyes, has traveled many years with me understanding music she shares with me on this life journey," I explained.

"So, you have your own personal muse?" she said. "What makes you so special?" she added.

"I don't know, but I got one, and we talk when I'm being mannerly or in trouble," I confessed.

"I'll leave that alone. She may not find me good for you, but I would like her to."

"How strange that your father gave you his collection. That's special, and you have just become more to me in so many ways. You're going to force me to make some hard choices down the road. For now, add Nancy Wilson and Ramsey Lewis's *Simple Pleasures* CD, and play 'Like In Love.' You might have to dust off the turntable in the corner to add that one to the playlist. Then you can come back to me and let me kiss you all over," I said.

"OK. It's a lot here," she said.

"I've been handling it," I said.

"Better than anyone has ever and forever, baby. Loving you is easy. Leaving, I will never," she said.

"We'll see, Lynn," I said. "How can you be so sure?" I pressed.

"Look at us, even though you haven't been here lately. All that living and loving produces, we're here with each other and happy," she said. "That's why I'm afraid to love you more completely. Strangely, though, I do love you, while always wanting to run away, but somehow, I see you in my arms, until the very end, as we are now," she concluded.

We kissed. I kissed her, and we listened to CDs and vinyl albums and made love one more time. The night came quickly after rounds of love-making. We fell asleep so close that I found my face nestled in her breast and a mouthful of titty. As a grown man lying there, I felt it, something that made me think for a moment that everything would be all right, something in the security of her bosom, and I wondered if one ever truly loses the desire for the security of a mother's breast. When I looked at Lynn's peaceful countenance as she slept, I pondered why I had brought up Ms. Angel Eyes, she who was the purview of my thoughts, into this relationship.

Morning came swiftly, and I would leave with the sun's rising. I had an early work call and work to catch up on. Women can make a person like me push work to the side, finding passion and perhaps love.

# Chapter 10

## DON'T MISUNDERSTAND

*Maybe, I'm not to be happy.*

*This journey that I'm on has a price.*

*Stricken with this desire from an early
understanding my course was set.*

*Will I have regrets?*

*Climbing higher, wandering all over, playing
the field and women coming and going,*

*Their time and my time seem never to
gel in support of the dream.*

*Life takes its prisoners and produces winners, both
seeming to end up in the same place of emptiness,*

*However, those who escaped found the balance
between love and sharing in the glorious quest.*

*We're on the same team, we're one.*

*Will I have regrets?*

*Now in the August of my life – should I change now?*

*I would have to ask myself – why did I
start if I wasn't going to finish?*

*Of loves loved and loves lost*

*Joy found and of the same wonderful joy of having known love
Regrets. Yes.
But new love comes in the morning for those who endure.*

I told Lynn I would call her at the end of the workday. Running my own company had its advantages because I hired great people to support me. I kept my personal life separate from my work environment. I did not allow women to call me on the company phone lines or even stop by. Life for the most part was being in control of the left and right hand, but also meant not showing all your hole cards to everybody.

I had meetings all morning with executives representing a German company for our unique fertilizer products, which produced a 20% greater yield per acre. All proprietary products were owned by GEN Fertilizer, Inc. This would be an important client to sign. During the meeting, my mind ran wild with thoughts of Yvette and Lynn. It wasn't about sex, but about whether I could get it right with the woman to be with. I had to stay focused for the next several hours at least, however, and I would because business came before relationships. If I lost a woman over it, there was no decision to make. It's no different than them having to make a decision between their career or me. I would always say choose your career.

My team presented a very good rollout of our company structure, our products, and distribution and delivery capabilities. At noon, we went to lunch in Center City at an upscale restaurant. We dined for about ninety minutes and thereafter, we escorted them to the airport in time for their flight back to Bonn, Germany.

The next meeting was with the staff on an office expansion west of the Mississippi. We met until 6 p.m. and would pick it back up in the morning. My day was over, and it was time to make some calls.

I called Lynn, and she picked up on the first ring.

"Hello, how was your day?" she asked.

"Fine. Thank you for asking. What's up with you tonight?" I asked.

"Nothing really," she replied.

"Do you want to meet me at the Four Seasons for a drink and dinner, although it's no longer the Four Seasons?" I asked.

"If you like me to," she offered.

"I'm asking," hunting for some certainty.

"What time?" she said.

"Seven or seven-thirty, whichever one works better for you," I said.

"Seven-thirty works better for me," she said.

"Then seven-thirty it is. See you then, I'll be at the bar," I said.

I was already on my way to the hotel. Upon arriving, I let the valet park my car, and I went to the bar and waited. Sitting there alone for a few minutes, I had time to think. Will I have regrets at the end of the journey? Time had a way of confronting one's choices over the years. My mother would say, "I worry about you, son," and I would say, "I'm fine." Closing my eyes for a moment, my life was reeling back and forth, still confusing and still needing answers. Hoping for an answer, Lynn tapped me on the shoulder and said, "You want to talk about it?"

"Talk about what?" I said.

"What?!" she retorted. She was used to me playing off such moments as if nothing was on my mind, but after last night, the distance between us had shrunk.

"Whatever you were deep in thought about," she said gently.

"Not today," I said. My tone even to me intimated that I might one day be able to share such thoughts, but that day wasn't today.

"I'm here when you need someone to listen, to hold you and give you my support for the wrongs or the rights we all make in our life's journey," she said.

Once again, Lynn's words were spoken gently. What was even more was that I seemed to listen to them more clearly; they were not words merely spoken, but notes played, notes heard beyond my hearing. I felt them. "You know what to say and seemingly how to help," I said.

"Well, I do have two master's degrees, one in business and the other in psychology, and I am working on my doctorate at the university," she boasted, but merely to comfort me, it seemed.

"I know, but thanks. Sit here. I was holding this chair for you," I said.

Gesturing to the bartender, "Harry, would you give Lynn a drink please?"

"Sure, sir," Harry said, promptly. "What would you like, Ms.?"

"A Matador. Can you make it?" Lynn asked.

"Not a problem. The lady knows a little something about a not-so-often-asked-for drink," commented the bartender.

"Not at all," Lynn replied.

"It's the way you carry yourself. I think you know a lot. One Matador coming your way," said Harry.

"Harold, how did your meeting go with the Germans?" Lynn asked thoughtfully.

"Very well. I think we'll end up doing business with them soon," I said.

"And the other meeting?" she followed up.

"That was just an in-house meeting, but it went well," I said.

"Hey, dear, let's drink to you and finding that one you seek," Lynn lifted her glass.

I just smiled at her. She looked curiously at me in return, but did not speak. She understood me more than I ever thought before, and I thought much more of her now than I had at first. Finally, I broke the silence. "Lynn, you continue to surprise me in all your giving ways."

"You're the giver, Harold," she said without delay. "And I truly understand a man like you and your complexities. Your compassion and fairness outweigh your bad habits, but they come to an end when you finally shake off living falsehoods for the truth, and finish what you've started with a good woman. The good woman is the one who will be waiting and standing with her arms still open."

"So, you're the one standing at the end of the rainbow with outstretched arms ready to care for a broken guy, or a mature and stronger man?" I asked.

"Either one works for me, dear. I know who you are. You can't make love like that without knowing where and how giving comes from way deep inside the heart, your heart—which lots of people over the years have probably taken advantage of—and you have paid a heavy price. But you stayed true to the course, the game, and your dream. And I like a man like that. Let me buy you a drink because you're a special person, Harold, and I knew that from the first time talking with you." She paused and looked down at the bar for a moment, and when she lifted her head, she had taken on another level of seriousness—or maybe it was the pregnant pause. She looked into my eyes, but I felt her peering deeper into who I was as if she knew something about me that I had never told her, game recognizing game. Then she spoke as if she were reading my future. "Your tomorrow is now. I want you to run with it, and give it your all, and I'll be around. Pretty faces and bodies, even mine, will go, but it's what we have shared; it's how we thought and cared for one another and, oh, how we love. Just my memories will have me in love with you forever, and we're far from done."

"Lynn, should I call you a doctor now?" I broke the mood to lighten up the conversation.

"No, dear, it's just that your true love and the music we play and share tell our secrets," she said. Who was she today? Loving her was amazing, and yet it seemed a preamble to these moments when something in me was open to listening to her speak truths to me like a soothsayer. I had told her yesterday that I did love her, too. Had that something to do with what was now occurring between us?

She continued, unfazed by my attempt at levity, "You might think this weird, Harold, but my dad told me that if I find a man who loves and understands the complexities of how jazz singers sing and interpret songs, I have found a cool cat who knows about that thing called love and how to love. He won't be an easy man to live with, but he has the grit to run long and deep without giving in, even in love."

"I would like to meet your dad," was all I could say, as so many thoughts were coursing through my mind.

"If you get to the other side and then heaven, you'll find him listening, too," she said.

I smiled. "You got me smiling lately. Let's get something to eat," I said.

"My treat. You have treated me all these many months, and since we're going to one of the most expensive restaurants in the city, let me treat," she said.

"No problem," I said, content in this moment to receive her generosity, even her love. "I made an eight-thirty reservation, by the way. Also, I'll make sure I have my dessert straight up, no chaser. Truly, what's on the restaurant dessert menu?" I asked.

"Since I'm treating, you can have whatever you want and with no life regrets. In the near future, when the morning comes, so will love, my dear," she spoke, again, as if prophetically.

"Let's order dinner, sweetheart," I said.

# Chapter 11

## KIND WORDS FROM A FRIEND

Another summer had ended, the leaves were falling again, and my relationships continued with Lynn and Yvette, or Yvette and Lynn. I had not chosen yet. I was still in deep, loving and spending time with the two of them between running the company and hanging out with the brothers. My friends would ask me, over the years, how did I attract, keep for a while, and then let go of so many fine women. Harold, they would say invariably, if I had just two of them in my life, I'd be married and settled, eating popcorn on the sofa.

"That's why I got them, and you don't," I said to them again on this night we were hanging out together.

Terrance, a profound thinker said, "It's not the popcorn, guys. Harold don't do popcorn on the sofa. Maybe popcorn with a woman perched 2000 feet up in the sky with her legs dangling off a mountain rock."

"That's nice, but that's not me," said one of the guys. "And that's the problem."

"Anyway, they tend to leave me, and not me leaving them. I'm a train headed at full speed, ready to crash into myself and survive to walk into another, two years later," I replied.

"Man, your list is long. You attract ladies," Terrance said.

"You as well Terrance. I've seen the fine ones you let go," I replied.

"I just enjoy myself while working hard and trying to grab the brass ring while riding on the edge. Most of the time I'm about to fall from one of the horses, being too extended, while I am reaching for it," I explained.

"This is what I mean, brother-man. The magnet is you—your life—what you are willing to do and to share and your willingness to wine and dine these ladies. You seemingly don't care, but they do. They want you and the aura of being with you. They complete you like a road partner on a long trip making the journey seem not so long. You need to find the one that completes you on your terms and give or take of yourself a little to make it work." Terrance was on a roll.

"I was just told that the other day," I disclosed.

"Then you need to pay attention, which you say you do," added Terrance.

"Terrance, when did you become my therapist?" I quipped.

"I'm not. I'm your friend, and you're my friend, and have been for many years," he countered.

"All true," I said, adding, "I'll get it right one day, soon."

"Maybe it's the one I've seen you with in the summer," Terrence offered.

"That's no help. I was with several this summer, but focused on just two really, and I'm still seeing them," I said.

"See, that's what I mean. You got that romance thing happening and making women ooze all over themselves without you even touching them. Women want to be in your space, and you're no Billy Dee Williams," Terrance warned.

"Hey, I'm OK," I scoffed.

"I think we both would place ourselves at a seven or eight on a scale of ten," he ventured a guess.

"I'll go with that, and I'll let my swag carry the balance," I concurred.

"And so will I," Terrence agreed. "So, what plans do you have between now and the end of the year?" he added.

"I got to go to California in several weeks for business. I'll turn it into a business and pleasure trip, of course," I said.

"Will you take one of your new friends?" he asked.

"You know I will," I confirmed.

"Well, my friend, enjoy yourself, but right now let's schedule a tee time for next week," he said. Then he asked with heartfelt concern, "Do you think the lady I seen you with is the right one?"

"What did she look like?" I asked, trying to determine whom he was talking about other than a real looker.

"She was your height or slightly smaller, which you like," he said.

"True that," we agreed and clinked our glasses.

"Very sassy in her mannerism, a little older than you're used to, and she's got one of those bodies that makes a man turn his head. She seemed different, because most women with those qualities need attention, but she was all into you. I noticed other men trying to get her attention, but she was oblivious to them. The two of you were one," he explained.

"The one you have described, her name is Lynn. She is all that and more," I said. "She's not the one I'm going to the West Coast with, though. The other is just as fine, slightly shorter, five-foot-six or five-foot-seven, and with similar qualities. Her name is Yvette," I said.

"Therein lies the challenge for me—similar qualities. Why go for the similar when you got the real deal?" Terrance spoke seriously.

"I met them about the same time. No, that's not true. I met Lynn over two years ago, but never followed up with her until recently. She was a hello and a dance. Then she said, 'You don't remember me, do you? We met two years ago and talked for about an hour and I really wanted you to call me.' We danced that evening at the club, and we've been doing some off-the-ceiling lovemaking since then," I said.

"You always do, from what the women say about you. I've talked to a few of them over the years once you left them or they left your ass. They came crying on my shoulder asking me, 'Why doesn't he want me?' or 'Why doesn't he care?' 'We can work things out. You're his friend. Tell me what I need to do. I want to be with him,'" Terrance elaborated.

"'Help me, Terrance,' they would say. I had no answer for them, except to explain to them that you're committed to your work more than making a relationship work at this time in your life. I would say keep trying; things are dynamic. I would buy them a drink if we were out in a club and move on," he said.

"Terrance, I know I've passed on some nice ladies that would have made me happy, and I'm sure I would have made them happy, as well. My work and bad-boy habits have just kept me unfocused on settling down before I complete what I want to do. However, time is no longer on my side, so I'm going to play this hand all in. Win or lose. When I win, I'll do those humanitarian projects waiting for me. If I lose, I'll resolve myself to being an OK businessman who gave his all without selling his soul and who had fun along the way. Hopefully, I did no harm to others in pursuit of the brass ring. I'll jump off the merry-go-round for good at that time."

"Well, Harold, no one can ever say you didn't give a lifetime to it. And the best part is, you still have a successful business to go to every day and to leave behind a legacy. Your fertilizer company has to be worth millions," Terrance consoled.

"I know, but achieving the 'big one' will allow me to do what I think I'm capable of for thousands of people," I said.

"Well, yes. You also screw women like you eat dessert, but you got the heart of a lamb. My friend, I'm glad I don't have that thing that drives you, but I'm glad you do, and this go-round I see a winner in you," he said.

"You're my friend, so of course you would say that," I said.

"I am; therefore, my words are true. No puffery. Men like you win even when they lose. Finish your race, get your reward, do right by others, and rewards will keep coming like a bucket of water overflowing," Terrance was offering part solace, part cheer.

"That sounds great and heartfelt, but, my friend, I'm getting tired," I said, feeling weary.

"What do you say to me all the time about starting something?" Terrance pressed me.

"Terrance, why start if you're not going to finish, for it would be a waste of time, which one can never regain," I repeated, words I had said to him many, many times.

"That's right. And your completion and reward for staying the course is just over the next hill, but this time, you're on top of the hill ready to walk into the valley for doing something well for yourself and others. Play the endgame out, my friend. It's the hardest part to see when the end is in front of you. Be patient and stay diligent to the vision you carried all these years. God has been on your side from the jump. Enjoy playing the endgame, which may be in other people's hands now, but they know you and your spirit have touched their spirit. Winners find winners, and losers will wish they stayed the course with you through the wrong and the right choices of life." Terrance labored to reach me, and I was appreciative. We had been friends for many years, and moments like this one reminded me why. We'd been there for each other, and that was a win, in and of itself. I needed to count my blessings.

"You know this is the second time I've heard that phrase 'through the wrongs and the right choices of life,' this week," I remarked.

"The wind is telling you something. My grandpop would say, 'When coincidence happens twice, the wind carries our secrets and our wants to meet up with the secrets and wants of others, weaving them together, an interlocking, if you will, to create a picture of our times well lived,'" Terrance quoted.

"Smart man. Those old guys listened in their youth to the older men of their time, which allowed them to travel righteously, thus finding wisdom, and you just shared some of it with me," I said, expressing my gratitude. How long we'd been there chopping it up, I don't know, but I was buoyed by the exchange with my dear friend.

"Thank you. Let's go find something to eat and drink before the balance of the day is over. Besides, since you now got two new ladies, you can tell me about your other cultural beauties," Terrance said.

"Oh, and you can tell me about yours as well," I countered.

"Oh, no, we're talking about *you* for now, brother," he joked.

"Hey, you know I've had them all, at least most of those cultural beauties. Terrance, for my taste, African-American women with all their shades of melanin are the finest on the planet. Just ask all the rich guys marrying them today," I said, extolling the virtues of women in a nice, not-so-nice way, I guessed. "European-American women, well, once you get past the hair flipping and makeup, they look very different, and I've dated many of them. My last one was a young Italian-Irish woman from South Philly named Tina. Asian women, I like them a lot, but I would like them a little taller. And they are no more or no less smart than anyone else. Smart is whoever is sitting their asses down and studying. I've dated a few very pretty Persian women, love them with that hint of African blood in them. And the Hispanic and Latina women got it in spades, and sassiness too, but hey, they got that Catholicism thing happening with them," I said, further extolling the virtues of women in a nice, not-so-nice way.

"You went around the globe in less than thirty seconds," Terrance chortled.

"Truly, women are fascinating to behold, and it's been said before. Whoever said it knew what the hell he was saying and probably had as much fun as we are having even with all the consternation that comes our way at times," I said.

"Harold, you're a different kind of guy. You know women are a lot of work. And we are too, from their perspective," Terrance said.

"I'm sure you would agree," I said.

"I do. By the way what other rules do you subscribe to?" asked Terrance.

"Terrance, let me tell you about Trip Hoes and Trip Pimps," I said.

"What?" Terrance cried with laughter.

"You heard me. Trip Hoes and Trip Pimps," I said.

"I think this story might be long and very funny from the sound of it. Let's finish our food and head for a club for some eye candy for the evening."

# Chapter 12

## TRIP HOES AND TRIP PIMPS, NO WINNERS

"No, Terrance, this is short and to the point, kind of a crazy rule of the game, played or got played. First, a definition is needed for the two, although on its surface, it sounds straight forward. A trip ho is a woman who falls for a brother's bull when he meets up with someone in a club or some gathering, and he has sized her up as to what's needed to get the shot. Cool questions about life, work, and kids, are all fair game. Finally, after a drink or two, he drops the question, 'Would you like to go to Aruba with me? I'm planning a trip next month or soon for a long weekend.' Ask 'What do you think?' and again, 'Would you like to go?' Her obvious reply, 'I don't even know you.' The trip pimp replies, 'I'm not leaving for a month or so. We got time for drinks and whatever to see if we want to take the trip together.' Of course, the trip pimp then says, 'I got the ticket and the trip money, even separate rooms.' But he holds back on the separate rooms line, if he thinks it's not needed. Some women will say to themselves that this is a free trip and a chance to have some fun, and they tell themselves that he seems like a nice guy. Let me say they tell themselves these things only to justify the trip to themselves. At that point, the trip pimp is the winner; the trip ho is the loser and has just set herself up for whatever, and soon finds herself being pimped and becoming the player's trip ho over and over.

"She going to get fucked; maybe not the first night, but the pimp got one or two days and nights left to pimp the trip ho for some pussy. Check this. All he may have to do while there is to buy her a pair of funky sunglasses or something she wants. Pussy's paid for, and now the pimp gets more than the value of the trip or money, because the woman has sold her body for trinkets and her self-respect for a weekend in the sun.

"I have and other guys have mastered the trip pimp game, and if you're good at it, you're traveling all the weekends you want, and you get all the pussy you want even after the weekend is over, for months until she realizes she has been played. She finds herself no longer under the sway of the trip pimp and is now asking herself why. Them liking each other is no longer enough. Even wanting access to his home or friends is not enough. She had a home and friends, all left behind for some bullshit hype the trip pimp ran on her. In the long run, she'll find herself the loser. She had more freedom and self-control before she succumbed to the game, and perhaps she left a real love at the kitchen table to become a trip ho unwittingly. Oh, if women only understood the songs sung by the great female jazz singers, and their songs were as much for men as for women, they would come to know it's all about love and heartache, Cupid and the arrow through the heart. Finding love. Holding onto it. Fighting for it. For a sixty/forty percent love, even an 80/20 percent love, can be more than one hundred percent of what's on one's desired score card.

"The trip pimp had laid the trap taking weeks or months to score and devour the feast. Strangely, trip hoes get caught all the time, and their only rationale is to continue some sort of relationship to caress their vanity and diva images of themselves, but trip hoes they are.

"Understand Terrance, I'm not glorifying the pimp or the pimp game here. He's taking advantage of a situation. That's why I don't play that game anymore. And women soon find themselves not liking the individual anyway, or at least looking at him differently, even though his story and life situation might be what they think they want. It's better for a woman to know what they want and keep clear of the 'whatever' mind set. This way the trip pimp can't score, and the woman's womanhood is properly respected by others, but most importantly, by herself, and so finds more integrity in her being. She needs to fight for what's in her yard before wanting what's across the street. She'll generally come up empty, and she's left with a wet pussy and most of the time not a great fuck. So all she gets is peanuts, and she's trying to justify the relationship or event by saying, it's not just about sex. These girls, and the guys, too, need to wake up! That's reality. She's just there thinking about the other guy who completes her—fun, laughs, a touch that moves her. She needs to learn and make sure she stays with the one who she turned up with, for the next guy won't be feeling it once her bad habits and, maybe, low self-esteem, are exposed.

"Men have a way of backing off and shutting down when others know about the woman they're walking down the street with. A woman needs to be the lady and hear the songwriter as they write of love, being lucky in love, being loved by the one who cares, and that she will know him by his attention to loving her and by his works. Men must know and many do, that women are to be protected and respected every day of their lives. We must be men continually revolting against false societal conditioning. We must find our humanity in all that we do, say, and believe. Yes, Terrance, the trip hoes and trip pimp game reaps no winners; civility reigns not, brother. You know I talk a lot of stuff, and I enjoy the sexual pleasures between a woman and myself, but in all my wildest—responsibility is first to myself as a man, secondly to the woman I love, and finally to the family and society as a whole."

"Harold, I get it and truly understand your point of view, your take on love and humanity, but this story, well, that's about the craziest thing I have ever heard. However, coming from you, I truly get it. We really need to go and get some food and check out the clubs now!"

# Chapter 13

## MANHATTAN

Two weeks had passed since Lynn and I went to Manhattan to see a play. I had stocked the limo that took us to the Big Apple with enough liquor to keep us happy on the drive up I-95. We were cool going. We talked, laughed, and listened to music, and in an hour and forty-five minutes, we were in the Big Apple. I directed the chauffeur to drive up to one of my favorite restaurants in Midtown for dinner before going to the theater. We continued enjoying ourselves discussing political and economic topics of the day. Lynn was a worthy debater. Her ability to be objective in her points of view merited my respect. She kept me on point in my responses to her positions on the various issues. I loved it. She was witty, sassy, and good to bite when I got hungry for dessert, and that was coming.

I pulled her over a year ago, and I've been laying pipe regularly, although she was landing hooks like a boxer, even if I wasn't feeling the pain. She was throwing 'I'm gonna make you love me' hooks, and I was being knocked out without knowing it. That was what I allowed her to think for the moment—or was I the one fooling myself? In any event, next week I would be on a plane headed to the West Coast with Yvette for five days or more. For now, however, Lynn had a hundred percent of my attention, and feeling even much more than I realized, and I was what she was looking for. Somehow, I knew what she wanted, and it wasn't any different than what I was looking for, to spend time and maybe a lifetime together.

Now these two women, Yvette and Lynn, I liked more than most other women. How far past two years we would make it, I was not yet sure. I had had long-term relationships in the past reach my two-year rule. Indeed, a few had made it beyond the two-year rule. Now I had two of them. For the moment I didn't have to decide, and indeed, I didn't want to decide at this point in the relationships. I was having fun with these two fine ladies and exploring all of them mostly on my terms. I knew the table would turn. It always did, but for now the arrow of the spinner was pointing in my direction.

I have seen it, though, when things have flown in the opposite direction. It was the beginning of the end because one or the other wasn't willing to compromise on what he or she wanted. I had refused to date mainly because my work had taken priority over relationships and what others wanted of me. I was willing to give, if any of those with whom I had relationships in the past would have allowed me to achieve what I had started out to do. However, each woman had her own timetable, which was why I developed the two-year rule in the first place. I came to realize that there were some women who may go longer than two years, and if they did, they were the ones who really loved me. The others had their own agendas of the wants they desired and valued more than love. "I want excess," one woman told me, and she got it with someone else. I was OK with that. I would let time determine which one of us was right, she who wanted excess, or I who waited on love.

Over the years, I noticed that women tended to pick what they wanted most of the time unless they were weak-minded. Some women, it seemed to me, needed to wake up and stop making bad selections in men. Unfortunately, they did not seem to appreciate how a decision about the man with whom they were dealing could seriously, if not irreparably, affect their quality of life. Selecting bad men had caused many upwardly mobile women to lose it all and to forgo achieving their dreams. These types of guys knew why they wanted her, but a weak-minded woman would always fall prey to a guy with much less on the ball and to a bullshit rap.

Now, Lynn was not a weak-minded woman. She had strong role models, her parents, to emulate, and from them was able to learn many of life's lessons. Yvette was also a strong woman, even though she had to box her way up from a problematic family environment, one in which role models to emulate were few, but were still there if you looked. I appreciated Lynn's and Yvette's strength and loved that they were strong women. So many unexpected developments had occurred between Lynn and me recently that my mind had been replaying those thoughts and the rationale behind so much of how I conducted myself in relationships. But I was aware how much keener Lynn was to pick up these introspective moments, so much so that I refocused my gaze on her, our dinner, and our evening together.

Indeed, Lynn and I enjoyed a delicious dinner with a bottle of wine. Then I paid the bill and called for our limo to pick us up in the next ten minutes. We were off to see the play.

Arriving ahead of time, we found our seats and continued talking. The conversation turned to the actors and their bios in the Playbill. Three hours later, we were back in the limo and headed down the interstate. We were really into being with one another, and then without the usual precursors, it just happened. We kissed, and it was on. Our emotions—hidden somehow from us behind a veil of simple serenity induced by holding each other—suddenly revealed themselves. I reached for a button along the door handle and the divider went up. I muted communications with the driver, and while I was doing that, she got undressed.

Moments later, she started undressing me. Kissing and caressing, I rolled her legs up over my shoulders and had her sitting on my lap with a wide-open pussy to enjoy, to enjoy while we cruised down the interstate. We would fuck against the background of the limousine's motion along the highway until we reached her place. She pushed so much pussy at me in the car that if she had asked me to marry her, I would have said yes. She didn't know the control she had at that moment, nor did she care. She was a long-term player for love and not excess.

We got ourselves together upon arriving, hit the button to unmute, dropped the divider, and had the driver open the door for us. I had him bring our things from the limo and place them just inside the house. I tipped him very well as was customary, and we continued making love on the sofa until we fell on the floor and lusted ourselves into mutual submission. Throughout the room, a hot sweaty fog, the smell of orgasmic pussy, enveloped us, and I loved it. Within that fog, sheltered in each other's arms, we fell asleep on the floor until morning.

# Chapter 14

## WEST COAST

The next week Yvette and I flew first class to Los Angeles for a meeting I had in Santa Monica, California. The company had an office there, so it would be business before pleasure for the first two days, and after 5:00 p.m., we would explore Santa Monica and Beverly Hills. My meeting, though, started early, so I had one of my employees pick me up, which allowed me to leave Yvette with a brand-new red Mustang convertible rental in which to drive around all day. She made herself busy, and we talked throughout the day between my meetings as the first day was full of nonstop meetings and travel to different job sites and client facilities. Yvette spent her time cruising the freeways of Cali. With the top down and wind from the Pacific Ocean blowing in her hair, she drove seventy plus miles an hour to wherever, getting lost by design, and using the car's GPS to find her way back to the hotel.

We planned to rendezvous around 6:30 p.m. back at the hotel to shower and change for an evening on the town. We stayed in a Hilton Hotel in Santa Monica, close to the office, the night we arrived in Cali. We would upgrade the next day when we checked into the Waldorf Astoria Beverly Hills for a couple of days, after which we would drive down to Palm Springs to stay at the J. W. Marriott Hotel and Resort for another day or two.

Unbeknownst to Yvette, I had an adventurous surprise in store for her. We would leave Palm springs and we would drive through the desert straight to the Las Vegas Four Seasons hotel for three days and two night. The resort was well known to be lavish, and we would take full advantage of its amenities while enjoying the dry desert air and scenic oasis beauty. Our flight home would be delayed by only three days.

That was yet to come, however. At the moment, I was tired from traveling and meetings all day, so we dined at a lovely restaurant by the water in Santa Monica and walked the pier. It was dark, and I pulled her close to me, and it went beyond kissing. She got hot and bothered quickly. I turned her around, bent her over the rail, and entered her. Then, it got crazy. So crazy, we almost fell thirty or forty freaking feet into the damn Pacific Ocean. Catching our balance—no, me catching her from pulling us both into the ocean below—we stopped and laughed. Pitched against the railing now, safe, adrenaline nonetheless raced through my body. I said to her, "Yvette, we need to stop this shit before all of your people and all of my people end up at our damn funerals." We both laughed hard and continued to make jokes about what almost happened to us. And what did we expect after all, from out-of-control intercourse on the edge of a cliff.

"Let's walk," I finally said, the nervous laughter subsiding. "We're safer doing that," I added. That fresh sea breeze had been blowing on her pussy when she was bent over the railing, and it had been driving me insane. Call it love or call it sex, we were the laughter in our laughs. We wanted each other too much. That's why we loved so insanely when we found each other after being apart, even if only for a day.

The preceding events were funny but sobering, and I was prompted to admit something she hadn't known. "Yvette," I said, "You know I hate swimming. If we went over, did you have me?"

"Baby, just like you got me now. I had you even in the air before going under," she said, and though she was grinning, she said it like she meant it, and I believed her.

All we would have been was two wet asses trying to get our story straight if security had come, like having to explain the strawberry incident to the doctors in the emergency room.

Yvette smiled and winked. "Please know, baby, for sure that I got you. OK, let's keep this thing going," she added, holding and squeezing my hand as we continued walking. We smiled at each other as we walked, and I said, "That's enough excitement for my tired ass tonight. Let's go back to the hotel and wind down."

Returning to the hotel, we skipped the bar action and went up to our room where she put on some sexy lingerie. I saw the lingerie, and damn the boy popped back into action with a little foreplay that included me watching her twerk. Really, all she was doing was shaking her ass, but that was enough for me, along with a nightcap. Seemed twerking had taken society by storm. It was an acquired talent that took some practice, but to me it was vulgar. Just naturally showing off the flesh made it for me. We enjoyed each other that night, and it was good. As we lay there, I was ready for the day to end. "I'm tired. I'm going to sleep. Here is the remote," I said, her head resting on my chest.

"Big daddy, do you want me in the morning?" she asked before I closed my eyes.

"You know that's a yes. I might be late for my meeting, but I can't say no to you," I remarked. Then, I pointed out, "I know you want to relax and enjoy exploring the city tomorrow. So, I'm done tomorrow at one p.m., and then the rest of the week is ours to explore. I got a surprise for you, too, and the best way to share it with you is in a convertible."

"Are you sure we'll be driving?" she said emphatically. A little laughter accented her remark.

"It'll be OK. The temperature will be over a hundred degrees, but we will have a cooler filled with beer, as well as water, of course," I assured her.

"What kind of surprise is this?" she probed.

"Sorry, you got to wait until tomorrow. So you might as well stop being so inquisitive. Let's go to sleep," I said.

"OK. In the morning then," she acquiesced, clicked off the TV, and closed her eyes. We rested well together that night, and Lynn was nowhere on my mind. I was completely present with Yvette, and our adventure was just beginning.

# Chapter 15

## SANTA MONICA, THEN BEVERLY HILLS

The next morning, I woke her up to a brick-hard dick. The kind you got when you were sixteen. Instead of pissing it out of me, I went to work calling forth those bad habits that hounded me. Why? Lately I didn't linger long on those thoughts, for she was there, a fresh peach to slide in and out of, until we were totally and completely sexed. We started at 5:30 a.m. and finished at 7:00 a.m., which left me just enough time to shower, shave, get a cup of coffee, and be ready to do business at 8 a.m. sharp.

However, an hour into our lovemaking, she started crying and asked me to stop fucking her because she was tired. All the while, though, she was saying she couldn't get enough of my dick. She was scratching me, pulling her hair, and grabbing and trying to suck her own tits. And her eyes, they were rolling to the back of her head. She had had several orgasms, and now after this last one, she was shaking like she had gotten the Holy Ghost. The last one had pulled everything out of her. I heard her and felt her, but I had her on call, so she could scream if she wanted to, and she was screaming now.

"Baby, baby, I need you. I love you, baby," but I was not stopping. She would sleep until noon or later when I was finished with this pussy. She wouldn't be talking that big daddy shit anymore. She would be toast. I would soon be leaving to go to my meeting. In fact, she might just be getting up when I would be coming back in from my meeting around 1 p.m. It didn't matter, I was zoned out in that place where only lovers go and where she traveled freely and willingly. She would sleep eventually and let love have its way. As I had planned, I showered, shaved, dressed, and left, stopping in the lobby on the way for a cup of coffee.

I left her a note to pack our things because we were leaving and checking into the Waldorf later that afternoon. We were going to be ballers from Beverly Hills to the J.W. Marriott in Palm Springs first, then onto the Four Seasons, and finally onto the Wynn Las Vegas to gamble. One o'clock came quickly, so I wrapped up my West Coast business. I was now ready to enjoy the heat and our time together on this West Coast vacation.

I walked into our hotel room to find her sprawled all over the bed, still unable to get up. I left her there and went to eat lunch. She needed her rest because it would be an after two p.m. check-in at the Waldorf. No chance we could miss a memorable night of lovemaking at the Waldorf Astoria. I couldn't. I wouldn't. But things weren't always what they seemed. I was laying down love vibes and driving her mad, but this woman had me in love with her more than she knew, and I was going to show her on this trip. I had opened myself up to Yvette, to love and to lovin', to the joy of just being together with her, and furthermore to sharing these new experiences with her. I was affected by all of it, by her. They said falling in love was a wonderful thing, but I had found over the years, it was more painful than joyful. Yet, like her wanting more and begging for it not to stop, I wanted love, and I would have to accept at some point that the joy came with the pain if I were ever to commit to one woman. I mean, wouldn't I? I had just left Lynn on the living room floor after an evening in Manhattan, limo sex, and all the gushy stuff. Now, here I was. "A brown-eyed girl with curly hair will make a good wife for life," my grandmother would say, and Yvette was certainly that. I was fucked up. But maybe I wasn't. Maybe I was just trying to figure this shit out. Terrance wasn't around, so here I was, holding my own therapy session. This was my short lunch conversation sitting alone at the table, but I had to get back and get Yvette moving. The California sun was waiting for us.

I knew she'd be famished, so I'd have to eat lunch with her again, but that would be OK. We'd do lunch at the Waldorf in all its grandeur. Love those environments. I'm sure that's why I work so hard to afford this quality of life, this life in an upper-class world.

"Yvette, wake up my dear. Time to check out. The note I left, you never got up to read it. Please shower, and I'll start packing our things. I already checked us out of the hotel and ate lunch," I informed her.

"Why didn't you wait for me?" she said. She was squinting and rubbing the sleep out of her eyes. Even still, she was beautiful and sexy no matter when I saw her.

"I'm still joining you for lunch at the Waldorf. Is that OK?" I said tenderly.

"How sweet, Harold! You know you're the sweetest, right?" she said.

"Thank you, Yvette. You're sweeter though. I know you are exhausted, but get ready, OK?"

"I am. Morning sex like that, and that was not normal morning sex, zonks me out, baby," she explained.

"It's the afternoon, so let's go find the sun and fun," I said. I'd hoped to remind her of what the day held in store for us.

"OK," she acquiesced. She smiled at me through those morning eyes, stood up, and entered the bathroom.

I was feeling great despite all my bad-boy habits. In moments like these, I acknowledged, or better yet accepted, who I was, for better or for worse. How much could a man stand of critiquing himself? Peace was made in the doing, and there was nothing I could do, or would do, if I were honest, about it at this moment. I needed, however, to get another name for this behavior, this 'bad-boy habits' personality that seemed to burst out when I was with women, women who drew me into themselves from simple eye contact alone, women who wanted to express their sexuality in parks, in cars, on walks across bridges, and on ocean piers damn near falling into the ocean, for goodness' sake. Why at that moment it occurred to me, I don't know, but I really wanted to see if I could screw a woman parachuting from a plane. Wouldn't that be the ultimate sex high? Maybe Yvette would come along and jump with me. I was reminded of her, and it seemed like she had been taking a long time in the shower.

"Yvette, how are you coming? Let's speed it up—we're only on the West Coast for a few days; let's make the best of it," I said.

"I'm good. Give me twenty minutes, and we can go," she requested.

"Cool. I'll take the bags to the car, except for your small carry-on, while you finish getting ready," I said. I grabbed the luggage and headed out the door.

As I walked down the hall with the luggage, Lynn called. I didn't want to answer and wouldn't, during my time here with Yvette. I had told her I was traveling and would be extremely busy on this long trip. I didn't lie. I was busy and working. I was just doing a few other things on this trip. Where did time go? Wasn't long ago, I was there with Lynn, and now I was here with Yvette. But I would never have another love like Lynn. I needed Ms. Angel Eyes to sing "Where Do I Go from Here," to help me answer this question. Perhaps it wouldn't be a future question. However, I would know the answer if I listened to Gloria Lynne sing "I'm Glad There Is You." I loved Gloria, but I loved Ms. Angel Eyes more, so I needed to work on these bad-boy habits of mine. I wouldn't call Lynn at all during our time out west, because I heard Ms. Angel Eyes singing the songwriter's words to "A Fool In Love." Oh, how her songs could have a brother placing himself in the songs, even though she was singing from a woman's perspective. She wasn't done with me yet. I heard her leading me from "A Fool In Love" to "Now I Know," the songwriter's sweet lyric. She sang and sang to me. I could hear her, but was I ready to listen to all that she was saying? She would continue to sing anyway.

In the end, she would help me solve this life mystery of mine, if it was a mystery at all, for Yvette was getting the best of me. As I loved her, I found myself wondering why my heart rang and skipped with joy, but why it never beat was such a mystery. I needed more than this West Coast trip to find the answer, or at least to make the decision I knew needed to be made. I was locked in a hurricane of feelings wanting so very much to understand love in the limited time given to a man and a woman. I sought help and envisioned that Ms. Angel Eyes would stretch out her hand as she did on stage so elegantly and pull me forward, and within her voice to find a love affair now with Yvette—or was it with Lynn? I needed to travel a little more on this life journey even though time was not on my side anymore. Here now, at this point in my life with these two women, I had another opportunity to find this thing called love. At the moment, I needed to put the luggage in the car and head back to the room to get Yvette. The afternoon sunlight was waiting. When I returned to the room, she was ready and looking like a million dollars, stacked.

"What took you so long to put luggage in the car?" Yvette asked. I didn't answer. I just asked if she was ready to go.

"Yes, I am," she said. I was moving about, but I could feel her eyes on me. Where had I gone, really?

"Good. Well then, let's go. We got things to do and a red convertible to do it in with the California sun shining above," I said, lightening the mood. Yvette asked me to carry the remaining things to the car as we walked out of the room. We decided to cruise the freeway for a while before going to the Waldorf to check in. We wanted to enjoy the breeze as we drove along the coast, talking and playing road games.

Driving with the top down made the afternoon even more enjoyable. We ate lunch at some café overlooking the water and were now on our way to check in at the Waldorf Astoria. Our room was lovely, and we were going to enjoy all that the hotel had to offer. We began with a shower together and lovemaking, which started on the bed and led to plastering her against the floor-to-ceiling glass window naked while she allowed me all the pussy I wanted. She was enjoying love and lovin'. We were on a high floor looking over the city. After some wonderful sex we lay together on the bed. I was tired, but Yvette was smiling, and softly squeezing and pulling me close to her, finding comfort in my arms after an orgasmic outburst inside her vaginal walls of cum and sperm splattering all up in there. We slept for hours before finally getting ourselves together for an evening experience in Beverly Hills.

It was about eight o'clock when we left the room dressed in our finest evening wear, looking like millionaires. We started with cocktails at the lounge bar before our 8:30 p.m. dinner reservation at Jean-Georges Beverly Hills. We dined on a light but elegant dinner, an over-the-top experience for two people falling in love. I was the conductor of this romantic jaunt, but I was getting caught up, too. It just seemed to happen, as was the case when the aura of two people was just right, so perfectly right, they both would fall prey to Cupid's arrow shot through their hearts. Then they were locked in time and space, and they would never want to leave that place they've known, the place of feeling loved and of being in love. At the same time, each somehow knew it would be too early to express these deeply felt feelings vocally. However, if they never verbalized their feelings, how would the other know? An old-school response would be, any response would be, too much weight for words to carry. What a person did, not what a person said, was what mattered. This I knew, believed, and subscribed to. So, I would continue this jaunt with the hope that she would know how I felt by what I did. Like so many good men did and still do today. She would have to come to understand that the win or the loss would be based on her mental maturity or lack thereof to discern the difference.

Yes, *Hollywood* and all its trappings could turn out the best of us, but obedience to something greater than ourselves, one's own self likes and lustful desires, could have one stuck and imprisoned, not letting one ever figure out that life's a journey to be traveled through and in which to grow. If one is lucky or fortunate enough to discover these truths, then he or she would ultimately find that growing and maturing is the answer for one's stay here on the planet. Who was I or where was I in my own discovery? Well, the reality was that I was caught in the middle, not between two women, but between my own self-likes and lustful desires. I was trapped, but I was digging my way out of it. The difference for me, if there truly was one, was that I figured out the journey, and I decided that I wouldn't stay stuck because otherwise there would be no growth. After more than a year of spending time with these two women and developing relationships with each of them, I had come to realize my struggle, how I was trapped. Meanwhile, I was also shown what would be required of me.

For now, though, I was here in *Hollywood* and about to leave and head southeast to the J.W. Marriott Desert Springs Resort & Spa. So, we finished up our late lunch, and did some shopping at those upscale stores where I bought her a pair of Christian Louboutin bootie boots and a pair of Jimmy Choo snakeskin heels that cost over three thousand dollars. I didn't care. While she tried on shoes; though, I had stepped out and went into a jewelry store to buy her a bracelet of the best quality

18-carat gold, diamonds, and tsavorite stones. I had the jeweler engrave our initials and the date on the inside of the bracelet. Ten thousand dollars I spent at this local jeweler next door. When I returned home, I would place it in one of her favorite handbags to find with a note from me saying, "Please know that I care more than you'll ever know."

"Hey, where did you go?" Yvette asked when she saw me return later.

"Just walking around. Let me pay for your shoes," I said. I pulled out and placed my American Express card on the counter. "Do you want anything else?" I asked, my hand gently stroking her hair.

"No, I'm fine," she said.

"OK," I said.

On another day, Yvette would be surprised when she found this tastefully wrapped gift from a Beverly Hills jeweler. After shopping and stowing the bags of goodies and the bracelet safely in my travel bag, we popped the top on our red convertible and continued on Route 10. Wind in our face, Valentino sunglasses on and dressed perfectly for the drive, we were in our fun mood again, as we found ourselves so often. Fantasia played on the radio. Then Yvette piped through the car sound system her favorite Spotify downloads to make the trip very, very hip. We were the perfect traveling companions. How did I find such a person in my life, and would I fuck it up as many men had done in life? Time would tell, but I was mindful women had fucked up, too. That was part of Cupid's arrow and the heart of love and life.

# Chapter 16

## PALM SPRINGS

Now Yvette and I were on Route 10 heading for paradise to find more love again and to enjoy poolside fun and a couple days of fine dining. Then we would be back on the road of our epic drive through the desert and through the Mojave National Preserve, four hours of sheer adventure on the back roads to Las Vegas. Wow! This stretch of highway and adventure would be a first for me and a surprise the two of us would remember for a lifetime.

After about an hour and forty-five minutes on the road, we pulled into the resort. I'd been here before, but I just told her it was for a business conference, a very plausible story I thought. She seemed unfazed by my comment. Maybe it was because she was with me. I didn't know, of course, but I wanted to believe that was true. Songwriters write about the inner peace that two people find when their two hearts are so caught up in one another, and storytellers create memorable pages bound in novels with some romantic titles. Perhaps our story would be memorialized in song or text one day.

Yvette was awestruck walking into the resort hotel, all of its beauty surrounded us. Most prominent was the water canal that flowed beneath our feet and throughout the hotel and its grounds. We were on top of the world on this journey, and we were together. Starry-eyed she was, and I the captain of our starship. Though the better part of the day had passed, the day still seemed young judging by the brightness of the sun, so we checked in, showered, and changed into our swimwear before we strolled the grounds in the desert heat. Finally, we made our way to the pool to relax and enjoy a light snack and colorful drinks. Yvette was a water girl, and if she found water, whether at the beach or a poolside, she would be in it all day if she could. Today, for some reason, the pool area wasn't very crowded so we ordered. Then as expected, Yvette made her way into the water.

Beckoning me to join her and enjoy a swim together, I obliged by jumping in the pool like a crazed teenager trying to impress his first teenage love. I wasn't one for swimming laps, but she nudged me on further still, and without much of an effort, we actually swam a couple laps together, almost stroke for stroke. I imagined a mating dance between flamingos or something of the sort such as I had seen in one too many wildlife shows. But here I was doing the dance in the form of a swim, and I chuckled to myself. In fact, as we glided to the wall for the final time, our eyes met, and we smiled that smile that exists only between lovers. As we stood up out of the water, our eyes never broke contact, and I was that teenage boy whose heart was pounding as much from the swim as from the feelings I felt for her. The moment intensified as we stared at each other before she joked that she had to slow down so I could keep up, at which we both burst into laughter and fell into each other's arms. I kissed her, cementing that moment in both our minds, and then I got out of the water. True to form, Yvette stayed in the pool until her food got cold and her drink became watered down, but she didn't care. She was loving the water, and I loved that she was. We stayed at the pool for a couple of hours before heading up to our suite, which was elegant. Even more, our suite contained a cool room that overlooked the pool beneath us and the desert hills in the distance. It was breathtaking—indeed, some real romantic, idealistic state-of-mind shit.

And in that moment, my mind wandered. Thought about one of them brothers in the NBA, about when he's balling and when his game is so tight he's dropping shots from anywhere and everywhere on the court like AI, so much so that not even Shaquille could stop his shots, even if he'd pay the price for entering Shaq's space. But no matter, he doesn't care because it's game time. And when it's game time, let the players play and the watchers head for the bleachers. This I knew well, and so it was with Yvette and Lynn.

Each knew I was a player. Problem was the price to pay when going to the hoop was nothing so mundane as an elbow or referee's whistle. No, it would be the breaking of a heart, and I wondered why even now in so beautiful a place as this, with so enchanting a woman as Yvette, I had brought up Lynn. Was it guilt? Maybe, but I felt these two women in many ways were just one person to me. Then I heard Yvette move about the room, and I snapped back. Turning toward her and the bathroom suite, I proceeded to get cleaned up before relaxing on the landing. We enjoyed the resort view from the penthouse after fixing ourselves drinks from the bar.

Yvette and I sat there on the landing and talked and explored our inner thoughts about our wants for tomorrow and for all of our tomorrows together. It got deep, but we wanted that conversation. In fact, it was needed after being together for well over a year, closer to two in fact, which she brought up. The thought of my two-year rule invaded my brain, and the jinn on my shoulder was frantic, agitated, and emphatic, and reminded me that little time remained of my self-imposed time frame. I didn't want to hear that. Go away, let me think only of us, and for now, it did, and I did. Yvette winked at me and asked if I was OK. I assured her that I was and asked if she was OK.

She replied with a smile and, "I really do love you. You know that. Right?"

"Yes, I do. And you know I do," came spilling out of me as if a baby were smiling and slobbering copiously from his mouth. That did it. Those words sealed the deal for her or perhaps for me. Right then and there on that landing, our hearts one, could only bring forth Ms. Angel Eyes singing in my head "The Very Thought of You."

"**Harold, my dear foolish man, you gotta stop, for the very thought of her completes you, and the very thought of you completes her. What more do you want or need? I must go now, but I'll return, for I need to sing to you as much as you need to hear my voice, and if I wasn't in the October of my life and still earthly, you in your August time, our hearts would be one**," and she winked at me as she looked away, her playful smile adorning her face still.

"You like me a little, Ms. Angel Eyes?" I asked.

"**No, just a man like you**," she replied. "**Go to her now before love passes you by**," and like that, Ms. Angel Eyes was gone from me.

Yvette's glowing warmth brought me back, and she reached over to kiss me, and I leaned forward to kiss and caress her for the thousandth time, it seemed. Soon that balcony, that landing upon which we relaxed together, was wet with our bodies' sweat and the pulsing of our forms in the desert heat under the early night sky. The bombarding and the colliding brought us once again to a climax in heaven's gates. There she was now, looking at me once again with that feeling of completeness, as if we had just met on the moon. Philly internationally famed recording artist Phyllis Hyman sang in the background with Ms. Angel Eyes' approval. Oh, to travel through love's promised land fraught with highs and lows, but certainly for now, I was lost in Erroll Garner's song, "Misty." If Yvette and I were to never meet again, our love that day was to be forever. Our hearts knew, but it would for sure take time and perhaps more highs and lows, pain and maybe even separation in our future to cement what we knew. But on that day and in that moment, love came to stay for the both of us.

"Let's get up from here and jump in the shower and ready ourselves for dinner," I said to Yvette, and we did. An hour later we were leaving our suite for an evening in the shadows of darkness and light; we continued sharing sweet nothings, all in laughter in the cozy desert air. Walking down the grand stairway to the boat dock, we boarded the boat that meandered along the canal to our dinner reservation. Now she was dressed in white and high heels; she was lovely, and I was just a cool, laid-back brother. Knowing that after many years of relationships and families and after doing so for so many others out of the love of our hearts, we found ourselves now with time to think about and experience love and lovin'. I thought I had been here before. I was certain though that this was Yvette's first time enjoying such a luxury of knowing love.

I whispered to her, "Trust in me?"

She smiled and said, "I do."

Dinner was special—the desert nights here at the resort were exquisite. We were now ready to hop back on the boat and enjoy the balance of the night floating and saying hello and good night from time to time to others entering and leaving our floating haven in this desert paradise. We drifted there until the hour was late, and then we headed to the bar for a nightcap before retiring for the night.

We fell asleep quickly and slept soundly under the morning sun piercing through the windows because we forgot to close the curtains. We laid there though, oblivious to the sun upon us, it seemed, for hours, just the two of us, free of all our worldly cares–family, friends, and work. In the corner of my mind even within my dreams, my muse came again singing, "Never Let Me Go." What would I be without Ms. Angel Eyes these past years? What would I be without Yvette? I was free to think and walk with Ms. Angel Eyes in the expanse of the universe. We understood our times, our moments. As she said, "**Go now, wake her up with a kiss, and ready yourselves for breakfast and an early visit to the pool**," and so I did. Yvette's head just then rolled toward me as if Ms. Angel Eyes gently turned her to me. She was waiting to be kissed. I awoke from that dream, that conversation, with Yvette's lips touching mine, and we saw for the first time the morning desert sun. It warmed our bodies and our hearts, magnified our dreams, and swept away our unending cares. "Did you sleep well, my dear?" I asked Yvette.

"Yes. And you, Harold?" Yvette replied.

"I did," I replied. I added, "Let's do breakfast early and head for the pool."

"Why so early?" she asked.

"Oh, I was told to," I quipped.

"You were told to," Yvette repeated. A curious glance from her, and I knew she didn't quite get my meaning.

"Yes. Just come along," I said matter-of-factly, and upon her face, I placed my hand, looked into her eyes, pausing for a moment, before kissing her gently. I turned to get out of the bed, and as she had so often along this journey of ours, she followed my lead without hesitation, not because she had to or because she could not do as she pleased, but because she loved me and trusted me, as I trusted Ms. Angel Eyes.

Breakfast was great in the open air. Now walking toward the pool, we found the whole area empty of hotel patrons. Yvette immediately found a pool pillow, climbed aboard, and floated slowly around the vast pool. Music flowed from the perfectly mounted speakers around the pool, and it seemed we were in a dream, and from it I took my cue, and without thought or care, I began to sing to her "Don't Misunderstand Me" in my baritone voice, while I video-recorded her wafting on the pool of never, never land. She was beautiful. Six minutes recorded would be for our tomorrows. Another recording to be tossed in the album of forgotten things, things we would find years later to recall being in love again and again. The softness of her there in the pool reached out to me as we kept our eyes focused on one another.

"How did you know we would have the area to ourselves?" Yvette spoke excitedly.

I looked up and heard Ms. Angel Eyes saying, "**Go on. She is waiting. Jump in and swim over to her. Continue to be the gentleman you can be. I know you. What song would you like to hear me sing to you**?" I gestured, "Someone to Watch Over Me." She smiled. "Or 'The Song Is You.' In fact, yes, I'll hear 'The Song Is You.'" Hearing her sing to me, I swam toward Yvette.

"Are you enjoying yourself here in what appears to be your private pool for the moment?" I asked.

"Yes, I am," she said gently, emphatically, lovingly.

"I'm glad," I said, and I loved being able to bring her such joy. I knew it was not entirely of my own doing. Sometimes we have to listen to the voices that know us best, that can and will guide us if we listen. I didn't always listen, but I was listening now. "Give me a kiss. I'm going to swim back over and relax in the lounge chairs. For a moment, I just felt the need to be closer to you," I said.

The morning hours at the pool were special. I continued to hear Ms. Angel Eyes singing to me about being aware of the many places I had visited and of the importance of sharing time, for it was fleeting. I relished all her advice and her knowledge. I sat drinking a hot cup of freshly roasted Columbian coffee under the beautiful desert sun and sky. I would remember this morning. The afternoon came and went, and we were still at the pool. The crowd had now grown, but we had had our special hours alone at the pool, so company was now welcome. Meeting several people lounging close by and in the pool with

Yvette, we had fun as the day faded away. Breakfast and lunch at the pool was fitting. It gave us space to be apart, but close in thoughts, even though we were never more than fifty feet away from each other. From time to time, I was still taking snapshots and videos while I read a book I had brought to the pool with me. Meanwhile, she played in the pool and, I imagined, also in her thoughts about how she could imagine her life now. As our day at the pool came to an end, I began packing up our things.

Back in the room, we showered and changed so that we could venture out into the town of Palm Springs in our red Mustang convertible. I had called ahead, so our valet had our car waiting at the front entrance. Without a moment's delay, we went off for several hours exploring this place created in the desert. Then, Yvette exhaled words reminiscent from our earlier days, "I wish I met you earlier in my life. How different things would have been for me, and you, us."

I smiled and offered, "Perhaps, but now is our time to fight for whatever time we have."

"I still wish that I met you when I was young and you slightly older," she reprised.

"My dear, perfect is perfect when it's given, and we accept it as our time. It's for the living and for the sharing, and time has chosen us to be more than just a dream, but a dream no more. You know, Yvette, it must be this desert air in our heads. You think?"

"I think it's so much more," she said as if dispensing wisdom about a long unknown riddle.

Quickened by the truth she spoke, I was reminded of all I had planned and said, "Hey, let's turn around and head back to the resort. We got another evening here before we head out tomorrow."

"Where are we headed from here?" she wondered aloud.

"Trust me. You'll like the adventure," I said.

"I will," she said, affirming my words.

The drive back was quiet, as if our thoughts carried on a conversation, and that was fine with me. Walking into the hotel, we stopped at the lavish, open bar to have a drink before heading up to our room. In the room, we showered off the desert dust and fell asleep. And again, I heard Ms. Angel Eyes. I asked playfully if it was she who was speaking. "**You know it's me**," she said.

"I know," I said. "I was here thinking about my day. The morning was great as you knew it would be. Can you sing 'Can I' to me, because you're making dreams come true, because the young lady is setting my soul aflame, and because my emotions are exploding. If she was lonely before, she will be no longer," I shared.

"**You may be right, my dear. If the two of you can weather the storms ahead. It won't always be like this. You know it won't, but the joy comes in the trying, the finding, and understanding. It's why you first met. Continue to store up the good times for shelter in and from the storms that will come**," she said. She added, "**Stay in tonight and just hold her.**"

"OK, Ms. Angel Eyes," I said.

"**And that I am and more**," she said.

"I know and so very much more. Thanks for the sharing, the caring and for all of you. A life well lived and sung about."

"**I don't know about my life well lived, but I lived it with its joy and a lot of pain. I'm fine now, though**," Ms. Angel Eyes assured me. "**Harold, you're a special one, but complex and a handful for most women**," she said.

"You think so?" I asked.

"**I know so, my dear. Go now and stay in tonight**," she said, and as effortlessly as she had come, she was gone.

Waking up from our rest, I suggested to Yvette that we stay in for the night.

"I was going to suggest that. You read my mind all the time," said Yvette.

We stayed in that evening, the two of us, and enjoyed movies, popcorn, hugs, and kisses.

# Chapter 17

## YOU COMPLETE ME

We arose early, packed our bags, and readied ourselves for the desert trip. It was early enough for another morning alone at the pool, and we enjoyed it, as if it were still yesterday. Soft jazzy-like music still coming from the poolside speaker, I offered up another baritone menu of lyrics to Will Downing's, "Nothing Has Ever Felt Like This," singing back to Ms. Rachelle Ferrell's melodic voice. While Yvette floated about on a water pillow with her thoughts, I went up to change and called for the bellboy to get our luggage, except for what Yvette had left out, a change of clothes for traveling. Afterward, I stopped by the pool one last time to let Yvette know to meet me at noon in the lobby.

As I headed over to check out, I saw my car parked out front and decided to make a quick stop at a convenience store to fill up the gas tank, and to buy another styrofoam cooler and some more items, namely ice, water, paper towels, beer and a few snacks, for the four-hour trip through the Mojave National Preserve. These would be essential for traveling through the hot, scenic, and seldom-traveled desert route, as opposed to driving Route 115 with all its traffic. As it approached noon, I was mindful that Yvette was a stickler for being on time, if not just a little ahead of time, and sure enough, as I pulled up to the hotel there she was, ready and waiting. She called out to

117

me. "Harold, I'm over here." I gestured in her direction as we traveled toward each other.

"Are you ready to go?" I asked, stopping the car and getting out.

"Yes. But where to?" she asked.

"Las Vegas, through the desert," I said.

"Harold, are you sure about traveling through the desert?" she said with no observable reservation.

"Yep," I replied.

"It sounds exciting. I'm game. Hey, we got each other, and you did promise me an adventure. I'm an East Coast city girl so all this shit is different out here. Let's go, but let's promise ourselves a return trip here for a longer stay," Yvette said, asking with a smile and looking up at me from under those lovely eyelashes.

"OK, I'll promise, if you promise we will do it again and return here in twenty-four months from today's date," I said.

"Why twenty-four months?" Yvette asked.

"Well, if we're still together after two more years have passed, then it's an easy return. If we're not, perhaps the thought of being together again somewhere in the future will cause Cupid's love angels to shoot another arrow and bring us together again," I said. "Would it be a promise unkept?" I asked her.

"Hey, don't think like that. I'll never leave you. In all my years, this is the first time I've truly fallen in love, and it's with you. True, I'm no longer in my thirties, and I've a couple of husbands and kids behind me, but was I ever in love like this? No. Hell, no! I want it and you, as well. You complete me, and the dream, I don't have to dream anymore. The dream is behind me now, thanks to you," Yvette said. She wanted me to know that for certain.

"No thanks to me, thank coincidence," I said as she grabbed me and kissed me, while saying don't go. "Well, let the valet open the door for you and let's go," I said, still in her grasp. Tipping the valet, we hopped in the convertible and drove over the bridge leaving paradise, and headed toward Twentynine Palms. While we left, I heard Ms. Angel Eyes saying, "**You're on your way. Try not to go astray**," while she sang the song "People Will Say We're In Love," by another great songwriter.

# Chapter 18

## THE TRIP THROUGH THE DESERT

Now on our way and in front of us the ride, the desert, and the City of Neon, Las Vegas. With love in the car and the top dropped, her hair was blowing in the wind as we traveled seventy miles an hour after passing the quiet town of Twentynine Palms. Now, we were in the desert preserve, Mojave National Preserve, an American park, but, oh, so different than our East Coast national parks with their lush green trees reaching toward the sky. Here, we were seeing the barren landscape devoid of greenery and water, where the air searched for a simple breeze, a breeze filled with moisture that could not be found. Here the earth was parched from the burning sun. The desert, with fissures wide and deep enough to stand in, waved goodbye. The desert so vast seemed as if one could simply sink into the sea of sand, the incalculable granules that shifted and blew over time and people, over past lives and histories in this dry oasis. If you slowed yourself you would hear the sand, the dunes, the breakers and perhaps see them waving and saying, welcome, come along, it's for all to enjoy. Leaving my thoughts, I turned to Yvette who was busy videoing the hills, the landscape, and us, all about us, memories to keep forever of our first trip in and through the desert.

We were only into our first hour or so of travel in this place, and it was truly breathtaking how we felt all alone. How alone?

Well, we drove for over an hour and saw maybe three other cars pass us from the opposite direction and no cars in sight behind us. None! Imagine that. We were digging the drive and the view in our brand new, candy-apple red, Mustang convertible. The temperature was 115 degrees; no need to find the temperature in the shade for there was no shade to be found. The many saguaro cacti, the large tree-like giant columnar cacti with funny arms, were our company. They seemed to wave us on. Yvette requested that we stop, the first of several, to have me take a picture of her, and then me, standing side-by-side with Mr. Saguaro Cacti. A good call, for we were not in a rush. Our destination was ours to plan, and we existed in a timeframe known only to the two of us. The desert has its way of slowing you down. That East Coast hustle neither works here very well, nor do you want it to. One cannot even find oneself thinking about speeding up time here.

Picture-taking took about twenty minutes to record our times and our moments. Once again, we found each other finding ways to say through our smiles and expressions how we were feeling. And then Mr. Saguaro Cactus seemed to lower his arms to nudge me forward to kiss her as she stood there with her iPad capturing all of me and the desert and I, all of her, yes, in my head, to hold for eternity.

Back in the car motoring our way toward Vegas, the heat was getting to this East Coast couple, and an hour later we pulled off at one of the scenic rest stops. We parked. I opened the trunk and got the two of us a bottle of cold water and two ice-cold beers. Yvette drank that beer in one turn-up and that was rare for her because she was not a beer drinker. She blurted out, "This is the best damned tasting and coldest beer I ever drank." The beer was followed by several short swallows of bottled water. The sun out west will have you doing things you don't normally do. I continued drinking my water and moved closer to Yvette for a kiss. She kissed me on the lips and worked her way slowly to my left ear and said, "I wanna get fucked in the desert."

I smiled and said, "You do?"

"Yep," was her reply.

With the two of us wearing only a few pieces of clothing, and my bottle of cold water in my hand, I quickly poured it onto the trunk, then took off her shorts and her thong. I laid her beautiful ass on the wet trunk top and poured on her what water was left, and the love-making in the desert sun was on. And it was good, too. No, *better* than good. Brothers and sisters, intercourse in 115-degree heat gives a whole new meaning to fucking outside. East Coast concrete heat can't compare, but I'll do it in the desert anytime and especially on the trunk of a red Mustang convertible. The heat dried us up quickly while we took another bottle or two of water to wash off. We were back in the car with another ice-cold beer and again destination bound, but on our time. Settled comfortably into the passenger seat, Yvette looked over at me and said, "You're a nasty ass, but you're mine, and it almost took a lifetime to find you. You can get some of this pussy anytime you want."

"Don't lie on your pussy. It might dry up on you," I teased.

"Oh, don't say that," Yvette gasped, as she burst into laughter.

"Then don't tell a lie on it," I reiterated.

"I'm not. I mean what I say. You can have this pussy, Harold, anytime you want," said Yvette.

"Well, I'll accept that, and I think you mean it for as long as you and I fit like a hand in a glove," I said, the ghost of my two-year rule appearing still in the desert sun.

"We'll always fit together even though we may not wild-out like this always," Yvette said, speaking quite sincerely.

"I understand. Let's change the subject. Soon you'll be telling me you're seeing water ponds in the desert," I said.

"You know, I was going to tell you earlier, I been seeing them in the distance and was going to suggest we go in one for fun," she said. "If we do ...," she began to say before I interrupted her.

"We'll be jumping into sand," I said.

"Seriously, look sweetheart, over to your right. There is one right out there," said Yvette.

"It's a mirage. The desert heat is playing tricks," I said.

"Can't be. Are you sure?" she asked.

"Positive," I said.

"Did you see those road signs saying don't pull your car off onto the side of the road? It says stay on the paved road, otherwise your car will sink into the desert's sandy earth." I'm an inquisitive person, but not that inquisitive to get stuck in the desert with no cell phone connection and no cars passing by in either direction.

We were still about two hours outside of Vegas. Yvette wanted to stop at the general store ahead, just to cool off in their air conditioning. I agreed. Walking into the general store was a treat. We ended up buying some of the local crafts before getting back on the road.

Yvette started reviewing all the videos she had taken of the desert topography, its mountain ranges, desert animals, etc. The pictures were memorable. She had really captured the trip in its totality so far. Apparently, she had been much busier than I thought. She had enough footage for a movie and would still have more to film including our entrance into Las Vegas. Despite having been quite busy, Yvette was restless, and sensing we would be back in civilization soon, she wanted one more bite of the apple in the desert heat. She suggested that I move my seat all the way back and take off my shorts again. Apparently, that I could have her pussy anytime also meant she could have my dick anytime. So she sat in my lap with my dick all up in her pussy while she drove us to Las Vegas.

"Now, I got this all the way to Vegas," she said, and I was down with it all. It was time for me to enjoy the drive while she drove the car, and me crazy. That was a delightfully wild sex suggestion. This woman, a mother at a young age, was catching up on lost time and experiences. Spreading her cheeks, I dropped the back of the seat lower. Yvette had more than enough room to drive me to the moon and the car toward Vegas. And afterward, she played everything from Herbie Hancock and Wayne Shorter, to Stevie, Aretha, Mary J., Yusef Lateef, Teddy, and the artist Joe. I was truly relaxed hearing truth.

This desert trip was surely ending on a high note. Forty-five minutes later seeing a sign that read "Las Vegas 40 miles," Yvette decided to pull off in an authorized parking area. Pulling additional bottles of water from the cooler, we washed off again, which just about used up the roll of Scott paper towels. Finally getting through the desert, I asked Yvette, "Was the adventure a good surprise?"

"Baby! Surprise is not the right word. It was amazing, incredible, educational, and a sexual revelation, doing it in the desert," Yvette said resoundingly expressing her joy. "I'm ready for Las Vegas."

# Chapter 19

## LAS VEGAS

With the Preserve behind us along with some great desert sex, we were ready for Vegas. Merging onto Route 115, we rolled into Vegas to check in at the Mandalay Bay Four Seasons. I had reserved a suite for us, and after checking in, a long hot shower was primary for the two of us to wash away the desert dust and the airy smell of desert pussy. Laughing and snacking on the remaining items in the cooler, we jostled for who would get to shower first. Yvette won since she argued on creative grounds and proved to be an excellent car-seat lap dancer while driving over 65 miles an hour at times. However, lap dancing in a convertible, I would strongly argue, ought to be done only in the desert on empty lanes, for at times, it was hard to stay focused on the highway, and in our lane!

Yvette was staying in the shower way too long, so I decided to join her, which she welcomed. With her tits and ass before me, she asked if I wanted some more.

I said, "Sure."

"No, I was only joking," she said quickly. "My pussy is pussied out. No more for you. I told you you're a nasty ass," she laughed, and wagged her finger at me.

"I thought I was *your* nasty ass," I said, reaching for her pussy in jest.

"You are, baby, and don't be giving my dick away," demanded Yvette.

"Listen to you, getting possessive," I said with a yelp.

"OK, you need to get out of the shower and let me have some me-time, OK?"

"This shower feels great, dear," I said.

"It really does. That's why I'm still in here, sweetheart," she said.

I thought then I would acquiesce, but not before just a few more minutes and so I just stood in the shower with her. As she faced the shower head, the warm water washing over her body, silently, gently, I just held her from behind, and we stood there motionless, the water washing over us both. The water's splash audible, noticeable, palpable, at first, after only a short while could not be heard, known, or felt any longer. Time stilled itself. I thought I was about to see Ms. Angel Eyes, but I did not. But as if spoken in my head, I heard, "This trip, and you, our time in the pool, at the pool, out here, the time coming through the desert, this suite, this shower with you, every minute with you, since we held hands that first day we met makes me never want to leave you." Had I heard these words or imagined them? Yvette had not moved. Was she speaking? I couldn't tell. Then she turned, faced me, and looked up at me. I couldn't tell if she had tears in her eyes or if her face was wet from the shower. But I realized it didn't matter. This moment was different. She wasn't joking. She wasn't being emotional, but I could feel her emotions as if they were my own. Calmly, deliberately, softly, tenderly, but clearly, her gaze unbroken, she spoke. "Harold, don't leave me." A man knows when his woman has reached the point of no return, and Yvette had arrived. She did not ask a question, she was not making a desperate appeal or plea, she was not looking for an answer. Her eyes were locked onto my eyes for a lifetime in but a moment in time, and throughout it, she did not blink, not once. She didn't so much as look at me as to imbibe me, so as to know me, and I think in that moment she knew who I really was. She couldn't control me, and she didn't want to, I felt, so she said her piece and I wouldn't ever be able to deny that she had said it. Then just before she averted her eyes, just before she stepped out of the shower, she seemed to cry without dropping a single tear, without even the expression on her face changing at all. Then, in fact, I did hear Ms. Angel Eyes say, "**Love her, if you can. I know you can.**"

Being who I was, I would love her, but the ghost of my two-year rule loomed, and the jinn was on my shoulder, too. In a moment, in an act as true to myself as I could muster, I said, "Girl, you'll be the one wanting to leave." I was trying to lighten the moment. She seemed neither to take offense to my levity nor felt the need to make me feel more or less uncomfortable. Most of all, she seemed committed to finishing what she started and to making peace with herself about the depth of her feelings for me.

"I am in love with you, Harold. I don't think I can ever leave you, really. If I did go, it would be our Aries egos getting in the way, but please know, I'll come back somehow, some way, to you. You're in my soul, my brain. A woman just can't stop loving a man like you, even if she wanted to, and I am being completely honest with you right here, right now." When she was done, she just stood where she had spoken, just outside the shower. I couldn't help but notice that she had laid herself bare, literally, before me, and made it clear. My tomorrows, as far as she was concerned, were my choice. She had made hers. Yvette was light, my light, along a path I had been seeking for a long time, and she had just made it clear that light would always be on. But I said, "We'll see if you know how to stick. As my mother would say, 'Is the woman a stayer or a goer?'" I asked her indirectly. But my Ms. Angel Eyes would say, "**Let the music play.**" Then I said tenderly to Yvette, "Why don't you go get some rest. Later, we'll eat and visit the blackjack tables." I assured her of a great evening together.

I stayed in the shower it seemed for an hour before finding my way to the bed to join Yvette. We slept until early evening. Shortly thereafter we got dressed and found our way to the elevator and into the midst of the Vegas nightlife. We were still on a West Coast high–LA, Palm Springs, the Mojave Desert, and now Vegas—for two days before flying back home first-class. We chose one of the restaurants in the Four Seasons Hotel. Looking at each other across the table we both agreed that we were tired. Eating our fill, we decided to just go back upstairs and sleep. It was still early, and we set the alarm for 12:30 and would do Vegas late-late nightlife. This town never sleeps anyway.

We nestled together, kissed briefly, and fell asleep. Time was ours to do and enjoy as we so desired and going back to sleep was the right call that would propel and sustain our energy levels to hang high in the Vegas nightlife of clubbing, gaming, and drinking.

Awakened by the alarm clock, we struggled with what to wear as clothes were everywhere, but we pulled it together and headed for the casino. We began our night out at the blackjack table where I bought $10,000 in chips. We gambled for about an hour, betting aggressively each hand, which resulted astonishingly in us being up $4,500. We cashed in the chips and enjoyed the balance of the night on our winnings. We were rolling high and balling. Next we checked out a dance club where we spent a couple of hours dancing, drinking, and interacting with strangers. Leaving there, we called for a town car to carry us to the Bellagio where we kept the action going. On our way into the hotel, I placed a crazy bet of $2,000 on the blackjack table and won. Yvette was ecstatic and even more so when I gave her all the chips to cash in—and keep.

"Let's go!" she said.

"You sure?" I asked.

"Yep," she replied.

And off we were to the next club to drink and club some more. It was almost 5:30 in the morning when we looked at one another and knew it was time to call for another town car to take us back to our hotel. After the driver dropped us off, we searched for a place to eat an early breakfast or a burger and fries to absorb the alcohol. We found an open restaurant and again ate our fill before we headed for the elevator and bed. We got undressed, showered quickly, said good night, and got in the bed. Almost asleep, Yvette raised her head and shook my shoulder to simply say, "You make me happy and I love you." We kissed again only to wake up later in the late morning around noon. I was in no rush to get out of bed and neither was Yvette. We did decide to call room service and have breakfast in our suite.

We had the casino winnings, so we ordered stupid stuff and too much of it: hot coffee was the first thing we ordered, followed by waffles, maple syrup, creamy scrambled eggs with caviar, potatoes, breakfast meats, fruit, a bottle of champagne, and orange juice, plus some other stuff. We were funnin' on the house. We ate, laughed some more, and still wanted each other. Our bellies full, we decided to go back to bed and then we would walk over to the hotel pool and take pleasure in a swim together.

Crawling back into the bed for now, I lay on my back. Yvette followed behind me and straightened her naked body atop mine with her head tucked close and softly between my neck and pillow. Immediately, she started biting my neck and talking shit in my ear again. I relished every second of her words and voice, melodious and rhythmic with a cadence all their own. We fell asleep again.

"**Hello, Harold**," said Ms. Angel Eyes.

"Ms. Angel Eyes!" I said, surprised.

"**Yes. How are you?**"

"I'm doing well. Who's with you?"

"**An old friend. Mr. Jimmy Scott.**"

"I know him. Beyond great, the jazz singer, Mr. Cool," I said.

"I know you do. That's one of the many things I like about you, young man," said Mr. Scott.

"Mr. Little Jimmy Scott, if I can refer to you that way, how are you, sir?"

"Please do and pleased to meet you, Harold," Mr. Scott replied.

"Gosh! The two of you together! How can it be?" I was lost for words.

"**Music is beyond magical, and like you have found Yvette, voices find one another,**" replied Ms. Angel Eyes.

"You know, I'm hearing songs like 'All the Way,' or 'I'll Be Around' and 'Someone To Watch Over Me.'" You made songwriters' songs special, Mr. Scott. Sing it as you like. I'm just a huge fan," I said.

"My man! You're much more than that; I'm told so by Angel Eyes," Mr. Scott said, speaking in the high-pitched voice of his.

"Mr. Scott, you're so cold. A very cold cat wearing your thick-rimmed glasses, standing at the mic in complete control of the room and notes only coming forth on your command. Seeing you two together is like heaven's gates opening, so do I hear a song or is Ms. Angel Eyes going to address my 'bad-boy' habits?" I said.

"I'll leave that to the two of you, but I'm just hanging out with her," said Mr. Scott.

"And you are 'the Gentleman,' Mr. Scott," I said.

"Thank you, Harold," Mr. Scott replied.

"Wow! Jimmy Scott your CD –*All The Way*— my favorite," I said. I always felt that if the brothers would go find this man's music, just maybe they would understand the merrymaking of romance, but they shouldn't let it get too wild like I have the tendency to do at times.

"**All right, Harold, I like you better when you're finding the best of you. I see it working between the two of you**," Ms. Angel Eyes said.

I smiled all the while offering up a huge, "I'm sorry," to my Ms. Angel Eyes.

"**I know you are, Harold**," said Ms. Angel Eyes.

"You two masters, what will you sing? Mr. Scott first," I said.

"OK, you got it, my young brother," Mr. Scott said.

"'All the Way,' and Ms. Angel Eyes, your song, 'Where Do I Go from You,'" I said.

"Oh, that's a great one," Mr. Scott replied.

"I like how you sing that song," I said, referring to Ms. Angel Eyes.

"**Harold, get some rest and get home safely. We'll talk soon**," said Ms. Angel Eyes.

"I hope," I said.

"**Young man, it depends on you growing. Maturing is the journey of life. You need some work still**," Ms. Angel Eyes quipped.

I smiled and closed my eyes to listen to the voices and images of my dream. I heard their voices charm and beguile me restfully to sleep. The vision was clear. Yes, I was up close, and it was personal. There in the room digging the vibes back in time. Maybe I was the club owner or just a cool cat with a pocket full of dough and certainly not coins, and access to all—women, the nightlife—and the two masters on stage in this smoky jazz room performing for the evening crowd. You know jazz crowds. We're different intellectually; we're hip and street savvy. I always knew that I would be backstage with them and their friends eventually, and that list was always long, but my name was on it, as well as the lady with me that evening.

Yvette was trying to wake me from a deeply euphoric trance, like sleep that I fell into just after the very last note of the songs.

"I didn't know you were that tired. I like looking at you while you sleep for some strange reason. It's as if you're finding peace with others. An eerie, soothing aura seems to be all around you at times," said Yvette.

"I wasn't tired, but peace comes more than just in the morning rising," I said.

"Wow, what brought that profound statement forth?" said Yvette.

"Maybe one day you'll know. Let's get up and go to the pool." I quietly asked her to ready herself.

"I'm ready sweetheart," rang clearly from Yvette.

"OK. Give me a minute, or you can go ahead," I said.

"No dear, I'll wait and walk down with you," she said.

The pool was crowded and there were only a few spaces available, but we "found" two after I tipped an attendant to secure us two lounge chairs, towels, and an umbrella. We were still in the desert after all, and the temperature was 109 degrees. Yvette found the water, and I brought a book to read that I was really interested in finishing by the end of the trip. After about twenty-five minutes of reading, I heard a woman's voice say, "Harold!" I looked up, and there was Diane, my old girlfriend from about six years ago. She was one of my two-year-rule romances. "Hey, Diane, what's up? And what are you doing in Vegas?" I said, as we embraced.

"Here with my husband," Diane said.

"You got married?" I asked, somewhat surprised.

"Yes!" she said as emphatically as I had sounded surprised.

"Are you happy?" I asked.

"Yes," she said.

"Shall I say completely?" I asked Diane again.

"Well, if you're asking how we wilded our days and nights away? Then, no, but you're looking great, no change I see and in more than one way. I thought it was you tipping the attendant and putting him to work," Diane said, as she smiled at me.

"Vacationing or work?" I asked.

"I'm here with my husband, who's here for work. They hold an annual conference, and every three or four years they host it in Vegas," she said.

"Married long?" I asked.

"No. It took some time to get over you. About twenty-four months, no, more than that. I moistened up when I saw you. Memories are funny things to box and forget, and then place on a shelf. You know, we were special." Diane stated firmly.

"I think we still are," I said.

"Are we?" Diane asked, wanting to know.

"Very much so," I replied.

I embraced Diane again and invited her to sit down. She did, and we talked while Yvette floated about in the pool. "And who are you here with?" she asked.

"A friend over there at the far end of the pool," I said.

"I see her. She looks like your type," she said, her frown apparent.

"You mean like you?" I asked.

Diane squirmed. "I don't think so. Anyway, what happened to us?" Diane asked directly. Seemed she really wanted an answer.

I told her, "I thought you wanted more from me at the time, and in time, I think you would have gotten all that you wanted and I, all that I wanted. I did find all those wants in our togetherness. We were in love," I said.

Diane looked at me, paused while seeming to resist the urge to look in Yvette's direction, and then said very candidly, "And I'm still in love with you, Harold. Why did you not return my calls, and there were plenty," she asked.

"I didn't quite know back then, why I didn't," I said.

"Well, I wasn't sure if I still loved you, but I am now. Seeing you confirmed my feelings for you. Harold, I miss you," she said.

Rather casual about it, I asked her, "You want to give me some?"

"You're still you, and my answer is yes," she admitted, adding, "and it's not just the sex, which was great, but it was always how we held each other, kissed each other. You always made my body explode into pieces and then you would collect them all before leaving me for the evening, and then, well, let's just say there was so much more, Harold. People don't get it until it's lost. Like my grandmother used to tell me, 'It's like water – a true love doesn't get missed until the well runs dry.' I miss my water and the well is dry."

"I'm water now, Diane?" I asked, smiling my smile.

"There you go, making me laugh. Do you want to be my water again?" she asked.

"You're married, and just recently," I said quietly.

"One shouldn't get married for their wants. I'll accept sixty of eighty percent of you now for a hundred percent of what I have," said Diane. She straightened up as she spoke, as if she needed to be strong acknowledging a truth—against her better angels—she might never have spoken had she not seen me this day, a truth she seemed willing to defend if it came to it.

"Liking and loving are vastly different, honey," I said.

"I'm still your honey?" Diane asked, a little bit surprised.

"Forever and always," I said.

"That's wonderful to hear," she said, asking, "Harold, are you staying here in the hotel?"

"Yes, of course," I said.

And with that same strength she had spoken her truth, she said, not in a playful way, but in a "you better" way, said, "Maybe, if you can find the time, I want you to fuck me."

"Just like that?" I asked.

"Yes, just like that! I want you back," she said.

"Diane, you are married!" I repeated, this time it was I who was fighting his better angels.

"I know that better than you, Harold, but I understand now what you tried to tell me in so many ways about love and lovin'," she confessed. "I'm here, you're here, and you know how we do it," Diane said, all smiles. "Look, here's my business card and my new number."

"What's your number? Just give it to me. I'll remember. I'm not promising anything," I said.

"Your friend is heading toward us. I better go," said Diane.

"Would you like me to introduce her to you?" I asked.

"No. She looks too much like me. Just a different shade of black. Hope we talk soon," she said. "Kisses and hugs from me to you," she said as she left.

Arriving as Diane was out of ear shot, Yvette asked, "Hey, who was that?"

"Diane," I answered.

"And what's up with Diane?" Yvette said, her effort to be cool apparent.

"She was an old girlfriend of six years ago. She's out here with her husband," I said, better to come clean, a nod to my better angels, I thought.

"Kiss me, and I hope she's looking," said Yvette.

"OK, Ms. Possessive. Let me order you a drink," I said, trying to help return us to our hermetically sealed world, one in which only she and I existed.

"Are you going to have one, too?" Yvette asked.

"Sure," I said. "Your usual Tito and tonic?" I asked and she affirmed with a nod.

Getting up to get our drinks and walking toward the bar, I wondered if both the ladies were looking to see what direction I would cast my eyes and attention. I made it a point to look back at Yvette because I knew this would give her a comfort level that she needed. Yvette has a Ms. Diva personality about her, even though she would deny it vehemently, and I needed to make sure she felt like the only one who was attracting my eye while we were here. As my body followed through on such, sending a wave to Yvette, who was watching me and who waved back, my thoughts wandered and the idea of having some more of Diane was an exciting one. She was still foxy as hell, every inch of her against my 5'9' frame. I was glad I had stayed in the gym and worked out regularly. I was pleased that I was looking good and feeling good, but I also was thinking my ass needed to be in shape if I was going to do Diane like she wanted, and like I would be obliged to do if I decided to call her.

But emotions were colliding for If I went there, my muse, Ms. Angel Eyes, might be my muse no longer. I had to think about this. I was here with Yvette, and we'd been on vacation for almost a week. I was able to block out Lynn when here comes Diane as lovely as the morning sun, sweeter than sugar candy, finer than wine, and a gripping pocket to fit my hand into as tight as a pair of tight white jeans, if you get my meaning. What you didn't see, you didn't miss, but seeing it again made my temperature rise. And she knew she still looked good walking it—her body was moving geodetically and still showing perfect in every mentally known dimension. Yes, walking toward me in damn-near nothing covering her ass, and tits falling out from her top. Her cocoa-brown body blackening in the desert sun. Damn, she was still beautiful, in her late forties, looking like 32. That old lines still ring true, "the blacker the berry, the sweeter the juice, when it gets even blacker, the juicier the juice," and "Black don't crack." She had me smiling again. This kind of stuff is why men become fuckups. It's other women. Damn, the Western lifestyle is trying.

Well, I would let that subject die its own slow death for now. At the bar, though, Diane was on the brain, and yes, I finally did cast my eyes in her direction and made eye contact. I told myself to let that be for the moment, but Diane was right. There was something about certain relationships, the ones that were *right*, that were beyond just a dick and a pussy giving and receiving scintillating nerve ending explosions, something even beyond the caressing of the bodies, even if it was some heavenly made stuff. That *right* love felt between two, this part was hard to move away from, and the *right* sex and the memories stored in the recesses of the body, this part was harder to let go. In those *right* relationships, the major parts of the two individuals are tied into knots, and untying them is damn hard. Not even time itself can untie us from those tightly tied love knots. No, one cannot just unbind the *right* relationship fashioned in and by perfect love and perfect sex. It comes in very rare packages and at unexpected moments, but it comes. It's generally the battle for more that moves the two apart, but not the love and the thoughts; they remain forever. And so the problem really is that we're no good for anyone else, even though we're with someone else. I would like to think there are at least a few exceptions to the rule, but are there really? No, I didn't think so.

As I carried the drinks back to our lounge chairs, Yvette saw me and cleared a spot to set down our drinks.

"What took you so long? Did you stop by your friend?" she asked, again her efforts to be cool apparent.

"You saw me walk directly to the bar," I said.

"I saw you. I just wanted to bring her up," said Yvette.

"I don't know why," I said. "She was just an old girlfriend, nothing more," I added.

"Why did you break up?" Yvette asked, but not really wanting to know.

"I guess for the usual reasons couples do," I said. "Why did you, Yvette, break up in your previous relationship?" I asked.

"Being with you, Harold, makes the answer easy to reply to," she said.

"You know why. We talked about our baggage many times. Let's put it behind us," I reminded her.

"OK sweetheart. You know you're my sweetheart," said Yvette sprightly moving her 5'6" body around, having more hips than the average sister and getting darker from the desert sun.

"So, you have told me," I said.

"I'm going to keep on calling you sweetheart," Yvette said. "The pool area here is a lot different than at the resort," Yvette complained.

"You're right. We gotta go back," I said.

"I'm going to keep my twenty-four-months promise, and I hope you will, too," Yvette swore aloud and raised her right hand, as if taking an oath.

"Twenty-four months works for me," I said nonchalantly. "How's the drink, Yvette?" I asked.

"Not as good. And nothing will taste as good as the ice-cold beer in the desert followed by laying wet on a wet convertible trunk as we dried in the sun," Yvette said, showing a smile that could hardly be contained.

"Last night was fun, and we still have more house money to continue 'funnin,'" I said.

"Why do you use that word?" asked Yvette.

I asked, "You don't like it?"

"It's cool and different, but you're quite different as well. Maybe that's the attraction. You're a complex person and probably hard to deal with, but I give way," said Yvette.

"You're the second person that said the same thing," I said.

"Pay attention then, Harold," Yvette said. She was trying not to be salty, and I appreciated the effort.

I reached over and kissed Yvette. If I were honest with myself, she was good for me, and if I wanted this woman, this amazing woman, in my life, I needed to make her feel secure. Today's event was a real challenge to that security.

"Hey, it's getting close to five o'clock. Let's have another drink and later let's find the best Mexican restaurant on the strip," Yvette suggested.

"OK. Are you going to have the same or something different this time?" I asked.

"Just get me a bottle of water. You need to drink more water in this heat, too," she said.

"OK," I answered. "You're right. I'll get two bottles of water and drink one, as well. When I come back, I'm going to take a quick dip in the pool," I said, but noticing a waiter nearby, I got his attention, ordered for the two of us, and then ventured toward the pool. I was feeling better that my full attention was focused back on Yvette, but I didn't realize until after I entered the pool that Diane was already in the water. We made eye contact again, but I stayed in the other end for about ten minutes until I saw the waiter return with our drinks. I completed a lap and then returned to our lounge area. Yvette handed me a towel, and as I dried myself, I reached down, looked into her eyes, smiled, and kissed her again. Then I noticed, wow, her tits were falling from her bathing suit top, as well. What was a brother to do? The right thing, of course.

We lay around the pool area for another hour or so and then headed to our suite. I was getting a little hungry, and Yvette wanted Mexican. Maid service had the suite cleaned and stocked with fresh towels. The hotel service was good, but the J.W. Marriott Palm Springs Resort and Spa was a couple of notches above this hotel.

"We got just the night and the afternoon before we must return the car and head for the airport. Let me know if you want to do something special between now and then," I said to Yvette.

"Harold, let's catch a comedy show after eating," Yvette suggested.

"Sounds doable. Google comedy acts in Vegas for the night and check available tickets," I said. And she did.

"Hey, Katt Williams is in town. There's a ten o'clock show and tickets are available," she replied.

"I'll call the concierge to secure two tickets at will-call," I said.

"Great," she said.

"Let's get cleaned up and get dressed. I asked around on the way up to the suite when you were stopping in a couple of shops about a good Mexican restaurant, and they suggested Javier's, an upscale dining experience at Aria Resort and Casino along with a world-class tequila lineup. The best in Las Vegas. They suggested several things: their ceviche, enchiladas, and steak. And we must try their hand-shaken margaritas. I'll make an eight o'clock reservation for dinner, and we'll call for a town car from the restaurant to the Katt Williams show," I said.

Dressed and ready for another night in the City of Neon, we were excited about having a great night out. The concierge had a town car waiting out front and show tickets at the front desk. From the hotel to the Aria Resort & Casino was a short trip, and we were hungry and ready for a delicious meal. We sat at a table that offered a view of the casino floor, ordered drinks, and looked over the menu together. We started with an appetizer, which we shared, and then I ordered for the two of us. We dined and drank until 9:30. Our food was literally everything we hoped for on this last night in Vegas. With Katt Williams serving up comedy for dessert, our trip would end on another high note.

The show was laughter-filled with Katt running across the stage dropping funny lines with a serious message. He has been real with his thing for many years. I had the driver return exactly at midnight to drive us to the hotel. He was there waiting to open the door for Yvette, and I followed her in. Once back at the hotel, our heads turned toward each other with that gambler question – do you feel lucky tonight? We smiled and said why not.

"OK, let's make a bet together," I suggested.

Yvette asked, "You mean like me matching what you bet?"

"Yes," I said.

"OK, how much?" Yvette said hesitantly. I could tell she wanted to hold onto her winnings.

"One thousand dollars each and one bet, win or lose. I'll love you to sleep," I said.

"All right, baby!" Yvette said, letting go of any apprehensions. She was immediately back into the spirit of having fun and pulled out her cash from her purse.

With her $1,000 and my $1,000, which was still all house money, I told the dealer to let the money play. The first card was an ace. Yvette grabbed my hand and squeezed tightly. The second card was a one-eyed jack, good enough for blackjack. She screamed. I guess the whole casino heard her. We collected our winnings, headed to the cashier's window, cashed our chips, and divided the winnings equally. And I kept my promise, and I loved her to sleep.

When the morning light snuck through the curtain, we were already up, perhaps the earliest all week. Winning can do that. Taking turns in the bathroom, we packed our bags and counted our money.

"Almost a free week of fun," Yvette joyfully screamed again.

She had no idea about the $10,000.00 bracelet purchase, and she wouldn't for now.

"You know I don't gamble, and I will only go into a casino with you," said Yvette.

"It doesn't happen like this a lot, but sometimes it goes well when you're 'funnin' with the one you love," I said, teasing Yvette, who laughed.

"You love me, baby?" she asked.

"I guess I do," I said. "I'm only going to tell you once. I love you." I smiled at her as she came toward me to give me the biggest, wettest kiss of the week. Bags packed, money in our pockets, we went to find a different place to eat breakfast than in the hotel. We decided to have breakfast at the Wynn, walk the strip afterward, and then return the car while we waited for our afternoon flight. We would be home soon with memories. Waiting for us was work and, even more, our personal lives, and the baggage that came along with them.

## Chapter 20

## BACK TO HOME AND LYNN

Lynn was not personal baggage, but she was waiting for a phone call, and I had to make the call. After dropping Yvette off, Lynn's number popped up in my cell. I called her to ask what was up and what she had been doing the past several days. Of course, the answer rang clear.

"Missing you. How was the West Coast? Did you miss me?" she asked.

"Great. Yes, I have missed you very much, and I want to see you tomorrow," I said.

"Not tonight?" she asked.

"Lynn, the flight and the workload was just grueling. I want to rest, go by the office first thing in the morning, and then in the evening, take you to dinner and be surprised by how much you missed me these past few days. All in that order," I explained.

"It has been more than a few days, my lover man, but that will do," said Lynn.

I was hit with a load of files placed on my desk in the morning with yesterday-like due schedules attached to them. In fact, I would be working on them late into the night. Lynn, too, was complaining somewhat about the stack of files on her desk.

The MALAs (multi-affair love angels) had done me a big one. Surely, those angels have been helping us guys over the years juggle our multi-love affairs with women. Understand, these aren't heavenly angels, and they're not a hundred percent your watchers, especially if you go afoul, such as doing that crazy, insecure stuff. One can't be a fun guy and be insecure. That's why fun guys are hard to find. I just got saved, and my tired ass needed some rest.

Lynn texted me what would foreshadow our reunion.

"You got me smiling," I said.

"For a minute, I was feeling some kind of way," whined Lynn.

"You were?" I said. "Lynn don't go there. We both gotta earn the work-a-day coins to pay the bills and afford our life-style," I stated in order to take control of the matter.

"I know, sorry I tried to make you feel like that," Lynn said. She sounded guilty, and that was enough for me not to belabor the point. I let it go.

"I know what I got for you is more than enough," Lynn continued.

"What about what I got for you?"

"I've been waiting and wanting to spend more time with you, and this past year together, almost two years, has me thinking about us all the time. My work, though, is requiring much more of my time and mental alertness lately," Lynn said. She seemed to feel that she had to explain or justify her work and our time apart, but she didn't.

I said, "Look, it's great to know we both need to pay much more attention to our professions this year. We know how we feel about each other," I said.

"I was going to talk to you about that. I hadn't realized how much time we were spending together, and the sex thing, we should cut back just a little," Lynn said.

"Lynn, are you serious? Why? I was thinking you wanted more time together," I said, surprised.

"I just said why. It's work. I'm in line for a promotion, and I must be a hundred percent every day," she said, and I could hear it in her voice. She sounded determined to do what was needed for advancement. The MALAs were working overtime for me today. If I heard right, I just might be able to squeeze some time in with Diane. Since Diane was married, her time would be limited. Seeing Diane again, and so unexpectedly in Vegas, looking like a bowl of ice cream and cherries, got my dick hard talking to her at the pool. That's a crazy thought, three women, I said to myself.

Diane and I had stopped talking over the dumbest thing. I said she was getting fat, and I think she was going through a lot at the time, maybe even talking to another guy. She told me to get out that evening.

I said, "You're putting me out, Diane?"

"Yes, I am," she said.

"You know, if I go, we're done," I said.

"I don't care," she replied without hesitation.

I left, and though she tried calling me several times, I never responded. Not my best moment. I think that's a line in a movie somewhere. Now six years later, we have found each other by a pool. Seemed appropriate as we spent most of our time back then at the beach during the summer months. It all seemed so perfectly tee'd up, but I was not sure if I wanted to start talking with Diane again. She was married, and divorce can be such a headache, although I had been spared the worst of it. I'd been married, although mostly separated, for over twelve years before finally divorcing my ex. My attorney, John Worth, did a great job. It was a complicated one; however, my ex and I agreed not to run up legal fees and do a 50/50 division of everything except our companies and our houses. She kept her company and estate house, which was worth millions, and I kept my house, the family farm, and my companies, equally worth millions. Over the years, I tended to let all the women know my history, but not my net worth. We're both OK today, and it was long overdue. As my mind wandered, I began to think how Yvette fitted me well. Maybe she's the glove I've been looking for.

Realizing the pause in the conversation as my mind had drifted, I said to Lynn, abruptly, "Tell me about the possible promotion and how soon."

"It's a senior vice president position opening in Manhattan at the end of the year."

Diane in Washington, D.C., Lynn and Yvette living on opposite ends of Philadelphia—that's work. Diane is not in the equation, really, just yet, but my 'bad-boy' habits surged, and I thought I could work that distance between the ladies quite well.

"Harold, are you listening to me?" Lynn said, mild annoyance in her voice.

"Yes, Lynn, I'm listening," I said. "You said promotion at the end of the year."

"'Where?" she asked to see if I was truly attentive.

"Manhattan," I said right away.

"Oh, you were listening," she said, surprised.

"I know you think I'm one of your employees at times," I said.

"No, I don't," she said.

"I think so," I said.

"Well, I know you're not," she said.

"I'll never get caught not listening, maybe not hearing, but not listening, no way. Romance requires listening intently. You have to feel your way into the heart, everything else follows," I philosophized.

"Harold, you may be right, because you're a romantic ass. I'll give you that and more," said Lynn.

"You're tired, and I got files in front of me. Go home. Get some rest. We'll find our time together tomorrow evening," I said.

The next day came quickly. I had to be in the office before any of my employees. However, I did rest well, falling asleep as soon as my head hit the pillow. Staying in that first night I returned from Vegas was the right move. I needed the rest. Thanks to hearing Ms. Angel Eyes wanting the best for me. Maybe because of the songs she has played of love and loves lost, pain, infidelity, high times, and aging, I have made better decisions. Her understanding of time was so insightful, and the compassion in her words and voice made me think that she wanted us men to be *better,* starting with me. If she comes again, she'll know about Diane.

The staff handled the work at the office, and the morning meeting brought me up to speed on current issues. It was a full and busy day in the office, between phone calls and meeting after meeting with all the divisions. At the end of the day, around five o'clock, I called Lynn and asked would seven o'clock work. She said to come earlier if I could. "By the way," I said, "I got the text from you. It was a surprise. A picture of your pussy spread wide open. With a handwritten note. That was some creative shit to begin an evening."

"You liked that! Well, there's more when you get here," said Lynn.

I arrived at seven o'clock, and there was more! Her front door was left ajar, the initial sign of my being welcomed back. Playing loudly was a famous jazz track single from her father's collection. She had her sound system loaded with his CDs. Upon entering, I followed her presence. Her perfume filled the air and drew me toward her. She was in her sunroom, the curtains were drawn, and she lay there virtually naked before me. She spoke up, "You miss this." It was hard to say no. One could only say yes to what she offered, and she offered it on a *regular basis*.

Lynn was special—naked, ass, titties, intelligent, money in the bank, and she was all the holidays in one package, one package that was laying there before me.

"Come here and tell me about your business trip, or we can talk about it later."

I opted for later, and somehow, I undressed myself, not even recalling unbuttoning my shirt or removing my tie. I'm sure I would have started with the tie, but I can't remember, nor was it important. There in the warmth of her, I wanted to cum like a teenager, but she deserved and desired more, and I was up for it. Her thick lips painted ruby red had marked me all over, for passion was blowing off like a teapot with a high flame driving the steam to scream. We were delivering springtime to each other once again, as if we had never been apart. She squeezed me one time so I could feel all of her. I thought she was going to break this brother's back, but I picked her lovely ass up and started wailing on her, plastered against the wall, then rolled onto the rug. We were sweating and breathing like athletes now. After more than forty-five minutes of this, I came up for water, drank some, and poured the rest on us. We stayed wet. I was no longer in the desert heat. Working my way back to the sofa, I went for the lift one more time. Her legs were already wrapped around my back, locked for a sit-down. With her hands still free, she grabbed the back of my head and buried it in her glistening titties. She was squeezing me so firmly, she damn near suffocated me with titties of pleasure. Every now and then, one was stuck in my mouth, and she held it like a nursing mother. This was why men sometimes left women; their woman just liked to fuck too much. As for me, I liked those kinds of women.

Ms. Angel Eyes was taking the underwhelming approach to bringing to light my bad-boy qualities. Her songs suggested being with and away from men like me. Still, she understood me and sang through the passion and the loving required to take this journey with me. For sure, Ms. Angel Eyes had some racy history herself before passing over.

We finally rolled on the floor together, somehow unlocking her thick thighs and long legs. We lay there for a long time it seemed, embracing each other, and our orgasmic memories over the past eighteen months and counting. Over the course of nearly two years of being close, I had made it through all the special days and holidays merely by letting both Lynn and Yvette know that I only did birthdays. Their birthdays were coming again, and I would just do the simple, but special things for each of them. During the other big holidays, they were to be with their families and I, with mine, otherwise we would all have family coming and going and talking under their breath. "Look at her, she had a different guy here last year, and who now is this one. I wonder how long this one will last." Or my kids would say, "Really, Dad." We all have those relatives, so why feed into it. Privacy was not totally dead in America.

"Hey! Harold to Earth. Are you hungry? I got off early and cooked a beef roast, vegetables, potato, et cetera." Lynn shook me out of my thoughts.

"Yes, Lynn, I'm here," I tried to recover.

"Harold, you'll have to warm it up yourself, because I'm worn out from these missing-you sessions," Lynn said.

"No problem. I'll fix myself a drink, too. Would you like a drink or a glass of wine?" I offered.

"Shit! I need a stiff drink. A dry gin martini with a lemon twist. The way you do it – the gin chilled over ice stirred, not shaken. You know where the martini glasses are over there in the far cabinet. I'm done. You just make my pussy cum so much, and that last one shook me like I was having convulsions," Lynn confessed.

"Well, I know your vaginal walls just gripped my dick like it was in a vise. You got some good-ass pussy, Lynn," I told her. "Every woman ain't got good-ass pussy like yours. And yes, I had to say it just like that," I added.

"Good!" Lynn smiled, "But you know how to put the work in to make it all that it can be."

"You got educational jokes. Now!" I laughed out loud.

"Getting back to that vise grip you got. What if we were stuck like two dogs in the summer heat like we would see in the neighborhood growing up?" I queried.

"Oh, no. You got jokes. That's a funny thought," Lynn started laughing uncontrollably. "That doesn't happen to people. Does it?" Lynn tried to be serious all of a sudden.

"Maybe, maybe not, but it would be an embarrassing phone call to make if I had to," I said, and we both laughed some more at the thought of such a spectacle and then finished our drinks together.

Lynn was happy to see me and to have me blow her back out one more delightful time, but there was also a moment where I slipped, one might say, and my dick started to slide into her asshole, and she immediately hollered, "Oh shit, not my ass." We laughed at such moments and others throughout the night, which we would spend together alternating between drinks in hand and lying naked and looking exhausted before one of us would invariably incite the other's wild side again and again. No, this night wasn't going to be popcorn, kisses, and hugs. Lynn wouldn't have it any other way, and well, neither would I.

# Chapter 21

## THE TWO-YEAR RULE

I had experienced a great trip out west with Yvette, and since I had returned, I enjoyed an amazing night with Lynn. I hadn't expected, though, to add a third woman, in the form of Diane, an old flame, into the mix with these two women. What was a brother to do? I didn't know, but I knew I would figure it out as I always had. How badly this could all go down if they ever found out about each other never crossed my mind. Yet, as I lay alone in my bed, one thing was for sure: I knew the two-year rule would soon rear its ugly head, and the questions about what to do, how to do, when to do, and with whom to do whatever, and so on and so forth, would begin cascading. Would my own self-imposed rule come crashing down on me? I never thought about it because it never occurred to me. Maybe that was a good thing.

I did wonder though, where this relationship with Lynn was going. Was there more to it than just sex? Did I even want us to be a couple? The questions would start like clockwork beginning in the tenth or eleventh month of this year. Maybe Yvette and Lynn would each go their own way or maybe each would push beyond the two years and close in on two-and-a-half years or even three years. I didn't know, but I knew the time was coming. Being certain it would come, I decided to go with the flow this time and see who would be standing at the goalpost, or which one would stick a stake in the ground and give me an ultimatum to be decided right then and there just as Diane had done. That ended something that could have been great, evidenced by what we still seemed to have when I saw her out west. She had given me an ultimatum and I left, and I chose not to call her back. So as for Yvette and Lynn, each could just walk away quietly or create some nonsense to use as an excuse for leaving. The unknown was just that, the unknown, so I would move forward with each woman in search of the love and oneness I wanted. Yes, I would move forward, but then again, I also knew in the recesses of my mind that a decision still had to be made, whether I would finish the race or leave it and them *all* behind.

For the moment, both Yvette and Lynn were telling me they were mine. That was incredibly exciting, and perhaps one day when this was all over, I would write a book about love, how it leads us, and how love is about traveling together in our loftiest feelings, the ones about the dream of a future with another. Say what we all will, we all wanted that, and whether anyone or everyone would come to that realization as I finally had was another story. Thinking about such an ending, I wanted to stay in this dream-filled world of mine thinking about a future with either of these gorgeous and amazing women. I wanted to avoid life's realities for a little longer, as well as the pain of having to ultimately leave one of them whom I also loved.

Time simply spent together with another and time expressing our feelings with another created bonds, unending bonds, in many ways of which we were unaware. Over the course of my years, I had seen those bonds, love bonds, broken. Bonds broken for any reason, even the right reason, however, did not remove the love that had taken hold of us. So, we'd come and go still with that love in our hearts, really in our bones, having never forgotten our time together and the feelings shared, and so at least for some, the rare opportunity to have experienced a lifetime of joy never to be found again, is lost. If I only had such memories so be it, but for now I was looking forward, and I was glad these women were here with me sharing all that we had so far, and thus pushing us into that dream-filled tomorrow.

I would have to choose one of them not simply because I had to choose, but because if I didn't, life would choose for me. I didn't relish the thought of life choosing for me as it might not be the choice I wanted for myself. Besides, I believed in making my own choices, shaping my own destiny, and living out the future of my own making. Life didn't require, I had always believed, that we be heroes who rode in to save the world. No, it only required that we saved ourselves, for in so doing we could save others. When traveling on a plane, we were told to put on *our* oxygen mask before helping others to put theirs on in the event of an emergency. Was not life, the choices we made, and how we loved, the same?

With much mental and emotional energy spent, I began to fall asleep, and as I did, I wondered if Ms. Angel Eyes was around. I could go for hearing her sing and someone tripping the ivories on the piano.

The next morning, while on my way to the office, I became stuck in unusual traffic delays. It was no problem; I simply started making client calls to use the time as well as possible. This was a standard practice for me, and my secretary was well aware of my habits. Therefore, it was troubling that she continued blowing up my cell while I was on a client call. Consequently, I finished up the call as quickly as possible and called her back to see what was so urgent.

To say the least, it was a bombshell. "I opened the envelope, sir," my secretary began, "Well, sir, having read the papers, sir, you, well, you have a court date and a child who is three years of age."

"What? I can't believe this shit," I said. "Domestic Court is sending me papers about a three-year-old child who is supposed to be mine?" I asked her, though I was really just expressing my surprise. "I'll be in the office within the hour," I said, ending the call.

The Domestic Court had papers delivered to me through the mail apparently for fathering a child three years ago with a woman named Tina DiFilipo. I knew the woman, but the child could not be mine. I heard Michael Jackson singing "Billy Jean" in my head, but this one was not mine. I hadn't even seen her for more than three years. My first call was to my attorney to get on top of this. I had children, but not being a responsible man when it came to children, uh, that was not me. I was like my father, a hawk and a provider. For now, I consoled myself with the understanding that this was the risk that came with the lifestyle I was leading. That same lifestyle Ms. Angel Eyes kept suggesting, if not outright telling me, that I needed to change and grow away from.

Tina DiFilipo, she was about thirty-two or thirty-three when I met her at a summer gathering. She stood out and caught my attention right away. We talked and then met about a week later for a late breakfast, after which we started up a relationship. And yes, the sex was all that, but protection was always a requirement, always. A little over a year later, I ended the relationship because she was looking for someone to have a child with, and I wasn't going to be the one. I was sure I was tapped as the child's birth father because I had more zeros behind my numbers than the alternative, the child's real father. I would have to deal with it and have the appropriate testing done to prove that I wasn't this child's father. For now, I had my secretary make an appointment with my attorney ASAP to discuss legalities and next steps.

Was life trying to make some decisions for me? I wasn't sure, but it crossed my mind. Nonetheless, this matter was going to consume time, time that I just didn't have. Regardless, it had to be dealt with properly. Even still, I didn't get it.

Something must have happened to Tina because this wasn't like her. Life was on the upside for her, and we left on a good note. For several months after, we had a couple of lunch dates to talk about stuff. No lovemaking was involved. It was genuinely just a platonic friendship. We hadn't talked or seen each other since our last lunch date more than three years ago.

When I arrived at the office, my secretary had finally gotten my attorney on the line, so I took the call in my office and explained what just happened, scheduled a late lunch with him. In the meantime, I scanned the documents and emailed them to him. Our lunch was in two hours, so I cleared a few things off my desk as best I could with this matter suddenly looming over me. While the time didn't pass quickly, I eventually met with John Worth, my attorney, at a nearby restaurant where we often met during happy hour.

Our meeting was productive. We walked through a time-line, talked possibilities, and concluded that I couldn't be the father. However, we still had to do the legal rigmarole, as required. The DNA test would be the decisive factor, and I was sure about the result coming up negative. The attorney said it would take several months, but he would do what was necessary to conclude the matter as quickly as possible. I also let him know that if my recollection was inaccurate and I were the father, then it was what it was, and I would just have another kid and would do for that one no differently than I had for my others. We ordered another round of drinks and changed the subject. We caught up for a while since I had been out of town and busy as of late in any case. He assured me again, and I left with my mind relatively unburdened. There was still the matter of what was going on with Tina. It would come to light I figured, and fortunately, my mind found time to think about the other women in my life.

In fact, I wondered what was going to be next with Yvette after such a great time in the desert and in what direction my relationship with Lynn would take. But for the moment, I needed to stay focused on the business, my health, and my employees. I decided I would stay home tonight and off the phone except for a short call with Yvette. What a day of surprises! But some time at home enjoying a quiet evening would be worthwhile. By the time I arrived home and got settled, it was about eight o'clock. I called Yvette then, and she had been waiting for my call.

"Hello, Yvette," I said.

"Hey, what's up," she asked.

"Nothing much," I replied.

Yvette knew me well enough by now, and she immediately picked up that something was different. "You sound a little depressed. A long day at work?" she asked.

She couldn't have guessed what had suddenly dropped in my lap. If she only knew. I said, "Yes. Very long, unsettling, as well." Then I changed the subject before she continued down that path. "I got the Gloria Lynne CD on. I got a glass of wine in my hand, and I am listening to her song 'I Wish You Love'. You'll have to listen to it one day. It's one of my favorites by her."

"You and your ladies of songs. You should write about them," she said.

"Maybe I will somewhere in tomorrow's land of voices I hear from time to time. You know in many ways they are everything and all things–songs. They will never stop coming as long as people live, work, love, fight, make up, and on and on," I mused. I was loosening up a bit; I found myself back in that space where I expressed a little bit more of myself to her.

"I guess you are right about that. It's a good thing, right?" she said.

"Yes. I believe very much so," I said. "Have you been thinking about the trip?" I added.

"Yes. And sharing with my girlfriends the fun we had," she said. I couldn't see her, obviously, but I could hear the smile on her face as she spoke, and I felt myself smile, too, a welcome feeling after the day I had. "They asked me if I really liked you, and I told them yes. After the times when you and I have been out with them, they think you're good for me. They also said, 'He likes you, girl.'" Actually, more than one has said that, come to think about it," she went on.

"How many do you have?" I asked.

"Five or six close friends," she said, "and a few more." She named them one at a time.

"Hear the questions," I began. "What do you think and what are you going to do about it?" I asked.

"Ride the wave of love to where only lovers go, babe," she replied, silky were her words, a whisper, like a secret, as if at once, she was telling me what she was going to do and what I should do.

"Ride the wave, huh? Well, speaking of waves, you know the more I think about it, the more I realize just how dangerous it was when we almost fell into the damn Pacific Ocean off the pier, and for what? Well, for some amazing pussy, I guess," I laughed as I said it. "Even though we did end up laughing about it. We hype up each other, although it seems so impossible to be able to sustain our energy level," I added.

"We make the impossible real by believing and wanting the best for us. You know if things get stormy, Harold, let's try to work through it. Will you promise me that, that we will work through it, Harold?" asked Yvette, suddenly more serious.

"Sure, Yvette. Will you promise me, too?" I said. Again, I was opening up to her unexpectedly again. There was something about Yvette that I could not put into words, but maybe that was it. Somehow she helped, allowed me, shit, I didn't know, but somehow, she got me to share more of what was inside me, the more of me I, myself, was even unaware that I wanted to share or even needed to share. It always surprised me, but I wasn't mad about it.

"Yes, Harold. I promise you that we will work through it," she spoke, soberly, lovingly, and despite my doubts, I believed her.

"That's always good to hear, and I needed something good to hear to end my day," I said.

"What happened today, babe? You don't have to tell me if you don't want to, but if you do, it will stay just between you and me. That's a promise too, babe, I make to you. You know that, right? You know you can tell me anything because I love you, Harold?" she said.

It seemed she didn't want to pry, but like so many times before, she continued to open herself up to me, and I increasingly felt compelled to match her. So, it was hard not to tell her. "Not now, Yvette, but in the near future, good or bad, I will tell you," I said. Even as I said it, I realized I had said more than I wanted to, if not as much as I needed to.

"Good or bad! What could that be, babe?" Yvette asked.

"It is not a good or bad thing. It's just a thing," I said, trying to put the genie back in the bottle. I wasn't sure how successful I would be, but I had to try. Just wasn't ready to tell all yet.

"Just a thing, huh, babe?" she said. She didn't say another word, but I could hear the "uh, huh!"

"Let's change the subject," I said, adding, "How was work today at the hospital?"

"A couple serious cases, but other than that, pretty normal. Around three o'clock there had been a shooting, and several teenagers were rushed in. One died on the table, and the other two are in critical condition. Their parents were there. It's sad the way these kids are dying, and for what? If they could project ten years ahead, they could see the foolishness in their actions. Parents have to do more, and we all have to do more to help figure out this problem and push humanity forward," Yvette said, expressing her grave concern.

"Yvette, I'm hearing a different person talking about saving humanity. You're right! I believe in that wholeheartedly. We should care every day and in every way. I think when we do, we sleep better, and our tomorrows will be better, too. The noise level in the world is too high and not enough people are listening," I said.

"You're right, babe! I see it daily in the hospital and especially when I work the emergency shift. I must work at not becoming jaded or narrow-minded though, to the problems right outside our doors. In fact, I've been thinking about doing more community service work. There is a need out there." Yvette's voice rose higher and higher the more she talked.

"We all can do more, and we will. Well, I'm tired, Yvette. It was a long day. What's on your schedule tomorrow?" I asked.

"I'm free after work, but I'm going out for drinks with my girlfriends. They want to hear more about the trip," she confessed.

"OK. Enjoy yourself. Hey, I'm going to go," I said.

"OK. Here's a kiss. Get some sleep," Yvette said and blew kisses through the phone.

"Goodnight, sweetheart," I said.

"Goodnight," she said.

# Chapter 22

## TINA WITH A BABY

I hate the phrase "baby momma," so I don't use it.

While working in the office the next day, I was still thinking about Tina, and what had been going on in her life had me concerned. I wanted to reach out to her, but my attorney had counseled me against making the call. He warned this case could get expensive, not including the possibility of a long-term bill being clamped to my wrist. I thought about calling her just this once, but I decided to let my attorney handle it. Even still, I couldn't help thinking it didn't add up. The timeframe didn't work, and I knew me. What did she get herself into after our brief affair? The sister was fine, but unfortunately vulnerable to many guys' bullshit in the streets. Being older, I tried to school her about those kinds of guys and where to go shopping, so to speak. Finding a good guy was like going grocery shopping—shop at Save-A-Lot, get a Save-A-Lot brother. Buy an Oreo-like pack of cookies, but they won't be the quality of real Oreos.

It was after 11:00 and I was listening to WDAS. Patty Jackson was blowing up the airwaves with a driving playlist and conversation. Just then I could hear her saying, "What's a Save-A-Lot brother?" Now if you go shopping at Acme, you'll get an Acme kind of brother. Go shopping at Whole Foods on the other hand, and you'll get the right kind of brother. Patty would also have the sisters and the whole city calling in talking and laughing about, "what kind of brother you got." It would be all-in jest, for certain.

I'm guessing Tina found a Save-A-Lot brother, and she found herself in a difficult situation dealing with the consequences of such a choice. Not a nice place to be in as a single woman I would assume, but time would tell the story. I decided to have my attorney put a private investigator on it. I wanted a detailed history, pictures, the works, so we were ready to defend our case or to become a new dad to a three-year-old. While I liked kids, I didn't want to pay for another man's child unless I agreed to do it. One interesting aspect was that the child was a little girl, which was nice, since I only had boys.

Tina was soft and fine. She was not too heavy on the back end and had well-defined breasts. She was happy being with me, but her maturity level was another question. I enjoyed her, but it was something I didn't want to deal with at the time. I had big fun loving and sexing this 32-year-old Italian-Irish babe with brunette hair and light brown eyes that were pretty to gaze into. She might have been a great fit if, at the time, she had been older and if she hadn't wanted a baby. My phone ringing disturbed my thoughts. It was John Worth.

"Yo, brother, we got a problem," John said.

"What do you mean? What kind of problem?"

"The young girl, Tina DiFilipo," he said.

"Yes. What's up?"

"She just killed herself or she was murdered," he said.

"What!?" I exclaimed.

"Check the news. It's on all the channels. It's looking like her male friend might be the likely suspect," John explained.

"Man! What a crazy twenty-four hours," I said. Yesterday, I had received court papers claiming I was the father of a three-year-old, and today, that girl's mother was dead.

"No less," replied John.

"Tina was trying to reach out to me. I felt it, but why hadn't she just called me or come by the office, John? I mean she knew me, we left on good terms, and we wanted the best for each other. Seems so unnecessary what has happened," I bemoaned. "What do you know or what's being reported by the police about the killing and the man she was involved with? How long were they together?" I asked John.

He didn't want to get ahead of what was being reported, and just said, "Let's wait and let me get my guys on this ASAP."

"What do you want me to do and what does this mean for the domestic case and papers I was served?" I asked John, seeking to understand how this might affect the court case.

"Well, it sure complicates things. Do you know anything about her parents? Is there anyone who will take the child other than the system?" he asked me.

"I'm not one hundred percent sure. I met her grandmother once. Her parent scene wasn't the best. No father to speak of in her life and a mother too busy in the street. I recall her telling me her mother had a drug problem," I said.

"Man, Harold, you picked one this time to say hello to," he said.

"I guess you're right, but her problem was apparently stacked against her long before we met up," I replied.

"You're right, but you're now implicated from the root," John explained.

"It appears so, my friend. Does this make my problem worse than it already was?" I asked.

"It may. We gotta get the blood testing, you know, DNA, done ASAP. Was the grandmother you met a responsible person?" Worth asked.

"Not really. I don't think so, but I'm sure at her age she doesn't want a baby to raise," I thought out loud.

"Better her than you," John said.

"Maybe," I said casually.

"Don't go there on me, Harold. You need to look at the long run here, the future, and a three-year-old girl in that picture with no mother," John cautioned.

"Yeah, you're right. Please do whatever is required to find out the truth about the killing and who the real father is," I said, trying to take John's advice. "I'm sure it's not me," I added.

"I believe you, Harold, but the courts will want more than that to let you off the hook," he said.

"By the way, what will this cost me?" I asked.

"Upwards of twenty thousand dollars. That is expensive for a brief period of fun in the streets," he responded.

"That's why I spend my time with older women these days," I said in my defense.

"I know. You can send me five thousand to start," he said, referring to the retainer.

"OK, my friend, this is not good, and I don't need this headache currently in my life. I have two wonderful ladies that I'm digging and would like to spend my time thinking and being with them," I explained.

"I get it, but this is now on your plate," John stated flatly.

Oh, Tina, what have you tossed on my plate, and why me, dear? Again, time will tell. I then said to John, "Please, I need you to drill down on this and find the answers ASAP."

"No problem. Send me out a check tomorrow," he said.

"I will, John," I said, adding, "OK, gotta go. Lynn's calling me." I hung up the phone and immediately picked up Lynn's call.

"Hey, what's up, Lynn," I said.

"Nothing, just calling you. Here at my desk planning to work late," she said.

"Ready for round two?" I asked.

"Sure, but I need to work. You knocked me out messing with you the other night, Harold," she said.

"You left the door cracked and gave an open invitation to you," I said.

"Yes, I did, and it was RSVP'd personally," she said.

"Nice reply, Lynn," I said.

"You're funny, Harold," she said. "No, really, though, just having fun with you, and having you in my life right now is great," she added.

"I hope it's more than fun," I replied.

"Hey, what's up, Harold? You don't sound great. What's wrong?" Lynn asked.

"Nothing," I said.

"Hey, did you hear about the young woman who was killed in her apartment? They say it was by a boyfriend."

"Yes, I heard," I said.

"That's so sad. They say she has a little girl. What will happen to her?" Lynn thought out loud.

"Time will tell. Let's change the subject, though, Lynn. What are you working on?" I said.

"It's a commercial company, a financial restructuring they dropped in my lap. Major work and head of the class stuff, if I handle it right," she said.

"You will. I have all the confidence in the world in you," I said.

"Thanks, dear. But again, you sound depressed. What's the matter? You can tell me," she said.

"I don't want to talk about it at the moment. I'll share it with you in the near future. Give me some time. I need some time and space to deal with what has just been tossed on my plate, so to speak," I said.

"If anyone can handle it and come up smelling like roses, you're the one. Just be fair as you always are in your deals and things will work out fine for you. Trust me it will," she assured me.

"OK, Lynn. I hope so," I said. I really appreciated her encouragement. "I'm headed home after I leave the office, and I still have a few calls to make before getting home. I want to call it an early night though and get a good night's sleep in. Let's talk tomorrow. Can we do that?" I asked.

"OK, I have about three hours of work before I head home to a nice hot bath and my bed, which reminds me, Harold, you complete me with your sexy ways of making love," she said.

"Play some old songs for me. It'll help me sleep better with both our music players turned up like we were," I said.

"You got me smiling. I'll play some old and new music for you as soon as I unlock my door. I'll head to turn on the music, then to draw me a bath and finally to bed for a good night's sleep, as well," Lynn said.

"OK, Lynn, call me tomorrow," I said.

"I will. Good night," she said.

With the morning sun came an early call from my attorney. "John, what's the call for so early?" I asked.

"The police will be coming by to talk to you," he said.

"About what?" I asked.

"Somehow, they got tracks on you from Domestic and want to investigate your relationship with Tina DiFilipo," he informed me.

"What kind of questions will they ask and what do I tell them?" I asked.

"Don't say anything, and tell them you have legal counsel. I'm trying to arrange for you to come in now with me and to be interviewed in my presence. If they get to your house before I get there, call me and put me on the phone. Please don't provide them with any information," he urged.

"I don't have any information. I haven't seen the woman in over three years," I said.

"I know, but I need to be there when they ask you questions. This is a homicide," he said.

"I know, I get it. Why me? I'm still asking myself that question. Tina, Tina, what has been going on in your life? You had it

165

all—beauty, body, brains, confidence, and a degree. John, have you found out anything to update me?" I asked.

"Yes. She was murdered about four or five in the morning two days ago in her apartment in the Northern Liberties section of the city. Her body was found by a tenant on the same floor. Her door was left open. As I understand it, the tenant knocked on her door, and hearing no one, pushed open the door and found her body lying on the floor, apparently beaten with some kind of blunt instrument, and struck in the head several times. I'm trying to get the police report now. Who and why would do this to her? Do you have an alibi as to where you were at the time of the incident?" John asked me.

"It was around that time I was in bed, at a friend's house or in Vegas. Let me take a minute and think about this. I got into work around my regular time, nine o'clock in the morning, and the employees were already here at work. If I recall the exact date and time of her death, I'm thinking, I was with Lynn Underwood and prior to that I was just getting back from Vegas with Yvette Marshall," I explained.

"Well, you were busy, and we don't need these two women finding out or for their paths to cross," John said, knowing me well enough.

"John, you're right, so please do what you do to minimize my problems, which seem to be mounting by the day," I pleaded, adding, "My career and my business are at stake here, John."

"I know, my friend, and I'll make sure you're kept in the background. Besides, you haven't seen or talked to her in over three years. Right?" he wanted to confirm.

"Oh, look, here, John," I said. Right at that moment as I was looking through my mail that had piled up for a week, there was a letter from Tina. "John!" I exclaimed.

"What!" he said eagerly.

"I have a letter here, in my hand, from Tina DiFilipo," I said. I couldn't believe it.

"Don't open it. I'm about fifteen minutes from you. Put it up and out of the way and don't open it. Do you understand!" he stressed.

"Sure," I said, thinking this was not the time to ignore my lawyer's advice.

I placed the letter on the fireplace mantel, and as I did, my heart was beating in triple-time. My head was pounding worse than a migraine headache, and my body became warm and then heated up to a temperature that brought forth a complete body sweat. I heard cars then pulling into the driveway.

As this surreal scene was forming outside my house, I reflected quickly on my life. It had been a good life, even great, living here in the suburbs in a nice house that I built when I had very little and was married with two kids. Together, we had worked hard to afford them the best education possible. But here now, the picture of their smiling faces, faces of their happy childhoods, was juxtaposed to the thought of a three-year-old little girl who was now without a mother. Was this good life I had coming to an end with the opening of this envelope, propped against a picture of my two happy children?

The doorbell rang. I answered it. It was a detective and several police officers who were accompanying him. "Come in, please. My attorney told me to expect you," I said to them. I glanced outside and I noticed John Worth had just pulled up, but he still had to pass six or seven cars to get to my door.

He called out to me, "Harold, keep the door open and let's talk briefly before I say anything to the detective." I replied, "I'll wait right here at the door." I slowly turned and asked the detective if he would give me a minute with my attorney who had just arrived. He nodded as he moved—not gingerly—in the direction of the fireplace. I called out, "Detective, can you and your men stop moving about until the attorney speaks with me?"

"No problem. You have something to hide?"

I didn't even dignify that question with an answer, but said, looking at my lawyer, "John Worth, glad you're here."

"Let's talk. The letter. Where is it and did you open it?" John asked intently.

"No. I didn't open it," I said, adding, "although, I really did want to open the letter, as some mental discrepancies swirled about me."

"Whatever your thoughts, get me the letter, but first hear me out. Let me do the talking. Keep quiet no matter what I say or what you hear, even if you want to say something. Are we clear?" John said, eyeballing me as if I were a schoolboy who needed to mind the adults when they were talking. I knew he meant no harm or disrespect. He was just trying to keep me protected, and that's what I paid him for. I was grateful to be able to afford such a great lawyer.

"Yes, very clear," I said. I asked in jest however, "Is this a scene from *A Few Good Men*?"

"No time for levity, my friend," John retorted. "This is a serious matter."

"All right. Go ahead. What's next?" I asked.

John was going to tell the detective that I was just returning from vacation. He stopped, thought for a second, and then decided not to let the authorities know about the letter, though, at this time.

To this, I said, "OK, fortunately, I had redirected the detective from heading toward the fireplace."

"Where is it? Give it to me, but not now, later," said John. "I will take it with me when I leave. This is important evidence. Whatever is written inside can be explosive. Now let's go and find out why the detectives are here," John further instructed.

"You know why," I said.

"Don't assume anything and remember what I said about letting me do the talking," he repeated.

"Let's go in now. I got it from here."

"Hello, officer, my name is Attorney John Worth."

"I have heard of you. I'm Detective Roberts," the detective said.

"I know your chief. He's an old friend," John said, trying to establish some rapport as well as to let the detective know we weren't some kind of okey dokes, I gathered.

Detective Roberts said, "That's good to know," even if his expression conveyed that he didn't give a rat's ass who we knew.

"Please tell me why you're here," John said, getting down to business.

The detective said, "As you know, your client Mr. Harold Longston is involved in a domestic case with the deceased, Tina DiFilipo."

"OK. That's just a domestic case of which he was informed by papers that were mailed to him," John said. "So, why are you here?" he asked.

"We want to talk to him regarding the murder of Tina DiFilipo since there is a relationship between them," the detective said, clearly trying to rile me up.

"No, detective. Not any longer, and they have not seen each other for years.

Undeterred, the detective, said, "Well, I need to verify that and more."

"He's more than willing to cooperate with the authorities, but my client has legal representation now," John informed him. "If you want to talk with him, let's set a time at the District and go from there," he said to the detective.

"OK. I'll order my officers to leave now. Let's exchange numbers. You can call me to set a time and date within the next couple days to bring your client in for questioning," the detective said, and left shortly after his officers were ordered to leave.

John and I moved to the kitchen. He sat at the island bar, and I made coffee for the two of us after finally handing him the letter. After inspecting the envelope, he opened it,

"Harold, this is serious. It was postmarked six days ago. Does this look like her handwriting?" John asked.

"As closely as I can remember," I said.

John opened the business envelope. There were two separately folded sets of papers, a handwritten letter and a formal document. John started to read the handwritten letter aloud.

*Dear Harold, I hope all is well with you. Since leaving you, which I should have never done, I have been in and out of a couple relationships. I guess looking for someone like you. It has been hard. I fell in love with you, even though our time was brief. I should have listened. You taught me so much about myself and the world. I was so single-minded about what I wanted, and I took your love for just someone helping me, not realizing that you really cared. I wouldn't allow myself at that time to see us in any different kind of way, although I should have. You were good for me, and in time, even if we ended up only having a friendship, we would have been the best of friends.*

*My life is a mess. Shortly after you left, I got pregnant. You knew I wanted a child more than anything. I believe that's the real reason you left. I needed you and you left me. I would have listened to you and done anything and everything you would have wanted me to do. Why did you leave me? I have longed for you, your caress, the lovemaking. You just made me a more complete woman, and I've not been right with any man, since. When I'm with them, I find myself talking about you and us to their displeasure. That has not helped my relationships with them. You're indelibly etched into my brain, Harold. You touched every part of me. I needed you and wanted you, but you never came or called. I turned to other men, who seemingly had your qualities. They all fell flat, even though I was with them and at times we enjoyed each other. Then something would snap in me knowing he could do only for the moment. He wasn't you or what I wanted, nor did I need that type of man anymore. Before you, I thought they were the men for me. I thought it was good enough to have access to them and spending time with them was good enough. Access isn't what it's about, though. It's about love. I know that now—a selflessness kind of love, not that 'me' kind or 'me first' kind of love. I know that now, and if I had time in life, perhaps I would find it again.*

*Now I have a three-year-old daughter named Lynette, and she's such a beautiful little girl. She's a blessing, but I'm caught in an abusive web with a man who won't leave me alone. I've asked him to stop calling me and to stay away. I have called the police many times to get a restraining order on him, but somehow there always seemed to be a technicality that prevented me from getting one. I'm really fearing for my life. I can't sleep, I can't eat, and I'm so very tired. Also, I don't know how, but he found the pictures of us. All of them. He became so angry. I'm sorry to tell you he has promised to kill the two of us.*

*Harold, this man is crazy. I'm afraid for me and my daughter, and I'm afraid for you, as well. Right now, I need to make things right and warn you about him. His name is Taye Wells. Please don't take this lightly. So that you know and get what I am saying, he's a Save-A-Lot dude cloaked in a Whole Foods persona, and he's good. You know, he fooled me, and I would have thought that having grown up in a rough neighborhood, having gotten a college education, and with having all of your watchful insights about men, I would have seen him for what he is, but he still fooled me. Watch out for him. He hangs* out like you in similar places, but he literally hates you and the life you have. As you taught me – "We don't have any control of where we start out, but we have everything to do with where we want to end up." You were good for me, but I made some bad calls. So, like I said, this last dude has hatred leaking from his innermost core. He's dangerous! I'm repeating myself to make sure you get what I'm telling you, dear. If a younger woman can love an older man, then I am guilty of loving you completely. Taye hated that I couldn't get you out of my life, out of my brain. My thoughts of you many times made me velvety wet standing alone or self-caressing my body laying down. You were in me, and I was more than feeling all of you.

Finally, I did one of the worst things, I think, any woman could do, which is to falsely accuse a man of being the father of a child that is not his. Out of fear and concern for my life and the future of my daughter, I went to the court and filed papers claiming you were the father. I knew you would take care of her. Like I said, I've made some bad decisions, but for this one, I am extremely sorry. You're a good man. You like your women. I get that now, which I was a little jealous of, but I'll take jealousy over what I ended up with. Men who I met thought that I shouldn't want to be alone. They thought I needed to have a man just because, even if I didn't love him. But having known love, having been in love with you, it could never be enough for me to be with a man just to have one, not even because it made paying the bills easier. I would have been better off waiting and listening to you when you talked about where to go shopping for a man. I think if I had ended up somewhere between a Save-A-Lot and an Acme kind of brother, that would have been okay before being with you. But after you, it *wasn't enough. I hope you're smiling, Harold, because I mean everything I've said.*

*Harold, it may be too late to undo what I put in motion. This is exactly why I'm writing this letter to you. Please forgive me. You are not the father, and Taye Wells is not the father. If I'm still alive, I will make things right. I don't think I'm going to live much longer. This guy is beyond crazy. Please watch yourself because he may come for you next. He's about six feet tall, light skin, an almost yellow-looking man with dark brown hair. He carries himself much like you. He has a narcissistic personality and is dangerously possessive, which I found out much too late. He told me once, "If I can't have you, the Lord will have you." As you can see, I'm trapped. I hope this letter will clear up the mess I've created for you.*

*Harold, I do have two final requests of you. Can you please forgive me, if only in some small way, and would you please watch out for my daughter? I would have loved to have had your child, Harold. We would have had more than one, I'm sure. You know, I only have my grandmother to watch her, and she's not in good health. Please don't let my daughter become a ward of the state. Please know that I'm truly sorry for everything.*

*I love you. Always and forever.*

*Tina*

By the time John had finished reading the letter, I stood with my head bowed and my fingers seemingly netted together as if I were praying for Tina and her daughter. I felt terrible after hearing that letter, and as I slowly looked up at John, I said, "If I only knew."

Attending to the sobering legal matter he was keen to oversee, John brought me back to reality. "If this means what I think it means, then you'll be free of this problem and any responsibility for the child and her care. But I know you, Harold, and I know, even if so, your thoughts of her and the child will not so easily fade away."

"Yes, it does seem to mean that, and you are right, old friend. Will I ever be free of the thoughts and how to care for Lynette?" I mused unsure of what lay ahead.

# Chapter 23

## SOUTH PHILLY

John didn't need to stick around, and I thought since the matter was all but concluded, that he would start making his way toward the door. Instead, he said, "So, you never told me how you met Tina." I never knew why John uttered those words. Maybe he saw how the matter weighed on me, particularly why she didn't just call. Or maybe he just saw a brother who needed to talk it out a bit. Either way, I took the bait, and I began to tell him our story.

"South Philly. Yeah, that's where she's from. As you probably already know, John, there's a stew of ethnic groups each fighting one another for territory and identity there. Tina was in that mix, but she was a pretty brunette with a lot of swag. At about five-feet, five-inches with a fine body from which hung a pair of 36DD-cup breasts, she was a bit of an eye-turner. For some reason, we hit it off from our first smiles. I acknowledged her with a smile, and she smiled and said hello. From there our conversation flowed freely. It seemed unusual, but when the arc of the universe places two people together, there's nothing unusual about it at all. It was our time.

"And let me tell you about some of the craziest things we shared and did that year we were together. I've been kissing and hugging White girls since the first grade from the coat closet to under the trees on the playground at recess. From there it continued through high school and college, off and on, but when I met Tina, it seemed like it was going to be something special, and it was. She was younger and full of everything I still wanted, at least at the beginning of our relationship, anyway. From our second meeting we got close quickly and that was at the Melrose Diner, located in the fifteen hundred block of Snyder Avenue."

John replied, "Yeah, I know where it is."

"After several days and evenings of spending hours on the phone talking about everything, we met for drinks at Del Frisco's in Center City. We met up at the bar on the upper level where we embraced and kissed long for the first time with the bar crowd watching. She knew what she was doing. Tina was an exhibitionist, and I was fine with it, but it was also more than that. The babe dug me, and I was liking her vibe. She was wearing some kind of skintight dress that held all of her firmly, accentuating her breasts and ass, which called me to attention."

"Harold, you're crazy," John spoke up, laughing.

"Brother! Tina was the real deal and would give the sistas a run for their money at any man, if he was the prize. However, Tina's problem was that she was an uncultured young woman, of whom there were a lot like her in South Philly, but I didn't care. I had her back, so I would teach her things about life and the world. Basically, I refined many of her weaknesses into her strengths. Anyway, from the bar, I called for a table seating for two where we dined and enjoyed being together. Here was the crazy part, John. Tina had awful dining etiquette, but while at the table, she took off her right shoe and found my crotch and started playing 'toe tunes' like hitting keys on a piano. I thought *I* only did that kind of stuff to women in a restaurant. She also sang an Alicia Keys song and then belted out an R. Thicke song, "The Sweetest Love," and the restaurant crowd watched and listened. They were mesmerized. I'm telling you the girl had some chops. I was so totally impressed with that soulful sound rolling out from her diaphragm that I completely forgot about how she held her knife and fork. In defense of South Philly, Kensington's social and cultural awareness was the worst, truly PWT. After dinner, she insisted we go clubbing and then to her place, which we did.

"John, we got to her apartment about one a.m. She turned her Echo on as I wanted to hear 'Versace on the Floor' by Bruno Mars, followed by Avant and Keke singing 'You & I.' I made love to that woman all night long, and believe me when I tell you that this thirty-two or thirty-three-years-young, and perhaps a femme fatale, with her firm and statuesque pink titties and a body that housed a uniquely shaped chalice, was oozing cream juice like a fountain, releasing orgasmic rhythms of love. I might have made a baby that night because we romanced each other and loved like two possessed individuals finding that place where only lovers go, yes, and well into the morning when the rising sun called us to take a break. From that moment it was on, and so this kind of fun, lovemaking, and learning continued for over a year until I had to stop it. Since I didn't want any more kids and she did, I felt that I needed to end it. She was still very young and so she would be good for someone, someone who wanted kids and to start a family."

John always chose his words well; maybe it was an occupational hazard from being an attorney. After listening to all that I had shared, John said, "Harold, I now understand this letter and your relationship quite a bit better. Tina was a young woman who fell deeply in love with an older man. You sure this baby is not yours?"

He hadn't asked the question I was about to answer, but his inquisitiveness prompted me to say, "John, there's more I need to share with you."

## Chapter 24

# TINA AND ME

"John, I haven't thought about Tina much before this but as I have said, it really was a blissful romance, and it was totally hot too. Tina and I kicked it off like spending new crisp money and somehow, we were joined at the hip from the get-go. After the first night we spent together we seemed inseparable. Her hours of the day were my hours of the day so much so that I wasn't even going to the office and she wasn't going to work. In fact, she almost lost her job as a nurse. She was an LPN who worked at one of the city's rehab centers. We were just totally caught up in each other. She was young and hot, and I was mellow and searching. It was a crazy time, John. I mean, wow, I was giving her so much dick that I was flooding that pink pussy with sperm on such a regular basis that we had no time for anyone else, let alone anything else. We had ourselves, and at the time it seemed to be enough. But, she became worried about losing her job, so I told her not to worry and that we both needed to be more mindful of our jobs and responsibilities. In time, we adjusted. I started working more, and so did she, but then I began to stress to her that she needed to finish up her college degree. Sounds like from the letter that she did. We lived, ate, drank, laughed, played, and screwed our way into love and maybe out of a relationship, although, we never lost our love for each other. In fact, hearing the letter reminded me how much I still loved her. That she's no more, though, I wonder if I should have stayed with her. I will miss her."

John was listening intently, even if he was hearing more than he really needed for my defense, but with the decisions looming about Yvette and Lynn, not to mention, Diane, in the back of my mind, I wasn't really talking to him so much as I was talking to myself. I had to work out what I was going to do about them, and having just lost someone whom I loved, I was reminded of having experienced such a loss once before.

"It happened once before, John. I regretted not furthering a relationship earlier in my life with Bertha, a Southern beauty with a Southern name. Back then, I was running too fast in the street and so bypassed a love affair with a woman who truly loved me, and the truth was, I loved her. By the time I slowed down and understood that, it was too late and she had moved on. The game and the shit I was into, though, and I was playing back then, would have taken her down with me anyway. My point is that I couldn't go back or change things, nor could I just stop loving her or wishing I could get the time back. Now, I may have done it again because in a way Tina was Bertha. Yes, they were different, and the times were different, but I still loved Tina as much as I had loved Bertha many years ago."

John had gotten the picture by now, but in the flash of time that passed while John and I stood there and he took in what I had said, I could not resist the flood of images, memories, and emotions of all the time Tina and I had enjoyed together.

The last time I saw her, she had called me and said come pick me up and let's go down to Kelly Drive and walk along Boathouse Row. Tina loved screwing anywhere outside and especially in weird places as much as I did. She and I broke a hotel bed one evening having some delirious sex. That was the thing about us—we were the truth, much like what writers imagine.

I asked her, "Why?" She said, "Just come get me."

"OK!" I told her, and within the hour, she was in the car, and we were on our way down to Boathouse Row. When she got in the car with just a sundress on and nothing else underneath, I became immediately aroused. She had that effect on me, and she knew it. With that look on her face which I could not resist, she pulled up her sundress, spread her legs, and showed me her clit; her three forefingers of each hand slowly pulled it open as if to meet the afternoon daylight. I remembered how often I used to say, "All pussy is pink," and looking at her glowing smile, I said aloud to her, "Yours is definitely pink." She had laughed and said, trying to imitate my voice, "All pussy is pink," and I laughed, too. She knew my line and had me smiling before she reached over and grabbed me for all the world to see, though I was still driving and behind the wheel of my convertible. Her damn exhibitionist tendencies only encouraged my bad-boy habits, but I didn't care one bit. Also, during our time together I was never able, it seemed, to communicate with Ms. Angel Eyes, something I always wondered about.

"Pull over," Tina said to me that afternoon. I did not hesitate, for by now, she and I had damn near made love everywhere in this City of Brotherly Love. In a parked car on Hunting Park Avenue. Leaving Lou & Choo's very drunk. In Center City on the balcony of XIX Restaurant overlooking the city. At the top of Liberty One on New Year's Eve. In several restaurants in Rittenhouse Square with her sitting on my lap at a corner table while people watched us. All throughout Old City, South Philly, and West Philly. And in the surrounding counties and in wineries in Delaware, Chester, Bucks, and more. But on this day, she had one more spot where she wanted to get sexed by me, and it was at the top of the walk near the Art Museum, opposite the side of the building from where the Rocky statue stood. We took the winding walk to the top, stopping twice for me to push up into her wet cavity, while sitting on benches that lined the walkway to the top. Finally, at the top, we were at it again while people watched us. She told me often it was her fantasy to have people watch her while being fucked in public by someone like me. In fact, she wrote down and shared all of her fantasies with me in a short story. I often told her that if she ever wrote a book, to be sure to share some of the coin with me. She would never have that opportunity now.

I recalled when we were leaving the beach one afternoon, that Tina, who had been playing with herself as she liked to do, said to pull over into a strip mall she noticed coming up ahead just off of the Atlantic City Expressway, because she had gotten hot and bothered. And there we were, at it again. She had always enjoyed the beach, as much in fact as Yvette did, it occurred to me. We rocked the car at the far end of the parking lot until she complained that it was too private an area. She resumed her position again with her legs open wide and propped on the dashboard of the car after she made me pull the car closer to the storefronts and other cars that were all around. Those kinds of lovemaking sessions were quickies, but not too quick. We made love for hours in cars, it seemed, and often because she loved car sex and so did I with her, really.

As often as not, Tina would say to me, "You made this pussy yours. You know that, don't you?" And to that, I always replied, "That's your pussy and this is my dick; we just figured out how to make them work together. Why do women keep wanting to give ownership of their pussy to someone like me?" Usually, she laughed it off, but one time, she replied, "You just don't get it. It's rare for a woman to get fucked like you fuck me. I gotta say it that way. And it's not just the lovemaking. You got something different happening with your shit. So, yeah, a woman will say, 'You can get some of this pussy when you want it.' You see, baby, I'm all booed up with the shit you doing to me and probably other women, too. It's all in the song, 'Something About You' by Michon Young. You got her downloaded somewhere on your phone, I know you do, and let Chrisette

Michele blow a few 'A Couple of Forevers.' You can get some anytime," she said, concluding the conversation that evening.

During those times, I continued not to hear from Ms. Angel Eyes and her jazzy-self singing and talking to me, which I missed but I understood why, for I was deeply ensconced in my bad-boy habits during our time together.

On another occasion, one winter evening, I told Tina to meet me at the Hilton Hotel on City Line Avenue for drinks. She agreed and arrived in about 45 minutes wearing a mink coat she got from some hustler in South Philly, and she was looking fabulous. We had drinks and just a lot of fun being together. For the fun of it, I whispered in Tina's ear, "Follow me." I reached for her hand, and we started walking down the corridor looking into conference rooms and banquet halls that we could slip into and make love. One smaller banquet room had a black baby grand piano in the corner. I said, "You be the singer, and I'll be the piano player." She smiled with a devilish look and said, "OK." I lifted her onto the piano in her fur coat, and she added, "Fuck me right here on top of this piano." I said, "Sure. That was my idea all along to do exactly that in this hotel somewhere, and here is perfect. You know they got cameras in here," I informed her.

"Great, then love me and let's make a movie together," she said. Then she screamed quietly with excitement, which she did when she wanted to give herself to me. After I dimmed the lights, we made love like in the movies and periodically took short breaks between finding promises of love and of completeness in Loveland; I even played the piano while she sang to me about us. It was truly amazing no one walked in on us that evening as I think we were there long enough to have footage for two movies. We were so bad in one way, but good for one another also. We really were so completely into each other, or so I thought. After a year of being together, Tina started talking about having a baby in a very serious way, which made me check myself and how I was nailing that reservoir of sexual pleasure of hers. She was really in love with me and had grown in her understanding of many things, and I loved that about her, but her clock was ticking, and I didn't want to be the one. I should have seen it coming, but I was so into the time we were spending together, and I already had children. It just was not top of mind for me. Consequently, I started moving away from her as she continued asking why and why not. She told me, "I love you and I know you care for me. No one can love or want you more than I want and need you, Harold. I'll raise the baby, and you can do whatever you want and see whomever you want. I just want to be the mother of your child."

It wasn't until she came to me and told me she was pregnant that I knew things had to change. It shook me and brought me back down to earth. What was I doing, I thought. Eventually, she admitted to me she wasn't pregnant because she was on the pill. She said she just wanted to see my reaction. Her actions were over the top, and within several months, we separated. We talked, though, for several months afterward, but finally the calls stopped coming. She knew it was over between the two of us because she was hellbent on having a child.

In hindsight, should Tina's desire to have a child with me have been such a big deal, such a deal breaker? I didn't know, but her sudden loss made me question it, and the fact that I was questioning it left me spinning on a hamster wheel of uncertainty. I knew I didn't want any more children. I knew I had my company to develop, and I already had kids. Then again, at the time, I had found someone I really loved and who completely loved me; that was a rare thing. We were absolutely great together. I got her, and she got me. I accepted her, and she accepted me. In so many inexplicable ways, we completed each other. The longer we were together, the more she matured, and I could see how she would be a fierce partner and loving mother. How could I convey all that, all of this, to John? Not sure I could, but either way, her death, I realized now, was something that would haunt me forever.

Like Tina's life that had been taken in a flash, so had my recollection of us. John must have noticed a momentary vacant stare upon my face, oblivious to the life I had just relived because he remarked, "Not sure where you went, partner, but let's talk next steps if you're cool with that."

"Yeah, I'm cool, counselor. What's our next step?"

"Well, Harold, this Taye Wells character looks like he might be the one who murdered Tina DeFilipo. I need to call the chief right away and go by the District. I'll discuss this letter with him first. In the meantime, though, we got to get you some protection, and I mean immediately. If he murdered Tina, and if her letter is any indication of what this guy is capable of, you may be a target," John said.

"John, I can handle myself," I insisted.

"I know you can, but this is on a whole different level, my brother. Let's not take this lightly," he urged. "The dude may be crazy like the woman said. She has forewarned you with the letter and pleaded that you pay attention to everything she was giving you, to all this upfront knowledge of him. We need to find him, stop this guy before he gets to you or your loved ones. He's a nutcase. Since returning, have you noticed anything different or anyone following you or casing your home?" John continued. He was in full court press mode now, trying as respectfully as possible, to not cross the line of how much to push me to not underestimate this guy.

"No. I really haven't paid any attention," I said, adding, "You know how I live a carefree life."

"Well, I hope you won't have to pay the piper, my friend, anytime soon," he said.

"Let me continue to handle this, but I think we can both breathe a sigh of relief. On the domestic side," I said, exhausted from hearing the letter and trying to make sense of all of the thoughts that had run through my head.

"Hey, how long were you two together?" John asked.

"Not very long," I said, somberly.

"Well, you completed her. What're your thoughts about her asking you to watch out for little Lynette? You know it means financially and maybe a little more," John said.

"I'm not sure about what I'm going to do with Lynnette, so make sure we get a meeting with the judge in his chambers," I answered candidly. "I'll have to think long and hard on this matter. You just can't play around without consequences," I said, my voice trailing off.

"I got afternoon appointments and it is now close to noon," said John.

"Thanks, John. You're here saving me again, brother, and I truly appreciate it," I said.

"I'll send you a bill, my friend," he quipped, flashing a big smile.

The second document was from a law firm that John's office had done business with in the past.

"Harold, this document appears to give you custody of her daughter if you want her," John said, holding up the document for me to read.

"But I'm not the father," I said, curious about his comment.

"Yes, I understand. Look, I need to go see the chief and then into the office myself. Let me deal with this matter later. It's not as important now, as the dude possibly has you in his gun sight," John said. He was continuing his press undeterred.

"OK!" I said, and John left the house with a mission to keep me safe.

The morning had been overwhelming, so I decided to take the rest of the day off. Once I called my secretary to move all my afternoon appointments to tomorrow, I would call Yvette or Lynn. They're both one, it seemed, at times. I would meet one of them for an early dinner. I needed someone to talk to. Passion wasn't on the afternoon agenda, but sharing time with someone as I processed all that was happening was very much so on my agenda.

## Chapter 25

# DO I REALLY WANT TO TALK

I pulled out my cellphone to call someone without a thought of whom to dial. As I did, Yvette's number was illuminated on my screen. She was calling. I guess she was the one to have lunch with.

"Hello, Harold," Yvette said.

"Hey, Yvette what's up?" I asked.

"I'm calling to check on you. You didn't sound too good yesterday, and I been worried all night about you," she said.

"I'm fine, the morning has been like a long scene in a movie, with me in the leading role," I said.

"What do you mean? Are you busy? I'm calling to take you out to lunch or something if you want to talk," she offered.

"Yes, let's do a late lunch at FARMiCiA," I said. It was an Old City favorite of ours.

"Great, Harold. What time? I'll leave work an hour before and meet you there," she said.

"OK. Is two-thirty or three-thirty better?" I asked.

"Three-thirty works better for me," she replied.

"Yvette, see you at three-thirty. I may arrive a little early. I'll be at the bar with my heart and feelings mellowing in a glass of Malbec," I said, a little dramatic, but then again, I had quite a dramatic morning.

"Wow, you don't drink wine often, so I guess something, or someone has you worried," she observed.

I decided to rest for two hours before heading to the restaurant. I set my alarm and rested my eyes. When the alarm went off at 2:15 p.m., I cleaned up and headed to my car to meet Yvette. I looked around my surroundings for anything that might be out of the normal. Noticing nothing, I hopped in the Porsche, dropped the top, and drove off to meet Yvette. I arrived thirty minutes early as traffic was light. I parked the car, fed the meter, went directly to the bar, and immediately ordered my first glass of Malbec.

Sitting there, I reflected on life, my life, and the women who had come and gone. None was as final and tragic as Tina's life. I always thought that I was just a phone call away to past loves and friendships. Why didn't Tina want to reach out to me? It didn't quite add up. She liked being with me, sharing laughs, and answering her list of questions about many different things. We did that for hours at a time. I would often say, "Choose the face that fits you and wear it or change the makeup for a better looking and feeling of you." She would always smile, calling those kinds of lines corny. "But they sound so profound. I'll get it one day, Harold," she would say.

Did she ever get it? I will never know. Draining the first glass of Malbec, I called for another while I waited, still washing down my sorrows. Did I cause her death? Will I ever know? Was I good for her, as she wrote in the letter? I'll have to get that original back from John and keep it.

"Harold," Yvette called, walking toward me. She, too, was something to look at and in high heels even more so. I stood up to greet and embrace her. She smelled so lovely wearing the perfume I bought her. For some reason, she now claimed it was her favorite. I must admit I enjoyed her wearing it. She probably sprayed it on before coming in the restaurant to lift my spirits with her smile and the smell of marry me.

"Hey sweetheart! You feeling better?" she asked.

"Oh, I don't know. Glad that you're here to share a moment and a meal over a drink with me though," I confessed.

"My pleasure. I was concerned. This is perhaps the first time I've seen you with such a melancholy disposition. You're normally so upbeat and cheerful. What's got you so upset?" she said.

Whatever she did or how she did it, Yvette had made it comfortable to share things with her that I would not normally, and this was no different. "It's, well, it's pretty deep, painful, and very personal to talk about," I said.

"I'm here to listen, if you want to share," she said, as she had so many times before.

So, I began. "Well, I better tell you now before you hear it on the news."

"The news? It must be pretty serious if it made the news," Yvette said, concerned.

"Did you hear the other day in the news about a woman who was murdered in her apartment?" I asked. I was peering into her eyes now.

"Yes. What about it?" she asked.

"The woman was an ex-girlfriend. We were together for about a year, a few years ago," I said.

"How short?" Yvette asked. She wanted to be clear on the time period.

"About a year," I said again.

"Oh, I would call that a short relationship. Our relationship has been longer so far," she said, as she smiled.

"Yes, it has, and I hope it'll be much longer," I said, and I really meant it.

"I now understand the melancholy. I'm sure you had nothing to do with the murder, right?" Yvette asked as if for the truth and some greater clarity.

"No, nothing, but the police wanted to question me. They came by the house this morning, but my attorney intervened and scheduled an interview for later in the week. More importantly a three-year-old little girl is left without her mother," I explained.

"Are you the father?" Yvette asked in a soft voice, her hand touching mine as she spoke.

"No. However, yesterday morning in the office, I was served with papers stating that I am the father," I said.

"How do you know you're not the father? And if you're not, why were you served with those papers?" Yvette asked. She sounded like a mother talking to her son.

"I'm not. Please believe me," I said.

"OK, I do, but I don't understand why you were served court papers," she pressed.

"Happy to hear that from you. This little girl all is alone, and it has my stomach in knots. What do I do?" I asked.

"If you're not the father. Why are you so concerned?" Yvette asked. She seemed perplexed.

"I'm not. This morning, my attorney called me early to let me know that a detective and police officers would be stopping by my house to question me because they found out about the family court papers. They think I may have something to do with the murder so that's why they want to question me. Somehow, I just can't forget her vivaciousness, and I wonder how Tina ended up with such a man and in such a terrible predicament that ended in her death. I just can't see how. She was like a Valentine's Day person. If you know what I mean."

"I'm not sure, Harold, but it's good to see another side of you. I see where that romantic side comes from. It's your passion for others that dwells deep inside that fun-guy framework that walks around looking like he's got it all together. None of us isSuperman, dear. And if you need to cry, I'm here with open arms. Put your personal feelings aside. You need me now," she placed one hand on mine and with the other, she caressed my face as she spoke. "Go ahead and continue with Tina and her death," she then insisted.

"Well, this morning, Yvette, I was sorting through my backlog of mail while talking to my attorney, when I found an envelope from Tina. I was taken aback knowing she was dead already, so I checked the handwriting closely to assure myself it was from her. It was her writing. I told John that I had found this envelope from Tina, and he instructed me not to open it and said he was on his way over. He again told me not to open it and keep it out of view of the authorities. I did as he instructed, and he arrived shortly thereafter and then dealt with the detective and the officer. After they left, I got the envelope off the fireplace mantel and gave it to John. He examined it and found two documents inside. One was a letter from Tina, which he opened and read. Long story short, Tina stated in the letter that I was not the father and apologized for giving my name to the courts. She explained she was afraid of being killed by an ex-boyfriend who had snapped, and she even thought this guy would come for me because of her feelings for me that she apparently shared with him too often. It's beyond a mess. A woman is dead, a little girl is without a mother, and I may be in the crosshairs. Who knows what else is to come from all of this and her probable murderer."

"Harold, your heart is heavy, sweetheart, but I want to be by your side until the end," Yvette affirmed.

"Really?" I asked her. I wasn't sure what I expected from her, but what she said reassured me of our relationship.

"Yes, we're one, baby. Unbending, unbreakable, and to-gether forever through thick and thin. The external won't get us, although what might, is whether we can get out of our Aries' ego ways and keep the insanity at bay," she explained.

"I don't know what to say for the first time," I said.

"That's OK. You'll know what to say and do when the time comes," she reassured me.

"Are you ready for a late lunch or an early dinner?" Yvette suggested to changed the subject somewhat.

"Sure, dear," I said.

"Let's get a table, then," she said. I had always been the one to secure the table, and order the meal, but I was a bit off my game at the moment, and it mattered to me that she took charge of the situation. So simple a thing it was, of course, but it was less what she did but rather that she did it. She knew when and how to press, to encourage, to listen, and to lead. We were becoming a team tested by life's vagaries, and I felt with her I could win, *we* could win. We ate and talked into the early evening, throughout which she continued to heal my heart, as only a lover could.

# Chapter 26

## LOVERS OR FRIENDS

*How could I?*
*Oh, dear, my dearest, how could I?*
*Why does the morning dew cover the*
*hillside before the morning sun?*
*How could I find love without holding your*
*hand, moving us into Tomorrowland?*
*Why does a child need the love of their parents?*
*Oh, my dearest, how could I wish for anything other than you?*
*How will my tomorrow become today*
*without you caressing my needs?*
*For you're the wind engulfing me, carrying me to*
*that place where we are and always will be,*
*Oh dear, how could I?*
*Because I'm the morning dew, the sunshine, that caressing*
*need. I am without exception, the one who loves you.*

We left the restaurant on a high. I was no longer losing my way in feelings and deep thoughts about Tina's death, but felt a renewed warmth for what God has for us. Find it, seek it. The door is there for us to knock upon. It will open to a new-ness for friends and lovers and even for a little three-year-old. I knew this now. As I knew that Ms. Angel Eyes, my heavenly muse, was nearby, and I'm sure that's the reason Yvette called and came. We kissed, and I walked her to her car and opened the door. We kissed again and said good night. I walked slowly to my car, my heart no longer as heavy.

I thought about many things, but most importantly about this evening with Yvette, for no words were left to speak of the many things we shared. Yvette called them, each one, forward, that is, our memories of yesterday, all of them it seemed, as I caressed her in my mind. Each recollection, a wave of energy and hope of reaching our Tomorrowland, washed over me, over us. I was happy to be with her; she was good for someone like me. Time would tell. Would time share her with me in those golden years when we would throw pebbles in the stream not far from the house and when we would stride along during walks in the park throughout the seasons of our lives?

Driving the Expressway about sixty miles an hour, I was in my own world, until brought back to reality by a car that rear-ended me. "What the heck!" I shouted. The car pushed me into the guard rail, and it took all I had and prayers to stay safe. I was able to get out of the car, walk around, and check out the driver who back-ended me. It appeared that he was drinking. I could smell it on his breath. I called an ambulance and the police. The other driver was banged up but would live. He was in worse condition. Fortunately, I had stopped drinking after a few glasses of wine. We had talked, eaten, and shared single dessert, as we always did. It saved on the purse as well as the waistline. Within about fifteen minutes, the police arrived, followed by the ambulance. The police took all of our information, and shortly thereafter a tow truck arrived. The car was going to be towed to a repair shop. The police insisted that I go to the hospital as well, so I jumped in the ambulance.

I was in the emergency room for three or four hours. I was given a battery of tests before they would let me go. I thought I had said good night to Yvette, but I called her. She came to the hospital, drove me home, and we spent the night at the house, falling asleep in each other's arms. The television played as we slept.

Yvette and I woke up and I fixed us breakfast—a veggie omelet, fried potatoes with onions and green peppers, beef sausage, rye toast, and piping hot coffee with thick cream fresh from a dairy in the country. It was a breakfast that she liked me fixing for her from our beginning. We took our time enjoying breakfast, and the coffee was a real treat. We each drank a second and a third cup. Things were happening and sliding off the curve—a car accident last night, police officers at my door, an old friend murdered, a three-year-old without a mother, and a crazed individual I needed to look out for. What was next? For now, I was going to focus on the two ladies in my life and reach out to Diane for a hot minute. We had moved beyond our second year of my two-year rule, so what was next? I kind of knew. Would we last much longer? I was not betting this go around. Sure enough, about two hours after Yvette left, Lynn called.

"Harold, how are you? I been worried about you hearing your voice the other day. You sounded like the world was slowly rolling in on you," Lynn said.

"Well, things have been difficult lately," I replied.

"Are you ready to tell me about what's been occurring with you?" she asked.

"Yes. I'll stop by tonight to see you after I go into the office. I'm sure you have to work late anyway," I said.

"Yes, I do. Eight o'clock or nine works for me," she said.

"Nine is better and I'm only going to stay for a couple of hours and then call it an early night," I said.

"I just want to be with you and share some time with you," she said.

"Let me go now and we'll see each other tonight," I said.

"OK, dear," she said.

After breakfast with Yvette and after my call from Lynn, I drove to the office and expected to work until I drove over to Lynn's. My time with Lynn would be on speed dial to carry me through my past days and recent incidents, including the car accident last night. And it was on speed dial as soon as I arrived. I started with the detective stopping by, my relationship with Tina, her three-year-old girl, Taye Wells, and the car accident yesterday. Lynn couldn't believe all the things I was telling her, but she was really concerned, as much as Yvette in many ways, if not more. Offering to do whatever she could, and that I would ask of her. The heartfelt time spent together was again needed, and I enjoyed being with her. Lynn became upset when I told her about Taye Wells, his violent nature, and the likelihood that he murdered Tina. And that I might be his next target.

It was now 11 p.m., and I left as planned. Maybe it was the thought of being with Yvette so much lately or everything that had happened in the last few days, but I just wanted time to be alone to think and rest in my bed. Most of all, I didn't want to bring any harm to Lynn or Yvette if this Taye Wells was following me or trying to identify my travel patterns. I couldn't take this guy lightly, and I needed to be careful until the authorities had this dude under wraps. I would call John in the morning to see how his meeting went with the chief of police and what their plans were to find this man. Fortunately, I was licensed to carry, but I hadn't been carrying at all. It was time, though, to pull the Glocks and holsters off the shelf where they were stored away in the master bedroom closet. After loading them, I would keep one by my bed and one on the first floor in a closet near the family room. I had purchased my two Glock 43s several years ago because they were easily concealable, compact, lightweight, accurate, and easy to aim. But on second thought, I wondered if maybe I should carry the second Glock on my person instead of hiding it in the closet. In the morning,

I would decide, but tonight I concluded, I would sleep with one on my nightstand as well as activate the security system, which I also had a habit of never doing. If he came for me, I would be ready. Until the police had this man behind bars, I had to protect myself and the people in my life.

As if I had thought through all of the pros and cons while sleeping, I decided in the morning to carry the Glock on me every day. Over the weekend, I would go to the shooting range to practice my head and center mass shots. The more I practiced, the more I would give myself the edge.

# Chapter 27

## MY OLD SELF

I had to get back to my old self. Since I had come back from out west, crap had been happening and it was looking like not for the better. My meeting in the judge's chamber was coming up, I had a funeral to attend, and I had to watch out for a possible nut who wanted to kill me. John was handling the paternity matter since we had the notarized letter from Tina, but the other two were on me, and they were enough. With all of that going on, getting back to my old self meant I needed some sexual healing, and Lynn was the my choice.

Lynn was just that kind of turn-up girl. She would make me forget all my troubles and cares. She was the kind of sister who, knowing all my problems, would want to comfort me. I called her up and set up an evening together, although I was thinking that some back-seat-of-the-car sex would be what the doctor ordered, and I began smiling to myself.

"Lynn? Hello," I said.

"Hey baby! What's up?" she replied.

"You!" I replied. "I should have stayed last night and made love to you. Are you listening to Rihanna's 'Love on the Brain?' I'm hearing it in the background," I said. Just hearing her voice was relaxing me.

"Yes, I wanted you too, but after what you shared with me, your plate was full, and I didn't want you to, if you didn't want to," she said.

"Well, I want to, now!' I said.

"Yes, baby, so do I. We have some catching up to do. This thing is snapping even right now for some of your long pipe in me," Lynn said, getting me excited to see her.

"I told you it's not the size of the pipe. It's knowing what to do with it. My jawn is not a mallet; it's a living extension of my feelings," I retorted.

"Whatever! When I'm feeling that dick all up in my titties, oh, it's long," Lynn shouted.

"Your imagination is funny! You definitely got jokes," I said.

"No, just something you want," said Lynn.

"Funny!" I replied. By now, I was laughing, and with each passing moment, each repartee, I felt my old self surface, and the tensions pulling on my life were easing, little by little.

I asked her, "What about six o'clock? I can be at your house by then. What time can you get off?" I asked.

"Six o'clock," Lynn said warmly.

I could hear her chuckling before she said, "I can make that time work to give you this pussy and get some—you know how to love me," said Lynn.

The thought of just some raw, wet, passionate, all-night-long, tired-in-the-morning, body-sore, real sexual-healing lovemaking had me hard and rushing toward six o'clock.

I got what few things I needed done and headed to Lynn's house. I arrived a little early. I sat in the car outside her place and replayed the day at the office and scheduled a few office appointments for tomorrow. As I did, it suddenly occurred to me that I may have seen that Taye Wells dude on the street near my office as I was rushing from my building to my car. I couldn't be sure though, because I was moving too fast. Lynn was the only thing really on my mind, however. And right on time, she beeped the horn as she pulled in her driveway. Once in the house with her, I wanted every last succulent drop of her wet pussy, and it was wet before I even touched her. Within minutes, she reached her first climax. I was delivering like the mailman, delivering mail to her box. And to the rhythm of our motion, I said, "I've ... missed ... this ... pussy."

Lynn replied, "And I've missed this dick. How do you do this to me?"

"I know how because I'm doing it to you," I said, quoting the song incorrectly. If she only knew, however, what she was doing to me, the way I liked it, and such, I needed her as well. She was pushing so much ass at me, I damn near hollered like I had her hollering. Her older twin house neighbor would look at me and Lynn over the past years, whether I was alone, or we were together, and shake her head in disgust. But she was smiling at the same time as if recalling her years of merrymaking while driving around in a new import. She traveled a lot and weren't home a lot because she spent time at her other house in Virginia. I could tell the lady next door liked me because she knew I had Lynn all booed up. Lynn had told me that she would say things like, "You two had a good one going on last night. I could tell because you had your music turned up loud damn near all night."

I asked Lynn what she said back to her. "Only that you won't leave me alone." And she replied, 'I think you can't leave him alone.'"

"I just waved my hand in the air, turned around, and went back in the house," she said.

Round one of missed-you sex commenced once we entered the front door. It ended at the foot of the stairs. Afterwards, I went upstairs and ran a hot bath while she laid on the living room floor. When I called her to come upstairs, she just laid there on the floor, so I pulled her up the steps and into the bathroom. "Get in," I said. I followed. We talked briefly, and then round two was served up in the soaking tub with an unscented bath oil. With her legs wrapped around me and from time to time draped over the side of the soaker like a wet towel, we made love for an hour listening again to the Phyllis Hyman and the Whispers' CDs.

It's something about that snapper of Lynn's. It does a dick well, pulls it in deep, and reaches for that last succulent drop from me. I had to help Lynn out of the soaker. I dried her off, and walked her into the bedroom where she immediately flopped onto the bed and fell asleep. She said only, "I'm tired," before she was out. Looking at her there fulfilled, I knew then that no shade of color or of gray is needed; no external devices are required to enthrall a woman into completeness. I needed what we had just done. I forgot everything that was happening in my world, known and unknown. I would turn that reality clock back on in the morning at nine when I was back in the office working. Whatever the day would bring, I was going to look at things differently. A night of relief allowed me to hit the ground running with and against what was coming, and things were coming, I felt. I had to accept that and adjust my mindset to hold up under any situation and protect the two women, the child, and myself from this dude roaming the streets.

If the person I thought I saw on the street near my office yesterday was Taye, I needed to pay close attention and keep my Glock closer.

I called John as soon as I sat at my desk. He picked up on the third ring.

"I was going to call you, Harold," he said immediately. "Here's the latest. Our Taye Wells has been eluding the police. They had him cornered in a North Philly apartment complex, but he escaped. He is on the run and he knows the police want him. The news channels picked up this case, and now his picture is plastered all over the networks. The street talk is he left the state to lay low. The police are following up to verify that the word is on the street in order to take appropriate action. I got the chief to post a police officer at your house and at your office," John detailed.

"I thought I saw Taye yesterday near my office," I informed John.

"What?!" he said.

"Yes, I thought I saw him," I repeated.

"I need to let the police know that, ASAP. And you need to continue paying attention to what's happening in your surroundings," he warned.

"John, I started carrying my Glock with me everywhere I go, and I keep one by my bed," I informed him.

"Good. You may need it," he said.

# Chapter 28

## UP IN THE AIR

*When you're able to live your life for love and not security,*
*When you understand that life is hard and*
*perhaps too real, but never without hope,*
*Then you'll be able to see it differently, yes clearly,*
*that life is for the living, as often told.*
*Maybe, I got it wrong, maybe it was too*
*easy aided by looks in all its favors.*
*Yes, when you're able to move beyond the*
*physical, you will come to know the real.*
*When you're able.*

Things were up in the air, and I needed to land these balls bouncing in and out of my control. This Taye Wells, I had to pay attention to him, not so much because I worried about anything happening to me, but because I didn't want the people around me or my employees to get hurt. He could explode anywhere and endanger any of them. When and where he would explode was obviously an unknown, but of this I became increasingly certain: he would eventually explode. It was just a matter of time, unfortunately. I needed to be ready to call forth my skills from years of military training. I wanted to get to him before he got to me, and that was what I promised everyone dear to me.

This reality that seemed out of a movie was playing out right alongside my love life, which in equal measure dominated my mind. Fact was, I was in love right now, but I had to find my way to her, the one with whom I would travel to Tomorrowland, through all my life's baggage. Tragedy had a way of making things clear, earth-shatteringly clear, like a hurricane or a tornado blowing forcefully and whirling violently, disrupting one's comparably uneventful existence. It could make some lose their minds, fall prey to depression, drunkenness, or the wrong associations, real or imaginary. Yes, I had a battle on my hands, one for my soul, which I couldn't afford to lose and which meant I couldn't afford to lose my way. Fighting against the darkness in a man's heart to harm others. I would have to fight this guy just as hard and with the same intensity as I immersed myself in passion and lovemaking. If my passion and lovemaking was an extension of how I felt, then I would have to be at least as clear about my feelings in the pursuit of Wells, and I would be. He threatened me, those whom I loved, and my hopes and prayers for a life together with "her," whoever "she" turned out to be, in Tomorrowland. There it was, clearly now before me, everything that was on the line, and the chilling reality of what was likely to come and the inexplicable calm I felt despite my anger which had surfaced, revealed matter-of-factly that I would probably have to kill this man, and I was, more than most, damn capable of it.

If I had been adrift over these recent, maybe even many, years, I was focused now. I hoped it was not too little, too late. As my grandmother would say, "Son, it's never too late to start or to do right. You gotta learn to fight evil." Well, Grandmom, evil was now upon my path, so there was no time to lose my way, no time to go astray. I would mind my time, and I would fight this battle.

# Chapter 29

## DIANE

While at the office and experiencing a normal workday, Yvette called me on my cell.

"Hello, Yvette, how are you today?" I asked.

"I'm fine and you?" said Yvette.

"As good as can be expected given what has been served up," I said.

"I understand. I'm just calling to check in on you," she said.

"Thanks. I'm dealing with some stark realities these past few days after our return from the desert. Could you or I ever imagine the change from being on a towering high of fun and new adventures at our age to this mess right now?" I bemoaned.

"Nope. You can handle it, though. I have no doubts, honestly. Besides, maybe all this is for a reason, and only you and the Man Upstairs know what it is," Yvette said.

"Well, I know He knows, and I still got to figure it out," I replied.

"It's your life and not a TV show. I feel safe when I'm with you, and other people around you feel the same way. You just hold onto that and fight. You'll end up where you want and with the things you want," said Yvette.

"I don't want things. You make it sound like I accumulate toys," I said.

"No, I don't mean it to sound like that. Your heart needs to know someone cares for you, and I care for you. You must have had a wonderful and loving mother. You could be her expressing the love she had for you," she said.

"I did. What's got you going there today?"

"I don't know. Just felt like it needed to be said. So, I said it. Now, let's move on to a new topic," she retorted and that was that. "What's the latest from your attorney and the police?"

"John told me they had gotten close to apprehending the probable murderer. They tracked him down to an apartment complex, but he escaped," I said.

"That's not good," Yvette railed.

"No, it's not, but he said they're onto him, and with all the media attention and help from the public, they'll get him. In the meantime, I've got to be vigilant. John said the word on the street is that he left the state to lay low," I explained. Then I said, "I'm going to stay at the office late tonight and clear some of my work off my desk. You want me to stop by later, around nine o'clock?"

"Sure, please come," Yvette said.

After hanging up, I was back at cleaning up the paperwork I had for about an hour or so when my phone rang.

"Hello, this is Diane," a voice said.

"Hey, how are you?" I said, excited to hear her voice.

"I'm fine and in the city," she said.

"What are you doing in Philly?" I asked.

"I guess I'm seeing you," she said.

"Where are you?" I wanted to know.

"I'm at the Ritz Carlton on Broad Street," she said.

"We spent a lot of good times there," I said.

"For sure," Diane replied.

I asked, "What brings you to town? Business?" I inquired cautiously.

"Sort of, but since seeing you in Vegas I can't get you out of my mind. You got me. I thought I got you out of my system. I was wrong. Love reminds me of you. When I think of love or being in love all my thoughts remind me of you," she confessed.

"That's very sweet to hear, but I don't know about that, and you're married."

"I left him for the moment and told him I'll be away for a week to work out some things," she explained further.

"Diane, it is not a good time," I said.

"You don't want to see me?" she asked with a tone that was leading me on.

"It's not that, but a lot of shit is happening right now," I said begrudgingly.

"I can help. I've always helped you," she said.

"I know, but this is different." I tried to brush her off.

"How different?" Diane insisted, probing for an answer.

"I don't want to talk about it over the phone," I said, and immediately after the words came out of my mouth, I questioned why I said that. I had just talked myself into seeing her.

"Good, let's meet here in the hotel lobby and talk this evening," she said. I could hear Diane smiling on the other end of the cell as she spoke, seizing her opportunity.

"OK, what time then?" I said begrudgingly.

"I'm here for us. Whenever you are free," she said matter-of-factly.

"Call it seven-thirty then. In the lobby will be fine," I said. Hanging up, I wondered what can of worms had I just reopened. Time would tell. I tried hard not to like her, but we were in love once, and maybe still. Head down again, I was back to work non-stop. The Ritz Carlton was not far, but before I headed out, I sent Yvette a text message saying I was not coming by.

Having stayed a bit longer than normal at work, I was ready to go. I looked up at the clock on the wall, and it already 6:45 pm. I preferred to be a little early, so I packed up my briefcase in order to head out. As I did, I called for an Uber, and then took the elevator down to the street level to meet my driver. The

Uber driver pulled up across the street. I walked over, hopped in his car, and confirmed that the destination was the Ritz. A short while later, I walked in, earlier than 7:30, and saw her.

She was sitting at the open bar in the lobby. Even though her back was to me, I could still tell it was her. I walked up on her without her noticing and watched her take a sip of her favorite drink, La Familia Reserve Tequila, in a brandy snifter. I looked upon her for a moment or so before she noticed me standing there. "Well, hi," she said as if not excited, but we kissed and embraced for a long time, and her excitement was evident. Without letting go of me, she confessed, "I missed you. Why did we ever split up?" Then, before I could answer, she held me closer and kissed me again.

We slowly released one another and sat in the bar seats facing each other. "I see your drink hasn't changed," I said.

"Should I order your favorite?" she parried.

"Do you remember?" I asked.

"Sit your ass down and I'll order it perfectly for you, Harold," she said with a sweet, yet smug smile.

"I believe you will, Diane," I surrendered, which would be just the first of others that evening. Diane ordered my drink perfectly, and it was delivered perfectly. We drank and enjoyed ourselves at this very bar many afternoons and evenings during the years we were together. Memories flooded my mind as she talked, and I barely heard her say how surprised she was to see me by the pool.

"Harold, are you even listening to me?" she inquired with a playful huff.

"Yes, you were saying how surprised you were to see me in Vegas," I quickly recovered.

"OK. You're still the same. You always knew how to listen when you weren't listening," she said and laughed, as did I.

"Yes, I still do. So, you're in town for business?" I asked again.

"No, I told you. I wanted to see you again. You're all I can think about and the only thing that is cramming my brain since you shocked me by walking in the pool area. It took me more than a few minutes to get myself together before walking over to you. Also, I needed to wait until, and was hoping that, your friend would go in the pool, or at least move away from you to give me a window to come over. I wasn't going to miss talking to you for another six years, no way. So, I'm here for the second time after six years. Time has allowed me to freely and finally push ego away and come back to ... well ... you," she said. I could see and hear in her words, in fact, that there was no ego in her words, posture, or expression. Just like that, as if it were the easiest thing in the world, strong, poised, and confident, Diane said her piece and showed what genuine vulnerability and courage looked like. I admired her for it and for her singular focus and ability to be so sure about a thing so fragile as love.

"And you are here now. I can't say I haven't missed you, too," I said, empowered, I suspected, by her. But empowered, I said my piece as well. "What we did and how we departed over dumb stuff, I thought you were dealing with someone else and you created a lightweight excuse to kick me out of your house. You knew my ego, and so you got the right response, the one you wanted. I shut down. Also, I think you had gotten all you needed in terms of my help, and you were ready to move on. I know you tried calling me several times, but they were weak efforts to talk again. You had another agenda back then, Diane," I said to her and left the silence hanging in the air, pregnant.

But she had not come to play, and again without ego, spoke. "To be honest, you're right, Harold. I had other things happening and your instincts were right. I allowed myself to think you were too committed to other priorities to make a move with someone who was cool, but unfulfilling. I couldn't stay with you not feeling like a priority. Anyway, it was a way to move on. I had another relationship and unfortunately that didn't work.

Thereafter, I stayed to myself until I met my husband, and six months later, we were married. At the altar, I was thinking of you. What's a woman to do? My pride wouldn't allow me to just come to your office. Our egos, at least mine, got in my way, once too often. I lost a lot and haven't been really happy since leaving you. And seeing you again, I'm happy. If it wasn't for staying busy with my friends, well, who knows. I don't have any children, which I have wanted and miss having, but that was a life decision."

When she finished speaking, it was as if she had said what she'd come to say, or at least to say what needed to be said. Maybe there was more that I could have said in that moment, but one had to know when more explaining only risked losing what love remained, if any. Our mutual silence in that moment and the expressions upon our faces told the tale. Peace had been spoken, and any hardship or hard feelings had evaporated. The only thing that remained were the memories, the joy, and the passion we had shared, and they had been distracting me from the moment we began talking, however much I tried to keep them at bay. What would happen next, I didn't really know.

"By the way, how are Monette and your other girlfriends?" I asked. A fresh topic felt like starting anew.

"Hey, they're doing great, and they ask about you from time to time and if I've heard from you. I had to apologize to them for lying on you about something I wanted or needed to believe you did, but my guilt became too heavy, and I had to confess it to them. I didn't want them thinking that way about you. You didn't deserve that, Harold. I think they knew it wasn't the truth, but you know girlfriends, they'll side with you right or wrong," she replied.

"Apology accepted. Besides, I didn't really know what that was about back then. Anyway, you really look great, Diane," I offered.

"Thanks. You look great as well, Harold," she replied.

"Would you like to have dinner somewhere nearby?" I asked.

"Yes, in our favorite restaurant where we always dined for special occasions. I'm sure you still go there," she asked more than stated.

"I do indeed. That would be Davio's, right?" I answered.

"You know you're right. I missed that about you, too," said Diane.

"I'll make a reservation, or we can just eat at the bar. Your call," I said.

"Let's just get a table. You got me all warm being with you," she said.

"It's the tequila," I said. "I'm sure it's the drink."

"I'm not going to blame it on the alcohol. You, you do something to me when I'm with you. Yes, my temperature rises, and I get a little weaker wanting you," Diane uttered, gasping for air it seemed.

"Let's share a dish like we always did," I said.

"I would like that, Harold," she replied, this time in a soft-spoken tone.

"You got it. And you can share my dessert as well. Do you still not like sweet stuff, Diane?" I said.

"Yes, except for you," she quipped.

"Working on brownie points?" I returned.

"No. what we had … I don't know how we lost our way," she said.

"Ego, fear of sharing our deep and very personal selves. I don't know, but we should have recognized the signs earlier. If only I had the opportunity to redo our life?" I revealed.

"You know, Harold, I understand that statement. We were our best and worst enemy, but we were best as lovers. I knew we could never be friends. That's just the way you are. I'm here now to say I'm sorry, and I still love you. Those feelings I thought I could bury, I can't, and seeing you only confirmed I was just going through the motions with someone else. It works, and it doesn't work, if you know what I mean. It's not fair to the other person. I'm only being selfish. Sometimes a half of a loaf is better than a whole loaf or no loaf at all. I get it now. And I didn't like seeing you with another woman," Diane said. I thought amends were over. What was she really after here? Something more was occurring, so pursue it with her, I did.

"Diane! Why were you not able to share all these feelings back then?" I pressed.

"I think, I think that I wanted you to share your feelings with me first, maybe. I truly don't know, but time gave me the answer, seeing you in Vegas. Walking over to your lounge chair chilled me to the bone, and you know I'm a tough city girl. I don't let men bowl me over like that, but somehow you did. That thing came late in my life, falling in love, and I did it with you. Excusing a teenage love affair, men worked my schedule. I laid it out for them, men. If you didn't want to come home, you got my response, and it generally wasn't worth it from their point of view, so they came," she went on. "You wouldn't have cared, but I get it now. Truly, I do," she said, and at that, she reached out and took hold of my hands like she never wanted them to be unlocked again.

"Diane, we were good for one another, but both of us are easy on the eyes to others, which keeps us pursuing and being pursued, thus missing, walking, and maybe running past what's right in front of us, true love," I said, as sure of my words as time itself. And so sure of them that I heard them in the innermost part of myself, and I wondered what I had just said. Then, it rang clear. That's what I was going to miss or run past, true love, once again. My two-year rule was now passing into its third year. Was it a flawed rule? Was that what I was beginning to understand? I wasn't sure, and I didn't want to leave getting to Tomorrowland to chance. I had a plan, needed a plan, right?!

But, as if looking out upon a horizon, the panoramic view of my present life displayed itself.

There was Diane who just re-emerged in my life and whom I had loved, still loved; there was Lynn whose love was a rhythm and a vibe I could not fully resist, but whose workload and job required so much of her I wondered, at times, if there was even time for me; there was Yvette, who was asking questions about us and asking whether we would be together forever, who was that someone with whom I felt a life connection, but whose questions I had not answered; and then there was the memory of Tina and what to do about a three-year-old girl. Pillars on the horizon, substantial, real lives, with real feelings at stake, they were all asking me for time. Was it a coincidence that all seemed to be converging to a point right now? The proverbial pendulum of the clock still swung back and forth while time marched on, but was I effectively trying to stand still with my two-year rule, as if I could hold back time? This convergence of the women in my life was pushing me forward to stand and fight for true love, for that which was most desired in the universe, for that which was also the most baffling in it, and for that which an all-out revolution of the heart was required to win. These were the universal truths across time and space about true love. More than ever before, I was aware of the precipice upon which I stood—on the edge of a reality in which I would eventually, if not sooner, be called on to make a decision about whether I was going to fight, how I was going to fight, and for whom. The thought was emotional, terrifying even, yet the crystallization of the fight to come was calming as it clarified the enemy to be faced. But, would Taye Wells be or would I be ultimately the victim of the perpetual swing of the pendulum?

"Harold, you're wandering," Diane said in a friendly voice, wearing a bit of smile.

"Yes, I am, Diane," I confessed. "Yes. A little. I needed to. You're here sitting across the table from me after all these years.

Here now? Why? I was asking myself these questions as well as others about what I have going on right now." But I was getting too deep maybe, so I changed up to give Diane my full attention. I asked her, "What do you see on the menu? Any favorites?"

"I want to try something new for us to share," she said.

"What about the Oven Baked Lump Crab Cakes?" I suggested.

"That sounds tasty, and the chef here will not disappoint our palates," Diane agreed.

We enjoyed our dinner and drinks, left the restaurant and walked slowly, holding each other tightly as we made our way back to the Ritz Carlton. Walking into the Ritz, I suggested we have a final drink for the evening. She didn't have to ask; she knew we were spending the night together. At one of our favorite bars, a small, quiet, and intimate setting, we continued reaching back. I recalled the Ritz was one of the first places where we shared drinks and got to know each other. Also, we would come here and have drinks before going to the theater.

"Remember us going to see *A Bronx Tale* with the TV actor. Oh, what was the actor's name?"

"Harold, you were never good at remembering names. He was Chazz Palminteri," she said.

"Right! He's one of your favorite actors," I said.

"No. He *is* my favorite actor!" she said.

"OK, OK. You'd better get in line though, because he's a cool dude," I joked.

"You're right," Diane said, smiling.

I could see she was preoccupied with the memories of us together. In fact, they seemed to be flooding her whole mind and body with joy. We were really feeling good about being together again. Time spent in this favorite little corner of ours, our favorite place in this unapologetic city still looking for brotherly love, in fact, made the leap back in time that much more effortless, and soon enough, we carried our unfinished drinks to her room and closed the door behind us. Love embraced us from that moment, and our clothing seemed to slide off. Standing there, her warm, sculpted body pressed against mine, we just continued embracing one another for a time, for love lost that's been found again tends to overwhelm its beneficiaries. Diane's skin was soft, and her curves invited my hands to follow them wherever they led. The sensations I experienced just holding her led me to imagine her, and the taste of warm cream and peaches for which one could wait ever so patiently filled my thoughts. Yes, I would wait; I wanted all her peaches and all her cream.

We began our voyage into making love to one another without the thought of coming up for air. Time was spent getting back all the love we had missed, and with her first sigh upon penetration, she exclaimed, "Oh, how I missed you." Into me she melted, her words of ecstasy spilling and flowing out of her. And as they did, she opened wider, pulling harder, yet wider still, and squeezing oh, so much tighter. With each subtle movement a degree raised in temperature until, like a kettle, she blew. Out came an outburst. "I love, oh, I still love your ass." I knew then that she was all mine, and I was all hers, again. Though the morning came quickly, the night had been an odyssey in pleasure of love lost and found; we had made love time after time after time, and our bodies bore the marks of passion and the marks of possession. We awoke to kisses slow and gentle at first, and then more of each other before I headed for the shower. Standing on the threshold of the bathroom, I cast a glance back at Diane, whose beautiful hair tossed here and there and the easy smile upon her face told a tale of how it is for two to be so at home with each other and within each other. Once in the shower, the spray upon my face, I saw Diane still in my mind lying on the bed, and as if just awaking a second time, I told myself this needed to end before it began, again, and it most certainly would if I didn't deal with it and soon. Easier said than done, for I, nonetheless, told myself that for now, I still wanted more.

While I was in the shower, Diane ordered breakfast. She finally got up and made her way to the shower. We hugged and kissed as we passed. She didn't want to let me go until I tapped her rear end, squeezed more than a handful, and said, "Go take your shower and get dressed." She did, and I exited.

As I wanted to check my messages, I dressed right away, and began perusing through my phone. I had both texts and emails, and I realized I needed to respond to some of them promptly. Diane showered for quite some time, but emerged rejuvenated, it seemed, by her quickened pace about the room. While I continued going through my missed calls and emails, she began reading hers, so I was able to continue without interruption. After a bit, she entered the room wrapped in the hotel's Turkish bathrobe, wanting to talk. I gestured to her that I was still on the phone and needed a bit more time and privacy.

I was now on the phone with my attorney who was updating me on the status of the court case and Taye Wells' whereabouts. The case was going to be heard in the judge's chamber, which John thought was to our advantage as he felt confident about the evidence we had and his ability to persuade the judge of our desired outcome, especially with Tina's letter. As for Taye Wells, John said authorities suspected he had entered Ohio; consequently, the police were now working with the FBI and the Ohio's authorities to widen the search. "John, do you think they'll catch him in Ohio?" I asked.

"Harold, I surely hope so for everyone's safety. We need to talk very soon here in my office about both situations," he said. "How about Monday?" he continued.

"I need another week beyond this mess, John, and besides, I don't want to deal with it for the next few days." I replied.

"OK, fine. We got time. You call me when you're ready to focus on what's at hand and we'll let the police do their thing and get this guy in the meantime. I got some background on the child including some pictures sent by the court. She's a cutie, brother. Maybe even looks a little like you," John said, although I wasn't sure why. Did he really think I might actually be the girl's father?

"John, I am not the father," I said emphatically.

"Whoa, man, I believe you, but she's still a cutie," he countered.

"Well, her mother was very pretty," I said, relaxing as I spoke about Tina.

"I'll email or text you the pictures and background report from Domestic. Let's talk soon, Harold," he said.

"OK, John, have a nice day, and I appreciate the update," I said.

Though things felt like they were looking up, a murderer was still on the loose and who was gunning for me. I was less concerned for myself, though. Rather, I more worried about those around me whom I loved. My life, as life does, took some unexpected turns, and like always, I would adapt, roll with the punches, as they say, and do me, which was the only way I knew how to do it, and, hey, the record showed, I wasn't too bad at coming out on top. I felt a sense of confidence, but I was a soldier when it came down to it, and the worst thing a soldier could do was lower his guard. So, my guard was up, but watching Diane in the robe, moving about the room, was disarming. As in the past, I was still taken aback by her beauty. No makeup, her hair down, curves that gave shape to an otherwise shapeless robe, this dark woman of color was stunningly gorgeous. She moved about gracefully without effort, but purpose, drive, and passion adorned her face, and I remembered why I loved her, still. So, despite what may have been on my schedule, I decided to spend the day with Diane. Taye was in the back of my mind, but at least at this moment, Diane was at the front of it.

Today would call for music, no doubt, and so the Spotify playlist was loaded, and we would be serenaded by the likes of our dear brother Gerald Levert, whose live voice I'm still missing, Miki Howard, Jean Carne, Phyllis Hyman, Marlena Shaw, and especially Regina Belle singing "What Goes Around." Office work on hold, Diane my diet plan for the day, we finished breakfast, planned the afternoon and the early evening together, and rested the balance of the morning engaging in small talk and sharing about our years apart. Many of our highs and lows seemed to have been similar, how we had been in and out of relationships for a while until we each decided just to be alone for a period of time. We both agreed that a period of being all by oneself gave us time to find out what were the most important things in life to us. Who could have predicted that after so many years apart a chance meeting would bring us together to share and to appreciate what we really meant to each other? Although we would do nothing about it now, we agreed to bury the egos, that Aries thing that haunted each of us over the years. Somewhere in our tomorrows we would find the peace of being without each other as it seemed the ordained plan for our lives, at least for now. Perhaps we were just the memories of love lost and wants of the heart, still empty for who and what was to come. Indeed, Yvette was ever present in all my thinking even in my being here with Diane. Why was she? Was it the reason we wait and want, being so unsure of our feelings, or maybe just being too afraid of them? I didn't know why, but Yvette was in my mind, and Ms. Angel Eyes probably knew why, but she was not here.

Just then Diane reached over and kissed me. "What was that all about?"

I was absent, but present here, too, with her.

"Bring your thoughts back to me," Diane asked softly.

"I was here," I replied.

"OK, well, know I'm here, too," said Diane.

"Yes, you are. I'm unbottling all these feelings I have colliding inside. Let's take it moment by moment. Can we do that?" I asked, hoping she would understand.

"Sure, I will, if you will," Diane said again in her soft voice, assuring the two of us.

"Sure," I said. Forever for always for us, let the songwriters and the jazz voices sing and bring us together, or at least to a not-so-distant place where our union, what we have now, could exist for eternity. Maybe she wasn't the one who would ultimately fill my tomorrows, but I still did not want to lose the memories, the feelings, and the love we had for each other. Was that wrong? Would it get in the way of my tomorrows or would she be the one waiting for me in Tomorrowland? I thought it would remind me, the me with the two-year rule, that rules are just that, guides; they are not the passion, not the vulnerability that must be risked to experience the exquisite, not the unbounded love of which the songwriters write, about which the singers sing, and to which we, the lovers, listen and dream. With that in mind, the music changed up in my head to Eddie Kendrick's "Can I," to the Whispers' "I Love You," and to Lalah Hathaway's jazzy, soulful voice. All of them played somehow in my head, so then I changed our conversation. The voices of love sang song after song, and for some reason compelled by something I couldn't restrain, I reached out for Diane's hand and asked for a dance. We danced slowly for a long time, at least a song for every year we were apart. The very last ones were by great R&B groups, the Intruders and the Originals singing "I Wanna Know Your Name" and "Baby, I'm For Real." The dance got slower, and the dips tighter, and I began to sing to her, my voice being in the same key. The words "I'm for Real" floated silky as she raised her head from my shoulder, tilted it back, and looked into my eyes. She was all smiles. She parted her tender full lips, and from her soft genteel voice came, "You are," like the whisper of a secret she wanted no one else to know.

I didn't let go, couldn't let go. Told myself in that moment I was not letting her go. I was her vocalist now, and so I continued to sing Phil Perry as we waltzed and twirled around the room. We were high again. It was always so easy for us to go there. We danced into the afternoon, across the floor, and the graceful rhythm of our syncopation ushered us into more of her and more of me. My lips no longer moved, yet I still sang. No longer on our feet, we still waltzed again and again. We loved each other. Where she or I began or ended, I did not know, for we moved as one and unabating euphoria was our crescendo. I know we fell asleep only because we woke up, because in my dreams the singing and the dancing never stopped, never ended.

When we woke up around 3 p.m., we still embraced each other, our lips nearly touching. As if we knew words would fall flat, neither of us spoke; we just closed our eyes, kissed each other and got ourselves ready to move about the city. Walking along the sidewalks, we stopped in familiar shops and laughed, kissed, and hugged our way to a bar for happy hour and half-price appetizers. There we ate and drank. A couple of women at the bar couldn't refrain from asking the question, "You two are the bomb. Did you just get married or something? Because you guys are having so much fun together, and it's so real. We're envious."

Up until then, silence and the romance of the morning hermetically sealed us. Unaware of anything else and almost anyone else, we had dressed, left the hotel, and enjoyed teenage-like, puppy love tunnel vision. All of it must have incited Diane to wonder why not us, now, this time. And if I hadn't preferred to stay in this bubble, safe, as it were, from the outside world, I probably would have known the questions were coming. And come they did, hard ones.

"Why is it a bad time for me to come and see you? I want you to level with me, Harold. I hope I deserve that," Diane said, playing on feelings of love she knew I had for her.

"You really want to know?" I asked.

With a deep breath and quick glance down at the table, she looked up and said, "Yes."

Yvette and Lynn knew nothing about each other, and I could have said less to satisfy Diane; however, I was beginning to appreciate the strength in feeling free and so chose radical honesty in that moment. I said, "The past two years, Diane, I've been dating two women, although at times they seem like one. I really like them both, but my two-year rule is starting to rear its head. I think you women have ... it's like a body alarm clock. It goes off after two years like clockwork." I felt cathartic talking about my two-year rule, almost as if I hoped to get some feedback on it, to check myself.

"I know about your rule, about us. I won't say it's not real, Harold; it played a role in our separating, I believe. I was wrong to go, and you were wrong, too. We need to accept that and forgive. I think we have in our own way and that's why we can pick up where we left off so easily, falling in love at the sight of one another," she said.

"Diane, you have reflected on our separation and why it happened for a while," I said.

Diane reaffirmed the time she'd spent thinking about us together and in love. She acknowledged, "I have, and I still do."

"And so, do I. It creates heartaches, the kind Gregory Porter and Lalah Hathaway sing about most appropriately in the song 'Insanity.'"

Diane spoke up quickly, "I know the song. Beautiful." She continued, "Harold, you need to understand a woman wants a man like you. Some think they can't have you for whatever reasons, and they run away clothed in their ego for protection. I was that woman, and it may have cost me my greatest and only love. Hell, I'm here six years later. If I could have stopped the insanity sung about in the song, then I'd be OK. I'm sure of that now, no question in my mind."

"Diane, you're right, and time will call me again to pay attention and make some hard decisions soon," I said. "Getting back to what you asked me, listen closely. After coming back from having a wonderful time in the desert and Vegas, I was greeted by an unexpected legal matter, having received papers demanding I appear in court regarding the custody of a three-year-old little girl; then her mother was murdered, and the police questioned me about it as a possible suspect; and finally, I discovered that her boyfriend, the probable killer, likely wants to kill me, and maybe even the two women I am seeing."

"You have a three-year-old little girl, Harold! I want her," Diane said miraculously as if hearing nothing else.

"Is that all you heard, what I said about the little girl?" I asked incredulously.

"No, but that's so nice that you have a little one," she said.

"I'm actually not the father, Diane, but her mother left a document giving custody of the girl, Lynette, to me if I wanted her," I explained.

"You want her of course, right?" she said excitedly.

"Diane, I'm not sure," I said.

"We need to talk about this, Harold. What a gift! I'm so excited for you," she said.

"You certainly see it a lot differently than many others," I acknowledged.

"Well, you know I never had children, and I always wanted one with you, if I were able to have them," she confessed.

"We can talk about the child after I get through the court process. I got a very good lawyer to handle the matter," I said.

"OK, please keep me updated daily," she asked.

"I don't know about daily, but I will," I agreed.

"Promise?" she asked.

"Yes, Diane, I promise," I answered.

"All right, what about your other problems?" she asked.

"The women, yes. They understand that situation. They know about the child and the mother, Tina DiFilippo."

Diane interrupted me. "I know Tina. She's younger. I knew her parents. They had it rough growing up in that neighborhood in South Philly. Hell, it wasn't easy for us, either."

"No, way, Diane," I said, astounded. "Are you sure? What does she look like?"

"The Tina I knew is an Italian-Irish mix girl about five-foot-seven-inches, a bob haircut, nice body, maybe a White version of me. Last I heard, she lived in North Philly, the section they now call Northern Liberties," Diane elaborated.

"All true. Maybe you did know her," I acknowledged.

"How did the two of you meet?" she asked.

"We met a while after you and I separated. No, it was a couple of years later. I was just working and trying to get over you, and she appeared one day," I explained.

"What do you mean just appeared?" Diane asked, laughing a bit as she spoke.

"I met her at a gathering and later we met again at a diner. It went from there," I said. "We clicked from the beginning, and we were together for about a year or so," I added.

"Harold, I want this child whether it's yours or not," she said, focused, determined. She was not joking. "What's that line you always quote by Einstein about coincidence?" she then asked.

"I would agree it applies here," I said.

"I can't be mad. I left you before you called it quits with me. It's the cost of making wrong decisions. If you only knew how much I still love you," she confessed.

She smiled at me with a look I'd seen before. It was that look she got in her eyes when she committed herself to a goal. This time the goal might have been me, but for sure it was Lynette. We continued to hang out and then we worked our way back to the hotel.

Back at the room, we settled in for the night. More lovemaking and her beautiful body to caress and work to my enjoyment made for an easy call to extend the stay for a second night. The second night was more fun and more intense than the previous night. How that could be was one of the secrets of falling in love. Clearly, whatever else was or wasn't true, we were still in love. And yet, there were Yvette and Lynn, women whom I loved and who hadn't left me yet, as Diane had. I liked having Diane all booed up and her breasts looking like shooting bullets, still sticking out firmly, calling me to a party at a place where only lovers can go. At that party, she and I explored every inch of each other, and she experienced her fourth or sixth orgasm that evening and shook violently like an earthquake full of desire erupting and begging me to stop. She couldn't take it anymore. "Hell, I am done. NO MORE, no more!" she exclaimed. She was done, and I was too, my face buried in her breasts; the fragrant smell of her perfume kept me close, and I slept like a baby. Before tumbling into a deep sleep, I knew we would repeat this at the drop of a dime if one or the other made the call, and we found the time.

We awoke to another great breakfast together and talked about seeing each other again soon. The balance of this week was out, with only a slight possibility that we would meet up three or four days later, if she planned to stay in the city. Diane decided to stay only an additional two days to rest and shop before leaving. Always having a change of clothes in the car, which I carried up to the room yesterday, I left around noon from the hotel dressed for work, and headed straight to the office with the intention of working late.

# Chapter 30

## MY GLOCK AND COURT

As I entered the office, my employees greeted me as they always did. I considered myself fortunate and I certainly was grateful to have such wonderful employees. Because of them, I was truly able to enjoy a fulfilling private life. I sat in on all of the office meetings and then returned calls and messages from the last two days. Both Lynn and Yvette had left me phone messages, but I had texted them over the past two days. John had called, but we, too, had spoken already. I would call him again later for any possible updates. While there were many calls from clients, they had been directed to my staff to handle. I was relieved that I had no pressing matters to handle.

That also meant no pressing matters, calls, or messages from Taye Wells so far. I felt some relief, but I couldn't afford to relax. The Glocks on my hip and ankle reminded me of that and how much, for the moment at least, my life had changed. Completing a full workday at the office, I left for home, eager to get some rest. I was on high alert, however, so I cased the street around the office. All looked normal. I headed for home, cruising the neighborhood to see if anything looked unusual. It all looked normal as well. I pulled into the driveway and entered the house. I climbed the stairs to the upper level of the house to reach my bedroom. It was 10 p.m., I observed, before I pulled back the covers on the bed and then stretched out underneath them. I fell asleep quickly. Lovemaking, not to mention being on 24/7 alert because a murderer was trying to kill me, required getting my rest, so I needed all that I could get.

The night flew by and the morning came swiftly. I was up at 7:30. I put on the pot to brew some fresh coffee, dressed, and then ate a hearty breakfast before heading to the office. It became second nature now to case the neighborhood. I cruised the block for anything that looked out of place. I found nothing, so I headed to the office. Another full day was planned just for office work, meetings, and returning calls.

My first call was to Lynn. We talked until my secretary buzzed me that I had a caller on hold. I had called Yvette earlier on the way to work, and we talked for about thirty minutes. I told both women that I was taking some time for myself, and I would see them several days from now. They both had work schedules that would keep them busy as well, anyway. I worked through lunch and dinner and left for home around 10:30. As I exited the building, the streets still looked normal for that time of night, empty. But the empty streets only reminded me that Tina's funeral was tomorrow. I had spent a lot of time and energy doing whatever I could to avoid thinking about this day, but it was here, and on the day of her funeral, I would probably see Lynette, her daughter, for the first time.

The service was held at a local funeral home. I sat in the back after walking to the front of the funeral hall to view the body. I wasn't given much to tears, and so never expected them when I felt my eyes well up as I looked down on her body. I had seen men die while serving in combat, but here, so far away from that life, it was hard to see her and even harder to sit through the service. Numerous police officers continually canvassed the area in case Taye Wells decided to show up.

Lynette was in the system now, Child Services, but she was at the service with her ailing grandmother. I chose to watch her from a distance. I wasn't sure what I would say to her or even what I would say to her if I met her. Moreover, I didn't want anyone introducing me as the father. She was a beautiful little girl, and seeing her, I thought what a gift she was, a bit of Tina who would live on and make her own way in the world, as had her mother. I left that day without saying a word to her, but whatever I thought of her before I saw her, she became more real to me now. I was not sure what would have to be done about her, but I began to think that I could not just let Tina's daughter, even if she weren't mine, be left to the vagaries of the system. That would need to be worked out later, however.

Since Tina's funeral, I worked tirelessly in the office. I saw Lynn and Yvette, but only sparingly. Both had allowed me space to deal with Tina DiFilipo's death and the domestic court matter, and for that, I was thankful. Diane wanted to see me again, too, but I only talked with her by phone. I delayed seeing her, telling her I needed to prepare for my domestic hearing in the judge's chamber and to deal with the police regarding Tina's murder. As much as Diane wanted to see me, she was also baby crazy. As I had promised her, I did keep her updated on the girl, even describing Lynette to her sometime after the funeral. The time I had to myself allowed me to complete a number of projects and to submit several proposals crucial to the company's growth.

Meanwhile, John had prevailed in getting the meeting in the judge's chamber scheduled, and it was to be held tomorrow, the twenty-eighth of the month, at nine a.m. I did several Q&As with John to ready myself, and I arrived at the court with mixed emotions. John and I were escorted to the judge's chamber before the judge arrived. When the judge came in, we all rose.

"Please sit, gentlemen. This is my chamber. Make yourselves comfortable. Child Services, please present your case regarding the minor, Lynette DiFilipo, and her relationship to Mr. Harold Longston," the judge said, getting right down to business.

"Your Honor, we have a copy of the deceased parent's letter in which she explains that Mr. Longston is not the father, but we are looking for your ruling on the matter," the attorney for Child Services said.

"Mr. Worth, would you now speak on your client's behalf?" the judge said.

"Yes, Your Honor," John answered. Then, he began. "Your Honor, I presented weeks ago a timeline of Tina DiFilipo's life as it pertained to the child, additional supporting evidence, and most importantly, the letter and notarized document of the deceased. While I also requested at that time the appropriate DNA tests, I believe, Your Honor, that sufficient information has been submitted to allow for a ruling."

John made his case, and the deliberations lasted for almost an hour, during which both sides strongly defended their arguments. Finally, the judge said he had heard enough, looked over top of his glasses and, after reviewing the exhibits for several minutes said, "Mr. Longston."

I replied, "Yes, Your Honor."

"Were you and Ms. DiFilipo close, and how do you feel about all this?" he asked.

"Your Honor, when I was first served with papers from the court, I was a little heated under the collar, so to speak, but finding Tina's letter later and reading Tina's story asking for my understanding—and stating that I was not the father—I was relieved. Then there is Lynette, and Tina's request for me to take the child and raise her. I felt good that she viewed me as a responsible person for such a major obligation; however, Your Honor, I'm not sure currently if I want to do it. I am sure that I'm not the father and that I don't want the courts to falsely saddle me with this bill Domestic Services wants to strap me with, but I am concerned about Lynette's well-being," I explained.

"Mr. Longston, thank you for your honesty. I think you're OK," the judge said, frankly, adding, "I will make a decision on this within the next ninety days or sooner."

The judge excused us from his chambers, and John and I left feeling pretty good about the outcome. We decided to go to lunch and found an eatery close by to grab a quick sandwich and a beer. Walking with John, I called Yvette to let her know how things went and to see if she wanted to have a light dinner somewhere this evening. She did, and we agreed to meet near her house, but not in the city. As she had the day off, we would meet at 7:30 p.m.

John and I discussed the next matter on the table, the murder case and Taye Wells.

"No one has seen him, and that has worried me greatly. Harold, this guy will show up soon, my friend, so you need to continue being vigilant," John said.

"Well, I'm still holstering the Glock right here inside my sport jacket."

"Good, I need to get back to the office. Let's talk soon and stay safe," John insisted as we departed.

"I'm going to my office, as well. By the way, old friend, thank you for handling everything regarding Domestic. I really appreciate all of your thoughtfulness and hard work. Anyway, see ya soon," I said. I headed back to my office, eyes scanning the streets as I left the restaurant.

# Chapter 31

## CANNES, FRANCE, LYNN

At my desk, I worked steadily with some sense that all I was going through would be over at some point. Progress on the Domestic case front was reassuring, and though it was not yet over, I felt some relief. The meeting in the judge's chambers seemed to have gone well. It was the first crack in the ice, and I looked forward to the thaw. However small the progress, I must have felt buoyed by it, for today, as over the past few days, I hadn't paid any attention to the time. It was already five o'clock. I told myself I would work a couple more hours and then head home. As I was thinking this through, Lynn called, excited about getting her promotion.

"Congrats! I thought that was going to happen for you eight to ten months from now."

"It was supposed to," she said, "but there was a death, one of the top executives. My boss was given the opportunity to move up, and so did I as a result." I could hear the exultation in her voice. I was quite excited for her and proud of her as well. She'd been working diligently for that promotion.

"Great, Lynn! Congratulations again! We definitely need to celebrate," I said. I hadn't had something to be so excited about for such a long while that every part of me wanted to celebrate her and her accomplishment.

"Of course! Tonight?" she asked hesitantly. She knew what I was dealing with.

"I was going home to rest, but we can celebrate. You've worked hard, and you deserve the opportunity. I'm very happy for you," I said.

"What time? It's five forty-five now."

"Can we do eight p.m.?" I asked.

"Sure. Where would you like to go?" she asked.

"Let's do Chops. I'm up for a steak and potato dinner," I said.

"I'll call for an eight o'clock reservation for two," she said.

"OK. Meet you there," I said.

I immediately called Yvette and apologized that I had to cancel, that something had come up, and that I would make it up to her. I was glad to get in a few more hours before leaving. I was the last one leaving the office for the night so I turned off the power and headed for Chops. We were seated and served drinks. Lynn's excitement was evident, and as she continued to talk, I found myself increasingly sharing emotionally in her jubilation. By the time we finished our drinks, I felt buoyed and said, "Hey, let's order some dinner."

"OK, you order for us." she said.

I knew what she would eat. I ordered for the two of us, a chopped salad to share. For Lynn, I ordered the barrel-cut, 8-oz. filet mignon medium, and I ordered the jumbo diver sea scallops for me. The sides were roasted garlic mashed potatoes and roasted asparagus, and to celebrate, I had them bring a bottle of champagne. As always, we ate our fill and drank the bottle of champagne. For dessert, I surprised her by telling her we were going to Cannes, France for seven days. She could not believe what I was saying, and said, "What?" so loudly other diners looked her way. I said to take a deep breath, even though I was smiling all the while.

"How did you come up with that, Harold?" she asked, still incredulous.

"I always wanted to take you there, but we have to leave within the next couple of days. I just got a feeling that things seem to be coming to a head, and I want us to spend some time together before it all does. We can leave on the fourth of next month, a few days from today, and we will return on the tenth. You want to go?" I finally asked her.

"Yes. Of course, dear!" she exclaimed.

"Now back to the dessert question. What would you like?" I asked.

"Baby, you know how we do dessert, and we're going to France. Well, that just got you two scoops of this pussy," she said. Her foot was now brushing up against the inside of my leg.

"Oh, you got dessert jokes," I replied.

"No! I got you," Lynn countered, truly elated with the surprise.

"Well, you figure out how to keep my ice cream hard until we get to your place. I see you smiling like Christmas is coming soon," I said.

"I've a lot of time banked that I can use. This will be fun for us," she said.

We left the restaurant, went to her house, and took a shower together. Serving dessert started there and continued damn near all night. That was my Lynn, and I got my Christmas and Kwanzaa gifts early that night. As I left in the morning, I remarked, "I'll have my secretary purchase the airline tickets and book the hotel reservations this morning." She kissed me long and sent me on my way.

Over the next several days, I planned to get everything just right. In fact, this morning, I was carrying contracts that I worked on a while ago that needed only to be signed today by a vendor who was stopping by the office. The many weeks of focusing on our business plan had paid off, and while I was away, the business would run smoothly in the hands of my great employees. My folks knew just what to do, and I had supreme confidence in them to execute it. Then, as I mentioned to Lynn, I had my secretary make the reservations for a suite at the Hotel Martinez for seven nights

I was going all out on this trip for some reason. Maybe it was the way Lynn made me feel or the way she held me. Whatever the reason, I was all in on this trip. I told Yvette that I would be away for six or seven days. She was OK with it. She responded so readily, I thought maybe she wanted some time to think about our relationship moving beyond two years. It was going to be what it was, given my two-year rule manifesting itself like clockwork. I surprised myself at how cavalier I seemed to be about it. Maybe I was focused on Lynn at the moment. With so much going on in my life, I continued to accept that I only had control over certain things. Yvette and I would talk further when I returned to see if we still had a future together.

With Lynn talking with me every day and night about this trip, I wanted to rush the days. Finally, the morning of the fourth arrived. We were on an early flight from Newark International to Aeroport de Cannes-Mandelieu, the international airport serving Cannes. In about 10 hours or so, we would arrive in Cannes for a week of sun and fun.

We traveled first class on KLM, and the food and service were excellent. Fortunately, upon arrival, we experienced no delays passing through customs. We exited the airport to find a town car waiting to transport us to the hotel about 30 minutes from the airport. As we headed to the hotel, I reflected on the fact that I hadn't even mentioned to Lynn I was thinking of flying us to Spain to see a bullfight or to Morocco for a day trip of shopping and adventure in Marrakesh. Morocco, I thought, would be an unforgettable experience for her as it would be her inaugural visit to the African continent, her first steps on the soil of our Motherland.

Once the driver pulled up to the hotel, he stopped and opened the car door for Lynn first and then for me. As we stepped out of the vehicle, the unimaginably lush surroundings took our breath away. As Lynn admired the wonder surrounding our hotel, I tipped the driver and instructed the bellman to bring our luggage inside. I checked us in, and the bit of French I spoke aided in a seamless registration process. Lynn was still entranced by the beauty of the city, and I patiently waited for her to come inside as I knew this experience was her dream fulfilled. Finally, she entered the hotel. She tried to play it cool like she'd been here before, but I could see in her eyes the disbelief that so much beauty could exist in one place. When we entered our luxurious suite, the fantasy continued. It was spacious and offered all the first-class amenities one could imagine. Indeed, they were consistent with those offered throughout this extraordinary and exceptionally beautiful hotel. We would certainly take advantage of the hotel's pools and beach daily. Lynn would do her foodie thing and experience the fantastic flavors of the local cuisines and not-to-be-missed local attractions of the city. I tipped the bellhop as he unloaded our luggage, and we immediately got settled. After we showered, Lynn stayed buck naked. I loved seeing her that way. While still moving about, she called me to come, and like a teenage boy on his first trip away from home, I ran, jumped over the bed, and then tackled her onto it. She screamed and with great delight asked, "Are you crazy or do you miss me that much?"

"Both, and do you miss me?" I asked.

"We just spent ten hours traveling, sitting next to one another," Lynn said.

"I know but you called me and said come here. So, I'm here, and you didn't say I had to walk to you," I said, rolling on the bed with her.

"My dear, I told you, you're crazy, but I love your crazy ass, all the way," Lynn said. She seemed happier than I had ever seen her.

"I know you do," I said.

"Let's get a quickie in," Lynn asked.

"What? We don't do quickies," I said. "And we've got a hotel and the French Riviera to see," I added.

"Come stick it in and let me squeeze you, baby," Lynn insisted this time.

"You're the nasty one, Lynn, not me," I said.

"I'm just weak for you. That's my story, and I'm sticking with it," she exclaimed, smiling. She then continued to get my attention with some playful, if nasty, gestures, beckoning me to come closer to her.

"My baby got jokes," I said. In the end, I obliged her, or did she oblige me? The outcome was the same either way; we were stuck for more than a few minutes while she squeezed and each of us enjoyed the other's release and the moans that made it all worth it. So, our vacation was off to a great start here in our suite with a balcony and a seaside view. After whatever we had just done, we cleaned up again, made a couple of drinks, and headed out the door to survey the scene, having decided beforehand where we would dine later on. For now, we walked and held hands.

Lynn was happy, very happy, and I felt great being able to share in her joy. Indeed, though we'd held hands so many times before, walking hand in hand now felt like the very first time all over again. She must have felt it too as she began squeezing my hand extremely hard before she stopped abruptly, turned to me, and said, "Strangely, if my tomorrows ended today, please know that you have been all that I have ever wanted in a man. So, always hold me in your arms and in your thoughts of us together." Just then, I heard Kem blowing sweetly his hit song,

"Share My life," as Kem called forth his words of dreams and joy.

"Hey! Why are you being so emotional?" I asked.

"I don't know. Time just flashed forward, and I could see you holding me," Lynn said. "Close your eyes," she said, after which she kissed me on both my eyelids, as if to balance out her feelings.

I had to change this river of feelings. "Let's go see what the shops here have to offer, and I'll buy you the world today," I told Lynn.

"You will?" Lynn asked.

"Yes," I said, as I could always hear Ella Mai when I was giving up my truth and being sincere through her words, through her songs, for Ella understood more about love and lovin' far beyond her tender years. She even sang songs about our love affair. Yes, I was in love with Lynn, and right there unbeknownst to her, I realized not only did I love her, but I was, in fact, in love with her.

"Yes, you can buy me the world today with one condition," Lynn replied.

"And that is?" I asked.

"I will need your arms and thoughts to forever embrace me always," she insisted with a voice of certainty. "And, sweetheart, I can assure you and promise you whether absent or present in this world, I will forever embrace the thought of you in every way," she added.

"Lynn, I never heard you sound so passionate about us. Why?" I asked.

"That's a question for our tomorrows together," she said. With those words, she grabbed my hand and began walking again. We shopped, enjoyed the remainder of the day, and looked onward to a week together on the other side of the Atlantic Ocean.

# Chapter 32

## OUR WEEK IN CANNES

After a day of shopping, although we didn't buy much, we did see some beautiful pieces of jewelry for her that were a must-buy before we left Cannes. By five o'clock, we had returned to the hotel bar for cocktails, which we enjoyed before retiring to our suite to rest and ready ourselves for an evening out. All smiles, we showered together and kissed as her body just engulfed me in all her finest. We were tired after a while and exited the shower. Gently, lovingly, we dried each other off and found the bed to rest and adjust to the time difference. Once again, I found comfort wrapped in her arms, my head nestled against her succulent breasts. I fell asleep first, I think, while she stroked my forehead; a woman in love, she had looked down upon me until I closed my eyes. After nearly three hours of rest, a call from the front desk awakened us. I had forgotten that I had told a friend that Lynn and I would be staying at the hotel for a week, and to stop by if he were still in Europe. The front desk connected us.

"Hello, Harold, this is Richardson," a voice on the other end said.

"Hey, buddy, what's up, and where are you, my friend?" I asked.

"I'm in Madrid. Several friends and I will fly over in three days to spend some time together and to meet your friend," Richardson said.

"Richardson, that's very special and kind of you, brother," I said.

"Hey, we go way back, you and I, so expect us in three days. Turn your phone on by the way, and I'll email you our arrival time. I booked us into the same hotel. This is more than a surprise. It will be a celebration of sorts. It will be good to see you," he said.

"Of sorts?! You know how we hang out, brother. We got money, time, and love for each other, brother. I will be forever grateful for how good you have been to me, especially how you have invested in my company. We're a multi-million-dollar business now because of your confidence in me. You better believe we are going to celebrate," I said.

"Hey, Harold, that's not necessary," Richardson replied, "that's what brothers do or should be doing for each other, help," he said emphatically.

"I get it, but you know it's true, and it's just my way of saying thanks and not forgetting the help offered long ago. See you soon, Richardson, and the others, too. Email me your details like you said, and I will send mine, also," I said with a smile of thankfulness.

Lynn had woken up sometime during my conversation with Richardson and wanted to know what all that was about. I told her that Richardson was an old friend from the neighborhood who had become quite successful in the movie industry.

"You never told me about him or any of your friends. I know you have them, and I know how you treasure friendship," she said.

"'I do," I said. "Anyway, Richardson is in Madrid with friends, and they'll be flying to Cannes in a few days to spend some time with us before we fly back to the States," I explained.

"Harold, why didn't you tell me?" She seemed a little bit alarmed.

"I wasn't sure it was going to happen, based on our last conversation about his schedule. He wasn't sure where they'd even be in Europe," I explained. Lynn listened intently. Once I finished, she threw her hands in the air and said I should have told her something so that she would be prepared for it. "Don't worry, you'll be fine, Lynn, and they'll enjoy meeting you and partying with us, and we will enjoy partying with them," I assured her. At least I tried. After that phone call and our short conversation, we fell back to sleep. We didn't wake up until around midnight. We decided to stay in and continue getting some much-needed rest.

The morning's sunlight peeked through the hotel room curtains. We awoke to find all of our hopes and dreams, all of our feelings of our yesterdays, still wanting and calling to us, lovers in this city of love, romance, and films. We had hoped to get an earlier start and to continue exploring the city and each other, but the day's pace began slower than expected, and it was a good thing Lynn and I spent this time together. I found that I was truly digging being here with her on the other side of the Atlantic. What a great travel partner she was—or was I just more in love than I had ever realized with this fine, dynamic sista? Whatever my feelings, we were finding love beyond the passion and the sex of the past two years.

Even from the moment our eyes had opened this morning, Lynn ushered in the day with a smile, and in her eyes shone the warmth of the morning's glowing sun. And, yes, I was lost in her obvious love for me, which I'd known in my mind, but had I really known it in my heart? Yes, I knew Lynn was a woman who had given unconditional love and great passion unselfishly and who would always be there for me. But time spent together was oh so different than time simply together. It was togetherness that warmed the body from deep within, thawed one's inner thoughts, and incited one to sing the words of Brainstorm. So, yes, I had to say to her this morning, "Dear, I really want to love you with all my being." Lynn sensed my sincerity, reached out, and called me to come closer, and we hugged our way, it seemed, into the late morning, missing breakfast. Our being together was our breakfast. She whispered, "Do you remember our weekend in the Capitol, Washington D.C., and the dive we ended up in? That young jazz artist we listened to who was just not that good? Then drove to a hookah bar where we hung out for hours with that sassy and sophisticated club manager? She was so cool!" Lynn reminisced with excitement.

"Yes, she was very cool, and I liked her, too. We'll have to go back. I lost so many cool points that night drinking those shots of whatever they were on top of the Jack Daniel's. Landed me on my ass as I recall, and she, her friend, and a co-worker had to help me up off the floor. Yeah, you had to remember that night, huh?" I said in jest.

"Oh, yes, that's right. I remember," Lynn said, laughing uncontrollably about that, about that evening spent in the town of world politics and world power. Then she said, "I knew that night, actually, that I would follow you anywhere, then, now, and perhaps forever."

"Lynn, it feels good hearing you say that and that we are still laughing about it, but we need to get out of this bed and get some lunch and hang out in this city of films, and, I'm sure, of much, much more," I said.

"OK, dear, you know we're joined at the hip forever, so you always say," Lynn reminded me.

"Go take a shower while I watch the beauty of you moving in lovely motion before me," I said.

Walking across the room toward the shower, Lynn looked over her shoulder, all the while her body moving, a harmony unto itself. "OK, you can come join me, if you like."

"No," I said, "we may not get out of this suite, and I want you to see what the city has to offer. Let's give ourselves an hour to get out the door. We'll have lunch at the café we passed by yesterday."

"I would really like that, Harold. I will be ready soon."

240

# Chapter 33

## EXPERIENCING THE CITY

*Why did I feel the need to love you?*
*Why did you let me?*
*We were having fun, as you called it*
*I was searching for perhaps, we*
*But somehow this affair was going to be a life trip*
*Whether together or apart, this thing called time—uncontrolled*
*Time—needing only her understanding*
*And yes, we know that story, as often told*
*So, we're here to find the answer*
*But our imagination is the infinite gift for lovers.*
*Therefore, we need not time, but each other.*

Seated at the café finally, Lynn and I turned our attention to the movement and energy of the city. We examined our tourist map during our light lunch, identified some sites to see, and began our escapade, walking and Uber-ing as we went about town. The French Riviera and the sun made for a lovely couple, and we enjoyed them everywhere we went. The rich and famous of the Cote d'Azur adorned our tour and gave us opportunities to discuss the latest gossip. So beautiful, so much to see, we decided earlier that before Richardson and my other friends arrived, we would spend as much time as possible traveling up and down the French Riviera digging the large and quaint villages. We would leave the noted tourist havens for another trip, however. We visited local marketplaces and found local artisans displaying their arts and crafts. Later we headed for Biot, Alpes-Maritimes, its cobblestone streets, and a town bubbling with art and culture in the hills of Antibes. We would spend the remaining hours of the day and early evening there before returning to our hotel. Cannes and the region were not places for American junk-food eaters, which was fine with us. Lynn was a foodie, and I was rather health conscious, so we were up for all the local delights and cuisine the area had to offer.

Biot was a charming village whose streets were lined with shady cafes, galleries, lovely bistros and restaurants overlooking the French Riviera. It was the kind of place two people could fall in love over and over again in the warmth of its summer sun, and its people. We found a place to dine and drank our share of French wine and enjoyed their French cuisine, dishes that were freshly prepared for us. Time was lost on us as we remained enchanted by all that surrounded us.

Once we realized the lateness of the hour, we headed back to the hotel. Back in our suite, we knocked off the dust of the hillside and the cobblestone streets and dressed fashionably for an evening out at a local jazz club named da Bouttau, Cotton Club a Cannes. We stayed until closing and called for an Uber driver to take us back to our hotel. Boy, was that an evening of treats that kept giving us memories that would endure for a lifetime. Still on a joy high, we simply took a shower together and once again nestled ourselves together and fell asleep.

In the morning Lynn woke me up with, "I want some. We're in France and believe me, I'm going to give you all this wet stuff the French way."

I smiled, and said, "What way is that?"

She replied, "It's yours, baby, do what you want with it, I've been letting you do that for these past two years, and now in

Europe, I gotta have some stories for my girlfriends. They think you got me all caught up, anyway. So, roll over Beethoven, and come wax this until I feel completeness all inside of me." Our way, the way we loved and made love to each other had always been seamless. With so much more time to share since we'd been here, we had been able to enjoy each other's company beyond the passion and the sex. That time I relished, the hand holding, the easy walks along the Riviera, the slow pace through quaint shops and the banter with store owners, locals, and even other tourists. This dynamic between us that stoked the fire that had melded us to one another was beautiful, and recognizing more fully my love for Lynn, I felt the desire to make love to her for hours. She was calling to me now, and truth be told, I loved her vibrations, rhythm, playful ways, and her sophistication. She was my lady and my African Hermetic keys to the universal union of one, if you will. Maybe that was it. She could be everything I desired, a balance and a counterbalance, and there was nothing false about any of it. She was complex, our universe was of the mind, and I could see that more clearly now, ironically, in this lavish, free-spirited, and beautiful world called Cannes.

Quickly, then, things got crazy, and before long, Lynn hollered, "Oh, goddamn." Twice I had to put my hand over her mouth. We were in a hotel room, and the walls had ears. So, we toned it down slightly, but didn't stop until we ended up on the balcony letting the chilly morning breeze blow over our sweaty bodies where her two legs met my third leg and where she found the completeness she desired. I carried her back to the bed and we continued wanting everything this love affair could and would provide us. I took a quick break to order breakfast in the room, and of course, I requested sliced apples. After ordering, I would love her until breakfast arrived. It was pleasurable and beyond memorable loving her on the opposite side of the ocean.

The knock came quicker than we thought, right in the middle of her outstretched legs on the cusp of shaking violently, and she hollered, "Don't stop, don't you fuckin' stop," and I didn't until, well, until the neighbors knew what we were having for breakfast. Thereafter, with our food still waiting at the door, I put on my robe, opened the door, and ordered the waiter to take everything onto the balcony, where we would eat breakfast, if Lynn didn't fall asleep on me. That last, "Oh, goddamn," might have anesthetized her, but I was determined for us to keep it moving, eat breakfast, and go down to the pool or beach where we could relax or swim.

Sure enough, Lynn was on her way to sleep, but I insisted that she get up and join me on the balcony to eat. She said, "OK, just let me freshen up first." I poured coffee for the two of us and waited for her. In her robe, she moved lazily as she stepped out on the balcony. She was beautiful just as she was. On the balcony together again, we ate our fill with lover's smiles upon our faces. We were in love.

Before Lynn and I would leave the hotel in the early afternoon, we decided to enjoy the pool for a while. Because Lynn wanted to remain in the pool much longer than I did, I went to rent a car for the day. Upon my return, I informed her of where I had been and that I wanted us to leave shortly to head for other adventures driving the streets of the French Riviera coastline with plans to end up at Le Cannet for a late lunch or early dinner, where the view from the terrace was breathtakingly beautiful.

With the plan in place, we changed clothes in the suite and hit the street in the Peugeot RCZ. Driving the French Riviera was a blast, and we relished every moment spent in the many shops, touring the various villages, and conversing with the wonderful people we met. The hours skipped along, so a late lunch was out.

When we arrived at Le Cannet for dinner, we let our waiter select our three-course meal after using both French and English to provide an idea of what we would like our dining experience to be. After dinner we took our time getting back to the hotel, and we decided to enjoy one of the clubs nearby and to walk the distance from the hotel. The nights in the Riviera were made for romance and certainly a sweet one. We would walk and talk, enjoy the city nightlife, and conserve our energy since Richardson and his crew would be arriving tomorrow. "By the way, Lynn, Richardson and his party are arriving around one p.m. tomorrow. He emailed me earlier, and I let him know that we would be at the beach. Sorry, I forgot to share that with you," I said.

"No problem, I'm looking forward to meeting your friends."

"By the way, it's a party of eight, four couples."

"Do you know them all?" Lynn asked.

"I think so, but I'll know tomorrow. My buddies have changed wives and girlfriends over the years," I admitted to her.

"I guess you have had your share, as well," Lynn spoke, already knowing the answer.

"Lynn, why go there? But, you're right. I may have had more than my share. Life is for the living, you know. I mean, talking about one's share, a woman will always want what they had if it was good. For it's like a hole that she can't fill unless he tracks back and makes it right."

"We're not good plumbers," Lynn said, trying to explain women candidly. "Funny, and I think you're right; we women carry more emotional baggage, though, with us. We just do, and some of us can suppress it well, until we run up against it. When I saw you at the club two years later, I was done. My heart started racing, and I got all hot and bothered. I was going to re-introduce myself to you, if you hadn't asked me to dance. I can only imagine how I would feel if we broke up, and then

I saw you out. So, don't leave me, Harold," she said. She was being a little bit melodramatic, but I could tell underneath it all, she was actually speaking quite candidly.

"Really, Lynn?" I probed a bit.

"Yes! Harold, you got some shit with your romantic self, but you have been everything I initially thought about you," Lynn said.

"Well, let's have a drink on that," I said, hoping to lighten the mood just a bit.

"I still have one. Go ahead order one, and we'll toast to being here in Cannes, and we'll walk back to the hotel," she said.

"OK," I agreed.

After the drink and the toast and a bit longer enjoying the club's atmosphere, we held hands and hugged our way back to the suite where we kissed and felt our souls wrapped in passion again and again before morning came.

Lynn was up early and flowing gently about, as if music were playing in her head. She looked at me and started to cry.

I asked, "Why are you crying?"

"I'm not crying— just my dreams and my eyes are cloudy no longer. Harold, I'm just happy. You know I had my son early in life with a man far from someone like you. He was smart and had some money, but all he wanted was a blue-collar job and the streets. He took care of us, but because of that, he thought he had the right to run around on me. I didn't deserve that. I wanted more. I took my son and left, moved back home, and continued my education with my father's help. You're like my father in many ways," she said, and after a momentary pause during which she seemed to be deciding whether to say any more, she continued, if reluctantly at first. "Recalling my life, it just hurts so bad at times, thinking about it, wondering if it would ever get better for me. Then I met you, and for once in my life, I knew you were a glove I could wear well. You never called, and my continued thoughts of you brought you into my life again. Yes, I'm crying, but I am crying tears of happiness because you complete me. Simply put, you are my dream come true, and the hurt and the loneliness was worth it to be here with you now. Yes, I love the French Riviera. It's been first class all the way. But since you've been here, you've shown me more of you, another side of you. You've made me feel like you are really mine and that you are in love with me. This makes my journey OK and validates my belief that I deserved better and that someone like you was out there for me. And oh my god, the sex with you, Harold, makes me wet in thought and body. What is it about you? Where were you earlier in my life?"

"Lynn, I'm here now. That's all that matters," I said.

"Yes, you are, and I'm more than glad, and something tells me that if I keep traveling with you our days will be brighter than even this moment. Loving you is easy, or maybe that's how a dream-come-true feels. Whatever, I know that it's real love; it's fun, it's heavenly, and yes, easy, and being here makes what my father said clear about a man like you: 'They don't come along often, but they run deep and true if you hold them dearly and just be there for them.' And I will be there for you, Harold," she said.

Lynn was talking to me while she was looking out the open balcony doors. The sea breeze was brisk and blew her full-length silk robe and hair as if she were in a Hollywood movie. She was one with the gentle wind, and the sun, and the Mediterranean with all it had to give its visitors and lovers who were all here stealing time in a world of exclusivity. I got up, went to her, and softly rubbed her shoulders and turned her to me. We kissed and held each other as tears continued falling from her eyes. I wiped them away, but they kept falling, and I understood. I was there to wipe her tears, mend her heartaches, and wash away all her thoughts of being lonely any longer. I knew then we could never be over one another. This trip we were on would have its own destination. Holding her, somehow a realization flashed before me, and I finally understood Paul of the Temptations' deeply moving rendition. Indeed, I could recall his YouTube version, seeing and hearing him sing, "For Once In My Life." Paul's voice and style so profoundly expressed his joy and pain of love and being loved.

Shifting thoughts about in my head, I decided to order breakfast. We would remain in to find solace in being together. We were feeling euphoric, and perhaps, we were a heavenly thought of another spring moving into summer, our life renewed for a moment.

"Let's shower and enjoy our breakfast on the balcony, and we'll watch the sun's rays gleaming off the Mediterranean to lose ourselves in each other's feelings," I finally said.

Lynn smiled and said, "OK, Harold. You have turned my world inside out and made me feel so very special."

To her I replied, not as one watching the clock tick away days and months in two-year increments, as one atop a castle's protective wall, but as a free man who dared to believe, free of apprehension and of time constraints. And so I said to her, "Lynn, I want you to always remember that your tears are our tears, your joy, our joy, and I'm the lucky one to have you by my side. So, let's go find our tomorrows, today."

## Chapter 34

# A BIRTHDAY DINNER PARTY

At around noon, I got a call from Richardson.

"Hello, Harold, we just landed and will be at the hotel soon. We'll meet poolside after checking in and getting ourselves somewhat settled," Richardson said.

"OK, great, Richardson. Lynn and I will be poolside waiting for you guys. I've reserved a table for ten. We'll see you there," I said.

"Great, see you soon," he said.

Lynn and I had spent quite a cathartic morning. Over breakfast on the balcony, we had shared our feelings and expressed them in ways they could never be misunderstood. We were now poolside, and Lynn was wading in the water. She loved being at the beach or floating in a pool, much the same as Yvette did, but the demands of her job kept her nose to the grindstone so she was not able to go to the beach or the pool, for that matter, as much as she desired. But now she was in her element as we waited for my friends to arrive. Spending time with them and doing some serious partying with them would be a fitting end to our time in Cannes. Lynn was still a little nervous about meeting so many people, but I told her, "You are making too much of it. In fact, they are probably more curious about you given what they know about me. I mean, for you to be here with me, they know you've got to be special, and you are."

"That's sweet, Harold," Lynn said.

"But true," I said.

Just then the waiters appeared at our table to work our party exclusively. I knew my friends, and these guys would not only require attention, but demand it, if necessary. I gave the waiters some instructions about what I wanted and how I wanted things handled.

I had a big surprise that Lynn knew nothing about—only Richardson, the hotel staff, and I. I was throwing her a birthday party tomorrow night complete with a five-star dinner presentation here at the hotel restaurant, La Palme d'Or. Champagne and the ambiance would be over the top. Lynn's birthday wasn't for another week, but it just felt right to surprise her and go all out. We'd be dressed to the nines, and it would be a most memorable occasion. We would be talking about it for years to come.

Richardson and friends walked into the pool area. I called Lynn to come over as they were heading to our table. I stood to greet them with heartfelt joy. We had traveled many roads together and many with failures and heartache. Anyone who dared to achieve great things would experience them. In this world of division and duality, the two opposing aspects of life, time walking the high wire with friends had redefined this world for me far beyond success, Valentine's Day, or Trick-or-Treat. I came to realize the world was about love and *love of friendship: in love, be a lover and in friendship, be a friend.* The planets are, and the universe will be, forever; let then love and friendship be forever, too.

Richardson and I walked toward each other and embraced. Likewise, I bear-hugged each of his friends, Nick, Rob, and Clifford. The women who accompanied them included Johnette, Richardson's wife since college; Nick's girlfriend of about five or six years, Tasha; Rob's girlfriend for the moment, Renee; and Clifford's wife and childhood sweetheart, Trina. It was good to see them all.

Nick and I had been friends from my college days. Another proponent of the two-year rule, he had apparently abandoned it, given how long he'd been with Tasha. Rob was the eldest in the group. He had befriended me early in life when I was trying to find my way as a young businessman. He and his wife, who had passed over ten years ago, had been very good to me. With his wife deceased, Rob usually traveled every year with a different lady, and each one tended to be young and fine—and Renee was no exception. Laid-back friends from the neighborhood, Clifford and Trina married as teenagers and were still together. I admired their love and relationship, and always told them so. All here now and doing well in life, it seemed, it was now time to introduce them to Lynn, and one by one they embraced her as their sister, which meant a lot to her.

I invited everyone to have a seat, and I waved for the waiters to come take the drink orders and to see if there was anything else they wanted. Conversation flowed freely around the table. Everyone wanted to know everything about Lynn.

Richardson said, "Harold, she's fine."

Johnette agreed and said, "Harold, you look happy."

"Harold is always happy," replied Richardson, but somehow Johnette suspected differently.

I ordered a round of drinks and food while we continued catching up and getting to know each other. It was good for all of us to be together again. The last time was about four years ago in the Virgin Islands.

The waiters were professionals and served the food promptly to us. I ordered another round of drinks for everyone while we ate, talked, laughed, and quietly gave thanks for our good health and blessings, all during the course of about two hours. By then, only the men remained seated at the table. The ladies had found their way down to the beach and were there until I went looking for them just to see how Lynn was fairing. Much to my pleasure, she was fitting right in. The ladies seemed to like Lynn, and she seemed to be enjoying their company. She had escorted the ladies to the beach and had one of the waiters carry their drinks to an area I had reserved. Complete with a couple of cabanas and bar setup, it allowed the ladies to continue enjoying themselves while there. I didn't stay long and returned to hang out with the brothers. We stayed late by the poolside and agreed we would meet up at 9 p.m. in the lobby to go to the jazz club Lynn and I had checked out a couple of days ago. It was about 5 p.m. now, so everyone would have time to rest and freshen up.

I requested the bill from the head waiter so that I could charge it to my room, but Richardson had intercepted the check. He grabbed it and said, "I got this one. You got a bigger one tomorrow night." The generosity between us never stopped. I thanked him, and we all headed to our rooms with the ladies leading the way.

Back in the room, Lynn was clearly feeling good about having met and spent time with my friends and their wives and girlfriends. Moreover, she was surprised that they all wanted to get to know her beyond our time together here in Cannes.

"Harold, these ladies like shopping," said Lynn, also surprised by their discussions about what they had been buying and were still planning to buy while here.

"Don't all women?" I said.

"Yes, but these ladies talk about spending money like rock stars," said Lynn in disbelief.

"I don't know about that, but they got their own money, and my boys certainly got dough," I said.

"I see that. I'm far from blind. How much you got?" Lynn asked, joking a little but equally curious now that she'd met my friends.

"Is that a soup question?" I said.

"What?" she asked.

"You know the line in the movie *Finding Forrester*," I said. "Let's just say I'm financially OK."

"The ladies say you are, and that you're a good catch," she said.

"They do?" I asked, adding, "Well, I guess you should listen to them."

"You always make light of things?" she asked.

"Yes, except love and friendship. Let's change the subject, why don't we. I suggest we relax and get ready to meet everyone at nine in the lobby."

I laid on the bed and closed my eyes and set the alarm for an 8 p.m. wakeup. I think Lynn was too hyped to relax. She started pulling out clothes and asking me what I thought she should wear of the four or five things she had brought with her. I told her whatever she wanted except for her evening formal, which she should wear tomorrow to dinner with everyone.

"Why?" she asked, quite curiously.

"Because at least one evening during our stay wherever we are in the world, we dress to the nines and share an evening of fine dining and dancing, and we haven't worn our formal clothes yet," I explained.

"Wow, I think that is so grand," she said.

"I do, too. Let me rest please," I requested.

"OK, dear," she said.

It was a little after six and I dozed off until the alarm chimed at 8 p.m. Lynn had rested as well, as best I could surmise, although not nearly as long as I had. By the time I awoke, she was already back up and still trying to decide between two outfits. And she wanted me to choose, so I finally said, "Wear the Gucci outfit." She was all smiles upon hearing my choice, so apparently, I had said the right thing. I didn't want to be late, so I felt relieved that I made the right call.

As for me, I planned on wearing a Versace suit and a silk shirt. I was ready in short order, and as Lynn had already been up and preparing to go out, she was nearly ready once she felt good about the outfit she planned to wear. I knew she was still focused on making a good impression, so I was happy that she had confidence in what she was wearing because it meant she would be able to relax and enjoy herself. Most of all, she would *be* herself, and my friends would have the opportunity to get to know the Lynn I loved. No doubt they would see what I saw, a beautiful woman who was looking so very fine in her outfit. We left the room about ten of nine to meet the group.

Lynn asked, "Are we all going to the jazz club?"

"Richardson reserved a limo for our time in Cannes," I said.

"Really?" Lynn said incredulously.

"Yes, dear, this is how we hang out," I said.

"I can get used to this in a heartbeat," she quipped.

As we exited the elevator, Richardson and everyone else were waiting so we all proceeded to the limo. The ladies all looked like money, including Lynn. Dinner and jazz were on the menu for tonight's fare at the restaurant. Arriving at da Bouttau, Cotton Club a Cannes, we exited the limo and were escorted to our table, which I had reserved earlier in the day. Lynn had been blown away stepping into the limo, and now that we were being escorted to our table, it was almost too much; but true to form, she handled herself as if to the manor born, which I knew she would. At the table, Rob took charge, calling for the maître d' to command an evening of the best French cooking paired with great French wines. The menu consisted of five courses. Lynn took out her phone and took several pics of the place and the menu. "My girlfriends will not believe this without the photos," she whispered to me.

"No problem. Are you enjoying yourself, my dear?" I whispered in her ear.

"Imagine this: my tears are going to come again, I'm so happy," she said, doing a stealthy job of hiding her emotions.

"You had your teary moment this morning. Now it's time for all smiles and merriment with everyone here at the table," I said. As I looked at her and spoke, I comforted her with my hand, which I placed on the small of her back. "*D'accord*, sweetheart?" I whispered. Lynn had picked up some French during our stay, and that I playfully used a little with her, made her beam again.

"*Oui*," she said. I smiled and kissed her on the cheek, and as if I had gotten down on one knee, the ladies all fawned, and Johnette commented, "Harold, you're still a romantic, we see." The fellas laughed aloud, and with that, Lynn truly relaxed and became one of the gang.

Dinner was *absolument superbe* as was our time together. The drinks kept flowing, and the jazz that came next was upbeat and created a fantastic backdrop against which we talked and laughed and told stories and laughed some more until we couldn't take it anymore. As we wound down, the jazz played on. We drank coffee after dinner with dessert, just what we needed before deciding to head back to the hotel about 2 a.m. We flagged down the waiter, but Rob picked up the bill unexpectedly and wouldn't hear anything else about it. Clifford, who had planned to pay the bill, took solace in leaving a generous tip, and it was indeed generous.

"Ladies, our limo awaits us," I said, and everyone started making their way toward it as we were all ready to go.

Back at the hotel, gathered in the hotel lobby, we all said our goodnights. Hugs, including bear hugs, and kisses were shared and heartfelt as if we were departing in all different directions. I loved these guys and gals, and the newcomers to the group by this point no longer seemed or felt new, including Lynn. When she and Richardson exchanged hugs, my heart was so glad, I smiled with both joy and gratitude.

We decided we would see everyone at breakfast, either poolside or at the cabana on the beach. We were all easygoing, so whoever arrived first would choose where we'd hang out, but no one was obliged to attend. See-you-when-we-see-you friends we were, except when we planned things. We had planned tonight, and the reunion exceeded all expectations. And we had planned the early birthday party to celebrate Lynn's birthday tomorrow, so while I might not see any of them at breakfast, everyone would be there to toast Lynn. Hugs and kisses done, we headed for our suite.

I was somewhat tired, but Lynn was wide awake and talkative, uncharacteristically, so I obliged her. I opened the door, but she shut it! She began kissing my neck and hugging me from behind, her fingers interlocked around my waist. She restrained me from moving forward and was biting my ear, before she started talking her sexy stuff—which is to say her nasty stuff—in it. What lethargy I had vanished, and the usual unquenchable drive to make love reared its head. We were slipping into our own world of love and passion. Lynn made it clear she was riding the horse tonight, and there wasn't a damn thing I could do to stop her, and knowing it would be another night of exploring the union of pleasures together, I didn't even try. I would not be able to mute her hollering this time. She dropped her Gucci outfit onto the floor where she stood. The curves of her body would devastate any who might resist her. Only her stunning beauty and seductive eyes rivaled her commanding breasts, round derriere, toned legs, and sculpted calves. That night, she was indeed the general, and she rode the horse long and hard. We would not rise early, for she tamed the night and sang her sweet, sexy love battle moans into the morning.

It was 10 a.m. when we rolled over and said good morning to each other. "Harold, last night, I'll never forget. Thank you. You're great," Lynn said.

"I'm just so glad you got to meet my friends and to have as much fun with them as I have over the years. That really meant a lot to me. They accepted you as one of us. You're welcome, but you really don't have to thank me. I love you," I said.

"A more amazing time I have never had. You've let me into your world and relationships in ways you haven't over the last two years, Harold. I treasure that, and I will never forget it," she replied.

I just smiled back at her in such a way that no more words needed to be exchanged. We were good. Finally, I broke the silence. "Lynn, darling?"

"Yes, Harold?" she said, anticipating still my every word.

"I'm hungry," I said.

"Oh, you!" she said and let fly a pillow at my head. She laughed, and so did I as she exited the bed.

I sat up on the edge of the bed, still laughing. "Let's get ready to go to breakfast downstairs and then let's go to the beach for the day. We've got another dinner party here at the hotel's main restaurant tonight at seven-thirty," I said.

"I know! Yes, I'm excited! You guys hang out like this all the time?" she asked.

"Yes, we sure do."

"Wow," she said. "OK, you go ahead to breakfast, and I'll join you as soon as I can get myself together," she added.

Within thirty minutes, I was on my way to eat a hearty breakfast with a couple of paperbacks I had started reading in tow.

In the café, Rob was eating by himself, so I joined him and ordered the same thing he was having but with coffee instead of tea. We talked about last night's events and about Lynn's birthday dinner party that was occurring tonight. He also asked me about her and our relationship, remembering that he saw me last year in Philadelphia, but with Yvette. He thought actually that I had come here with her.

"Harold, you know eventually you must pay the piper, so beware. Rob said.

"I have heard you say that before," I remarked, wondering where he was going with that comment.

"Be mindful, my friend. Your heart is good and stays out of the rain," he said. Again, more sophistry. Where was he going with this?

"I've heard you say that as well," I said, trying to follow.

"Call me if things get too complicated, and you need someone to talk to or need my help," Rob said, as if he knew something I hadn't realized yet, but should have.

"I will, I always have. You're like my big brother, Rob, always there and never far away," I said.

"Hey, I see you have a new friend," I said.

"Not a friend. Just a date," he said.

"I like that, just a date," I said.

"You know me, Harold. One love was enough for me, and since she has passed on, it's just a date," he said. He knew I understood, and I said no more about it.

"Perhaps, I'll find it, that one love, too," I said.

"I think you will. Between this one and the one in Philly, I think you will. If one was not thinking, one could mistake them for the same person, not in appearance but as a woman who fit you like a glove," he said.

"Funny you should say that. I have heard it said to me twice already, and once again just recently," I said.

Once breakfast arrived, we began to eat, and the subject floated onto other things. But as I ate, I felt how much I appreciated Rob, his friendship and guidance over the years. I was the eldest child, but Rob was a big brother's big brother, and I valued his advice, especially the way he helped me see things by just tapping me on the shoulder and prompting me to look around myself and pay attention to what he knew I already knew. He was clever like that. He believed, and so I came to believe long ago as well, that we are aware of most of the things in our lives, but for one reason or another, we treat them as if they are not there. Understanding this was important because it meant that if I had to be hit over the head with something, I was not ready to face it. After Rob's tap, I figured maybe I was ready to attend to what was upon me. Time would tell.

While we ate breakfast, Lynn and Johnette walked toward us wearing their beach coverups. We called them to join us, and they did. They stayed for a hot minute, and then headed for the beach.

After we concluded breakfast, I found a lounge chair, pulled out a book, and finished the first book of which I had brought several to read during the trip. Afterward, I went to check that everything was in order for the dinner party tonight. I wanted to ensure that the meal, the birthday cake, and the champagne for our 7:30 seating in the center of the restaurant were being attended to appropriately. The waitstaff assured me that everything was under control and that I need not worry. "It is what we do daily, sir," I was told. Rob and the others all knew it was a surprise, except for Lynn. I just hoped it stayed that way so that it would truly be a surprise. In fact, we would be celebrating not only her birthday, but also her job promotion. Once the party was over, we'd just enjoy ourselves as hotel bums, likely reminiscing about all of our adventures since we'd arrived.

I went back to my suite, set my alarm, and rested until 5 p.m. Once I hit the bed, I was out within minutes. I clearly needed the rest. When the alarm finally chimed at 5 p.m., it took me a bit to get to moving, even though I had slept well. Lynn wasn't back yet, so I went down to the beach, but everyone had left or was on the way up to their rooms. I knew 7:30 would come quickly, so I grabbed an espresso before heading back to the suite. By the time I arrived, Lynn had returned to the suite and was preparing herself for the big evening out. She was excited about the dinner party. Apparently, the ladies had concocted a story about the dinner being a surprise for Richardson.

Playing along, I said, "I was surprised the ladies shared that with you."

"Oh, yeah! They got me all excited. In fact, we left the beach early, and they treated me to the salon," Lynn said. "They're so cool, Harold. What a confident group of women. I really like them," she said, pausing and looking at me as she said it.

"So, a dinner party for Richardson, they told you," I repeated. I wanted to get more details so that I was prepared to play this out.

"Yes, you know about it, right?" she asked.

"Of course, You do special things for special people," I assured her.

"Wow, your friends are so lucky," she said.

"We all are and especially you. Sometimes we do things not knowing why, but it's the right thing to do, if you can," I said.

"Well, I'm hyped, and if it's anything like last night, well then, wow," she said.

"Absolutely," I said, adding, "It will be minus the limo, though."

"Harold what should I wear? I think the red formal, the off-the-shoulder dress," she pondered out loud.

"You have lovely shoulders on that frame of yours," I added.

"Thank you, dear," she said.

"Welcome. By the way, we can't be last," I said, warning of the time passing.

"We won't. These ladies are a stickler for promptness," Lynn said fretfully.

"One should always be at this level. It's just protocol and good manners, Lynn. But I'm sure you already know that. You wouldn't have gotten to where you are today, if you didn't know. The difference is that well-meaning people too often fail to extend deference to their friends and those whom they love most, but extend to strangers such deference out of some perfunctory social norm. That's backward. People will rarely tell such things, but when you arrive on time, for example, they register the respect that you have just shown them," I replied.

"I see! Wow! Makes so much sense. I just never really thought about it like that before. Guess that's what I was gleaning from the ladies, and I'm beginning to stress myself out a little bit. This is all so new to me," she confessed.

"Lynn, just breathe. You were meant for this and at this time in your life. You have arrived. We both have. Let's continue to enjoy ourselves. We'll be back home to our work-a-day-world soon enough," I said, encouraging her.

"This trip is far beyond my expectation of just spending a week with you. I just did not see all this coming, but I am so glad that I'm here," Lynn replied.

"Good!" I said before I kissed her. Then I said, smiling, "Now, stop talking and ready yourself for another wonderful evening with friends."

"OK," she said. "Freshen up my drink, and I'll reserve my excitement for me, myself, and I, as they say."

Getting ready and sharing another drink, we were finally ready to step out looking French Riviera glamourous. Lynn was completely clueless that this evening was all for her. I felt good that I could show her what she meant to me and what she was worth. She had long deserved a night like tonight. For now, though, she was ready to celebrate with Richardson on his special day.

Holding hands, Lynn and I entered the restaurant at 7:30 sharp. As we walked in, she suddenly gripped my hand a bit tighter and commented, "Oh no, Harold, they're all here already." Then, we were directed to our table and proceeded toward them when in unison, everyone stood up and began clapping enthusiastically for us  rather for Lynn, the reason still unbeknownst to her. Even tighter now, Lynn squeezed my hand and asked, if a tiny bit panicked, "Harold, why are they standing for us?"

"Well, Lynn, because you are special and they are excited to count you now as friend," I said.

"OK, but I don't think so," she doubted.

We were seated and everyone had come here dressed exquisitely, especially the ladies in their flowing gowns, glimmering jewelry, and glamorous makeup. Our evening together had begun superbly, and we had a long evening of celebration ahead of us. Waiters served drinks all around, and we all conversed about anything and everything. Notable was the ladies talking about the afternoon spent at the salon and the fun they had shopping. After a while, we began our five-course meal with small dishes of various sorts with the *remise en bouche* appropriately served between each course. After a couple hours of dining and great conversation, the time had approached for dessert.

Richardson asked, "Lynn, what would you like for dessert?"

Lynn, overwhelmed, said, "Richardson, we should be asking you. This is your night."

"No, Lynn, we should be asking you." At that moment, he stood up and extended his hand, directing her to what was occurring behind her. As he did, he announced to everyone, "Lynn, I hope you will allow Harold and all of us, for whom it has been so wonderful to meet you, to wish you an early happy birthday."

I reached over and said again in her ear, "Happy birthday! I do hope you're surprised."

From her puzzled expression, I could see she was indeed surprised. She still hadn't put it all together, I think, because she was focused on it being Richardson's night. But then she turned to see what everyone else was now viewing. She saw the elaborate birthday cake being rolled out on an elegant service table followed by six waiters, walking in pairs, each carrying a bottle of Dom Perignon champagne. Lynn's expression was priceless; she finally understood. It had been a surprise, a surprise all for her. She held it together—mostly.

"Oh, my goodness, Harold! You didn't?" she gasped.

"Oh, yes, I did," I said, as did nearly everyone else, in unison, "YES, HE DID!"

"This is, this was, all for me, Harold?!" she spoke excitedly.

"Yes!" I said. She had gone from a couple moments of an exuberant trembling to hugging me, to kissing me, and to hugging me forever, it seemed. Well, it was at least as long as it took Rob to say, "All right, that's enough," in reply to which some of the ladies said, "Oh, leave her alone." Everyone of course was cheering and laughing, and the spirit of celebration had formally been released upon us all. Up to that point, Lynn had still been holding it together, sort of, but when she released me from her hug and her kiss, her glassy eyes and, in particular, a single tear, betrayed her. Then the tears of joy came bursting forth, as we all stood up and sang "Happy Birthday" to Lynn. A week or so early, it was truly a surprise, and all was captured on video and photos to cherish for the lifetime to come.

"Cut the cake, Lynn," I finally said. She wiped her eyes with a soft, white linen, hand-rolled, edged pocket square I pulled from my jacket breast pocket. Somehow, I knew the soft fine linen would be feel gentle against her soft skin than my silk ones, just in case Lynn's excitement brought forth tears; apparently I had come to know her so well. Love gave her my pocket square and love extended her hand. While Lynn held tightly the tear-moistened pocket square in her left hand, the head waiter gave her a weighted silver knife to make the first cut, and from there, they took care of the rest.

The evening continued and was in every way marvelous, perfect, and of the first and grandest order. Seemed the merriment would never come to an end, and as on such occasions, neither I, nor anyone else, especially Lynn, wanted it to end.

It wound down, finally, with Rob saying, as the elder of the group, "Let such celebrations of and from the heart continue my friends, until we all see each other again. Let us raise a glass to our newfound friend, Lynn, whom we look forward to seeing again if fate would have it so." At that, glasses still full and near empty were raised and the clinking of glasses was heard in the wake of "Here, here." As everyone was sharing hugs, kisses, and goodbyes, I departed from the table momentarily to pay my compliments to the chef and the waiters and to pay the bill. After wanting it to be so perfect for her throughout the week, I likewise was all too pleased to deliver to the head waiter quite a generous tip with delight. His smile confirmed his appreciation, and I again thanked him.

Lynn had surmised why I left the table and when I sat down again, she pinched me and said, "Speaking of being generous, one great surprise deserves more than a great kiss."

"Meaning?"

"You'll see sweetie," she replied.

"Oh, now I'm a sweetie," I joked.

"There you go, again," Lynn replied, somewhere between tears of joy and laughter.

"My girlfriends will not believe this Cinderella-like week here with you, Harold."

"They will. You got the photos and the stories to share with them," I said.

"I do and thank you so much. You really went over the top, Harold, and took me with you. Thank you. I love you more than you'll ever know," she said.

With those words spoken, it was now after 11 p.m., and we decided to make it an early evening. We would see the others when we saw them, for nothing else was scheduled for us to do as a group. Lynn and I thanked everyone for coming, and we retired to our suite for a quiet nightcap and each other. Our night of celebration, imagination, romance, and lovemaking was memorable to say the least, a perfect ending to a perfect beginning, and Lynn made good on her surprise for her sweetie, as it were.

Lynn and I woke up late and dined on a late breakfast on the balcony just before noon. The sun and the beauty of the French Riviera intoxicated us as we sat on the balcony avoiding thoughts of returning home, because tomorrow we would be on a plane back to Philadelphia. We decided we would take the remaining time here to just hang out at the hotel so we'd be somewhat rested and thus ready to fly out tomorrow. Most of all, we would make sure to thank everyone again.

Just then the phone rang. The ladies wanted Lynn to meet them on the beach, which she said she would do in about an hour. I would find the guys after a while to chill for a bit as well, and, of course, they all agreed with me when I said, "I can only imagine the conversation Lynn is going to have with the ladies."

We'd gotten a late start, but we hung out for the balance of the day and once again into the night with the crew and again said our goodbyes. Still at the bar around 11 p.m., we celebrated one last time together. Again, we all hugged, kissed, and said, "See you guys soon." Lynn and I walked toward the elevator as she expressed her excitement about the warmth of the people in Cannes here along the French Riviera, the Côte d'Azur. We packed up our bags, which took a while, and laid across the bed and fell asleep.

# Chapter 35

## BACK IN PHILADELPHIA

Our last day in Cannes, we arose early to do some last-minute shopping. Before returning to the suite, I suggested Lynn order us one last drink at the bar while I cleared up the hotel bill balance. I instructed the attendant at the front desk to use the card on file so the checkout was quick and convenient. The drinks were served by the time I arrived back at the bar with Lynn, and we enjoyed our last drink together in Cannes. Once back in our suite, we called the bellboy to come pick up our luggage since we had completed most of our packing last night. Consequently, we were ready to head to the airport for the long flight home. Fortunately, we would be traveling first class, which would allow us to endure the trip in relative comfort. We left Hotel Martinez, said goodbye to Cannes, and headed home.

While in flight, I could see that Lynn was still riding high, recounting our experiences, the many different people we had met, and, of course, the special times with my friends. The city of Cannes, the hotel amenities, and the first-class beaches were spectacular, and she had loved every minute of it. Her facial and body expressions said it all, and I was so happy that she had enjoyed herself so thoroughly. At one point, Lynn reached over without warning and gave me the biggest kiss, 35,000 feet in the air above the Atlantic Ocean. Of course, I was all smiles.

We landed at Philly International some ten-plus hours later. Our flight was on time, and service was excellent as it had been on the way over, which made the hours float by. Upon arrival, we deplaned, and noticed our driver, dressed in his black suit and tie, who was waiting for us. He was holding up a prominent sign that read "Harold Longston," so I waved to gain his attention, greeted him, and gave him our baggage claim checks. While we waited for him to retrieve the bags and load up the town car, we continued to talk about the highlights of the week.

Within about an hour, we pulled into Lynn's driveway. The driver opened our doors, popped the trunk, and then brought the luggage into the house right behind us. In a festive mood, I tipped him a C-note and thanked him for being prompt and professional.

Lynn turned on the lights, and just like that, the feeling of home filled the room. We were home, finally. Everything seemed normal and in place, although Lynn noticed her trash can lid open.

She said, "I thought I closed that. Oh, I guess I was rushing and didn't do it."

I wondered to myself—so as not to alarm Lynn—whether that nut, Taye Wells, was in here. I led the way as we carried the suitcases upstairs. She unpacked her things while I cased the house. My Special Forces senses were tingling, so I retrieved my Glock from my car and finished inspecting the remainder of the rooms. Everything seemed fine, and nothing else appeared to be out of place or gave any other cause for suspicion. I dismissed the open trash can lid as nothing more than an overlooked task for now. We readied ourselves for bed as it had been a long trip. I fell asleep quickly, but awoke in the middle of the night, restless due to wondering about the latest update on, and whereabouts of, Wells. The house was secure, so I resolved that I would call John Worth first thing in the morning.

The morning came, but neither of us awoke early. Once wide-eyed, I arose and prepared a pot of coffee and poured myself a cup. I told Lynn I was going into the office to check on things, so she came into the kitchen and sat and talked with me for a while before I left. She sounded so profound in letting me know how much she loved me and how she wished we hadn't wasted two years from our first meeting.

"We missed those two years, Harold, but if I get no more time with you than these two years we've had since reconnecting, I want you to know it has been the most fulfilling time I have ever experienced in my life. By the way, you know my son means the whole world to me. I hope you two become friends, soon," Lynn said.

"No need to lament," I said, kissing her on the lips as I stood up from the table. "We will be fine. I should be back soon if there's not much going on. I just want to pick up my mail that's probably waiting for me on my desk. There's probably not much for me to do as I was in communication with the office while we were away, and the staff has had the company operations running like clockwork since we left. I ensured them that their 401ks would be looking good this year, as a little incentive, not that they needed any. There are several meetings, however, with vendors I feel I should attend now that I am back," I added. She walked me to the door and hugged and kissed me for a long time, it seemed, before I headed to my car. I was clearly back home as my radar for Wells was nearly back in full force, and I scanned the street for anything unusual as I departed.

Once I reached the office, the day somehow passed quite rapidly. Before I knew it, the first day back to work was over. I made a call to Yvette to check in with her. We talked for about an hour; though I never told her where I had really been for the past week.

"When will I see you?" she asked.

"Tomorrow. I'll come by after work," I said.

"OK," she said, making some inarticulate sound.

Then it was time to call Lynn. I kept wondering why I was spending this much time with her when I really wanted to be with Yvette—at least I thought I did. It was more than the fact that Lynn excited me; it really was, but I just couldn't put my finger on it. Even in Cannes, I was thinking about Yvette almost as much as I was about Lynn. One day in Cannes, I remembered that I had left Lynn on the beach. When I looked at her from a distance, I could see how the sun was bringing forth those reddish-brown and berry-black skin tones. Her body was oiled, and, wow, she was beautiful. Her full body image beckoned to me. At such times, I found myself sometimes still thinking about Yvette, but Lynn had a loving power that shone through her beauty. She was like an angel one dreams about. With all that in my head, I left Lynn that day to buy Yvette a gift. But while looking, I realized Yvette would not want the gift if she knew the origin of it. So ultimately, I decided not to shop for a gift for her. Anyway, if Lynn could tell that I sometimes had *something* else on my mind, she didn't bring it up at all. Maybe, I was just good at hiding my feelings? Then again, I had lived long enough to know that one had to take the crooked with the straight, as the old folks say. Maybe Lynn had some old folk in her, too. I dialed her number.

"Hello, what's up?" I asked Lynn.

"Nothing, I've unpacked, and I've been sleeping and resting all day. What time are you coming home?" she said without hesitation.

"Home is it?" I smiled and said, "Soon."

"You know what I mean, but you can make it home if you want, dear," Lynn replied.

"I'm a little tired. It has been a full day of moving around," I replied without commenting on her invitation. "Let's watch a movie and pop some popcorn when I get in," I said.

"I got your popcorn," Lynn said, obviously disbelieving I would seriously be interested in just watching a movie and eating popcorn.

"I want to rest a bit, I think. You've been resting all day, Lynn," I replied.

"Well, just get here," she said.

"OK," I said.

Once I arrived at Lynn's house, I showered, put on my robe, turned on a movie, and headed for the king-sized bed that was calling me to sleep, even if usually I heard a different call when I was with her. Later, after I had stretched out, Lynn came up with popcorn, and to my surprise, lay beside me. Soon, we both dozed off and slept with a movie watching us.

I slept soundly through the night, but Lynn thought she heard something and didn't bother to wake me. In the morning, we talked about it, so before I left, I walked throughout the whole house again with my Glock in my unstrapped holster. I was about to look in the utility room when she called me to come get a cup of coffee and stop acting like Shaft.

"OK," I said, and headed upstairs to spend some breakfast time with her before going into the office. We talked for about an hour, and I then left. I reached the office around 9 a.m., and I worked steadily throughout the day and into the early evening. Eventually, enough was enough, and I shut off the lights in the office and locked up. Heading for the parking lot, I noticed something looked different as I got closer to my car. My Jaguar was soaped up and spray-painted, "You're dead brotherman and I'm the one to do it." Also, with that same spray paint was drawn an image of a gun to what I supposed was my head. I instinctively drew my Glock and immediately started looking around.

I called the police, informed them as to who I was, and asked them to go by Lynn's and Yvette's houses and stay with each of the ladies to ensure their safety. They said they would radio for patrol cars and have the officers stake out the houses. I called both Yvette and Lynn to let them know that a police officer was coming and would post themselves outside the house or in the general area to be close at hand. The police told me not to touch anything, and that they would arrive at my office lot in a few minutes, as they had men stationed nearby. I called John Worth to let him know what was happening and what had occurred in the office parking lot with my car.

The police arrived and said they've been driving by regularly. "We don't know how we missed this guy."

A flatbed tow truck ordered by the police came and towed the car to the police compound. They would examine the car for prints and other clues. They were done with me after they validated my license to carry, as I told them I was carrying. I showed them the weapon that was holstered under my suit coat. I called an Uber to get home.

I went inside the house and retrieved my other Glock and strapped it to my left ankle. I was focused on Taye Wells. He just might have returned to Philly after some time had passed since he had been last seen. This dude was ratcheting up the game. People who I loved and wanted to be with were now in genuine danger. Saving their lives was the call, and the only thing that mattered now.

I had to respond and apply some pressure on him somehow. Maybe I could lure him to my place for a face-to-face encounter. It would be me or him. At the least, this would take others out of danger and help remove any feeling that they might be next. He's a punk. Killing a woman. No manhood there. I've got to figure this shit out. I picked up the phone to call John again, but as soon as I did, Lynn's name appeared on my phone.

I answered, "Lynn, what's up?"

In a tone of voice I had never heard from Lynn, ever, she spoke, every word trembling as she spoke it. "Harold, he's here.

He killed the police officer. He's here, baby, and he wants you."
I could hear the fear in her voice, and the faint sobbing she
must have been trying to hold back.

Then Taye must have grabbed the phone because next I
heard, "Hey brotha, I got your woman, Lynn, all five feet and
whatever of her. She's mine, for my pleasure, and I'm going to
kill her for dessert. You should have checked the utility room
this morning. I was going to do both of you, but I wanted a
little more fun. So I slipped back out of your lady's house and
went by your office and fucked up your Jag, your pretty import.
Did you drive Tina around in it? Don't matter, brotha. You
shouldn't park in those corner VIP parking areas. Too bad for
you," he said. Behind the maniacal laughter, the mocking, and
the crazy in his voice, I could hear the anger and the jealousy
that filled him.

He went on, "Then I came back here, slipped back in and
waited. Sorry about the police officer. Oops, dead! But you're
next. If you don't get your ass here in thirty minutes, she's
fuckin' dead and don't you tell a soul or I'll kill her without
hesitation. *You hear me*?" He was shouting now. I imagined
him peering at the phone as if frustrated I wasn't already there.

From the moment I heard his voice, my mind and body
shifted instinctively to a place I hadn't been in a long time. But I
was there now, cold, calm, calculating, almost detached. While
he spoke, I just listened. I knew how this was going to go, and
my mind was making numerous precise calculations so rapidly
that it was as if time was moving in slow motion and I had all
the time in the world. I spoke softly, "I won't. Why would I? I
want to kill you just as badly as you want to kill me." I spoke
with the killer's instinct within me, and I meant every word.

"Now, Mr. Swag, what's you gonna do? You the man with
all the ladies. How you gonna play?" asked Taye. From the
change in his verbiage, his words, his slang, I could tell he was
feeling cocky. I would use that to my advantage.

"Like a brother who's got nothing to lose. Just so you understand. I'm going to kill your neurotic ass more than once," I told him in no uncertain terms.

"Hah hah. You can talk that Special Forces shit all you want. Yeah, Tina told me all about you, your military background and your money, but I'm holding the cards, and I got *your* bitch," he said. The bitterness welling up in him was so evident now. Then he lost it completely. The veil had come off, and he spoke like the truly deranged man he was, "I still hear Tina talking about you, brotha. OK, Tina! It's making me crazy. I just wanna kill you. You can't fuck with me no mo'! Get your ass down here so I can end all this shit."

"Oh, Taye, I'm coming. You can bet on that. I play for keeps when people think they can fuck me over and the play is that you're a dead-ass fucker, for sure," I said. I wanted all his rage to be focused on me with the hopes of him losing some focus that I could use to help me to eliminate him. And I added, "By the way, don't call her a bitch. No man should ever call a woman a bitch. The one a man calls a bitch may become the mother of his children one day, oh, but I almost forgot, you're not a man. You're just a mentally ill, insecure, possessive, neurotic, dick-less, psychopath." I paused to let *that* sink in. Then I asked as calmly as I had been the whole time, "I'm asking one more time. What do you want? You want to live or do you want to die, Taye?"

"I told you. You, brother man, here, ASAP. No more rappin'," he said.

"One last time, you need to let her go, Taye. I'm coming, let Lynn go, and it'll be between the two of us. Stop being dick-less–you murdered a woman and a police officer," I added.

"Oh, I've killed others," he said.

"I don't doubt it, and I don't care. Deal with me man to man. What about it, Taye?" I asked.

"Brother, I still hear that bitch talking about you. It's making me crazy. I want to kill you. You can't fuck with me. Get your ass down here now so I can end all this shit," he shouted.

"Like I said, I'm coming. Oh, you can bet on that," I said again.

The back-and-forth continued for about forty minutes, and still I kept him on the phone talking to me because every minute I did was another minute I had to get closer to her house. From the first moment Lynn spoke and told me he was there, I immediately jumped into my pickup truck and started driving to her house.

I had pulled up about half a block away from her driveway. On the way, I had been running her house's layout through my head in order to determine how he had gotten into her home in the first place. Finally, I concluded it had to be through a basement window, and I was willing to bet that he hadn't locked it after entering.

Meanwhile, I kept the conversation going, saying anything to keep him on the phone, "Hey, Taye Wells, did you kill your mother? Did you let other men call your mother 'bitch' or something else out of her name?"

"What you asking me this kind of shit for?" he said. Taye spoke so angrily, he slurred his words.

"Tina told me stuff about you, too. How do you think I knew your name?" I said.

"*What*? What did she tell you?" Taye insisted.

"Now you wanna know what I know. Don't you?" I said, and I played that back at him for a minute in order to keep his thought pattern disjointed.

"It-it don't make no matter to me. I got your woman," said Taye.

"Hey, Taye, thanks for not calling her out of her name," I said, stroking his ego.

"Hey, I'm a good, brotha. I-I know things. I'm smart," he said defensively.

"Yeah, Tina said, you were a smart dude," I said, adding, "But your ass is crazy, though, brother."

I was now in the basement and had to quietly move up the stairs without him detecting my voice.

"Hey, Taye," I said quietly.

"What now?" he said aloud.

"Can I put you on hold just one minute? I just gotta piss. Just one minute, please, Taye. Can you let a brother piss? Can't you? You got a gun on my lady, and you're controlling everything," I said while hearing rap music blasting in the house. I was sure then Lynn's neighbor must not have been at home because she would have knocked on the door or called the cops by now.

"That's right I'm controlling everything. Do what you gotta do. If you're a long pisser then I'm gonna have to kill her because it sounds like you might not be taking this shit seriously," he reasoned aloud.

"Taye, no, brother, this is going to be quick," I said. At that, I put the phone on mute, crept up the stairs and into the hallway where some rapper's music could be heard clearly, words from men who would be idols, cared about nothing, had no integrity, spoke no truth, painted only disparaging images of me, my people, my culture. I loved music so much, but it seemed too fitting this psychopath was playing the music that characterized him, one unaware of his centralized manufactured consent to self-debasement and of his own self-damming influenced by a global system seeking more than economic control. Need I name this system. For we are in a war against this system for our souls, justice, and humanity.

Where was Professor Griff's conscientiousness that brought brothers to the table to break bread and speak peace and love? Where was Ice Cube, who understood the path to manhood, how actions today change tomorrow? Why was not the edifying knowledge of KRS-One and Sister Souljah blaring? Maybe the situation would be a different one. Maybe so, if he was taught that all innate creativity came from conscious and unconscious thought. Instead, garbage in, garbage out. Taye was lost in a cave of darkness, too late to free himself. How could he know he was playing out an end crafted by oppressors behind masks who distorted history? I would have to kill this man, but Taye was a man out of sync with peace, history, and truth. Music devoid of a message of harmony and of the universal laws, but filled with the numbing of syncopation. Couldn't hear the heart of humanity, never read *The Isis Papers* by Dr. Welsing, nor heard of W.E.B. Du Bois, let alone read *The Souls of Black Folk*. Style and creativity were things to buy not to live out, commodities for which we sold our souls for a measly dollar. Where was Miles Davis, who sought no acceptance but his own and created himself with the mind of the Creator as his guide? On this day, at this moment in time, there was but the lawless emptiness of that rap song to which Taye marched on a path to nowhere but death. Unbeknownst to him, I could see him now, and he was into the words and bouncing mindlessly.

Then I called his name, "Taye Wells." I thought he could not see me, but he caught a glimpse of me in the mirror between the kitchen and the sunroom.

"Don't shoot or I kill her now," he shouted. "Smart, brotha man! You got some special skills. You got in here, kept me talking, I see, but you slipped up, Cool G," he said.

We both had guns pointed, mine at him and his at Lynn.

"You know you gotta slide that piece over here on the floor. Slow-like, and move back. Slide it or she's dead," he said through gritted teeth with a modicum of calm in his voice, almost as if he were finally relieved, even happy to see me.

"Hey! Tina said you were smooth. Maybe I need to call you Silky-smooth," he said. "Hey, Silky, come on over here and have a seat at the island," he added. Then he blurted out, "Tina, stop talking to me about him. I just need to kill the two of them." He was hearing voices in his head, and for the first time, I began to feel like the situation could devolve without explanation or reason even more rapidly than I surmised while I had him on the phone. And then, as if he could read my thoughts, just like that, Taye shot me, hitting the inside of my left arm, just missing my heart, and then almost without further delay, he shot Lynn in the head. She died instantly. Instinctively, I hit the floor behind the island and simultaneously rolled forward up on one knee, drew my Glock from my ankle holster, and shot Taye Wells twice in the heart and once in the head.

Before Taye could hit the floor, I hollered in an inhuman way, like a wounded animal raging against the wild. How I crossed the room, I do not know, but immediately I had Lynn's body in my arms pulling her to me as if so benign a gesture could possibly save her from the tragedy she'd suffered. No, Lynn was dead, and I was there, a puddle of a man, crying and slobbering in pain, holding her tight, as tight as I could, rocking back and forth, back and forth, calling her name. More than I could ever have possibly fathomed seconds before, I needed her to be alive, smiling and laughing with me, but all there was now were thoughts and my arms full of her body that was so empty of her spirit. But her spirit seemingly wrapped her arms around me, held me, and whispered to me, "I loved you, baby, and I love you still." And then she was gone.

Maybe I just needed to believe that's what happened. Either way, I cried to summon Ms. Angel Eyes. I cried for someone to stop the pain, to comfort me as I sat there on the floor with Lynn in my arms. And there I would remain all night, it seemed like anyway, in her blood and in mine, rocking, rocking, rocking.

My Ms. Angel Eyes' voice I heard finally and then her music, and then lyrics, each word. Ms. Angel Eyes gave me then the bluesy sound of Donny Hathaway's "I Love You More Than You'll Ever Know." The music and voices rocked me to my feet with Lynn in my arms, the Glock still in my right hand. I stood over Taye's lifeless body and wondered why, why all this. I looked at him on the floor and emptied the clip into him. His body popped around like popcorn, bullets riddling his corpse. "You're not a brother. You're a damn weak-ass bitch. Never could you be the mother of a child. Fuck you! Shithead!" I tossed the empty weapon onto his chest and carried my love out the door and away from the ugliness.

Looking up at the night sky, grayish-black, beyond gloomy, the clouds loomed ominously as if tragedy had been foretold. They blanketed the night, but the night air of the late evening was surprisingly fresh, and I inhaled for the first time. As I placed Lynn in my truck, I called the police, and told them an officer was dead and my lady was, too. I called John Worth next because I was gonna need his Penn Law School expertise, bowtie and all, for sure.

"Hello," I said.

"What's up man? Hey, you sound awful," John said.

"John, I'm here at Lynn's house. She's dead and so is Taye Wells. He shot me first and killed her with a shot to the head, and then I shot him. He's dead," I said, matter-of-factly, devoid of emotion.

"Hey, man, do you need medical attention?" he asked immediately.

"I was only hit in the left arm. I'll be all right. Lynn is *dead*, John," I said before I wept on the phone like a little brother in the arms of his older brother. He listened without uttering a word. Then, through tears streaming down my face, I said, "She's got a son at the university."

"I'm coming to you. I'll call the police and an ambulance," John said.

"I called the police already," I said.

"I'm on my way. Don't talk to them until I get there. Please don't give any statements, including to reporters that will be showing up soon," he said emphatically.

"Unfortunately, I know the drill. See you when you get here," I said. But before I said goodbye, I gave John some instructions. It may have sounded odd to make such a request at that moment, but I said, "Also, John. I need you to call me in the morning at nine a.m."

"What's up?" John asked.

"I got some cleaning up to do. My life and relationships are not looking very bright, but I'm going to make some changes starting right now. I want you to call the judge and ask for a meeting with him, ASAP. I'm taking guardianship of Lynette. Can you handle that for me?" I said.

"You sure you want to be the father?" John asked in an overly concerned voice.

"No, I'm just going to be the financial person that provides for her. I'm taking her to Diane to raise. Diane will be a great mother to little Lynette. Diane and I were lovers a while back, and she's a successful corporate executive and married. It will be a stable environment for little Lynette, and Diane wants a child. She either couldn't have one or just didn't have one earlier in her life. I want this for the both of us. We have talked about it. I know now that our meeting was not coincidental and getting back together was for this reason," I explained. "John, you got to make it happen like in the next twenty-four to forty-eight hours. I'm asking you to move the bureaucratic hurdles that might bar the way. Call in your political chips and get it done. Lynette needs a new mother to care for her. I'll be Uncle Harold to her forever and for always. Let them know. You know money is not a problem," I elaborated, in a pleading voice.

"OK, all right, Harold. I'll make it happen. You have my word, whatever it takes," he said.

After he spoke, I realized that I didn't know if he knew he could really do it or not, and I also knew it was not in his nature to promise me such things, but I appreciated that he said he would make it happen, and I thanked him for it. He reiterated before hanging up that I shouldn't leave the scene, and should stay until the police got there, reminding me again that they may want to take me downtown. John was going to call the chief of police now to request that they let me go home after he got there and spoke to cops on the scene as it was clearly a case of self-defense. Hanging up with John and thinking about Lynn, my tears started falling again. I rolled my head over to meet hers, and we slept again, one more time, as we waited for the police.

## Chapter 36

# POLICE AND REPORTERS ON THE SCENE

The police officer tapping on the truck's window woke me up, and immediately he launched into his questions, which he asked through the window almost without waiting for me to answer, let alone open the door or the window. The need to think made me relive everything again while trying to refrain from answering any questions and yet trying to communicate that my lawyer would be here shortly. But it was no use.

Finally, I said, "Hold up, please! If I could get out of the vehicle, I would appreciate it." As I exited the truck, I realized it was one of the policemen whom I had gotten to know over the weeks of dealing with this manhunt. During my comings and goings from Lynn's house, we had conversed a number of times since they had started patrolling the area.

"Oh, sure, Mr. Longston, I didn't realize it was you. I'm sorry. What in god's name went on here, sir?" he said, noticing my clothes were covered in blood.

I wasn't supposed to answer any questions, but in the moment, I just said, "Hell! And I killed a devil."

"You mean that Taye Wells fellow?" asked the officer.

"Yes," I said.

"We'll want to ask you some questions, but first is there anyone else in the house?" he asked.

"No, no one else. My attorney is on his way here, and I know he put a call into your chief," I replied.

While we were talking, the other police officers roped off the crime scene and kept the reporters back. Several detectives or police officers eventually went inside.

"Just want to let you know a detective will come out soon to talk with you," the officer added.

"You should let him know that I'm not talking until my attorney gets here," I reminded him.

"OK. I understand. I'll let the detectives know, Mr. Longston," he said, and then joined the other officers to manage the scene and the crowd.

About fifteen or twenty minutes later, John was on the scene. He took control of the questions and made the ordeal so much easier for me. I think the police knew that they kind of blew it when they did not successfully apprehend this neurotic dick-less murderer on several prior occasions, and now they were being as understanding as possible, seeing the destruction that resulted from it.

I managed to answer all of the detective's questions, prompted by John. I explained in detail what occurred in the house and about our return from Cannes, a couple of days ago. During that exchange, I was rrunaware of a reporter from Channel 10 standing nearby, who overheard a bit about our time in Cannes. John told me that was too much information and to just stick to what happened here and at the office. Ultimately, the detectives were satisfied, and I would be allowed to go home after the EMT inspected and cleaned the gunshot wound.

"You're lucky. Two or three inches over and it would have been your heart," the EMT said.

After the wound was treated by the EMT, I stuck around for a bit as I first wanted to make sure Lynn's body was properly cared for in an ambulance and ready to leave when I was. We were leaving together in my mind, and I believed that was the way her spirit wanted it, too. Before we left though, I went to the ambulance to kiss Lynn one more time. As I turned to head back to my truck, uncontrollable tears, pain, and outrage swarmed about me. I couldn't hold it back, and so as I walked, those tears and feelings weakened me to the point that I collapsed. John suggested that another ambulance take me to the emergency room. I didn't argue. They put me on a gurney, pushed me into the ambulance, and hooked me up to whatever. I closed my wet eyes and listened in my head to Luther singing, "Because It's Really Love" as I heard both ambulances pull out together. I smiled through the tears and was in some way comforted by the conviction that I knew why we went to Cannes. There Lynn and I experienced our grandest time and her birthday together, and I had come to know unquestionably how much I loved her.

# Chapter 37

## YVETTE

They kept me overnight at the hospital. I awoke to the morning news with my face all over the television and on every major channel. Lying there in the warmth of the hospital room, I was now faced with another dilemma, how would I explain any of this to Yvette. When I paged the nurse's station, a nurse came rather quickly and asked what was wrong.

I told her that nothing was wrong, but that I would just like to know where my phone was. "Was it brought up from the emergency room with my things?" I asked her.

"Mr. Longston, I think your personal items were placed in the nightstand next to your bed," she said.

I looked. My things were in the drawer. I thanked the nurse and apologized for disturbing her.

She was very polite and said, "No problem. We're here for you."

I turned on the phone and waited for it to power up. Immediately the notification of calls rang out, and the call list populated with everyone who had been trying to reach me. I scrolled down the list, and it seemed everyone had tried to call me—everyone except Yvette. I decided I wasn't going to call her from this hospital bed. The news had certainly let her know that I was all right. I was being portrayed as a hero, the guy who took down the murderer, Taye Wells. I didn't feel like a hero, for sure, because I was not one. The media was always hyping shit up. The reality was that people were killed and lives had been impacted forever, for better and for worse. Whatever the news made it out to be, that was it. So, I moved on beyond the hype to what I was going to say to Yvette, that is, if she would even speak to me again. For the moment, I was at a loss for what to say to her.

Fortunately, I remembered that I wanted John to call me about Lynette. It was a welcomed distraction. I lay back in the bed and considered what I was going to do for and with Lynette, a three-year-old little girl without a mother or a father. Why would Tina give me such a responsibility? I grew up with wonderful parents and knew how important it was to have adults who were loving and caring and who had expectations and who placed hurdles, low and high, for me to clear, but who coached me all along the way. Maybe it was as simple as that; I would be a coach, a surrogate parent of sorts for Lynette. I had no doubt that Diane would be a wonderful mother to her. I wouldn't be surprised if she quit her job altogether and concentrated on Lynette's care. In fact, after all that's occurred in her short life so far, she would likely need all the love, stability, and mothering Diane could share.

Fortunately, Diane was the mothering type. I remembered during our relationship, I had to say to her more than once, "I'm not your child," or "I had a mother already and a great one, I don't need another." We would laugh, and she would invariably say, "You think that's what I'm doing?" but she already knew it. She was self-aware like that. It was one of the qualities that made her so endearing. I would say, "What do you think? You should just adopt a child." She'd reply, "Maybe someday, Harold. I'm too busy now and too old." I'd say, "You're never too old or too busy to care for the young or the old, sweetheart," to which she always agreed. Yes, Diane would be the perfect mother for Lynette.

Life seemed to be hitting me now with some hooks and straight body shots—or was it that I'd been missing those hits, slipping and sliding, weaving and bobbing, all this time? If so, I was now in the thirteenth to the fifteenth rounds, and it was imperative that I rise above everything much like Ali and Frazier had done in those last rounds. It was like an out-of-body experience seeing them fight those rounds all from a force within that brought them out of themselves, being themselves, conditioned mentally and spiritually, willing their bodies to do on-command all that was needed to win. And for me, they were both winners, the two that history would crown true winners. If no Frazier, no Ali. If no Ali, no Frazier.

It has been said about those final grueling rounds, that is when the body and the brain are the most susceptible to injury and long-term damage. I was in those rounds and being hit with boulders. Get up Harold! You have life and one to live. Until now, life had given me a pass to run the hall of the world peering in classroom doors, smiling at girls, breaking into vending machines in the student union center. Now, though, I was grown, running through women's hearts and breaking into their vending machines. Well, the school principal of time had just gotten me by the collar, and so now here I lay on my back luckily, inches from laying on a gurney in a morgue. Instead, I was here in the warmth of a hospital room with all of my thoughts. Tina was gone. Lynn was gone. Yvette, doubtless, was feeling lied to. Diane was replaying why she kicked me out of her house and how my, or rather our, egos couldn't get out of our own way to see each other as two people in love. And then there was Lynette, representing all the responsibilities left and unaddressed in my life. They say time has a way of changing things. Was it too late? I could hear my father saying, 'It's never too late to start, son, so get up and get your work done."

Just then my thoughts turned to Ms. Angel Eyes—or had she turned my thoughts to her?

"Ms. Angel Eyes, is that you?" I asked.

"**You know it's me! How are you, sweetheart?**" she asked, smiling.

"Getting better," I said, not yet defeated, but not yet feeling I would or could be victorious, and she knew me well enough to know exactly how I was feeling.

"**And you will**," she said, "**get better**." Her eyes explained her meaning.

I looked into them, knowing I could not look away, and knew I would be victorious, even if I didn't yet know how. "Yes, I will," I said confidently. There was no other way to answer her, and I could hear my mother quipping, "Speak those things that be not as though they were."

"I'm getting out of here in the next few hours, Ms. Angel Eyes. Truly you were heaven sent. I never asked if you were the one the songwriter wrote about and Little Jimmy Scott sang about so beautifully," I said.

"**And I'll never tell. Go now. A lady like me will always be around. Listen closely to the music because the answers are always in the great music**," she said.

And with the will within me and the encouragement and wisdom of those who'd come before me, slowly, steadily, I got up and dialed John's number. It rang a while, long enough that I anticipated the call going to voicemail.

As it rang, Ms. Angel Eyes continued, "**I've been watching from afar. You know, I don't come around when you're into your bad-boy habits state of mind, and it seems you've been there lately playing in your diversions, and even though floundering, thinking it's all good**," said Ms. Angel Eyes.

"Yeah, I've been doing a little something, I suppose. The Pied Piper meanwhile has come and taken away ones whom I have loved," I said.

"**Harold, we all get taken eventually. It's whether we all have paid our Earthly bills. Otherwise, he comes to collect in** ways you might not like. The knowing is in whether we live a full and just life during the journey," Ms. Angel Eyes shared, asking then, after a pause, "Well, are you ... living a full and just life?"

I was honest when I answered, "Most of the time I believe I am. Sometimes I feel like I need a hand, though."

"Well, that's why I keep an eye on you, to give you a hand. I'm your muse, Harold. I got your hand, but you're just like a little boy wanting to shake loose and run and play 'sometimes' as you say. Harold, you haven't lived a bad life. In fact, it has been good, except for those tendencies of yours, which I know are about your search of the heart. But darling, you still got a lot more living to do. The question always is, how are you going to live it."

"I think I know now," I said.

She looked at me a long time before speaking again, as if studying me. Did she believe me? Maybe she wanted to believe me. When she broke her silence, she held my hand, and then she said, talking to that little boy whose hand she'd been holding, "Then good! Get out of this bed; you're all right. You need to get busy. There's a lot on your plate." She rested her eyes as she finished her words and let my hand go before she opened her eyes and kissed me on the cheek. When I looked again, she was gone like a faded whisper.

The phone was still ringing and seemed like it had been ringing so very long. I started to hang it up, but then, "Hello," a voice said on the other end. "Hey, Harold, sorry, I just hung up with the people over at Domestic about Lynette, and I spoke earlier with the judge. The judge and I have had several conversations and a few influential people, political and otherwise, made calls to him as well. I think it's going to happen, but I need until late tomorrow, and then you can pick up Lynette. I'll handle the paperwork."

"Brother, I owe you big time. Thanks," I said with a sign of relief.

"You're doing what's right so I'm all in with you, and everything is right, you and Diane, I mean. You both have the financial resources, and Diane is married. By the way, don't you mess that up, Harold," John said, and he spoke those last words in a sobering voice.

"I know. I know. No, I won't. I get it now," I said.

"Lynette is a big winner here. You're laying the tracks for her to have a good life," he said. Then he added, "I'm proud of you, brother."

I said, "Thanks, but we're not at the finish line yet."

"I'll get you there. Quietly, the political factions were thankful to you for removing Taye Wells from society. I leaned on that and your private history of helping in the community with your charitable foundations. They didn't really know about them or that you had established such well-funded city projects all these many years," John explained.

"We had agreed to keep that private," I snapped.

"And, Harold, I have until now," John retorted, not trying to be rude.

"I'm sorry. I know you have, John. Besides, I said to get it done by whatever means. I know you did what you felt you had to do. So, thanks again," I assured him.

"Of course, Harold. Now, I'll be in touch with you tomorrow, late morning," he said.

"Cool. Let me call Diane, now," I said and then said goodbye.

I knew it was perhaps the end of one relationship as a lover and the beginning of another with Diane, as a co-parent of sorts, and as the previous one died away, thoughts of us together raced through my mind, maybe for the last time. As for now, I was about to deliver to her a three-year-old. Storks drop off children in many different ways; this way I never would have imagined. Fortunately, it would end with a smile and with laughter, something she and I were always able to do. Certainly, such smiles and laughter were things I could use right now.

"Hello, Harold," Diane said.

"Hey, Diane, are you in D.C. tomorrow late afternoon, early evening, possibly?" I asked.

"Yes, Harold. Why? What's up?" she asked.

"Good, I'm coming to D.C. to see you. It's important," I said.

"OK, but can you tell me what's up?" she asked again.

"You'll see when I get there. Be patient. I'm your sugar daddy, right?" I asked knowingly.

"I guess so," she sounded unsure. Maybe the secrecy was too much, but she replied, "Call me and I'll meet you."

"OK, Diane, will call around one or two o'clock or when I'm on the road," I responded and hung up.

With John taking care of the custody matter for Lynette and me planning to meet Diane tomorrow, I was ready for a drink and some rest. I didn't want to talk to anyone, but I glanced at my phone anyway. No calls still from Yvette. I was going to deal with the remaining situations one at a time. Lynette and Diane first and then finally, Yvette, a heavy lift indeed. For the moment, I decided to go home, leave the noise, the press, and my pain on the shelf. I just prayed that love found its way back to me.

When I left the hospital, I departed a bit euphoric. The Lynette and Diane matter was being working out. Tina could rest. Her baby girl would be loved and would live the life she dreamed of for herself. My truck was likely still at the scene of the crime or impounded by police for evidence. I didn't know. Didn't much care. I called for a town car to pick me up and drive me home. Alone in the backseat, it was daylight, but seemed like it was dark outside; maybe it was the pall over the rapidly changing landscape of my life, of my whole world in fact. My eyes followed the road as we traveled, as I felt the loneliness of a seemingly endless journey consume me.

As I arrived home, I tried to press forward, tried to handle the monumental tasks before me in a now-drunken state of loneliness. I hadn't had a drink, yet I felt woozy. Getting through my front door seemed burdensome suddenly, and I felt myself walking painfully slow, laboriously, as if trying to turn the world with each step. As I struggled through the doorway, Ms. Angel Eyes touched me for the second time today saying, "**Son, you're feeling lost, you've started to drift, and your feet are sinking in muddy waters. Lynette, Diane, those were easy. Yvette, though, hmmm. Well, son, I don't really have to tell you about that one, do I?**"

"No, you don't. You know, Ms. Angel Eyes, I've been searching for and am still pleading for a tomorrow, a tomorrow I know not how to find, but for some reason, I just know it's before me."

"**Harold, Yes, it is. But understand that in this infinite universe, with its changing personalities, it is truth that is unchanging. Life's journey requires us to seek that higher consciousness, to understand those jazz vibrations within us all that release us from the physical in order to see beyond to what is before us. Your many is one, and that one is Yvette. Those ladies you have romanced, or as you would say, sweet romanced, all these many years are one, she is, and they have, been your dreams. But, my son, you must come out of your dream. Lift your head and know that she waits for you. The lotus flower blossoms above the water in the sunlight, but its roots are in the muddy waters of darkness. You have matured into the man who can love without rules. I can say what a man, what a man twice, you have become. Guessing no longer and hiding no more in insecure dreams. You have realized what is good for you, and she has been there since** the first hello." Ms. Angel Eyes spoke as if recounting a love story.

"Yvette is the one!" I said, surprised to hear her say all that after so much had transpired.

"**Yes, indeed, but so much more,**" she whispered. "**In her quiet way, she's calling you to fall in love for real and to hear her voice. Listen, you can hear the music. Do you hear them singing? I'm playing their songs now. Hear them now, or you'll never hear them. Our times are but for a time, and that time is for living. Let your spirit live and learn to discern those spirits all about you. The songwriters are writing, and the singers are singing their songs to you and her. She will hear them, but time is needed. She doesn't want to be lonely. You hear what I'm telling you,**" Ms. Angel Eyes gently chided.

"Ms. Angel Eyes, I hear you, and I can see clearly, and the understanding is lovely," I answered.

"**The end of the journey is near, because you know, as she has long known, you complete her, and she, you. Like the nights complete the days, as a seedling needs the rain to grow, and yes, as the singer needs the songwriter,**" said Ms. Angel Eyes. "**My friend Donny Hathaway recorded a song years ago. Its lyrics were written by the songwriter Leon Russell, 'A Song for You.' It's many a man's journey. You have the CD. So, I'll finish with this. Know that life is music, though not all of it is great. Harold, you must find the great music of life and in your life,**" counseled Ms. Angel Eyes.

"The great Mr. Donny Hathaway, here, hanging out with Ms. Angel Eyes, how are you sir?" I asked.

"I'm fine," Donny answered. "Harold, know this, my younger brother—you said it in the beginning—I think your words were, love is 'You and me now wove into *we* finding ecstasy.' Find the *we*, the great music found in our living and in our imaginations."

"That's deep, Mr. Hathaway," I said.

292

"Peace be with you, brother," he replied.

"And peace be unto you, as well, Donny, if I may call you, Donny," I said.

"Sure," he replied.

That night, I slept and dreamt and listened to their great music that soothed, if just a bit, the malaise, and dissipated the cloud over me. I was grateful to Ms. Angel Eyes for taking my hand in my time of need.

# Chapter 38

## UNCLE HAROLD AND LITTLE LYNETTE

I was tired when I woke up some time after 10 a.m. I readied myself for the day. A big day awaited Lynette. She'd been through an unimaginable change and probably had no idea what life would be like with her mother gone forever. She might still be asking for her mother, as far as I knew. I had to ensure that this next change, this next adjustment, went well. I called John and suggested that the person with whom Lynette had spent the most time make the trip to D.C. with me and be prepared to stay during the transition period. I said I would double her pay, add a bonus, and pay her lodging; whatever was needed and for however long it took for Lynette to feel comfortable with her new family, I would take care of it. I was sure she would be staying with Diane and her husband, who lived in a huge home on their estate.

When I spoke to John, I discovered we were already on the same page. "Hey, I was about to call you about the very same concern," John said. He added, "In fact, the only way I was able to make it happen was if you would agree to have the temporary guardian travel with you today and stay until she was no longer needed and that you would cover all of the expenses," John said.

Happily, I said, "John, no problem, we're on the same page. Please have the people at Domestic refer to me as Lynette's

Uncle Harold." I asked John to let them know that would mean a lot to me.

He agreed and said, "I will text you the address where you can pick up Lynette and her caregiver. Be prepared to arrive by one p.m."

"Great! I will be ready. And again, great job, John. I'm exceedingly thankful," I said.

"You are welcome," replied John.

"Let me call Diane now to inform her of our schedule today," I said.

"OK, Harold, all the best," John said. We said goodbye and hung up.

I immediately dialed Diane, who picked up on the first ring.

"Hello, Diane, how are you?" I asked.

"Great! You still coming to D.C.?" she asked with anticipation.

"Yes, Diane, I am coming. I will be on the road sometime around one p.m., and I will have Lynette with me," I said proudly.

"Harold, you're bringing the baby?!" she said. "That's so nice. I look forward to meeting her."

"Yes, and I'm bringing her for you to raise, Diane. To love and educate her. Time to be a mother. Is this cool with your husband? If not, I'll keep her," I said emphatically.

"What? How, Harold?" I heard her say, before the faint sound of a strong woman overwhelmed with joy and surprise was heard weeping. Through those tears she mustered her lovely fortitude, "No, you won't, Harold! She's mine!" she said, offering up some laughter through the tears. I just smiled on the other end of the line and felt good about getting this right.

"Oh, my Lord, Harold, just how did you manage it? I heard about you and your friend on the news. I'm genuinely sorry for your loss. After hearing about that though, I figured anything that would happen regarding the child would be mired down in red tape. Honestly, with everything you had happening, I didn't honestly expect to hear from you for quite a while. I was so surprised when you called the very next day. I couldn't believe it," she explained. She was more composed now. And as if the rush of emotion opened up the dam, she mused for a moment, "Harold, why didn't *we* make it? Is it too late for us?" I heard her, but in the moment, I just let her words linger and never answered her. I understood where it was all coming from, so I just kept the focus on Lynette.

"Yeah, not my choice of making the evening news, but that incident changed me. I know you so well that I immediately called my lawyer and told him what I wanted and to make it happen by any means necessary, legally of course," I said with a chuckle. In the next moment, however, I said with my heart full of love for her, "Diane, in one sense, perhaps, our time has passed, but in another, this child will be our bond forever, even being apart."

With equal heart and her unique tenderness, she replied, "Harold, I understand our love never ended, and it never will. You have always found a way to complete me, and you have again. I will raise Lynette as if she were ours."

"I know, but I'm just excited to be Uncle Harold," I said.

"OK, Uncle Harold is it. Thank you, my love. You got your shit with you, but I can't love another like I love you," she acknowledged and confessed.

"By the way, I know you can handle it, but I had my attorney draw up papers securing Lynette financially," I explained.

"You didn't need to do that. I'm well off. I might even quit my job and spend my time with Lynette," Diane said.

I continued, "Also, the courts will grant you complete custody of her since the judge honored Tina's dying request. My attorney moved mountains to make this adoption happen."

"You were able to do that? You knew I wasn't going to say no, didn't you!"

"I know you very well, Diane. That's all," I responded.

"Yes, you do, and you have made me happier than you will ever truly know. If I never get another gift in life, I'm complete with her. A child is a gift that just keeps giving," she said.

"OK, then you have a wonderful gift from me to you, but I am the one who's really receiving the gift because I am able to do right by Tina and to cement our bond forever, and because I love you, Diane. See you in D.C. in a few hours," I said almost matter-of-factly, and I knew she understood. "Text me where you would like us to meet," I added.

"At the house of course. I'll have it all worked out with my husband. Sometimes, things are meant to be even before we can see them. His first child died at birth, and her name was Lynette. Imagine that, Harold. Can you believe it?" she said, her voice filled with wonder and joy. "Just call me when you're close," she concluded.

"OK. I will. By the way, I almost forgot. There is one small condition. I agreed to make this happen quickly, but it's at my expense," I started to explain.

"Oh, no, don't disappoint me," Diane said. Her joy seemed to have left her a moment, as if worried it was too good to be true after all.

"No, no, what I mean is that I'm coming with the lady who has been caring for Lynette. She'll have to stay a couple of weeks with you during the transition so that it'll be less of a shock to the baby," I elaborated.

"Oh, goodness. You had me worried for a moment. That will not be a problem at all. She can stay in the carriage house," Diane said.

"OK, then she's yours, my dear Mother Diane," I said exuberantly, matching Diane's excitement.

"It sounds grand, and by the way, my love, you still have me," Diane said, and again I heard the sound of crying, tears of joy.

"I need to hang up so I can go pick them up if you want to see the baby today," I said, changing the subject.

"OK, well then, you better get moving," Diane said.

I ended the call with a smile on my face and checked the time in order to plan the remainder of my morning. It was getting close to noon, so I fixed a cup of coffee, said my prayers of thankfulness, and kept it moving. Through joy of the morning, though, thoughts of Yvette asserted themselves, but I needed to stay focused. Diane, Lynette, and Uncle Harold. I didn't see it coming, but I liked it. I was running toward something somewhere. I didn't know what, but I was good with being part of the journey. I finished my coffee and jumped into my 1957 Thunderbird E-Code, a rare classic to travel, but changed my mind, turned around, and decided to drive the Jaguar, having gotten it back finally from the compound. Fortunately, I had my guy come by the house and detail the car so it glistened inside and out. Speeding off, I headed for the center to pick up Lynette and the caregiver.

Once there I met up with John. I was introduced to everyone, including little Lynette, as her uncle. An hour later, we were packed and on our way to D.C. for the start of Lynette's new life, home, and parents. I wasn't sure how comfortable Lynette would be with me, a stranger, but believing that I was family—even if she didn't really understand how—allowed her to relax and just be a kid. Consequently, if unexpectedly, we talked, laughed, and played games the entire way to D.C. Three hours later, we knocked on Diane's front door, and the next phase of this adventure began.

When Diane opened the door, it was as if she opened it to an entirely new world of possibilities of love, life, family, and more. Her bright countenance said it all. She greeted everyone with hugs and kisses. Then, she introduced us to her husband, Walt McCormack, a tall, distinguished gentleman, whom I would come to learn was quite amiable. However, Walt was not what I expected. He was reserved and projected a strong appearance in our presence, but an obvious weakness showed through—some health issues lurked behind that façade, and I knew why Diane came to Philly to see me. I quickly moved away from my thoughts and joined in everyone's excitement for Lynnette. We all moved into the living room while Walt went to the car to bring in their bags. There wasn't much, but he insisted.

After about an hour of pleasantries, we took a tour of the house and some of the estate, then returned to the spacious family room at the back of the house. Diane and Lynette talked about which room could be Lynette's and about decorations. Meanwhile, the caregiver asked about schools, and Walt shared that there were a couple of private schools in the area with which they made some inquiries in preparation for her arrival. After a while, I asked Walt if we could speak privately. He agreed without hesitation and led the way to his finely appointed study, which was more like a private library. Once inside, with the door closed gently behind us, I spoke promptly and from the gut. "You OK with this, Walt?" I spoke firmly and looked him in the eye. I wanted to know, needed to know, not only if he was on board, but also if Lynette would be in a home where both parents were invested in loving this little girl.

In a matter-of-fact voice, he said, "Oh, very much so, Harold. You just might have saved our marriage, to tell you the truth. I'm thankful to have a daughter, aga …," he paused and then just said, "to have a daughter," before continuing. "I understand you and Diane's history. It was before I met her. 'You take the cat with the kitten and sometimes a stray cat,' the old folks would say." I got a good feeling from him, and I appreciated his remarks, which let me know he was comfortable with me, Lynette, and these developments.

"I get that," I said, "and I'm happy for the two of you. I won't interfere."

"Thanks. I appreciate that," he said and immediately asked, as if he had forgotten his manners, "Can I offer you a drink?"

"Sure, I'll drink whatever you're having," I said to be polite.

"Oh, I don't drink. I'm diabetic, but please do not let that stop you. What will you have?" he asked insistently.

"I understand. In that case, I'll have a double of the Gentleman Jack I see on your shelf, please," I replied. I stayed late into the evening before leaving. I arranged to come back in several days to see Lynette. I didn't want her to feel abandoned. For all I knew, I was the only family she'd ever met, and I didn't want her to think I was disappearing. We all agreed that I would come back, and I was leaving confident that Lynette was in excellent hands.

I gave Lynette a big hug, and she said, "See you soon, Uncle Harold."

Hearing those words from such a tender and innocent child brought tears to my eyes and caused me to leave abruptly. Everyone noticed the tears as I was leaving but said nothing.

Once in my car, I sat for a couple of minutes letting the tears fall. I noticed Diane looking out the window waving, smiling, and giving me a thumbs-up. I waved back and slowly backed out of their driveway and headed for Philadelphia.

I decided to take the back roads north instead of I-95, the major interstate highway. The ride was quiet and long going back, but I needed that time to think. About halfway home, apparently due to being buried in my thoughts, I veered off the road and into a ditch. The car came to a jarring stop, so immediately I took stock of the situation, made sure I was all right as best as I could tell, and then exited the car. Slowly, I walked around and inspected it for damages. Right behind me, another car stopped to check on me. The driver was a woman, a physician as it turns out, and she was very concerned as she thought she may have caused me to veer off the road. I heard her first question clearly as she asked it so sincerely, "Are you

OK?" As she continued to approach, she asked, it seemed, a hundred questions repetitively.

I was OK, and I replied, "I'm fine."

As it was now dark, the lady asked me to drive to a Starbucks about a mile up the road so she could better determine that I was OK. She said she would follow directly behind me, so out of an abundance of caution, I agreed and within a few minutes we were in Starbucks parking lot and headed inside for coffee. Seated across from each other, she finally introduced herself as Dr. Vivian Jones. I told her my name and that I was traveling up from D.C. to Philadelphia. I only let her know that I was dropping off my niece, little Lynette, to stay with family in D.C. As we started this conversation, she quickly interjected and asked, "Do you mind if I touch you?"

I said, "What did you have in mind?"

She laughed and rephrased, "I would like to examine you. Check your pupils just to make sure you are really OK. I know you're a guy. You said you are OK, but I would feel better if I could take a second to check you out."

"That's not as much fun," I said with a knowing smile, "but sure. I still have a ways to go, so, yes, it might be a good idea to know that I am actually all right." I was surprised at how quickly she retrieved a pen light from her purse with one hand and placed the other one on the side of my face as if to hold it steady.

"Look left. Look right," she said in a firm but gentle tone. She switched hands and proceeded to check the other eye. Ironically at such a moment, I realized just how attractive she was, and she had even more of my attention now took I the opportunity to admire her body, all of it. We conversed for about an hour over a cup of coffee, and there was no doubt. She was awfully nice, which is to say, put together. That was my life. By way of nearly crashing on the side of the road, I would meet a physician who had a sexy body, was intelligent, and was beautiful. Once the coffee was finished, we exchanged information. Just before we both got back on the road, she made me promise to call her to let her know I had arrived home safely. I promised her I would, and just as she had insisted I stop at Starbucks, she doubled down on my promise to call her by saying, "If you don't call, Harold, I will call you."

"Vivian, I'll call you and thank you for being so concerned," I said, then I noticed, somewhat strangely or eerily, that she looked a lot like Lynn with an inviting sweet smile and body gestures that said, "You found me, come love me." Or was it my imagination?

Was it my imagination that I wanted her to be Lynn for an instant, who I wanted, and was missing, and will miss, so dearly? Unable to release myself at times from all our moments together, I recognized I was more wounded than I had realized. The hurt came down upon me like a torrential storm, riveted me to the pain of so profound a loss as I had not known, then gutted and afflicted me. The loss of this love, now palpable, made me understand finally that my time together with Lynn would be no more.

Was it my imagination or my feeling that was so painful, too painful for me now to think, think about us beyond a minute or more at a time? Was it now having to exist apart from this love affair between us, from this love affair that was yet unfulfilled, this love affair of which we wanted more that was driving me crazy? I could feel her touch and smell her intoxicating perfumes, and I could hear her voice calling me to come near to see her vividly in all her beauty. Whether it was my imagination, my feeling, or my love for her, they all reminded me and called to me to remember what we promised each other, to hold each other in our arms forever, and I would. Lynn was the goodness that a man yearns for in a woman. And perhaps, she'll become someone's muse somewhere in this timeless universe.

Dr. Vivian Jones was not Lynn, but she was fine.

Back on the road heading north, I thought of my Ms. Angel Eyes and if she would be proud of me and my newly developing relationship with little Lynette. Hours later, I pulled into my driveway, and immediately texted Vivian, "Home safely." What a day it had been, so long. I lumbered into the house, showered, and stretched out in the bed, which would be my friend until I woke up the next morning.

# Chapter 39

## THE ANSWER

*I will find what I'm after;*
*The search began before I knew myself.*
*I was placed on a path preordained before time*
*and the accumulation of spiritual wealth,*
*Looking, wandering, truly lost, and wanting to be found.*
*Not knowing what I'm after, but seeking because*
*human nature requires that of us,*
*My search is for you, an unbeknownst traveler on*
*and riding upon life's uncharted grounds.*
*A world of complexities, a world given and*
*to be shared, to seek, to understand.*
*WHAT?*
*That is the question that sends me forward*
*to acquire and to seek the answer.*
*Knowledge of self and that of the collective,*
*We the People, and to find me,*
*No, us.*
*Individualism is important, but a myth, a moral*
*understanding of collective cooperation for our existence,*
*A world of truth, and fairness, not one of serfdom,*
*I will find what I'm after, but it can only be*
*from finding who I am from within.*

I awoke around 9 a.m. and began my day. I searched for my phone to call Yvette. She didn't pick up. I understood. I felt miserable, but I decided to head to the office to work nonetheless. On the way to the car, I suddenly remembered the bracelet and went back in the house to get it. It was still nicely wrapped. The surprise, I guessed, would not be one now, with everything that had happened. *C'est la vie,* but I had bought it for her.

I immersed myself in the backlog of files that needed my attention until about four o'clock and then decided to head over to *South* on North Broad Street, Philly's best place for great food, drinks, and my favorite live jazz. I decided to sit at the bar and have a late lunch. I guess I was looking out of it, because the owner of the restaurant saw me at the bar and came over. "Harold, you're not your usual self."

"I'm sure you have seen the news," I said.

"Yes, I have, my brother, and I'm sorry. If I can share this with you, and it's a simple thing, I found taking a drive outside the city and digging the countryside works wonders. It clears the head and allows one to focus much better," he said.

"I just might do that before I stop by a friend's house," I replied. The countryside was home for me during my youth.

With a pat on the shoulder, he moved on. My lunch was served, and I ate my meal with a glass of wine. Then I paid my bill, tipped the bartender, and left. The drive outside the city I would do. Then, I would end up at Yvette's front door. Driving through the countryside calmed me. I was at peace and thought about what I did to Yvette. If it were me, I'd be pissed off, too. I was prepared to accept whatever the outcome, if she would even answer her door, assuming she was home. I made several more calls, but still no answer. Riding back to the city, Ms. Angel Eyes appeared and was sitting in the passenger seat.

"Hello. You must have known that I needed my muse," I said.

"I am your muse, baby, and you need to hear Phyllis Hyman's 'The Answer Is You.' The answer is the two becoming one. It's universal, Harold," said Ms. Angel Eyes affectionately.

"I love Phyllis," I said.

"Yes, I know, but you need to focus on Yvette," she said. "You messed up, and only time and the music of life will allow her to see that you're the answer. To find completeness is rare. She found it late in her life. Having things her way for so long has made it difficult for her to accept finding a man who shared everything and didn't want anything except to love her and to be loved. The two of you share a weakness: you attract people easily; therefore, the getting is easy for the two of you. But are they whom you wanted after you got them? That's the problem. It may work and will work for a while, but is it what you really want? Now, she doesn't want anyone but you, although she may be with someone else for a while, because she doesn't know how to backtrack when she has always gone forward. The way one runs from the poverty of their youth, she is fearful of going back, even looking back. This time, though, if she doesn't backtrack, she'll run past true love and the comfort of the security she has quietly craved her whole life, understanding finally that security without love is nothing. Wanting all of it, she may not know it's right in front of her with open arms. Hopefully, she will for the first time find a way to backtrack to you. Yvette was just a woman needing love, and you came and made it right, that is, her life. As many songwriters have written about, yes, the answer to her tomorrows is embodied in you. Two people, two different worlds finding completeness with each other, more than best friends, more than fun, simply love. Carry the passion of Phyllis and the song of Gregory Porter and Lalah Hathaway, 'Insanity.' Listen again to the words, and you and she will find your way back to each other, because that's what lovers always do. Thank the songwriters and the singers, so buy the CDs. I know you don't have that one, but you need to get it. I put it in your head to hear. Go spend some coin."

"OK, Ms. Angel Eyes." I came out of my daydream and said goodbye for now to her.

"**You're here. Go now. We'll talk later. Bye, Harold,**" Ms. Angel Eyes said.

Walking to Yvette's door, I held back my feelings and knocked on the door. I knocked again. I waited. Again, I knocked and continued to wait. It was not my nature to persist in such a way, but I could not leave, didn't want to leave. In fact, I wanted to be right there. After about ten minutes, though, of knocking and waiting, I thought I'd better get the message and turned to walk away when I heard the doorknob turn. I turned around. Yvette stood in the doorway. I could tell she had been crying. I wanted to comfort her and caress her. I held back, however, and just said, "Hello, how are you?"

"How do you think I feel?" Yvette shouted at me angrily.

"I'm sorry, but I was cleaning up things," I said.

"Yeah, right," she countered.

I didn't know what to say, but I remembered all that Ms. Angel Eyes reminded me. "Yvette, we were lovers, and I know we still are. Our time out west confirmed that for the two of us. Only time will give that back to us, and I'm willing to wait," I said.

"So, you are willing to wait? Why do you think I would wait?" she snapped.

I was parroting in part. I hadn't thought about her not wanting to wait, so I awkwardly replied, "Well, I don't. Only time will give up that answer. My muse said time is the music of life."

Yvette was incensed. "You and your damn muse. Why didn't she tell you to keep your dick in your pants?"

"She did, but not in those words. I just didn't listen," I admitted. Hearing myself, I sounded, well, not like I wanted, but she interrupted my thoughts.

"Harold! Why? I just don't understand. I loved you!" she declared. "Dammit, Harold!" she exclaimed, frustration and confusion echoing from her words.

"You still do!" I said.

"I don't know anymore," Yvette said, standing in the doorway, arms folded.

"I understand; that's why I've been getting my life together. Tina is dead, Lynn is dead, a police officer is dead, I killed a man, and as for the baby, I decided to become her financial guardian. Diane, the woman in Vegas, and her husband are going to raise her. And now, it is me and you. I need to work on it, and work it, I will. For the good, the better, and the best of us. I won't call you or bother you," I said. My lips were moving, and I meant what I was saying and not sure of what I was saying all at the same time. I wasn't parroting Ms. Angel Eyes any longer. I was finding my words, my voice, albeit I was raw. The cool me, easy-going me, easy-speaking me were gone. Before her now stood a man fumbling but trying to hold onto the woman whom he just didn't know he needed as much as he now realized he did. That was me.

"I have my memories of you to hold onto, to kiss, and to take long walks together with until, well, until the day comes when just maybe you'll fall in love with me again and we can be together, again. I know I've broken up a beautiful thing," I explained.

"No, it was more than a beautiful thing, Harold, it was love. How do you regain trust, respect, and love from a fall like this?" she asked, no doubt rhetorically because she was seething and crying and calm all at the same time. I didn't know what to say or if I should say anything, but the days of thinking it through, of biding the clock, were gone. Two years? Shit! Two minutes?

Hell, I didn't have two seconds in which to share with her the part of me that wanted her, that needed her, the part that I hadn't entirely let myself know that was asserting itself and needed to make itself known to this woman if a future was ever going to be possible, whenever that would be. And once again, my lips started moving, "All I ask, sweetheart…"

"Don't you *dare* 'sweetheart' or 'baby' me. I can't believe you. I thought I was your sweetheart, baby, whatever … but clearly I wasn't!" she excoriated me.

"I apologize. I apologize. You're right. … Yvette. Let me start again. All I ask, Yvette, is that you make a true and passionate search of your heart and that you make an effort to unshackle and let go of those deeply harbored insecurities, and if, if you find love for me, for us, hovering about there, then I know we can and will find each other again," I said in hopes of recovering. She just looked at me, said nothing, just stared at me angrily. And maybe I hit on something; or maybe for the first time she saw me unpolished, pressed, and unpracticed—not the Harold who had been to this beach before, to his favorite spot, and who had his approach down, seamless, who had everything under control—no, this Harold had never been here before, was in new territory, on unfamiliar ground, on equal footing and charting a path in the darkness like everybody else had to do. Or maybe it was something entirely different; I didn't know, and ultimately, I didn't care, but slowly the arch in her brow eased, the red fire in her eyes cooled to the burnt orange of the setting sun, and her tears of sadness were washed away by tears of love, if love in pain, and she allowed me to see her, she who loved me, and I felt some hope, and accepted that was possibly as good as I could hope for, today.

I didn't want to mess up again, and so I said, "A call from you one day would be nice. We shared more together in these few years than most couples share in a lifetime. You gave me your heart, and I gave you mine. We'll find each other soon." I started to reach out in order to hold her hand but resisted the urge. Her arms were still crossed. But she tilted her head to the side and looked down for the first time since she'd opened the door, and I felt foolish I had hurt this woman who loved me so, even in betrayal. But I could see she still loved me. "Just listen to the music. I've learned to listen, and the journey has brought me to you. If I leave, I can return. Good night, Yvette," I said, and as I dared not say any more, I started backing away from her doorway in order to leave.

"Just like that. I don't have anything to say about it. You get to come here, say what you got to say, try to make nice, and because, yes, because I can't help that I still love your ass, even though everything in me does not want to, then you get to leave, and I don't have any say at all?" Yvette was railing at me again, her voice reaching a crescendo, and I realized I was naive to think I was on better footing than when I arrived. I stopped backing up. Stood still and retorted without pretense or poise, "Yvette! I'm sinking in the muddy waters here because I know I hurt you and so now I just might lose you for good, even though I have realized that you are the one for me, the one I see when I imagine my tomorrows. I apologize, Yvette, for not being completely transparent with you." Such a raw statement seemed to have caught her off guard. I could see in her face, in the movement of her head and hands, her lips and her eyes, the war inside she was waging being fought right in front of me, and after a few moments, she spoke, though in a whisper, barely audible, this time.

She said, "I am so angry with you right now, Harold. But Lord help me because I love you so much, love you more than any man ever, it's not even close, and right now that scares the shit out of me because even with what you have done, I can't imagine not loving you, not being with you." As she spoke, she stepped closer and closer to me until she stood so close, she could have leaned forward and kissed me very easily. Against

310

all odds, I thought she might. Instead, she looked into my eyes as if she were searching them for evidence that I was really in there, really listening to her, really understanding her pain, and then she asked, "Can you even understand then how I feel and why that makes it so hard to let you in right now?"

"I would really like to think that I do, Yvette, but I'm only a man who knows love starts with freeing the mind. I have not always been truthful, and my judgment not always right, but I have been sincere in my feelings," I said. I could not help but look back into her eyes as I spoke those words and hoped that she discerned within me the spirit of the man who was seeing her, listening to her, whom she loved, and whom one day she could let in again. Then speaking as I reached into my pocket and pulled out the elegantly gift-wrapped box, I said, "By the way, I got this for you when we were on the West Coast. Open it on your birthday, which I know is coming soon." She stepped back quickly in surprise, all evidence of anger for that moment vanished; then she lunged forward, kissed me passionately on the lips and hugged me for what seemed like such a wonderfully long time, though it was for but an instant. Then she backed away as if she knew she had done the very thing she hadn't wanted to do, the thing I didn't deserve. But it was done now, so she merely excused her digression, and said without anger or joy, "Thank you, Harold," and nothing more.

"Know this for certain, Yvette, that everything about life is now a part of me, second nature to me, from life's morning smiles to her evening caresses. Life is the great music, yes, the jazz in me, the rhythmic melodies that I hear creating beauty in my life. Life waits for us in all its maturity," I implored, and before she could part her lips to reply, I turned and walked away.

"Harold?" Yvette's softened voice called out.

As she called out again, I paused and turned toward her. I heard her voice crack. "Harold, I'm beginning to understand,

and we will talk, and you keep listening to your muse and your ladies of song. As you tell me, the answer is in the great music."

I smiled and continued walking as I recalled her telling me once, "Words speak life," so I thought perhaps we would again talk, and maybe even allow ourselves to float away to that place, in our tomorrows, where only lovers can go. Engulfed in a cloud of memories, I began hearing my two favorite ladies of song whirling in my head, Ms. Nancy Wilson singing "One More Try" and Ms. Phyllis Hyman with the Whispers singing "Suddenly." As I got in my car and drove away, I hoped the interplay of our tomorrows would come again. As Ms. Angel Eyes had implored me to do, I had awakened from my cherished dream and my eyes were now opened to the universal truths and life's realities. Yes, Ms. Angel Eyes was and is right. Yes, jazz is the light, the soul, the spiritual, the ability to separate all things, but jazz, being all things and the harmony of all things, *is* not created from oppression or a broken spirit, but from the courage of free thought and the spirituality of the hue-man, *us*. This is my story, but is it also a story of many women, of one woman, or is it a story of you?

The End ... or will this be continued?

## 49 So Fine

Just a poem to read if you so dare

49 so fine, yet so unaware
Had exes, children, money, access
Though never a real love affair

With trip hoes and trip pimps she ran, all trippin'
All playin' for dollars, trinkets, (their) lives slippin'
49 so fine, she became many men's arm pieces
A singular vessel for their sexual releases

Hustlin' and Fun was her game
Shielding passion from that fine ass frame
Never knew love—nor ever came
Until Pierre, taking her to where only lovers reign

49 so fine, no one ever made her holler
49 so fine, void of expressing orgasmic rhymes
Until Pierre, long stroked, 6ed and 9ed her, so many times
There finding herself and feeling unknown to self
49 so fine, now awakened to expressing orgasmic rhymes
Now awakened to a real love in real time
From the dark murky waters of game—she has grown
Loved and being loved for the first time, so fine

Caressed in the warmth of Pierre's arms
A lotus flower she became
Beyond beauty–self-worth she gained
Beauty of the lotus, she'll remain

49 so fine, finding love and the joy of love
With Pierre she found—a love supreme
Driven no longer by the darkness of pleasure
Cloaked in the lie of saying I'm happy

But now knowing the difference between
Pleasure and Happiness are two different things
Pleasure that only begat loneliness
Oh, happiness, a cool spring, a life's dream

49 so fine, no longer, no need for exes and money and just fuckin'
49, becoming self-aware—willing to understand love and lovin'
Though it has taken her some time, and physical and mental wear
Yes, we'll all find it—haven't we too, already paid the fare

Yes, Love, if and when we find self—if we dare
True Love will find us all, when we become aware
Living without the blemishes of life's so many falls
Like an unblemished lotus flower upon the water fair.

Yes, 49, and wasted a lot of time playin', trippin', and slippin'
Yes, 49, redefining life, with Pierre, surrendered to a love
Yes, 49, touching the beauty of love and of the lotus fair
Yes, 49, a life finally defined now, and no longer unaware.

9 781735 302508